A NIGHT ON THE TOWN

"I ... uh ... feel   er winking trio of sh

"Nurse 'em,"   g show."

Van ached to t   thought of "his town" so far.

Then the gilt-fringed curtain rolled back its velvet folds, and all the lights, action, and glitter of Las Vegas pooled into a treasure hoard of onstage motion and music.

Van sipped her way through the shot glasses in the dark, watching chorus girls strut across the stage wearing rhinestone bikinis and enough feathers to furnish an ostrich herd.

The audience around her sat rapt. The curtain closed to thunderous applause and ovation after ovation.

"I bet you hated it," Nicky observed complacently.

"How *much* would you bet?"

Her challenge surprised him, but he pursed his lips consideringly. "A day at your command."

Her eyes outglittered stage-lit rhinestones. "Tempting. But I fear I'm a convert. The show was quite impressive, once one accepted the ... ambience."

He shrugged uneasily. "I lose, then."

"Yes, you do."

"What made you change your mind?"

"If I hadn't, it might have given you some satisfaction to see me turn tail and run," she answered, fixing him with a mock-stern eye. "And I don't ever wish to be accused of giving you satisfaction."

"...not like John Wayne," Van eyed h...
...bad glasses.
...Nicky advised. "This is a long...

Crystal Days

BY
CAROLE NELSON DOUGLAS

BANTAM BOOKS
NEW YORK • TORONTO • LONDON • SYDNEY • AUCKLAND

CRYSTAL DAYS
A Bantam Book / June 1990

ISBN 0-553-28522-X

Published simultaneously in the United States and Canada

Bantam Books are published by Bantam Books, a division of
Bantam Doubleday Dell Publishing Group, Inc. Its trademark,
consisting of the words "Bantam Books" and the portrayal of a
rooster, is Registered in U.S. Patent and Trademark Office and
in other countries. Marca Registrada. Bantam Books, 666 Fifth
Avenue, New York, New York 10103.

PRINTED IN THE UNITED STATES OF AMERICA

RAD   0 9 8 7 6 5 4 3 2 1

Prologue

Introducing Midnight Louie, Esquire

Las Vegas. It is Baghdad under glass, a neon bouquet to the whole world set in a doily of desert.

It is flash and flesh and glitter and cash. It holds enough busted bank accounts and broken hearts to pave the interstate from Needles to the Big Sur. It is bag ladies and chorus girls . . . guys, dolls and Mafia dons . . . potentates and small potatoes . . . tipsters and tourists.

It is my kind of town.

I am born here, weaned on a desert breeze and the sob of a showgirl's mother. I am on my own since I began walking and in my time I've hoofed every overheated inch of this burg. I know every grain of sand from the Strip's neon fringes to where a guy can find a high-noon shady spot to snooze downtown. I do not sleep at night; not in Las Vegas, and miss the action.

They call me Midnight Louie.

Now I am what you might call the unofficial house dick at the Crystal Phoenix Hotel and Casino . . . hell, all Las Vegas is one big overpopulated cosmic hotel open twenty-fours hours a day. Just like the wedding chapels.

Vegas. It can be a mean town, but it has a heart as big as the sun when it sinks over the mountains like a red-hot five-dollar gold piece. I never see a hunk of neon to compare to a desert sunset. And I never see real lovers leave Las Vegas unhappy.

Nowadays, I do more thinkin' than anything. The

1

*years catch up, even to an old tom on the prowl like me.
I do not say a lot these days, but I see everything, and I
hang out mostly at the Crystal Phoenix, where I got an
"in" with the management—okay, they owe me.*

*You could say were it not for Midnight Louie, the
Phoenix would not be the classy, world-famous joint it
is today. So I feel obligated to stick around and add
some local color to the establishment, you know?*

*Anyway, the lowdown behind the Phoenix is a story I
call "The Princess and the Prince"—well, let us lay it
on the green felt, folks. Mr. Nicky Fontana is a prince of
a guy, but the only blood that runs in his Family is red,
not blue.*

*Not that Mr. Nicky Fontana ever has any time for
that mob hanky-panky. Naw, he is a college graduate
and is set on adding some legitimate luster to the
Fontana es-cutch-eon.*

*So there is this abandoned hotel right on the Strip,
and there is Mr. Nicky Fontana with a few million in
genuine clean dough inherited from his grandma's pasta
factory in Venice—Venice, California, that is.*

*He is hotter than a Saturday-night poker player to
put his whole stash into turning the old Joshua Tree
Hotel into the handsomest, classiest hostelry in Vegas—
not the biggest, but the best.*

*Now Mr. Nicky Fontana's usual associates, they are
not exactly hoity-toity. So he does what a guy with
money and imagination usually does when he needs
something he does not have . . . like class. He imports it.*

I will never forget the day she blew in.

*I am discreetly eyeballing the lobby of the Joshua
Tree for salvage, as I am not as young as I used to be
and gotta take what I can. Besides, I do not have the
cushy job I have now, and the Joshua Tree was up for
grabs because of a fire.*

*Anyway, she comes in wearing pale summer linen
from her shoulders to her shoes; wearing a hat, one of
those wide straw jobs with a scarf built-in. Yup, a linen*

scarf the color of the desert sand first thing in the
morning when the sun is still cool.

So is she.

She just stands there dead center in the empty lobby,
peeling off some European-style sunglasses that are
darker than the custom-window tint on Boss Banana's
stretch limo, and stares. I stare, too, but she does not
notice me. Nobody does. That is why I am so good at
my new job.

Her you notice. Wow! Eyes like Lake Mead on a
sizzling July day—Independence Day, maybe—deep dark
blue eyes, so cool a guy wants to do the backstroke in
them. I gotta admit, I am smitten. Some kitten.

But she is not impressed—not with Walter Maxwell,
the top Vegas shyster who escorts her in; not with what
is left of the hotel; not with anything. She notices
everything but me. That is her first mistake. I know it
will not be her last.

Not with Mr. Nicky Fontana around. . . .

Chapter

One

"How long has the hotel been ... like this, Mr. Maxwell?"

"You mean vacant? About six years. It's not brand new, but—"

"It's at least forty years old. When your law firm contacted me in Athens, I was led to believe this would be a redecorating project, not a full restoration."

"Redecoration, restoration—it amounts to the same thing. You do have a seven-and-a-quarter million-dollar budget to work with, Miss von Rhine."

She turned to him, her blue eyes steelier than a midnight special. "Your letter said it was *eight* million. What happened to the missing seven hundred and fifty thousand?"

Walter Maxwell shrugged. "It's ... uh ... been allocated for a special project."

"The *hotel* is a special project, and it was to be all mine. Why would I travel thousands of miles to this oasis of kitsch if I hadn't been lured by a chance to redo the hotel in style? Now before I even get here, one-ninth of my budget is gone!"

"Ten percent."

"Is *everything* in this town a matter of percentage?"

"Please, Miss von Rhine. We're all risking a lot here. I know you left a prestigious position as assistant manager at the hotel in Athens, but you *will* be manager here. And I can explain. Even better, I'll show you. This way, please. To the private elevator."

5

She stepped gingerly over the lint-strewn, rumpled red carpeting, glancing down disparagingly from time to time, step to step.

"New Italian industrial carpeting. Number one," she muttered, mincing over the litter.

Her blond eyebrows lifted briefly as the elevator light flicked through the floor numbers in succession and stopped on the last one—thirteen.

"That'll be the second thing changed," she murmured as she left the elevator ahead of the lawyer.

"What?" Maxwell asked.

"The floor number. Traditionally, hotels skip the thirteenth floor. I'm surprised to find it here in Las Vegas . . . after all, gamblers are born superstitious. We'll simply rechristen it fourteen.

"He might not like that."

" 'He'?"

"Let me . . . uh, this way." Maxwell opened a numberless door with a flourish and ushered her through it the way Custer might have escorted the Seventh Cavalry to the Little Big Horn. "The, uh, penthouse."

"Penthouse? That's the least of my concerns, Mr. Maxwell. A hotel gets little return on a penthouse, unless as a status symbol to house certain insecure guests whose egos need boosting. I'd much rather see the kitchens." She began pinching off her beige knit gloves.

"Yes, but . . . he . . . really should meet you."

" 'He'?" You keep saying he, he, he. It sounds like you're giggling." She smiled to take the sting out of her comment.

"Please, Miss von Rhine, sit down."

She did, but first she had to remove some fabric-swatch rings, frowning automatically as her eyes skimmed the patterns. She calmly studied the surroundings, seeing a big, showy, empty room. Some cheap, outdated foil-backed wallpaper made dizzy Op Art motions over every wall. A chrome circular staircase with a rococo rail snaked up the farthest wall, its risers choked with shag carpeting. Life-sized statues of imitation white marble in fake Greek-god style stood in uneasy nakedness. Odds and ends of hotel furniture sat at careless angles, every horizontal surface aswamp with wallpaper rolls, carpet-sample books, and empty Styrofoam coffee cups.

"You *did* say the plans were for a quality hotel?" She asked softly.

Maxwell was spared answering. Muffled sounds erupted from a closed door leading off the main room; then the door itself exploded open.

A man stood in the doorway, his white shirtsleeves rolled up to his elbows, expensive cream silk tie roughly pulled out of its double-Windsor knot, dark head twisted to pinch the phone receiver to his hitched shoulder. An unlit cigarette dangled magically from his full lower lip as he spoke. Or cajoled.

"Nostradamus! Just quit trying to talk me out of it and lay the bet. Indian Summer in the sixth. To win. I got a feeling. Right, two-fifty."

He hung up, ran his fingers through his curly near-black hair, then noticed his guests.

His animated face, tanned, lean, and alert, froze in outright evaluation as he studied the woman sitting in the opposite chair. She watched dark eyes sweep inching approval from her arched instep up her ivory-hosed leg, then over the lines of the stark linen sheath and her bare white arms to her face, which was growing haughtier by the second.

"Terrific." The man came closer and perched on a broad chair arm, ignoring her automatic recoil. His square-fingered hand, impeccably manicured, took her chin in its surprisingly adept grasp and tilted her face to the desert light streaming through windows all along the west-facing wall.

"Class—even to the filling in her teeth. Maxie. Platinum, I bet, hmm, baby?"

His overheated olive-black eyes seemed to strike her

with all the finesse of scalding coffee, and she jerked angrily away.

The man spun to his feet, unnoticing. "You're thinking concierge, right, Maxie? I mean, she'd be wasted as the dining-room hostess. And get one of those skinny-legged, ladylike French desks for the lobby." He glanced back and down. "So you can see *her* legs. Class is okay, but sex appeal's even better. Make sure the new manager knows about the desk. When is that bozo getting here anyway?"

Indignation stiffened her into temporary silence.

"Nicky . . . ," Maxwell said, "This *is* the new manager."

The man wheeled to face the woman, then froze. "The von Rhine guy? *Van* von Rhine, you said. I'm not stupid—" she snorted delicately—"I remember names."

"*Miss* Van von Rhine," Maxwell repeated fatalistically.

They eyed each other, she and he; light and dark; ivory queen and ebony king across a cluttered board. The pawn was the only thing between them at the moment; Maxwell cleared his throat and kept silent.

"Miss . . . Van . . . von Rhine." Nicky was moving like a punch-drunk boxer. He extended his hand and gave her a confident grin. "Sorry for the mix-up. Nicky Fontana."

She was ignoring his hand and drawing on her gloves, finger by dainty beige finger. Maxwell quailed. She turned to him as if scenting rank panic and exploiting it.

"I believe your driver is waiting downstairs, Mr. Maxwell."

"Now, Miss von Rhine—" Maxwell moved between them, blocking her view of Nicky, who turned and strode to the window. "Don't let a misunderstanding upset you. The hotel needs you."

"I can see that. Desperately, to judge by these decorating samples."

"That's just for the thirteenth—er, *fourteenth* floor. The penthouse. Private. Nothing to do with the rest of the hotel."

"What a relief," she said acidly. "And who is this man?"

Nicky wheeled to face her. "'This man is the bank-roller. The man with the money, honey. I own the hotel."

"You!"

"Not publicly," Maxwell put in quickly. "Nicky is sort of a silent partner. All he'll do is live up here, uh, take a peek downstairs now and again, count the money. You know, kind of a—"

"Slum landlord?" she finished in overprecise tones.

Maxwell's already-round shoulders slumped, and he slunk back a few steps.

"Look." Nicky took a moment to scrape up an apologetic tone. "I'm, uh, sorry. What kind of a first name is 'Van,' anyway?"

"*My* name."

"Whatever... you're just what I wanted for the hotel. I don't even mind that you're a woman."

"All the better for 'class with sex appeal'?"

"Forget the sex appeal; I just failed my Nevada driver's-license eye test. Look, er, Miss von Rhine. A hotel is a business, you know that. Here in Vegas we sell flash, flesh, and fun. Only I want to do it first-class, see? Nothing obvious, but even class needs a little..." His right hand swayed back and forth all too expressively. "A little ooomph. Okay?"

"If you ache to hire 'oomph,' Mr. Fontana, I suggest you look in the chorus line at the Tropicana. You can't hire 'class'; you can't buy it; and *you* certainly can't recognize it!"

She threw a ring of samples on the tower of phonebooks that held the telephone. The books toppled in slow inevitability. "I'll say good day."

Nicky Fontana moved so fast, he was frozen into position by the door before she got there, one muscular forearm barring her way, the discarded sample ring dangling in his other hand like an ineffectual pendulum. But she paused.

"Okay," he conceded. "So I'm no connoisseur. Why do you think I had Maxie scour the world. And he found you. He says you're tops; you're what my hotel needs. I want to hire you. Do what you do. I'll try to keep my mitts out of it. That's why I'm a silent partner on the deal. All I got is some money and a vision of what another world-class hotel could do for Las Vegas. But I need . . ."

He glanced away, looking for words, his profile etched against a white column on the empty foyer walls as strikingly as a head on a Roman coin. His hand brandished the sample ring in frustration, then his fingers spread helplessly, the expression on his face becoming wryly appealing.

"I need you, Miss von Rhine," he said earnestly. "I need to hire somebody with class enough to tell me when to go jump in Lake Mead."

Nicky smiled the smile that always wore down Nostradamus the bookie, various hard-hearted chorines, and even his godfather, Mario, who'd always wanted Nicky in the Family business. He saw a sapphire glint light Van von Rhine's eyes for the first time.

"Now you tempt me, Mr. Fontana. I think I'd *like* to tell you to go jump in Lake Mead."

"I'm at your mercy." He looked as defenseless as a shark, all smooth, slippery facade and perfect white teeth.

She smiled coolly. "Not this afternoon. Mr. Maxwell promised to show me the rest of the hotel." Her gaze dismissed the gaudy penthouse suite. "The real part."

"Wait'll you see this done over. It's gonna be gorgeous." Nicky articulated the last word with passion. She looked away.

"I doubt it. But the rest of your hotel *will* be, Mr. Fontana. Or my name isn't Van von Rhine."

She swept out the faceless door, never turning her head to ensure that Maxwell trotted behind her. He did, of course, but first he cast an apologetic and beseeching glance at his boss.

Nicky remained in the doorway long after the elevator doors had pinched shut on the pair and the yellow light above them had winked out. He pulled the unlit cigarette from his mouth and tossed it dartlike toward the ashtray cylinder in the hall. It landed dead center, in the sand.

What are little girls with class made of? Nicky mused. *Rosewater and bath powder, spun sugar and ivory, probably. The sweetly elusive scent of . . . lilies of the valley.*

His face softened briefly, then his strong Roman nose wrinkled dismissively. *And icewater and vinegar,* he reminded himself.

Chapter

Two

"Nicky's an impulsive guy, but he means well," Maxwell said uneasily.

"That's hardly an excuse—or a recommendation for a good working relationship."

Van von Rhine restlessly prowled the seventh-floor living room to which Maxwell had shown her. Once, this had been part of a suite decorated in a garish ideal of elegance. Now the once-loud drapes hung faded and frayed. An air-conditioning unit strained and groaned like Atlas in its eternal battle to hold back the desert heat.

"We've, uh, just got this floor running—for staff—and the main floor where the kitchens are," Maxwell explained. "And the penthouse, of course."

"Of course."

Van lowered her large, floppy straw purse to the floor as if it bore lead ingots, reflecting that she'd been en route to this tawdry destination for twenty-four hours. Untying her scarf, she drew the hat off as wearily as she had her gloves.

"You should be pretty comfortable here," Maxwell said hopefully, privately doubting that Van von Rhine would find the Taj Mahal cushy enough for her taste.

"*My* accommodations are the least of it." She sighed and turned to face the room. "I really question whether I should stay at all."

Maxwell turned his hat in his hands like a Frisbee. "Getting your job back at that luxury hotel in Athens seems unlikely," he ventured.

13

"Yes."

"And that was your first official hotel position. I imagine finding another would take some time, even with your late father's connections—"

"Yes."

"But you'd do it," Maxwell said in a burst of confidence that was wholly self-generated. "Nicky, on the other hand—"

"Yes?"

"This is his only chance to make good. The Family has been pressuring him to join the Fontana enterprises. They didn't send him to some California college to—Going straight is his idea, and his grandma's cash is underwriting it. I guess I'm saying he needs you more than you need him."

"He needs *something*."

Van marched to the light switch and flipped it. The decor looked even shabbier, as Maxwell looked smaller and Van wearier.

"Do you mean to tell me," she asked Maxwell, "that a clan of hoodlums owns this hotel? That I've been hired by thugs?"

"No, no! Not them. Nicky. It's Nicky's joint. I mean, place. After a while, you get to talking like them. I've been the Fontana family lawyer for twenty years."

Van shuddered delicately. "I can't imagine trying to get any work done with that Fontana person squatting at the top of this hotel like a . . . a jaguar! It's really impossible—"

"Yeah, this old hotel would take a lot of work to get back on its feet again. Not much bark left on the old Joshua Tree."

"Not the hotel. Anything brick and mortar can be redeemed. And a Joshua Tree is a cactus and has no bark. I was talking about Mr. Fontana. Do you believe for an instant that he'll really keep his fingers out of anything—especially this hotel if it means that much to him?"

"No, but you need him."

Van glared.

"Yes, you do, Miss von Rhine. You don't know Vegas—
its history, its . . . uh . . . unique ambience. Nicky does,
down to his toenails. You can't bring the Joshua Tree up
from the ashes unless you know what goes in this
town—hotelwise. Give it a chance," Maxwell pleaded.
"Give Nicky a chance. If this doesn't go, that's it. He's
back in the bosom of his Family and the hands of his
uncle Mario, running numbers and learning the rack-
ets, just like all his brothers—"

"There are *more* like him?"

Maxwell nodded. "Almost a dozen. Rico, Aldo,
Eduardo, Armando, Ernesto, Emilio, Julio, Giusseppe,
and Ralph. The Fontanas believe in keeping it in the
Family, and there's a lot of Family to keep it in. Nicky's
the youngest."

"He certainly can't be the most diplomatic. You're
sure the financing for this hotel is sound?"

"Triple-A untainted money. Dough of the first water.
So help me." Maxwell pressed his palm to the lapel that
lay over his heart.

Van watched skeptically, then sighed again. "I'll stay
awhile then, and at least draw up a plan for the hotel's
revitalization—*if* Mr. Fontana can be convinced to re-
frain from making a nuisance of himself."

"I'm sure he won't, no problem," promised Maxwell,
backing out of the room.

As his heel and posterior entered the ill-lit hall, an
indignant yowl ricocheted off the corridor walls. Van
rushed to the doorway, but saw only semidarkness
arrowing into absolute blackness.

"Not—" she began, thinking the worst, as any hotel
manager might about a deserted building.

"Not rats," Maxwell reassured her. "Cats. They get in
somehow, trying to escape the daytime heat or nighttime cold."

Van shivered and ran her hands down the bare white

arms Nicky's espresso-colored eyes had warmed only a
half hour before. "You make this climate sound like a
hellish exercise in one extreme of discomfort or the
other."

"Not at all, Miss Von Rhine. You'll find Vegas as
delightful as Majorca or Scorpios—and Nicky Fontana
as tame as an iguana."

Maxwell was melting into the shadowed hall, an
insincere grin on his face. Van turned back to the room
and shut the door, automatically sliding the chain lock
into place. All her life had been spent in hotels as busy
as a Paris railway station, but this untended hulk struck
her as spooky in its emptiness, in the way its abandonment
imitated her own.

For thirty seconds she dueled an overwhelming impulse to pick up her hat, her purse, and her gloves, and
flee the Joshua Tree as fast as her sleek Italian pumps
could carry her. But she couldn't. She needed it, she
thought sadly, this decrepit hotel with its impossible
bankroller ensconced above. She needed a job history
longer than her three months in Athens. Nikos Skaliedes
had given her that job only because he felt sorry for her
after her father's death.

Van von Rhine had absolutely no credentials for a
hotel career, other than twenty-four years of spending
every waking and sleeping moment in hotels from
Bruges in the north of Western Europe to the Athens
Hilton on the edge of Eastern Europe as her father had
managed his way across continent.

Perhaps the unsettled life had contributed to her
mother's early death. Certainly Althea von Rhine was
only a name on an American birth certificate—Van had
come into this world at the Sheraton Russell in New
York City.

Now Erik Von Rhine, too, seemed as remote as her
unremembered mother. He had been an almost godlike
figure to his only daughter; his death last year at the

Venice Ritz had enshrined him permanently at a respectable distance.

There were a lot of things Van needed, she knew—a job; some time to think, to do something on her own, and not just because she was her father's daughter. The last thing she needed in this brave and battered new world she faced was a silent partner named Nicky.

"Give the kid a break, Nicky. She's fresh out of the eggshell."

"She's fresh out of the deep freeze. That chick could make a glacier look cozy."

"You're not hiring a chorus girl, Nicky. She's a pro. Her dad ran the best hotels in Europe. You said you wanted class."

"Class—not . . . not a Nazi in pantyhose."

Nicky slung aside an armful of fabric-swatch rings and sank onto the sorely tried penthouse armchair. He pulled a cigarette from a mother-of-pearl case and balanced it in his fine-tipped fingers.

"The old man was an aristocrat, but her mother was an American," Maxwell pointed out. "Say, are you going to light that cigarette with your eyes alone or go ahead and smoke the damn thing?"

Nicky looked up, a smile pulling his lips from a brooding to a sunny expression.

"Hey, Maxie, you're not letting our semiaristocratic lady get on your nerves, an ace mouthpiece like you?" He stuck the cigarette jauntily in the corner of his mouth, unlit. "I'm quitting smoking. Uncle Mario said this is how to do it. When I'm off the nicotine, I throw away the habit of having a cigarette in my hand." He glowered again. "That's just what I need when I'm quitting smoking, an uptight dame around."

Nicky stood, tossed his virgin cigarette into an ashtray overflowing with crushed but unsmoked cylinders, and thrust his hands into his pockets.

"I bet under that hat she even wears her hair in one

of those skinny, tight little rolls up the back of her head, like a schoolteacher."

"It's called a French twist, and it's considered elegant," Maxwell said prissily.

"Where? In the French Foreign Legion?"

"In society circles."

"Maybe this is a mistake. Maybe the dame is right; you can't buy class. Maybe me and Vegas don't need it. We've both done okay without it for a long time." Nicky laughed slyly at himself.

"Look, Nicky. Your grandma had a lot of faith in you. Eight mill was mucho dough to leave to a twenty-six-year-old guy, and only a grandson. Your uncle Mario's still steaming about it."

"Yeah. I sometimes wonder if he's more anxious to have me—or Mama Tinucci's money—in the business." Nicky brought a fresh cigarette consideringly to his lips. "Van von Rhine. It sounds like the name of a German railroad: the Van von Rhine Line."

"Get off that shtick with the girl! Think of her as a business associate, like me." Nicky made a derisive sound. "She can help you do what you want to do more than anything in this world, Nicky. She can help you put this no-name dump on the map, the Las Vegas map, right up there with Bally's Casino Resort and Caesars Palace. Think of it. Your name in neon: Fontana Hotel." Maxwell's small hands spread wide as they limned the imaginary logo on the air.

Nicky sat up, the cigarette rolling out of his mouth into his waiting palm as he lit up without benefit of matches.

"My name? You think so, Maxie? I hadn't thought about what to call the hotel. The Fontana Hotel." His mobile mouth kissed the air contemplatively. "Yeah, The Fontana. I like that. It's got class."

"Sure. The Dunes, the Sahara, the Fontana. It's as natural as nachos. But first . . ." Maxwell perched on the chair arm, his straw hat hooked on his dapper knee.

Nicky leaned close as the lawyer's voice lowered. "First you gotta research the thing. Get together with your new expert. Pick her brain."

"Brain. Now that I grant you. That doll has definitely got a first-class brain."

"Right. So all you have to do is take her out, show her the competition, and draw up a battle plan to make the Fontana the hottest hotel this old town ever set its bleary old eyes on."

"Right," Nicky said automatically. Then he frowned. "What do you mean, 'take her out'?"

"Show her the town, the hotels, the Strip."

"At night, like? Just her and me? Together?"

"Night would be a good start. Impress her with the Strip at full power, so she sees what a hotel is up against in this town."

The cigarette in Nicky's palm suffered from a sudden fatal crushing.

"Maxie, you want me to be seen—in public, all up and down the Strip—with this, this von Rhine chick? This ice-cube dame?"

"I think the term you're searching for is 'lady,'" Maxwell put in dryly. "If you're serious about remaking this hotel, you'll get on that phone, dial room seven-eleven, and ask Miss von Rhine out to dinner and dancing as pretty as you please. Prettier, in fact. Remember, you're not talking to Nostradamus the bookie or that Roxelle tootsie at the Tropicana. This is a *lady*, so you gotta play the little gentleman."

Nicky finally took the phone Maxwell extended and dialed the numbers. He held it on his shoulder, waiting for an answer.

"Maybe Uncle Mario is right," he muttered, his knuckles whitening on the receiver. "The hotel game is no business for a Fontana."

Chapter

Three

Nick dubiously eyed his own reflection, an image of sartorial perfection—or what passed for it in a flashy town like Vegas: open-necked ivory silk shirt, wool-and-silk-blend Italian suit the color of cappuccino, creamy Sicilian-lambskin loafers.

The dimly lit hotel hallway was straight out of the movie *Casablanca*. Nicky himself looked like a man bound for his own funeral.

Something rustled down the lengths of shadow stretching between each feebly beaming wall sconce; Nicky almost jumped out of his elegantly tailored clothes. Sweet fettuccine! He hadn't felt this nervous since he'd asked out Angel O'Malley, the Orange County High prom queen.

He frowned threateningly at his own craven image in the hallway mirror, turned and knocked briskly on the door to room seven-eleven, right below the tarnished brass numbers.

It opened instantly, almost as if she, too, had been pausing behind the door, nerving herself to face the inevitable—him.

"Seven-eleven," Nicky noted insouciantly by way of greeting, glancing to the numbers.

"I beg your pardon?" Eyebrows pale as corn silk elevated in scrupulously polite mystification.

"Your room number. I don't know if it's lucky or unlucky. How's your room, anyway? Maxie's been trying to have the hotel kept livable, at least, until it's redone."

She moved aside to admit him while Nicky scanned the shabby, once-grandiose decor. He shrugged.

"I've seen worse." Her earlier reaction to his own quarters rose vividly to mind. He grinned, looking more like the happy-go-lucky, devilishly winning Nicky his legions of friends, fans, and hangers-on would recognize. "So have you."

"Yes, but this is immaterial. It's what we do with the other rooms in this place that matters."

"Exactly right," Nicky said. "There are four hundred and forty guest rooms in the old Joshua Tree."

"That's a good size for a hotel," Van said. "Most European hotels are smaller; we're not used to Gargantuas with three thousand rooms, like your Bally's Casino Resort and Caesars Palace."

"That's nothing," Nicky rejoined quickly. "The new Goliath has four thousand rooms. And the Sultan copped a smart shtick; it's got one thousand and one rooms— you know, like the *Arabian Nights* stories. Tough luck that we can't do something catchy with four hundred and forty rooms.... But maybe class is better," Nicky conceded sagely.

Van von Rhine's face paled, if that was possible. She glanced down at herself with a self-dismissing fillip of her lips. "I hope I've dressed properly for... for what Mr. Maxwell calls 'Las Vegas's unique ambience.'"

That tore it. Nicky was forced to do what he'd been avoiding; he had to look at her. Now that she'd invited his inspection, he took his time.

She wore a cocktail dress, which was okay because some dames liked to dress to the incisors when out on the town in Las Vegas. The same silken cobalt hue that sleekly sheathed her body polished her high-heeled sandals.

"Looks okay," he said. "Might be a little warm though."

"Just how hot can it get here?"

"Hot as Hades," Nicky said authoritatively, opening the door for her exit. "Hot as... hell."

She sashayed out ahead of him, the dress's peplin waggling perkily. Nicky was in no mood to notice. He nostalgically fingered the gold lighter in his pants pocket. If he didn't fall off the wagon and light up tonight, it'd be a miracle.

They stood together at the intersection of Flamingo and Las Vegas Boulevard, a street better known the world over as The Strip. The traffic light took its own sweet time changing. Nicky had Van by her stiff elbow; it was about as sexy as a pump handle. Around them, Las Vegas's eternal kaleidoscope of pedestrians pressed together like a catch of thronging kippers.

"I hear this is now the busiest intersection in the world," Nicky explained with tour-guide pride. "It's out-jammed even Times Square."

"They have a lot in common," Van commented.

Nicky steered her into the icy blast emanating from the Barbary Coast casino's open doors. All the casinos were low-lit deep freezes in savvy contrast to the hot, neon-bright night outside.

Van von Rhine wore the same dazed expression she'd had since Nicky had pulled his custom silver Corvette into the valet parking line at Las Vegas's most dignified hostelry.

"Caesars Palace is across the street," Nicky said, figuring it was time to point out local landmarks. "See that big statue of the draped dude on the horse? That's Caesar. Or one of 'em. There were a whole bunch of Caesars. Must have been a big Italian family..." No chuckle from von Rhine, not even a smile. "So. You're the boss. What do you want to see first?"

"You're the guide, Mr. Fontana. I'm at your mercy." She shivered, whether from a surefeit of escaping air-conditioning or something more internal it was hard to say.

"Everybody calls me Nicky," he responded, annoyed. Her eyes darted to his face, their color as electric as the bright blue neon edging Caesars' rooflines. "I'm not everybody, Mr. Fontana."

"No . . . I see what you mean." He dropped her elbow like a hot potato. Let some baize-blind craps player plow right into her; he wasn't a nursemaid.

Ahead of them the colossal white erection that was Caesars Palace unrolled its magnificence. A semicircular facade of columns fronting the hotel sheltered looming marble goddesses, each the replica of some world-renowned statue.

"*Venus*." Nicky spoke reverently, pausing at the foot of one white giantess.

"I know the piece," Van said. "I've seen the original. The whole point of classical statuary, Mr. Fontana, is its uniqueness. You can't simply copy them wholesale and line them up"—her hand gestured to the row of semi-draped female figures—"like hookers waiting for a pick-up. It's hopeless, trying to make you understand! It's simply not a very classy thing to do."

Nicky swallowed. Behind the marble ladies, a smat-tering of all-too-fleshy life-size women plied their trade. Hookers were as ubiquitous a Las Vegas commodity as casino chips.

"I'm just showing you what's considered classy in Vegas," Nicky extemporized. "I didn't say *I* thought it was."

The interior of Caesars Palace offered a string of vast, marble-pillared casinos and cocktail lounges. They strolled along its echoing Appian Way of expensive shops until they came to another sculpted reproduction—Michel-angelo's *David*, a towering tribute to the naked male form, placed so that it could be viewed only at a sharp upward angle.

"I suppose you've seen this guy before too," Nicky said glumly.

"I've seen the original 'copy' in a square in Florence near the Pitti Palace where the real original is displayed for its protection," she agreed.

"Tacky, too, huh?" Nicky stared up wistfully at David's yeasty Renaissance thighs.

At last they emigrated down the Strip to the Dunes' geodesic Dome of the Sea Restaurant, where they were seated immediately. Van glanced up from her menu long enough to study the adjoining casino area's crystal-hung chandeliers.

"Apparently Las Vegas has a crystal fetish," she observed. "I haven't seen so much cut glass since the busboy at the Athens Hilton tripped and brought down the entire water-goblet-supply table.

"Yeah," Nicky admitted defensively. "That's what Las Vegas is for—lights. And glitter. And having fun." Nicky, who wasn't having any at all, had enunciated the last phrase darkly. "What are you going to order?"

She sighed. "Overpriced, all of it. The fish of the day, I suppose."

"Oh?" He studied his menu with mock care. "Carp?"

"Not classy, Mr. Fontana."

Nicky glanced up to see that his jibe had sparked the crystal glitter now refracting from her eyes.

"Nobody," he said disarmingly, "calls me Mr. Fontana. That's my uncle when he's in a bad mood and every body's walking on glass. If we're gonna be working together—"

She lowered the menu to regard him. "I don't suppose anybody ever called you Nicholas."

This time *he* winced. "Not since Miss Pribble in third grade, and she got glue in her drawer."

"Heavens! I'd hate to think what you'd do to retaliate now that you're all grown-up. How about Nick then?"

He shrugged. "I'm used to being Nicky. Why not? I'm the youngest."

"You're not in your family now... Nick."

"All I can say is, it was good enough for Nicky Hilton."

"You should do so well." But she smiled.

Nicky smiled gamely back. "Order what you like," he advised her. "It's on the house. My house."

"A house is not a hotel, Nick. And what you have sitting on ten acres of prime Las Vegas Strip is only an idea waiting to happen at the moment."

"Reopening the Joshua Tree is a great opportunity, you know," Nicky said suddenly. "Most Vegas hotels are owned by big corporations now—not much room for the personal touch. Things either go big in this town, or they don't go at all."

She looked at him for a long moment without answering, until he started feeling as if he should fidget—as if he were Nicky Fontana, all right, back in fourth grade, and he'd been caught playing with a pocketful of dreams in geography class.

He'd stood up to his nine older brothers; he'd defied his uncle Mario, which nobody who wasn't Family—and some who were—did without paying for it; he'd staunchly resisted the pleas of his widowed mother.

All for what he wanted to do more than anything: Make a first-class hotel out of an abandoned hulk of empty rooms and run-down dreams on the Las Vegas Strip.

Now, with nothing between him and Van von Rhine's chill, assessing eyes but his heart and soul, for the first time Nicky Fontana wondered if he could really do it.

But dinner was better, almost amiable. She ordered the most expensive entrée, lobster Pernod, having taken Nicky at his word. Van sipped the anisette that accompanied her coffee as if thinking of something else—as if she were somewhere else . . . or wanted to be.

Nicky got up to leave the banquette. "Ready? The late show at Bally's starts soon."

They stood together again at the interminable red light, heat heavier than molten lead pressing down upon them from the opaque black sky beyond the pulsing canopy of lights.

Van saw a single sequin of half-lit moon hung in the night-jet sky. Down the street the Flamingo's show sign neurotically twitched its pink neon tailfeathers. Behind them orange-and-green neon palms swayed electrically against the black-glass Deco donut of the Dunes's casino.

Van clutched her purse, starting at the brush of the unfamiliar fabric of Nick's jacket. He matched the world around them. His lush dark handsomeness seemed suddenly as high-calorie as hot fudge—and just as forbidden to her.

He was sincere in his desire to make something of the old Joshua Tree Hotel, out of himself. But he needed her to do it, she told herself with some satisfaction.

Inside the icy Bally's lobby, an immense vista of confetti-pattern carpeting and crystal-strung chandeliers sandwiched the hotel's main-floor casino between them like roast beef on rye.

Nicky propelled Van past lines of people to the theater entrance where swagged velvet ropes separated the mob from the VIPs. A long pink card in Nicky's hand wafted them past the guard to a *maitre d'* who ushered them into a red-velvet banquette inside.

Van studied the opulent house, its semicircular tiers of tables and a stage as vast as the Milan Opera House's.

"Eleven hundred seats," Nicky boasted. "One of the biggest in Vegas. We won't have anything this size. I figure a nice intimate revue. Not too nude."

Van didn't comment, even when the waiter, after taking Nicky's order, returned with an ice bucket, six shot glasses, and two lowball glasses crammed with ice cubes as big as uncut diamonds.

"Straight booze keeps best over the show," Nicky explained, bartering a ten-dollar tip for the drinks.

"I . . . uh . . . feel like John Wayne." Van eyed her winking trio of shot glasses.

"Nurse 'em," Nicky advised. "This is a long show."

Van ached to tell Nicky what she thought of 'his town' so far.

Then the gilt-fringed curtain rolled back its velvet folds, and all the lights, action, and glitter of Las Vegas pooled into a treasure hoard of onstage motion and music.

Van sipped her way through the shot glasses in the dark, watching chorus girls srut across the stage wearing rhinestone bikinis and enough feathers to furnish an ostrich herd.

Something tickled Van's ear and she jumped.

It was only the faint vibration of Nicky's nearby whispering lips.

"*Jubilee* cost ten million bucks to mount. It's run for nine years. Pretty hot stuff, huh?"

"How do you know the statistics?" she asked.

"I . . . uh, used to know somebody in the cast."

"Somebody . . . ." Van echoed knowingly, mentally separating the single word into its two, more accurately descriptive components.

Act II revealed a set as elaborate as one for *Aida*. While a chorus sang, lead performers danced the tale of Samson and Delilah. It climaxed, following an erotic pas de deux between the title couple, when the chained Biblical strongman pulled down the pillars of the Philistine temple. Forty feet of artful set tumbled interminably against a backdrop of hellish red flames.

Nicky Fontana leaned so close, Van felt his warm breath infiltrate the sheer neckline of her dress.

"I bet," he whispered, "I bet you find all of this somewhat—"

"Yes?" *Let* him *put the obvious into words for a change*, Van thought righteously.

"Oh, the leather-clad chorus boys, the dancing girls, the topless Samson—not to mention . . . ." His eyes flicked stageward. "Not to mention Delilah. I'd bet a bundle that you find the whole sordid little story and its reenactment pretty . . ." Van could hardly wait for him to finish.

"Philistine," he hissed silkily into her ear.

She jerked around to face him. He was laughing at her. Van turned back to the stage and watched a between-act magician make a sequin-draped female assistant vanish. She wished she could trade places with the woman masked in stage makeup and sink through the invisible trap door into obscurity.

But the audience around her sat rapt. The curtain closed to thunderous applause and ovation after ovation.

Finally benumbed from clapping, Van found her palm curled around an empty glass. A slightly scratchy sensation impinged on her shoulders. Van discovered that she was unconsciously leaning into Nicky's arm along the banquette behind her.

She sat bolt upright. "Well—"

"Yes?" Two hours in a passive spectator's seat had mellowed Nicky. "I bet you hated it," he observed complacently.

"How *much* would you bet?"

Her challenge surprised him, but he pursed his lips consideringly. "A day at your command."

Her eyes outglittered stage-lit rhinestones. "Tempting. But I fear I'm a convert. The show was quite impressive, once one accepted the . . . ambience."

He shrugged uneasily. "I lose, then."

"Yes, you do, because you're going to owe me several days at my command. You're going to introduce me to the finer points of everything in Las Vegas, from buffet lunches to shows in the buff. And we won't stop until I'm suitably impressed."

"What made you change your mind?" he asked.

"If I hadn't, it might have given you some satisfaction to see me turn tail and run," she answered, rising from her seat. Van von Rhine paused before entering the crowded aisle, fixing him with a mock-stern eye. "And I don't wish ever to be accused of giving you satisfaction."

Interlude

Midnight Louie Injects a Word

One thing about Vegas is crystal clear: Word gets around very quick in this town.

So it is not long before insiders all up and down the Strip are chattering like a pair of hot dice over Mr. Nicky Fontana and his "new lady."

They go out together morning, noon, and night, which is when the word starts buzzing that something is up, and all Mr. Nicky Fontana's friends start showing up like lost puppies at the Joshua Tree, which crowds my act somewhat, but I am a generous fellow.

And every morning Mr. Nicky Fontana's eyelids hang a little heavier, but Miss Van von Rhine, she is tough stuff. He does not so much as see her wilt, even after a day in 119-degree July heat pounding the Strip's sidewalks from A to C, the Aladdin Hotel to the California.

Every once in a while he tries to make a joke of it when they come back to the Joshua Tree, but Miss Van von Rhine is not amused. Rome, she says, was not built in a day, yet he expects his hotel to be rebuilt in six months, so no time is to be wasted in checking out the competition. This is the worst thing to tell someone like Mr. Nicky Fontana, who has made wasting time into an art of high dimensions.

Like I said before, none of this is unexpected to an old Vegas hand like myself, and while some might be laying

31

cash money down on how long it will be before Mr. Nicky Fontana runs for the airport and puts this particular kitten back on a plane for parts unknown, I keep my hand mum and play it two ways—to a straight or a royal flush.

Chapter

Four

Van shook herself briskly and moved away from the hypnotically barren view outside her window. She'd told Mr. Fontana—Nick—that she could convert a sow's ear into an Ultrasuede purse, and by Miss Piggy, she would do it! Much as the man irritated, confused, and unnerved her, he had given her a job.

This morning she planned to explore—solo—the Joshua Tree, from basement vault to rooftop. Nicky had the day off.

"I probably know more about what's to be found in this hotel than you do," she'd told him airily on parting at three that morning after a sultry walking tour of Glitter Gulch downtown.

The patent relief that had flooded the blacks of his eyes had been curiously disappointing. Van was beginning to enjoy running Nicky Fontana ragged, especially since she had perceived that he found no pleasure in her company. Yet his energetically ingratiating presence sapped her composure for some nameless reason. She needed a vacation from him.

She began with the kitchen, eager to meet the skeleton staff that supplied the few people still quartered in the hotel with their morning biscuits, afternoon tea, and an unceasing flow of Nicky Fontana's all-time anytime favorite food—hamburgers. Naturally.

So far, Van had spied only the mute Oriental waiter who delivered her breakfast. She telephoned her daily orders to an unseen someone nearly as mute as he, except for an invariably cheerful "Okey-dokey" sign-off.

She marched through the stainless steel doors at the hotel's rear to find a domain of polished steel tables and copper pans. "Hello . . . is anybody on duty?"

Only silent spit and polish answered her. Van explored her way through the suspended pots. The kitchen was empty, so she left, following the nondescript hall to the unrehabilitated lobby, perversely pleased to confront some benign neglect in contrast to the unassailably efficient kitchen.

But the lobby was not deserted. A narrow man reading a tabloid occupied one of the lumpy lounge chairs. She'd noticed him haunting the lobby before but she'd never seen the other person, who stood tapping an impatient foot.

"Can I help you?" Van began politely.

"I hope so, honey, 'cuz I sure ain't getting anything out of Nicky lately."

The woman drew herself to full height, a loftiness abetted by three-inch heels held to her instep by a curve of clear plastic embroidered with pink sequins depicting a Mexican market scene.

"That is to say," she added pointedly, "I have been unable to contact Mr. Fontana of late."

Van smiled. "Mr. Fontana has been out late—of late."

"I shall go up unannounced." She tossed a long ponytail of sorrel-colored hair.

The prospect of seeing Nicky Fontana awakened beforetimes by this tiger lily of a woman was too much, even for Van's innate restraint.

"You may go up unannounced, surely, but I'll be right along myself. I have some questions about the hotel staffing that only . . . Mr. Fontana . . . can answer."

"Then Mr. Fontana has a lot to answer for this morning." The woman's contact-lens-intensified green eyes flashed. "I am Roxelle, an old and very dear friend of Mr. Fontana's. And you must be?"

"Van von Rhine, the hotel manager."

"How do you do," the giantess said carefully. Painted nails as long as caviar knives pressed Van's palm. Van tightened her clasp despite this strong disincentive and smiled even more serenely.

"Please go right up, Miss . . . Roxelle. I'll be along presently."

"You can come up later," Roxelle said defiantly.

"That's what I meant. I'm afraid I don't speak Las Vegas-ese fluently yet."

" 'Las Vegas-ese!' That's rich." Roxelle's laugh was predictably throaty. "Listen, honey; the secret to life in Las Vegas is written right in the word itself; it's a *gas!*"

Roxelle kicked up her interesting heels and departed with enough clacking to imitate Western Union. The man now burying his mirth in the racing form echoed her parting laughter.

"I don't believe that we've been introduced." Van hovered over him, in no mood to be put off.

He jackknifed to his feet, his head coming only to Van's chin. This contrast of uncalled-for tall and surprisingly short was beginning to make Van feel like a shrinking and expanding Alice in Wonderland.

"Greetings to the lady who comes from o'er the sea," the fellow responded, bowing. "Who's here in Las Vegas to save the Joshua Tree. The name, fair maid, is Nostradamus. I'm known in this town, although not famous."

"Did . . . did Indian Summer win the other day?" Van asked.

"Ah, the lady has a mem'ry and no excusin.' That's one nag that gives Nostradamus a bruisin'."

"Then if you owe Nicky and are in no hurry," Van responded absently, "you can see him tomorrow, and not to worry." She froze, aware of what she'd just done.

Nostradamus grinned, exposing amiably crooked teeth.

"I'd be pleased to avoid the lovely Roxelle," he added in farewell. "She seemed in a mood for the dispensing of hell."

"Curiouser and Curiouser," Van murmured as the man merged with the hot blot of sunlight beyond the hotel's glassed entry doors.

Van marched for the penthouse elevator. She hoped Miss Roxelle was as adept at the giving of hell as she was at walking on her ridiculously high heels. Nicky Fontana could use some hellfire.

But as the elevator door hushed open on the empty hall of the thirteenth floor, Van paused. Indecipherable voices ebbed and flowed behind the numberless door Mr. Maxwell had shown her last week. She became again that only, lonely child who called a house of hundreds of bedrooms home, who considered doormen and desk clerks playmates. The blank door became one of legion.

Her father had often disappeared behind such a door, escorting a woman with glittering throat and wrists. Later, more worldly wise Van understood why the jewelry-decked ladies had so discreetly come and gone in her father's rooms.

His sudden heart attack had happened behind a closed door, too, with the assistant manager rushing one of the dimly glittering women from the scene. But it was the closed doors Van resented—not the death that had finally checked in behind one of them. It was the act of being shut out she minded most.

Van's hands had curled into fists during her mental journey into the past. One lifted to rap sharply on the closed, unnumbered door.

Chapter

Five

"Yeah!" Nicky Fontana shouted.

"Van von Rhine," she called crisply.

"Come in," he replied.

Van turned the knob and pushed the door into the room.

It had changed since the previous week; more flotsam than ever floated in its wide-open spaces. Nicky sprawled on a zebra-print loveseat, three unsmoked but crushed cigarettes screwed into the ashtray before him. A pristine fourth danced in his nervous fingers.

Roxelle's arrival had obviously hauled him from the shower. His wet hair coiled like ebony rigatoni. Waterdrops dewed a bare chest. Wearing only trousers and a rolled hand towel around his neck, Nicky glanced up at Van like a punchy prizefighter trapped in his corner between rounds nine and ten.

His sullenly percolating eyes poured out a relief as frankly naked as Nicky himself at her arrival.

Surprised, Van turned to the woman pacing impatiently before the mirrored bar. Roxelle's striding figure fumed in triplicate.

"This was a private conversation," Roxelle said huffily. "Me and Nicky have to settle how much time this hotel thing is going to take from our personal . . . relationship."

"I see," Van said sagely. "And what is that relationship—kissing cousins?"

Nicky concealed a sudden grin by dabbing his upper lip with the towel.

"Something like that. Anyway, you should know that daytimes are the only precious hours we can share. Your demands on Nicky's time are most inconvenient."

"I don't see why. I take him out mostly at night."

"You *do*! He swore he hardly had anything to do with you! At all!"

"Funny," Van said thoughtfully.

"Well! I never!" Thinking for a moment and not unearthing exactly what she "never," Roxelle stalked to the door. "Perhaps if it's your duty to show Miss von Ryan Vegas, Nicky, you could bring her to the Stardust to see what *real* Las Vegas floor-show fireworks look like."

"I don't think that'll be necessary, do you, Nicky?" Van speculated sweetly. "I think I've had a pretty good floor sample right here and now."

Slam! Van faced the closed door. A white dart hurled to the door's wooden surface, then fell to the carpet—Nicky's last cigarette, unsmoked despite deep provocation.

"Dames," he complained. "She doesn't get that this hotel is important!" Van turned to him, expecting to share in the abuse being accorded her sex. His look turned wry. "And what's this 'Nicky' business all of a sudden, von Rhine?"

"It seemed the thing most likely to drive her away. Besides, I give up! You can't make a Ritz out of a Holiday Inn. I guess you were born to be a Nicky."

Sun-browned arms stretched wide in a gesture either inviting embrace or proffering self-display. "That's me—no class, right?" Nicky summed up good-naturedly. "I know it, and now you know it. You'll just have to beat some into me."

Van smiled skeptically. He jumped up, mistaking hesitation for discouragement.

"Why don't you relax for a while?" Nicky urged,

leading her to the door. "Take a dip in the pool, sunbathe. You've practically got the joint to yourself. Then we'll go out tonight—but not your usual white-glove inspection. You've got to amble to gamble. We'll hit some casinos and end up at the Goliath. There are some things there you gotta see to believe."

"Not as many as there are here," Van muttered under her breath when the door had closed behind her. "Not by a long shot."

Van nodded uncertainly at another nondescript little man of late middle age staking out a spot in the empty lobby. The hotel crawled with anonymous casual visitors, yet each time she questioned one's right to be there, she found a Nostradamus or some other acquaintance of Nicky's.

Now she ignored them all, although—having taken Nicky's advice—she felt uneasy about parading her silky-cut French maillot swimsuit past a strange man.

Once at the hotel's rear, Van's bare feet slowed. She studied the surroundings, her managerial mind toting up substandard features and visualizing improvements.

The hotel was hourglass shaped—a broad curve of lobby, restaurant, and casino up front narrowed to a shopping arcade and then flared wide again to curved wings of guest floors. Nestled at the rear between the building's embracing white stucco arms, a blue rectangle of pool glistened like a giant emerald-cut aquamarine drying in the sun.

Van sighed to see the Mediterranean-style courtyard, its palm fans scouring the cobalt Las Vegas sky. Within the hotel's shadow grew a stand of sunset-hued calla-lilies as tall as she. An Oriental rock garden rambled over stone-formed hills, silver threads of water trickling into a still pond.

Something dimpled the pool's dark surface—a glitter uncheapened by sunlight, rich and elusive. Van leaned down to view a pirate's ransom of scaled gold writhing beneath the watery wine-dark surface—carp: not the plain-Jane kind that populate bodies of public water like Lake Mead, but the enamel-bright schools of showy goldfish that ornament private ponds.

Van, hands on her bare knees, bent to watch them. An airy scarf of sensation drifted past her ankles. She jumped back as a boa of black fur wreathed her knees.

"Why, what are *you* doing here?"

The creature that had silently approached looked up with noncommittal eyes of jade-green. A cat, Van realized. The fluffiest, fattest, blackest feline Van had ever seen. Snow-white whiskers sprayed from above its eyes and bracketed its midnight nose.

"Aren't you handsome?"

Its eyes had a lean and hungry look. "Poor kitty," Van crooned to her protégé. She slipped into the hotel kitchen, snatched a soup bowl and some milk, and rushed back to the pool.

The cat had settled somewhat nearer the forbidden carp pond. Van put down the milk and crouched happily beside it. "Oh, but aren't you a *beauty*!" she said, smoothing the cat's head. European establishments considered hotel cats a source of good luck. Even her father had tolerated a "house" cat or two.

But not black ones, Van thought, rising slowly. Black cats were universally unlucky. Van edged carefully around the blot of black fur shading the patio stones. It hadn't yet crossed her path; perhaps it would move on to a more occupied hotel.

On that hope she stepped into the searing sunlight. Feeling as if she moved in a sauna, she dropped her towel by the pool's deep end and sheathed herself in the cool blue of the water in the pool.

Later, Van chose one of perhaps seventy empty lounge chairs, applied sun lotion, and lay back. This world so near the Strip's noise-ridden fringes was silent, a place of soft wind and slowly drying waterdrops on her skin.

She could almost hear bees buzzing in the nearby bushes—large bees—very large bees.

Van sat up, alarm opening her eyes. Sound thrummed all around her, but the air was empty. Finally, in the shadow of her lounge chair, she spied the vibration's source. The cat, motionless and opaque as cast iron, napped under her chair.

She tiptoed away. Waking it would only encourage it to cross her path. She went slowly, looking back, walking straight into a pillar that hadn't been there before— a sun-warmed bronzed column in the Italian style, composed of firm bare flesh. Nicky Fontana in swimtrunks.

"Oh!" Van clutched her towel to her air-dried suit, *Rotten lucky already!* she thought.

"No harm done." Nicky Fontana's hold on her arms kept her from sidling past him. "I'm glad you took my advice. But I don't recall prescribing a dish of milk."

She glanced at the near-empty bowl near the carp pond.

"It was for the cat." She nodded over her shoulder, looking back to find Nicky studying that shoulder, as bare as his now and a good deal paler. *Of all people to be caught seminaked by,* Van fussed mentally. She wouldn't make that mistake again.

"I wouldn't do that again," Nicky said gravely.

"What?" she croaked, confused. Did black cats cause mind reading too?

"I wouldn't feed that jaded old tomcat plain milk. He likes Scotch in it—or rather, a little milk in his hooch."

"You know the cat?"

"A local layabout."

In the muffler of shadow the high-noon sun cast around Nicky's neck, a gold charm glittered hypnotically. His eyelashes, luxuriously long enough to add mystery to his angular face, threw tiny fringed shadows of themselves on his strong cheekbones.

Van could see that the charm at his neck dangled from a thick gold chain, both glinting against smooth, swelling chest muscles as hairless as those carved into

Michelangelo's *David*. Clothed, Nicky seemed hirsute
enough to ape King Kong; unclothed, his statue-smooth
chest struck Van as intriguingly vulnerable, temptingly
tactile . . . .

"How do you like it?" Nicky was asking with a grin
that seemed knowing.

"What?" she rasped back, appalled, wringing her
hands tighter on the towel clutched to her breastbone.

"The grotto." Nicky's eyes finally left her for the
scenery. "I thought I . . . we . . . could maintain it."

"Very peaceful," Van said too enthusiastically. "Most
refreshing! I wouldn't change a thing about it—not a
thing." She brushed past him and slipped through the
tinted glass door into the hallway beyond.

By the time she reached her floor her heart was
pounding as if she'd been running for her life. She
followed the hall to the single end window that overlooked
the swimming pool. Seven floors below, Nicky Fontana
was a lithe mahogany toothpick hurling itself onto a
sky-blue lacquer tray.

She watched him dive, striking water with speed
enough to make her catch the useless towel to her
throat again. There was no else there—no one—except . . .
From beneath the lounge chair that had been hers, Van
could have sworn a pair of solemn green eyes were
gazing precisely at the window where she stood.

Chapter

Six

"So what do you think?"

"I don't.... know what to say," Van said quite honestly.

Above Van and Nicky loomed the limitless black Las Vegas night sky and the gargantuan thighs of a plaster figure whose dimensions dwarfed even those of Michelangelo's *David*.

It was, of course, *Goliath*. The several-story-high figure of a man straddling the hotel entrance at least wore a kilt, knee-high leather-strapped sandals... and neon bulbs that twinkled as ribaldly as his lofty expression.

Nicky guided Van under the archway while she fought an irresistible impulse to look up. At least one couldn't stroll beneath the ersatz *David* at Caesars Palace, she thought with relief.

"This is the biggest sign on the Strip," Nicky was explaining, and "the Dunes's minaret is twenty-two stories. It's based on an ancient Wonder of the World—the Colossus of Rhodes. This place has got it *all*," Nicky promised happily while Van mentally inscribed "Abandon taste, all ye who enter here" on *Goliath*'s flashing belt buckle.

"Now, this is a little flashy," Nicky cautioned sotto voce, escorting Van through the dark-tinted revolving doors by slipping them both into one slot and ushering her through in the close custody of his arm.

Inside the Goliath, icy air and darkness—a reversal of the Strip's daylight-bright, overheated nighttime extrav-

43

agance—momentarily blinded Van. She blinked in the
shelter of Nicky's shoulder, her ears absorbing the rush
of voices, the brittle clink of coins and bar glasses, until
her eyes adjusted to the deliberately dim nightscape of
a Las Vegas casino.

While she attempted to focus, a dancing girl attired
in seven mysteriously attached veils shimmied past
with a full tray of equally miraculously poised cocktails

"Now this is something!" Nicky said enthusiastically.

"Yes," Van agreed weakly. "Could we . . . could I sit
down, please?"

Puppy-eager to do exactly what Van requested, Nicky
squired her up some steps covered in coagulated red
carpeting into a murky cocktail lounge. There, sunk
into a rug-covered divan, Van dug her high heels into
the mushy carpeting for balance and studied the gilt
camel-saddle-cum-cocktail table for a spot to place her
evening bag. She stared bemused at the drink menu
when a slave girl in gold lamé dropped it off.

"Forget the 'Rhodes Map,'" Nicky urged solicitously.
"I want you to really see this joint, and that drink's
guaranteed to make your eyeballs look like thirty state
highways ran across 'em."

"I think," Van said without thinking, "I'll try the . . .
Philistine Sling."

Across the saddle, Nicky winced. "That Sling can
really knock you out," he warned.

Van frowned her indecision. "The, uh, Vizier's Re-
venge, I guess—" The waitress nodded and danced
away.

Van laid down her menu and the law when they were
alone again. "No cutesy names for drinks at the Joshua
Tree, all right?"

"Maybe." Nicky squirmed on the mushy divan. "But
that's what people like about this town. It's fun."

"Bad taste is not fun."

"Says who?" Nicky's voice had risen a little, perhaps
in response to the racket all around them.

His open-necked ivory silk shirt set off the gold neck charm he wore. Van wished that something so inherently flashy didn't look so seductively appropriate. Nicky pulled out a cigarette, regarded it wistfully, then focused his dark eyes defiantly on hers and jammed it back in its case.

"All right," he began. They leaned away from the camel saddle in concert as the waitress wiggled between them to deposit two high-rise drinks upon it. "We'll discuss fine points later. But we should find something else to call our hotel besides the Joshua Tree. That's past."

"Have you any ideas?"

"No..." Nicky looked as innocent as a four-year-old at a soda fountain as he sipped on the straw impaled in a blue-green froth christened a Kirschmet. "I want a name that fits the Vegas, uh, ambience. Something with a ring to it, like... Sahara, Riviera, Tropicana—"

"Or Fontana?" Van finished shrewdly.

Nicky sputtered into his straw. "Now that you mention it, why not? That doesn't sound so bad."

"Nicky." Van sipped the citrus-colored libation before her, which attempted to combine every liquor known to bartender in one goblet. "I don't care *what* you call the hotel as long as it's within the bounds of good taste."

"And what is that? What *you* say it is?"

"Perhaps," she replied primly. "Surely you don't admire this—?" Her waving hand indicated a scene reminiscent of some hellishly lit Last Judgment. "Every hotel in this town is flocked and gilded, crystal-hung and neon-lit, overdraped and—frankly—tacky to its toenails."

They both glanced down as their waitress flounced past, sandaled feet displaying lime-painted nails.

"Okay." Nicky stirred on his low divan. "So things are a little... loud. I meant we should look the Goliath over for ideas we could, uh, translate."

"With class."

"With class, sure. That's what I pay you for, right?"

"Right," Van said grimly, planting her palms to push herself out of her seat. It didn't work. Nicky twisted out of his cushion first and offered a helping hand.

Once vertical again, they glared at each other.

"This lounge is not designed with a view to guest comfort," Van pronounced.

"Maybe comfort isn't everything! I don't want one of your damn snooty bland white hotels, that's for sure. That wouldn't work in Vegas."

"Perhaps that's just because it has class!"

Nicky's fists jammed into his pockets as if to restrain themselves from a forbidden cigarette.

"Is there anything else you wanted to show me?" Van inquired with excessive politeness.

"Yeah."

She followed him through the cavelike casino. Ahead, another cocktail lounge flowed into an adjoining blackness lit by tiny fairy lights in potted trees. Here Nicky paused.

"This is . . . attractive," Van conceded.

"Yeah, and look at this." Encouraged, he led her to a miniature gondola upholstered in the ever-present red velvet outlined with gilt braid.

The boat rocked gently in the dark water of a canal perhaps twelve feet wide that meandered among the cocktail tables. Once Nicky had helped her into the facing seats, some mechanism propelled them oarless into midwater.

"Pretty neat, huh?" Nicky inquired happily.

"But what's the point?" Van asked in a bit. "The canal must cost a fortune, and the tree lights are pretty, but we could see them better from the cocktail area. Besides, gondolas hardly fit the Goliath's biblical theme. . . ."

"This is a *modern* attraction. It's called—are you

ready?—the Loh-uv-ve Moat." He coated the title in announcer-like ooze.

Van stared blankly at the tree-shadowed image of Nicky opposite her. "The Love Moat?"

"Yeah, there's this TV show here—"

"They run *The Love Boat* in Europe too; I just don't know why anyone would want to ride this silly machine through the ill-lit rear of a hotel lobby. And I really can't see—"

The gondola sallied forth silently into the dark mouth of an unseen overhang. Even the faint twinkle of fairy lights winked out. They floated in absolute dark and complete silence. After a long moment, Van's voice resumed.

"If one wished to go to a carnival midway, one would go there, not to a hotel. I really can't see why anyone in his right mind would want to—"

The darkness opposite Van rustled violently. Hands seized her, reaching from the cold blackness to pull her abruptly across the small vessel, pressing her into Nicky's arms, rocking the boat, making waves.

She wasn't afraid, simply utterly startled to feel Nicky Fontana's hard, warm side, to find his lips unerringly meeting hers in the dark. His knee pressed between hers. His belt buckle jabbed into her ribs. His fingers combed into her French twist and his mouth plumbed the surprised depths of hers. It was a kiss right out of a movie.

"That," his voice underlined near at hand, "*that* is why anyone would like something as stupid as this!"

She realized that he had stopped kissing her and blinked her eyes open. The darkness had been hers, apparently for some time. A silver-haired couple at a canal-side table was eyeing them curiously as fairy lights again illuminated the inside of the gaudy little boat.

Van's evening bag lay glittering forlornly in the gondola bottom, where it had dropped when . . .

Nicky was bending to retrieve it and plunked it ungraciously in her lap, not looking at her. Van smoothed her hair and straightened her legs. Avoiding each other's eyes, Van and Nicky waited for the gondola to glide dockside. Each managed to disembark without touching the other.

Nicky plunged ahead through the crowded tables to where the vista opened to display a casino operating at full Saturday-night fervor. He jammed his hands into his pockets and spoke quietly without turning to her.

"It's no use. You don't dig Vegas, and even if the hotel does need class, it needs some down-to-earth pizzazz too. The Goliath may be crass, but it's always booked to the gills, and I know numbers, even if I don't know class. It'd never work," he muttered, "us working together. I'll pay you a few grand severance money. You can go back to your fancy continental joints, and I'll put the Fontana together my way."

"You can't!" Van burst out without thinking.

"You don't know what I can or can't do." He finally turned fiery eyes on her. "Maybe I don't either, but I can try. What I can't do is work with a wet blanket!" His eyes cooled. "You don't understand Vegas, which maybe would be all right—but you don't understand *me*, and that's not all right. I'm not a fool."

She shook her head. "I know that, and I know Las Vegas is built on . . . well, exaggeration. But you don't want the Goliath, Nicky. I know you well enough to know that. I'm sorry if I don't know how to react to this town, to you . . . but I do want the Fontana to work as much as you do."

"You want to *stay?*"

She couldn't quite agree to that. "I need a job," she said quietly. "And, I suppose, I could stand to learn a thing or two. If you'd teach me."

"About what?" he asked dubiously.

"About what you know. This town. Vegas."

* * *

Nicky drove. He drove like a bat out of the hot hell that Las Vegas in August would have been without air-conditioned hotels and an endless gridwork of power lines.

The Corvette's sleek fiberglass frame flattened to the road like a pale panther as the powerful motor stretched its automotive sinews.

There was only the dark of the road, a white dotted line into the distance, and the flat black shambles of the mountains ahead huddling against a sky nearly as opaque.

Nicky glanced to the passenger seat. The T-tops were off, and the wind ruffled their heads. Most dames hated open-top cars, he reflected, swaddling their hairdos in scarves; a few ran their fingers through their hair, leaned their heads back, closed their eyes, and let the wind kiss them senseless.

Van von Rhine did neither. She sat calmly, the dashboard illumination frosting her wind-tremored hair with the faintest of auroras. She looked dead ahead into the featureless dark and said nothing.

That suited Nicky. His eyes slid back to the empty road and emptier distance beyond it; the needle slipped farther up the luminous dial. The 'Vette had been engineered to fly. No mere earthbound patrol car could catch it. None prowled this endless waste by night anyway.

Nicky's eyes caressed the chrome lighter knob; there was nothing so cheerful when you were alone in the dark as the ember at the end of your own cigarette. But he didn't smoke anymore, he told himself, and he was no longer alone—not in this headlong flight to solitude, not in his dreams of a hotel worth rebuilding.

He braked the 'Vette so suddenly that it performed a flashy TV-style about-face. Sand sprayed the windshield. The headlights drilled into an endless tunnel of desert scrub. He punched them off, along with the motor. Sound and motion had quelled to instant peace and quiet. The mountains hunkered at their back again and ahead, ahead... Nicky got out of the car and went around to open Van's door.

She wasn't afraid, he had to give her that.

"Where are we?" she asked in the polite, interested tones of a tourist.

"About halfway between the Spectre Range and Shadow Mountain, not far from Devil's Hole. Nowhere."

She turned to survey the bulky shapes looming against the sky behind them. "Can I see these mountains from my hotel window?"

He thought for a moment, figuring. "Yeah. Yeah—I guess you could."

"They look like misty pink marble in the daylight."

"Everything looks different at night. Vegas is a twenty-four-hour state of mind, an all-day, all-night kind of place. But night's when it really sparkles. Look."

Nicky tented his fingers on her shoulders and delicately swiveled her to face the intended finale of the long, silent drive.

"Oh..." Her awed, indrawn breath was more reward than any expression on her face, had there been light enough to see it. "Is that... the city?"

Nicky nodded in the dark, to himself, without answering. You had to come way out here to see it—Las Vegas, queen of clubs, spades, hearts, and diamonds, all rolled into one. Now, by night, she displayed her diamonds—the tangled webs of quivering light that flashed far away on the desert.

Nicky leaned against the 'Vette's fender and began explaining. Or trying to.

"Have you ever flown from L.A. to Tucson? Naw, but I have. It's five hundred miles of flat nothin', night or day or anytime in between. At night it's black as the queen of spades, just black—bottomless as the Grand Canyon.

"The plane's jets are droning, and the cabin is real eerie, and you're studying the ghost of yourself in the window... then, halfway between L.A. and Tucson, this exploding rose of light blossoms in the dark below you, like some mushroom cloud of life, not death. It's fairy dust and fever, every firecracker you ever dreamed of on the Fourth of July, every headlight that ever seemed to be hurling right into you. It just . . . explodes."

Van shivered suddenly. Nicky took off his sport coat, carefully because a wrong rustle might ruin everything, and draped it over her shoulders, his eyes still on the distant light show.

"That's the way you got to look at Vegas, see? At night, in the dark. Then you don't see all the noisy, gaudy stuff—the stuff that I kinda like anyway—the stuff that makes some people think she's a tramp. At night, she's a lady. *At night she rakes all of her ice out of the safe and shines*." He laughed, maybe at himself.

"Anyhow, that's how I see it. I used to come out here when I came home from school, just a kid with a driver's license and a crazy idea. Sometimes I used to watch those lights until the damn dawn came up and scared them away. And that's what I want the hotel to be—one nice, clean crystal-clear lightbulb in all that wattage. Just one little new light in the dark. But classy, so it stands out."

She turned to him, saying nothing. Nicky smoothed the lapels over her shoulders, then turned and opened the car door. She reentered the car as matter-of-factly as she had exited it.

Nicky boosted himself into the driver's seat without bothering to open his door, as he did when he was sixteen. He switched on and revved the motor, burned the headlights back into the night, and aimed the 'Vette's long, low nose straight at the exploding star of light ahead.

He didn't speak all the way back, and neither did she.

The Fontana-to-be looked disappointingly shabby when they saw it through the windshield again. Nicky swept the car under its unlit canopy and escorted Van inside.

Someone had left a few lobby lights on. Van paused

hile he reclaimed his jacket. The expression on her face was noncommital; tired, maybe. Nicky knew in his sinking heart that he hadn't proved a thing—not in the dark of the Love Moat, not in the deepness of the desert night—except maybe his own vulnerability. Swear words tangoed at the edges of his mind.

"Hey, hey, hey! Nicky! Wait up."

Together they turned back to the doorway. A man stubbier than a three-quarter-smoked cigar was bustling through the glass doors. He wore a Hawaiian shirt and an impatient look.

"Say, Nicky boy! Where you been lately? Your mama's been worried, she tells me on the long-distance phone."

"My mama's been used to me keeping my own hours for seven years now," Nicky retorted.

"So your uncle's been worried." The man scanned the deserted lobby with quick deprecatory glances. "Give me a break, kid; this place's got no more potential than your brother Ralph's got for keno. Is this all you've done so far? Nothin'? Jeez, what a dump."

"It's in the planning stages—"

"Planning, schmanning. Kid, forget this hotel. That's a lot of moola to throw down a rathole. Come back to the Family business where you belong. You don't stand a chance."

"This is not a rathole, Mr. Fontana."

Nicky stared. Van hadn't spoken for so long that he'd forgotten that she could. His uncle Mario stared too. He wasn't used to being contradicted by women.

"Of course," she went on in a dispassionate tone, "it takes a certain amount of capital to renovate a hotel into a first-class establishment. But the work itself should progress quickly once it's begun."

"Who's this mouthy broad?"

"That's no broad, Uncle Mario. That's my new hotel manager."

"Oh, yeah? You and how many good fairies? This old dump's a DOA. That's 'dead on arrival,' sweetheart!"

Van's hands moved deliberately to her hips, and her head tilted, jutting her porcelain chin delicately forward. Nicky edged back, not sure what from, except maybe a form of fireworks he'd never witnessed before.

"'Oh, ye of little faith...'" Van quoted for openers. "I don't see how a prominent person such as yourself, Mr. Mario Fontana, got anywhere at all in this cold, cruel world with that defeatist attitude."

She advanced a step, her eyes flinging bolts of blue lightning. Mario stepped back before he could stop himself.

"I'll have you know that this 'old dump' is a perfect candidate for a stunning revival. It could become the finest *and* flashiest hotel in Las Vegas. And it won't be done in cheap 'Miami Moroccan' or 'Hollywood Orgasmic' or 'Roman Orgiastic' or 'Organic Behind' style like the rest of the... the 'joints' in this town. Wait until you see it, Mr. Fontana," she almost threatened. One elegant handwave indicated the indifferent ceiling above them.

"Enough fountains, mirrors, and crystal to blind the telescope on Mount Palomar." Her wrist circled eloquently toward the dreary stretches of encircling wall. "A glass-enclosed circular pavilion with a running-water roof and a chain of lagoons, cocktail lounges, restaurants, carp pools, bridges, and whirlpools. Perhaps even a small waterfall.

"And right where you are standing, Mr. Fontana, will rise a Plexiglas column bearing a custom-commissioned Lalique crystal artwork in a form to mirror the hotel's new name—the Crystal Phoenix.

"The Phoenix, in case your study of the classics was interrupted by business concerns, Mr. Fontana, is a mythical bird that rose again from the ashes of its own body. *This* Crystal Phoenix will be the epitome of the architectural art as it is practiced in this rather tawdry town of yours. It will be the eighth wonder of modern Las Vegas."

Van folded her arms and glared icily at Nicky's uncle Mario, who turned hastily to his nephew.

"Sounds . . . uh, good, Nicky. Smart thinkin'. Sure, I was just sayin', why not give the idea a try? Say, uh, it's late. I just stopped by to schmooze a little. So I'll say . . . *ciao*, Nicky . And, uh—"

He stared at Van, then turned in a blur of shirt as lurid as a Hawaiian sunset and vanished back into the midnight limo purring at the curb.

Nicky looked around the lobby and along the length of muted slot machines and idle, blanketed crap tables. He looked up to the pedestrian ceiling, down to the litter-carpeted floor. He looked at Van.

"Ya-hoo!" An unpremeditated bear hug spun Van into his arms, around and around on the exact future spot of the Lalique column with the crystal phoenix. "Lady, you are on a roll tonight! Uncle Mario was speechless! What an act. What a bluff! Yahoo!"

A royal-blue sandal went spinning across the rug, then another. Nicky turned exuberantly until he was dizzy and breathless from laughing. Odd thing, he noticed. Van was laughing too. Nicky drew a deep breath. Her lily-of-valley scent enveloped him; he felt the satin of her hair against his cheek. He let her go quickly.

"What a great con," he said, going to retrieve her far-flung shoes.

She waited, calm as a barefoot princess in her throne room, for his return. Nicky found himself kneeling to offer first one satin slipper, then the other, while her fingers pressed his shoulder for balance and her small foot arched neatly into his hand.

He'd been right from the first; she had world-class legs. Nicky's eyes followed his own conclusion up a well-turned length of ankle, calf, and knee to the thigh. He stood abruptly.

"So. When did you dream up this face-saving fairy tale? On your feet?"

"It . . . came to me in the car, on the way back," she was saying, almost shyly. "I started thinking about everything I've seen here and what the hotel could be. Your uncle Mario simply forced me to say what I'd already decided."

"You mean all that's for real? The water, the crystal, the, the imitation Love Moat?"

"For real. Only better. And not an imitation, the real thing. You'll see when I get an architect to draw up some plans. Your hotel will *shine*, Nicky, I promise."

Her eyes mirrored her promise, mirrored other things, maybe, that Nicky didn't want to lean too close and spot.

"Ah, it sounded great. You've sold me, but—"

"I'm sorry about the name," she said quietly. "It's just that the Crystal Phoenix will be much more marketable. More in keeping with Las Vegas . . . glitz, if you know what I mean. It has oomph." Her hand wobbled in a way that Nicky recognized from some place far away and long ago.

He took a stabilizing stroll around the empty lobby.

"Okay," he concluded. "I guess that's what I wanted— for you to see what this hotel could become, for you to grab onto a piece of my dream . . ."

He looked at her again. She was shining. She knew what she was doing finally, and why. She cared. She gave a damn. His hotel was her hotel. It was a scary thought.

"Let's . . . let's get upstairs to bed," he said, wanting privacy. Instantly, he cursed the unfortunate implication of his casual words, even in a hotel of many beds.

Van had already turned for the elevators, apparently having thought nothing of it. Nicky felt vaguely insulted and definitely relieved.

He saw her to her room by the weak light of a single wall sconce, but stopped her fingers as they turned the knob.

"About tonight," he said. "In the"—he laughed

nervously—"the Love Moat. I'm sorry. That's not my style. I was just so damn exasperated."

She looked at him limpidly, every hair in place, her voice level, her eyes unblinking. "What is your style?"

"I don't know," Nicky said, rummaging for the words that usually came so glibly. "I don't know." He tilted her chin to the light, to his face, and gently brushed her mouth with uncertain, apologetic lips.

Interlude

Midnight Louie Reflects on Benchmark Events

So this is the first time I hear the name, the night Macho Mario Fontana gets read the riot act by this little doll in high heels.

The Crystal Phoenix, she says, like she has it tucked in the back of her mind all along. The name tickles my fancy even then, the first time I hear it, and I am getting to an age when not much tickles my fancy.

Naturally I am there on the scene, although the Crystal Phoenix is just a light bulb in the brain of a feisty little doll at the time and I am not yet prevailed upon to take an official role in the establishment.

My usual modest profile keeps the principals in this little drama from observing my presence, which is just as well, as nobody acts with characteristic grace that night. Mr. Nicky Fontana is a prince, but even princes do not take to being outflanked by feisty dolls.

So I keep my usual low profile, but already I scent some opportunity on the premises for a freelance fellow-about-town like myself. I resolve to hang around and see what I can turn up. For one thing, I have a way with women. And that little hotel doll does not scare me one iota. Indeed, I expect to have Miss Van von Rhine eating out of my mitt within the month or my name is not Midnight Louie and the Crystal Phoenix is not about the become the classiest flophouse in Vegas.

Chapter

Seven

Van stood marooned in the deserted lobby, her arms cradling rolls of architectural plans. She turned slowly, mimicking the wild carousel motion of Nicky's impulsive embrace, which seemed a mere figment of the previous night's excesses. Today, Van saw only cold daylight reality extending in all directions.

She must have been mad! Or perhaps she simply had been angry, angry to see Uncle Mario in the lurid flesh laying a wet Fontana Family blanket all over Nicky's fragile aspirations. Now her shoulders tautened as she contemplated the work needed to realize her bravado midnight vision.

Far down the hall, a slight, anonymous figure moved from one wall to the other. Van observed it indifferently; she felt like a David handed a paper sling.

"Hi! Is Nicky up?" a breezy female voice called.

Startled, Van could only blurt, "I don't know" at the lithe, long-legged woman who had materialized before her.

The young woman grinned. "I know what you mean. Listen, I hate to barge in this early, knowing what hours he keeps, but my pulled calf muscle desperately needs that rooftop whirlpool of his. I'm Darcy McGill, and I wouldn't be butting in on your territory, would I?"

"Me? Certainly not," Van sputtered, juggling rolls of plans like loaves of French break. "I have nothing to do with the man," she insisted emphatically if not quite accurately.

"That's what they all say," Darcy commented, laughing. She extended a slim, strong hand for a businesslike shake. "I'll just run up and rattle Nicky's cage, then. See you around later, whoever you are."

She was gone, sprinting for the elevator with agile grace despite the supposed muscle injury. Van sourly watched the silver doors of the penthouse elevator swallow her shorts-clad figure. Obviously, Van could expect small help from Nicky's quarter as long as he kept the chorus line coming, in eager rotation.

"Here, Miss von Rhine, let me help you with those."

Van turned to find a beaming Walter Maxwell, his balding head dewed by early-morning Las Vegas humidity. She gratefully transferred a third of the slipping rolls to his waiting arms.

"At last a logical mind! Where, Mr. Maxwell, can I find the erstwhile manager's office?"

"This way." Maxwell scuttled eagerly in the direction indicated, glancing back at her armful of plans. "Your additional luggage arrived safely, I see."

"So to speak, if anything can be said to be 'safe' in Las Vegas." Van marched grimly alongside the little man. "Including one's sanity."

Maxwell let that comment slide into home plate unheralded.

"And how are the renovation plans proceeding?"

"Peachy!" Van snapped.

"It's Nicky, isn't it? He's not taking this project seriously—"

"I'm here to renovate a hotel, not rehabilitate a . . . a playboy who lives in a penthouse," Van fumed, preceding the lawyer, into an office marked Manager.

"Do you think it's possible?"

"With Nicky Fontana, everything is *im*possible!"

"I meant revamping the hotel," Maxwell put in meekly.

"Oh, that . . ." Van perched on the Goliath-sized tufted-leather managerial chair behind the desk and tilted unexpectedly backwards. She stood. "Oh, get me a good secretarial chair from the reception desk, please; these overstuffed, oversprung status symbols are worthless for *working* managers."

Maxwell hurriedly skated a chair from the next room into place while Van herded the leather behemoth away from the huge desk.

"Seriously," he asked, "how does the project look?"

"Like a lot of work and a lot of money." Van thoughtfully unrolled the plans, using abandoned Coke bottles to pin down their curling edges.

"Sounds like a job for Superman," suggested a new voice. They looked up to see a smiling Nicky Fontana.

"I woke up early, so I thought I'd see what's cooking. Hi, Maxie. You seen anybody I should know lately?"

"Only Nostradamus, looking to pay you off on a bet."

Nicky laughed and went to sprawl in Van's rejected chair, looking like he belonged in it.

"I thought you had company," Van remarked shortly, still shuffling papers.

"Unexpected company," Nicky emphasized. "Maxie, see if you can find Nostradamus. I've got a feeling rhymin' Simon will be heard of but not seen around here, now that he owes *me* dough for a change."

"Sure," Maxwell said, rising. He was lawyer enough to recognize a client's dismissal. "Take it easy," he said. Then he was gone.

"Whatcha doing?" Nicky asked approaching the desk.

"Working."

"Uh-oh. You must have got up on the wrong side of a prickly pear this morning. What're you working *on*, then?"

"The hotel."

"Are all those plans for this joint?"

"Every last floor and broom closet. I'm trying to

adapt my . . . our . . . far-fetched redesign scheme to reality."

"Hey, those are my digs, aren't they?" Nicky prowled on silent Gucci loafers behind Van's desk to study the drawings from the proper angle.

His hand braced itself on the low back of her chair, the knuckles pressing softly into her shoulder blade. Van stiffened, then swiftly reshuffled papers until the lobby floor plan rested on top.

"This is the key piece," she explained. "Once we establish the hotel's new theme in the marquee outside and carry it through the lobby, casino, and restaurant areas, redecorating the guest rooms should be a snap."

"I'm redoing the penthouse all by my lonesome, remember," Nicky warned. "Something in this place should be my private . . . preserve."

"I wouldn't have it any other way." Van turned to punctuate her remark with a stern glance.

Nicky had leaned nearer to view the plans, his freshly shaven cheek pressing perilously close to hers, a tangy lime scent inundating her nostrils.

Van turned back to the desk, her knuckles whitening on the desk rim as she spoke.

"We have to, of course, follow the rules of Las Vegas 'ambience.' The nighttime exterior should outshine day light, and the casino interior should resemble a night sky, dark and faintly twinkling."

"Where'd you get all that?" Nicky leaned so close to study the papers that the back support of Van's chair cracked in protest.

"Here." Van tapped a slim book while Nicky articulated its lengthy title.

"*Learning from Las Vegas: The Forgotten Symbolism of Architectural Form*. You mean people write books about this town—*real* books, not just gambling guides?"

"Not 'people'—a study group from the Yale University School of Art and Architecture."

"Well, I'll be damned! You mean I'm not crazy! This town is worth something? We *know* something here?"

"I mean that *some* well-educated people have found method in its madness; all I have to do is decode it, and we'll have a hotel. Tom Wolfe called Las Vegas the Versailles of America, but then he's a journalist and prone to hyperbole."

"I don't care what this big bad Wolf character—whoever he is—thinks. I just want to know if my hotel will be the tops. First-class?"

She kept her eyes unflinchingly forward. "First-class," she asserted. "If I find the time to do some preliminary groundwork."

"I get it." He straightened and withdrew.

At the door he paused. "About Darcy. The lady upstairs." His dark head jerked upward toward the penthouse. "She's a friend of mine, that's all. She needed a favor."

"So do I." Van was rewarded by a shrug of Nicky's silk-clad shoulders and a last lazy parting glance.

Just as Van resolved to get down to work a presence catapulted to her desktop.

Four fat black paws pinned the plans as effectively as and much more decoratively than Coke bottles. "You silly courtyard cat! How did you sneak inside the hotel? You're interrupting my work. Do you think you can slide through life on charm alone? And you act like you *own* the hotel." Van leaned near to confide in the cat's alertly cocked ears: "Have I got the soulmate for you!"

Within a week, blue-lined floor plans wallpapered the office's empty walls, and both the stray black cat and the White Sheep of the Fontana Family came and went at their separate but lordly leisure.

The cat confined itself to curling up at Van's feet, sitting on the precise document she most wished to use or hanging soulfully over her luncheon tray.

The man satisfied himself with popping in unexpectedly, aiming unsmoked cigarettes at various targets on the wall-pinned floor plans and asking too many questions.

"Haven't you got anything else to do but watch me work?" Van asked irritably one afternoon when the air-conditioning groaned to repel a particularly suffocating wave of late summer heat.

Nicky shrugged, revealing the gold charm at the open neck of his knit sport shirt, and smiled, "You don't look like you're working," he noted.

"This is when I work most, deciding the theme. Once the architects and construction bosses come in, it's literally out of our hands."

"That's why I'm here," Nicky said in an I-told-you-so tone. "To consult at this vital stage." He pinched a cigarette between his thumb and forefinger, then threw it at the wall opposite. "Almost got the bar carousel that time," he crowed, rising to retrieve his makeshift dart.

Van rolled her eyes.

"What are you trying to get done?" Nicky asked as he sat down.

"Right now I'm assigning functions and names to the various public areas. The greenhouse restaurant will be the Rainbow Oasis, for instance."

"Greenhouse. Isn't all that overhead desert sunlight pouring through the glass going to cost big bucks to cool?"

"That's the beauty of this new German roofing system that runs colored water between panes of glass, any shade you want, to reflect or absorb light as needed. And you can spotlight it at night too. Tailor-made for Las Vegas sparkle."

Nicky leaned forward, elbows atop her desk, to trace the first-floor outline with an impeccable fingernail. "I suppose you don't want to call this exterior waterway the Dove Moat—to go with the bird theme?"

"Certainly not! Something like the Crystal Promenade should do it. It'll be an informal area anyway, with cocktail service and walkways. And"—she watched him warily—"I've closely examined the square footage of the penthouse and adjoining roof."

"How closely?" Nicky's eyebrows raised in an expression that was kissing cousin to a smirk.

"Close enough to decide that—look, Nicky, where's this infamous whirlpool of yours located, exactly? It's not on the plan."

"I added it," he confessed, turning the paper around to study the faint blue lines crisscrossing it before targeting a spot with his thumb. "Yeah, right here. Big enough to seat six, yet small enough for two, if you get what I mean."

Dark eyes smiled up with impish significance. Van got precisely what he meant but wasn't about to admit it.

"It really doesn't matter *what* size your spa is! The point is that the unused portion of the roof should be converted into a starlight whirlpool area for the guests— if you don't mind commercial considerations impinging on your 'private preserve.'"

"Object, hell! That's a great idea!" Nicky snapped erect, his eyes widening to visualize the possibilities.

"Sultry starlit nights on the roof," he intoned in a husky radio-smooth baritone, "a split of champagne, bubbles in the glass and fiberglass, a discreet wash of piped-in music—the guests will love it! Who would have thought the great von Rhine would come up with a sybaritic stunt like that?"

Van glared, more disconcerted by his use of a classy word like "sybaritic" than his implication.

"What'll we call it?" Nicky mused. "Midnight at the Oasis? The Crystal Seraglio? The Phoenix Nest?"

"Don't be ridiculous! Where do you get all that nonsense?"

"I did go to college, you know. I learned a *little* something."

"Not so you could prove it," Van snapped. "We'll

worry about names later. All I need now is your permission to appropriate the area."

"Hey. . ." Nicky rose to leave, but first he leaned over the desk and took Van's chin in the palm of his hand, as he had the first time they met. "You don't need my permission for anything, Van. You're the boss lady. You don't need anybody's permission. Remember that."

She blinked into his Coke dark eyes as another name for the whirlpool deck popped into her dazed mind— the Velvet Maelstrom.

"And don't work too late," he admonished from the doorway. "You were in better shape when you were running me ragged all over town at all hours, von Rhine. You look terrible lately."

Van stared at the door after he had exited, then sighed and rotated her head on her neck. "Terrible."

By the time Van rolled the plans away and returned to her room, the sun had long since set. She switched on the TV and kicked off her shoes. Then the phone rang—the first time in days.

"Yes?"

"You sound worried. You must have been expecting me to call."

"Don't be ridiculous, Nicky. Is something wrong?"

"Yes. It's nine o'clock, and you haven't eaten dinner yet. Why don't you meet me in the lobby and we'll grab something along the Strip?"

"I was planning a quiet night in—"

"I know. That's why I called. Incidentally, you shouldn't stay down in the office this late alone; there're some unsavory characters roaming around."

"I know. But I almost never run into you."

"Not bad. I see I'm in for a tongue-lashing. Meet you downstairs in ten minutes."

Van sighed as the dial tone growled soothingly into her ear. She looked terrible. Nicky had seen every decent dress she had packed. The Strip depressed her. She didn't know what was wrong with her but was certain that Nicky would tell her, given the opportunity.

Ten minutes later she emerged from her room, having paired her blue silk heels with a matching blouse and the white suit-skirt she had worn that day.

The lobby, still half-lit, was deserted. Van paced, expecting promptness as the least Nicky could do in making a pest of himself. Instead, the nameless cat greeted her, massaging her calves with luxuriantly furred sides.

"Left your office hidey-hole, did you?" Van bent to pat it, then froze in midstoop, her every sense alert. Something was wrong, something about the lobby, and it was ordinarily so unremarkable that she hardly noticed it.

She looked around. For once, it was truly deserted, its ever-present peripheral denizens absent. Except... Van walked toward the rear hallway, aware of a subtle halo of unauthorized light leaking from somewhere.

Her heels moved from carpeting to institutional tile, ringing loud all at once. Behind her, the cat stalked on velvet paws.

Voices murmured from behind closed doors—one angry, another too soft, too strangely soft, to be heard. Van's heels tapped out a reckless faster beat.

The light came from the executive offices, from under the closed door that led to them, she realized, which she never bothered to shut or lock.... She slapped her evening purse under her arm as she tried the knob, expecting resistance for no reason.

The door sprang open, hurling her into the long passageway with it, casting her into its full light. The voices stopped. She went to her office. Four men stood in it now, making its managerial spaciousness seem suddenly cramped. Four men—three middle-aged men in dark sport clothes and Nicky Fontana.

"I'm sorry," Van blurted. "If I interrupted anything, that is . . . I'll wait in the lobby."

Nicky nodded curtly, his face taut. "Go on, then," he said harshly. "Get out of here."

She planted her feet, as she had with Macho Mario Fontana. "It's my office," she began in a too-high voice. "Van—leave!"

She stared at Nicky. And then she looked beyond him. Her carefully pinned-up plans hung askew. Her desktop was a worse mess than she had left it. Everything had . . . shifted.

One of the men had edged beyond her now, between her and the door.

"I'll see you in the lobby, then," she was saying, backing away from what she saw, from what she thought she saw. A secret meeting; men—mob types; Nicky, the hotel . . . Ugly questions, with uglier answers, lurked just around the corner.

The man behind her made himself into a door—a closed door—and she stopped.

"Let her go," Nicky said, his voice low, angry, and quietly desperate.

"Maybe this is a sign," the man behind her said. "Hotels are a dangerous business, Fontana, especially for parties who don't know what they're doin'."

Heavy hands dropped without warning to Van's shoulders. She stiffened without turning, recognizing that a reaction would only incite a greater one.

"Is that why you're here, to give me a few pointers?" Nicky demanded with reckless, attention-drawing tenacity. "Is that it?"

"Yeah, that's it." One man spoke, but it could have been any of them. They looked like the three little pigs, Van thought—beefy and possessed of a brutish shrewdness. "You got nerve, Nicky boy, askin' *us* what we're doin' here, like you own the place or somethin'."

Thug Number One, the spokesman, jabbed Nicky in the chest, right below the small gold charm, which twinkled wickedly in response. Numbers Two and Three, including the man behind Van, moved like swift lethal machines to Nicky, their porkchop hands sliding ever so lightly down his silken arms, then tightening to restraints.

"No!" Van stepped toward the intruders.

"Little lady..." Number One warned her off, not bothering to break eye contact with Nicky but holding up a forbidding hand.

"Stay out of it," Nicky said between clenched teeth.

It infuriated Van, the way they all acted as if she were not there, and yet all seemed obsessed with her presence.

Number One did something with his other hand, hard and fast to Nicky's stomach. Van never saw the blow, only Nicky sagging in the grasp of his jailers. The charm jiggled obscenely in the light of the overhead fluorescents.

Then Nicky was twisting like a fish on a line, flailing his arms. Thugs scattered as they lost control. Blows landed, air expelled in savage muttered bursts from male throats. Van felt trapped inside the life-sized silver screen at the wrong kind of movie.

"Stop it!" she shouted, unable to follow the action.

A man behind her grabbed her arm. She stepped back into him and ground her stiletto heel onto his instep with all the passion of a Spanish dancer.

A curse turned into a sharp pained wail. Behind her, a winded voice gathered to grunt a warning.

"Maybe this'll give you the idea, Fontana! Get out of the hotel business. It ain't healthy."

Number One swaggered over to pat Nicky's cheek in a parody of affection right out of *The Godfather*. And Nicky—there was fire in his eyes, but the thugs secured his arms, and blood oozed slowly at the edges of his face.

The men brushed past Van on their way out, Number One pausing to address her as he left. "Maybe you should get yourself a new boyfriend, girlie. This one's got no brains and less class, not to mention life expectancy."

He was gone. Van turned back into the room to find Nicky watching the door like someone on a leash. His eyes lowered as she stared, and he turned to sit on the desk.

"Are you hurt?" She edged sideways into the room, her purse clasped before her, her back to the wall as if she expected bogeymen to leap out from everywhere. "What was that about?"

"God knows," he said, then laughed. "Beating the kid to a pulp if you hadn't happened in, I guess. I heard something while I was waiting for you. When I came down the hall, I ran into the Three Stooges ransacking the office." He glanced up, looking like a real prizefighter this time. "Trust dames to be late and get a guy in trouble."

"I wasn't late!" Van was angry, she didn't know quite why or at whom. "And they wouldn't have been here at all if you hadn't had this crazy idea about a hotel—or your uncle Mario hadn't been in the Family business up to his Havana cigars! And I wouldn't have been here, either, if you hadn't had your heart set on bringing 'class' to a city that wouldn't recognize the meaning of the word if it was spelled out in neon twenty stories high!"

"Hey. . ." Nicky was coming toward her, an expression on his battered face as if it were Van who had been attacked and needed soothing.

"Stay away from me!" The wall was at her back now, and she edged even farther along it until she felt the right-angle reassurance of a corner. "Stay away! I don't want to see you. I don't want to know about things like this. It's crazy, Nicky. You can't do anything good in a rotten town like this! I should never have come. I wouldn't have, except . . . except—"

"It's nothing. I'm fine. Those bozos couldn't dust off a fruit fly. My brothers did worse when I was nine."

Nicky had her in the corner, and Van didn't know where to look so that she wouldn't see his worried face coming at her wearing an expression of cautious solicitude, as if *she'd* been hurt when any fool except Nicky Fontana could see that it was he who needed help.

"Let go of me!" Van ordered in her best Uncle-Mario-banishing voice as his hands clasped her arms.

Nicky's face came closer, the blood already drying on his cheek, the bruises already setting alongside the cuts like small swollen purple suns.

"No," he said softly, dangerously determined. *"No."*

Interlude

Midnight Louie Registers a Grievance

I am used to being overlooked, as I have said before, and I do not really expect a guy and doll who just repel three of the more repellent extant examples of Las Vegas muscle to pay much attention to me. And then I am in my retreat at the darkest corner of the lobby, and I am discreet normally, so when I am trying to be subtle, I am almost invisible.

So my not inconsiderable person is successfully camouflaged, and neither Mr. Nicky Fontana nor the little doll see me when he escorts her back to the lobby.

Well, needless to say, the thought of dinner does not sit so good on anyone's stomach, including mine—although I am not adverse to slipping by Dome of the Sea for a small snack later. Miss Van von Rhine is one subdued doll as Mr. Nicky Fontana leads her to the elevator, and I can discern, even from the dark, that she is upset more than somewhat.

But Mr. Nicky Fontana is a prince, as I indicated before, and he just guides her along with his arm around her shoulders, whispering whatever guys whisper to more than somewhat upset dolls.

I have never seen so spirited a lady undergo such a change in my whole lengthy lifetime. And I am not optimistic about Mr. Nicky Fontana's being able to bring this little doll around, not with his personal performance record with same little doll.

It is a long, dark, lonely night, and I am not optimistic about anything, I decide.

Chapter

Eight

"This is *your* floor!"

"They're *all* my floors." Nicky grinned as he escorted Van along the corridor to the penthouse door. "At least you're noticing where you are now."

"Yes," she agreed with a start, her shoulder shrugging off his custodial arm. Nicky stiffened at the rejection, then relaxed and elaborately backed away before speaking.

"I, for one, plan to clean up before I decide if I still want to go out for dinner—" He winced while massaging his stomach with his palm. "That guy's fist was packing a roll of quarters, or I'm an anteater."

"Oh." Van trailed him into the darkened penthouse, as if realizing just then that Nicky's wounds were more than a Technicolor effect on a distant screen. "Does it . . . hurt?"

He turned on the overhead track lighting and faced her with another deprecatory grimace. "Yeah." He lurched down the hallway.

Van waited. Under the bright penthouse lighting, it was impossible to forget that Nicky's wounds were real. He looked as if he'd been run through a wringer backward, despite his glib jokes. He looked, in short, awful.

Van set down her evening bag with sudden resolution and moved purposefully down the hall after him.

She found Nicky bracing himself on a black porcelain pedestal sink. He was dabbing at his facial cuts with a black washcloth, in the process sprinkling more water on his silk shirt than on his wounds.

"This is atrocious decor," Van noted, glancing grimly around the half bath and appropriating the washcloth.

Nicky made no protest but sat against the sink edge and studied the room while Van rubbed his already tender face with stringent German efficiency and some alcohol she'd found in the medicine cabinet.

"What's wrong with this decor?" he asked truculently.

"It's cheap . . . tawdry," Van retorted, slathering on alcohol despite his winces. "Black, white, and gold went out as a bathroom color scheme with Attila the Hun. The orgy wallpaper is gauche, the filigree lighting fixture belongs in a brothel, as does most of what passes for decor in this town, and the tap handles don't turn easily."

She savagely tweaked the gilt tails of brass peacocks posing as sink hardware and released a stream of rapidly overheating water.

"Take it easy, lady," Nicky pled only half-jokingly. "First you try to scrub me to death. Now you're trying to boil my backside!"

He jumped away from spattering hot water and began unbuttoning his now fully sodden shirt.

Van turned to shut off the water.

"Thank you, Miss Vanessa."

She whirled. "Why do you call me that?"

He shrugged, plastering the wet silk more tightly to his torso. "Van . . . Vanessa. Makes sense. And a Vanessa would be an efficient, well-controlled female, a cool hand in an emergency, organized to the point of folding a wet washcloth into fours and putting it neatly away—"

Van jumped guiltily and hurled away the washcloth her hands had absently been quartering in just the manner he described. Nicky was busy now peeling himself out of his shirt muscle by finely articulated muscle.

Van found the process prolonged and rather suggestive. She concentrated instead on the curious medallion at his throat.

"You're lucky those men didn't walk off with that. It must be worth something."

Nicky clasped the small medal in a protective fist as if just remembering it. "It's worth something to *me*."

"What is it?"

He paused in disrobing, looking first sheepish, then cunning. "If I tell you, will you tell me—?"

"No baptismal names."

"—then promise not to laugh?"

"I never laugh, remember? No sense of humor."

"If I tell you, will you tell me why that scene downstairs tore you up so much?"

"I don't know," Van said. "I really don't know."

He looked at her for a long time, then released the charm as if it no longer needed guarding. It fell against his naked chest, bright as a coin spinning on a rich walnut tabletop.

"St. Jude," Nicky confessed. "It's a medal of St. Jude. The Saint of the Impossible."

Van had nothing to say in the face of this childish and somehow touching faith, except finally to smile. "I always said you were impossible."

"You don't know the half of it," he began, edging nearer.

She eluded him by going to examine the clear vinyl shower curtain with its drawings of Greek gods and goddesses in imaginatively compromising positions.

"I didn't put this stuff in, for God's sake!" Nicky exploded. "I just live here, remember?"

"What are you going to do now?"

Nicky shrugged. "I don't know. Hit the jets, I guess, before I stiffen like a corpse. Those guys and me, we tussled more than it looked."

He left the room and Van followed. "Jets?" she asked uncertainly.

He grinned at her over his shoulder, one eye already swelling slightly shut. He would look hideous by morning. "Jets. Come on. You can view the infamous whirlpool."

En route, he paused at the mirrored bar, regarded his battered face, winced, and poured three fingers of brandy into a snifter. He handed that glass to Van and poured six fingers into another.

"Without dinner?" Van inquired sharply.

"Lady, it's my stomach, and right now it needs an anesthetic."

Pushing aside the sliding glass door, Nicky ushered Van onto the open rooftop. The heat felt unexpectedly heavy.

Unlucky or not, the thirteenth floor loomed high enough above a mostly low-profile city so that Van and Nicky seemed alone with the darkness. Above them, the night sky opened its robes to reveal a black velvet lining stitched with stars.

"Any complaints about the decor?" Nicky was swirling the brandy in his glass.

"None," Van said simply. She carefully minced her needle-narrow heels around the cracks between the redwood planks leading to some risers. At the top of the steps, under a latticework gazebo trellised by climbing roses pregnant with full-blown scent, the inset whirlpool foamed.

"I fail to see the attraction."

"It's not so bad; soothes the savaged soul." He came over to take her brandy snifter and set it down with his on a bench. "You should try it. Your muscles'll feel like they lifted weights in the morning. You were pretty uptight down there."

"I don't ordinarily encounter thugs in the process of accosting my acquaintances!" Van turned away, as if the sight of Nicky Now reminded her too painfully of Nicky Then. "What did those men want? And why? And what will you do about it?"

"I'll worry about that later. Now I need some tender loving hot water."

Van froze as a belt buckle clinked behind her, followed by the grate of a zipper.

"Come on," Nicky urged, "hop in. There are some extra bikinis around if you're shy."

"There *would* be!" Van exploded, so outraged that she swirled to face him.

Horrified, she let her glance drop to check what she should have ascertained before turning—his dark Jockeys were no more modest than European-style swimtrunks, which was not saying much for their efficiency.

But Nicky's attention was totally focused on her now. Barefoot, he was unnervingly even with her high-heeled height.

His face seemed conspiratorially near as he crooned, "Relax, Van. It's over. Things like that happen all the time in Vegas. I know how to deal with it, but I don't think you do. Just get loose and let go a little. . . ."

He reached for her, and she backed away, jamming a heel in a crack.

"My silk blouse—you'll get it wet! Oh damn! My shoe!"

He knelt to work her foot loose, finally pulling her instep free while he twisted the recalcitrant heel loose. One-footed, Van was forced to balance herself with one hand on Nicky's bare shoulder and recall a similar, more emotional scene the night before.

The whirlpool was veiling them with a warm mist, and the subtle play of the muscles under Van's fingers sent shivers up her arm and down her spine. How, she wondered, had she gotten herself into this ridiculous position?

"Free at last!" He flourished the liberated sandal. "Better take off the other one."

While Van again stooped to use him for a hand rest, Nicky patiently waited to claim the second shoe. When he had the pair, he quickly tossed them aside, bent, slipped an arm under Van's knees.

"Nicky, what are you doing?" She was screeching like a teenager, which only made him chuckle as he lifted her.

In three quick descending steps he was in the whirlpool, sinking into the fevered water with Van in his arms. She was screaming in full voice now, her fists clenched clichés beating on his arms and chest.

"Stop it! You . . . you thug! You unmitigated *savage*! I'm getting all wet . . . My silk blouse—Nicky, you're impossible, and you're drowning me! Oh, my *beautiful* blue blouse . . ."

She rose from the bubbling water like a vengeful dryad as Nicky reclined on his underwater bench, arms wide along the spa's curved fiberglass sides, and surveyed his handiwork.

"See, it's not so bad. Kind of relaxing, actually."

"'Relaxing'! You're a Vandal! A Hun! You've ruined my clothes . . . even my hair's soaking! Hasn't anybody ever taught you any manners?"

"Hasn't anybody ever taught you anything else?" he retorted, suddenly leaning inward.

His hands kept her from thrashing in the water that roiled around her hips. They were suddenly close to each other; the night was their private spangled black umbrella, and thugs existed only as a preface to a much longer and more involved story.

Nicky's fingers rose from the foaming water to tease the silk-covered top button of her blouse. "It's ruined already. Why not get rid of it?"

His voice had gone low, and the intensity of his eyes deepened as he lowered long dark Italian lashes over that uncommonly fierce expression. His face drifted nearer to Van's, his cut lips moving toward hers.

"You're—depraved," Van breathed without conviction.

Nicky's hands relentlessly descended the seam of her

wet blouse, rending loose one button after the other. They were everywhere—at her waist underwater, at her shoulders easing silk and thin lingerie straps off her body, at her French twist, pulling hidden pins loose and letting damp waves of hair brush her water-misted shoulders.

By the time their lips met, Van was conscious only of floating in a benign, bubbling environment while pieces of her everyday skin flayed away into the midnight distance. All she could hear was the soft, persuasive rise and fall of the voice so near her ear, it seemed an echo of her own thoughts. All she could feel was how divinely right this moment, these sensations, felt.

"That's a pretty baby," Nicky was saying.

His wet eyelashes fluttered against her cheek as he worked the blouse sleeves down her arms. In a moment something went spinning into the darkness, followed by another lacy something. Wet skin slid along wet skin, paradoxically like velvet. Van could no longer tell which sensation was her own and which came from him as they rocked together in the lulling water.

Suddenly Van giggled and writhed away. "Nicky! That tickles!"

He splashed after her, his dimly lit grin devilish. "Oh, so that's your Achilles heel—your ribs!"

He pinned her against the spa's opposite side, along the built-in recliner, his tongue stopping her bubbling laughter in her throat as he kissed her hard and long and fierce.

Every time their faces slipped underwater their heads would struggle back above the froth-boiled surface for gasps of air. Then Nicky would take quick advantage of Van's parted lips, and they would be lost in an embrace that bridged two opposite elements, air and water, and two opposite but mated bodies.

Van felt Nicky's tireless hands working the straight white skirt down her legs; she sensed sudden freedom when he rose to hurl its wet length over the gazebo rail. Then his thumbs were pushing down her clinging pantyhose, prodding into more and more intimate territory until Van broke away, heaved herself back in the water, and looked at him.

Mercurial Nicky at last was still, statue still, looking back at her. Laughter and lust had vanished like bubbles. Only the jet-propelled water moved, restless and caressing. Underneath it, Van lifted her hips to tug the hose down to her knees. Nicky's hands met hers there and quickly peeled them from her feet.

This time when he stood to throw the last of her clothing to the wind, the limp hose snaked back and twined his forearm. Grimacing, he unwound it and finally tossed it aside, bending to dredge up one last article of apparel—his this time—and toss it in a wet lump to the redwood decking.

Then he sat back in the whirlpool, opposite her, and they viewed each other across the small expanse of foaming water, as fighters do, accustomed to marking their encounters in the measured cadence of rounds.

"You look like a Southern belle," Nicky said suddenly, with a smile.

Van glanced down. She crouched in the hip-high water, a ruffle of white bubbles unfurling around her bare shoulders. He turned away, reaching for the brandy snifter. Van caught her breath. Nicky turned back and stretched out an arm in mute invitation. She could have lunged full length in the water, kept herself half-hidden, and still have reached his side in two seconds.

Instead, she stood—slowly, shyly, the warm water curdling away from her body like a second skin. It ebbed first from her breasts, then inch by inch along her ribs, her elbows and waist, her hips—then stopped, the foam forming a modest bikini line beneath her navel.

"Now you look like a Vegas show girl." he said. "No.

Classier. Like that Venus that's all hair and skin in that famous painting by... by Vermicelli—"

"Botticelli," she corrected indulgently.

"Whatever." His dark eyes were drowning in visual pleasure. "Us Italian guys sure can paint." His outstretched hand reached for her. "We can do other stuff too."

She moved toward him, step by step, her thighs cutting through the viscous water. He waited until she stood directly in front of him before curling his arm around her back and pressing the arch of her torso toward him. He brought his bruised mouth to the tip of one wet breast.

Van shivered at the contact, taking a deep breath and thrusting her face at the stars. Nicky murmured something, his free hand suddenly supporting the weight of her other breast before he wrenched his mouth from one to the other as if even twin aspects of her each held an insatiably individual lure. His lips and teeth worked with inciting skill; when he broke away to rest his chin on her midriff and tilt his face up at hers, she was looking back down at him with a hot calm and mutual intent.

He laughed suddenly and pulled her down beside him into the crook of his arm, offering her mouth the lip of the brandy snifter instead of his as she had expected.

"Clear your senses. It kind of unnerves me to see a classy lady looking like she's thinking of doing a striptease."

"How could I be? I don't have anything on to tease you with."

"Want to bet?" Nicky asked tenderly, tilting the brandy to her lips, then setting the goblet quickly aside and kissing her as if to share the heady sizzle of the taste.

Nicky was a verbal lover; he vocalized uninhibitedly, purring and chirping and growling and nipping. Above the water their lips ground and their tongues delved; below it, they slid off each other's limbs with tantalizing confusion, and Nicky's sure, delicate fingertips were toying with the tops of her thighs.

"Oh, Vanessa mine, you are not only efficient by day but a tigress by night," he was teasing.

Van's hands left the cable-hard shoulders they were kneading and hit the water flat, sending up a plume of spray. "I'm *not* a Vanessa! Why can't you just call me Van, like everybody else?"

"It's not very romantic, sweetheart," Nicky answered, doing something not very romantic but most effective to the back of her thighs. "And I'm not 'everybody else,'" he added, proving it by kissing her until their mouths seemed to merge.

"Now was that first class or not?" he demanded on parting.

"I don't know how you can——" Van was serious again, appalled by how natural it felt to be cavorting naked in a whirlpool with a man she hardly knew in any real sense.

"How I can what?"

"Laugh off things, like earlier tonight . . . and now."

His thumbs stroked soothingly along her jawline and ended up massaging the tense muscles along the top of her shoulders.

"What's eating you? Is it something you're afraid of?" His expression sharpened with an unwelcome thought, then turned solicitous. "Are you still a virgin?"

"No!" She had shouted the word from the rooftop almost before the last word emerged, so it was impossible to tell which question she denied so violently.

In an instant she was pressing close to him, her legs wrapping his waist, her arms around his torso, her tongue drawing a wet spiral around the convolutions of his ear.

"I'm not a virgin," she whispered wetly in his ear. "Does that take the fun out of it?"

"No. I just wondered what hurt you——"

"You," she murmured. "You hurt me when you stop

touching me and start talking. Kiss me again, Nicky, touch me. . . ."

It was too blatant an invitation to resist. Even though a frown had creased Nicky's forehead, it soon eased into an expression of concentrated sensuality. He was as lost as she. It was so surprising, this fevered lovemaking between two personalities seemingly oil and water.

To Nicky, it held a poignancy—a feeling as foreign to him as the word normally was. A preciousness. A magic. His mind searched for a way to name it, this surprising meeting between two creatures from vastly different worlds. He felt as if he'd picked up a porcupine and found a kitten.

She was murmuring feverishly now, too, all the right words, or rather *the* right word over and over. "Yes," she was saying whenever their lips parted long enough for one or the other to get a word in edgewise. "Oh, yes, yes, yes. . . ."

He pulled her to her feet with him, ran his hands down the undulations of her back as far as they could reach, melding her to him.

Separation seemed an obscenity, but he stepped out of the still-churning water and made sure she didn't slip on the way out. In the rooftop dark, she paused and looked at him, all of him. She reached without shyness to his face and let her hand stroke down the naked field of his chest and his belly to the dark vulnerable coil of hair at the hinge of his legs.

Then her hand dropped, and they went barefoot and dripping through the ankle-deep shag of the living room and up the spiral staircase to the bedroom.

Nicky hit the light switch with a sure touch in the dark. Lights sprang into life all around them, but their eyes were already linked as if by something that didn't require illumination to connect perfectly. They sank onto the bed.

Her body, untouched by the desert sun, seemed whiter than the haughty Carrara marble statues outside Caesars Palace. He was beginning to fathom what "class" meant, and it wasn't the cold, distant thing he had thought it was. Nicky swallowed.

"You're sure?"

She only nodded her grave face, the pale ripples of hair around it dipping onto her shoulders. He wished he were that hair, that he could touch her with such exquisite lightness. He brushed back the hair from her temples and began encompassing her face with small, neat, endless kisses. Her fingers combed into his hair and pressed his lips closer.

"Nicky . . . you're so . . . sweet." She sounded surprised.

He smiled through his kisses and let his fingers curl through the hair between her thighs, finding hidden warmth and a liquid welcome.

"Tell me afterward if you think I'm sweet," he advised, strumming her like a guitar until she gasped at the sudden surge of his passion, until she opened to him and lost herself in sighs and moans. She kept incitingly still as he eased the damp contraceptive sponge into place, making necessity into a sensual exercise. It was a popular notion that Nicky Fontana was the quintessential eternal child, but he prided himself on being responsible when it counted. He came to her invited, drawn in, sinking into her rampant complicity with relief and incalculable pleasure and shuddering satisfaction.

They moved together, deeply isolated in their separate cells of sensation, joined by a mutual melody of the senses. Nicky sheathed himself. She was a glove and he was cold.

When it had finally trembled to a stop and they lay in each other's arms, their faces buried—hers in his shoulder, his in her hair—as if to hide what was ordinarily most visible from this extraordinarily hidden intimacy, when it was over as any human act must be, they were silent.

Nicky pulled the covers over them, feeling a little

like an Adam who had just been shown the flaming sword and the fast way out of Eden, with Eve to look after. Why he felt that way he couldn't have said; Van would have bristled at the fancy of being "looked after" by anyone, especially him of all people. Of all people.

He smiled his lazy satisfaction and fell soundly asleep. It was probably exactly what Adam had done after the Fall.

Chapter

Nine

"Rise and shine, Evangeline."

Van's upper lip twitched at the featherweight touch of a fingertip. Her eyes blinked open. Nicky's forefinger was rhythmically stroking her eyelashes upward.

"You look awful!" she told him to his bruising face.

"It's a good thing I've been looking at you all night, then," he commented calmly.

She rolled her eyes heavenward, uncomfortable as the focus of such concentrated attention, and found slices of herself and himself reflected back. Surprise provided a pretext for pushing herself up against the headboard and away from Nicky's morning-after ardor.

"What is that?" she demanded. "Mirror strips inset between red velvet—*padded* red velvet?"

Nicky rolled onto his back to consider the upholstered ceiling while the long slivers of mirror above and behind them reflected censored portions of his anatomy.

"I inherited it," Nicky said, disclaiming the decor, "like Mama Tinucci's money. It's not my fault. Round waterbeds normally aren't my style."

"Round?" Van bobbed up in horror, "*Waterbed?*"

Her fingers tightened on the sheet as her widening eyes began to apprehend the room's screamingly overblown decor. Her fingers tightened on the sheet . . . the *red satin* sheet . . . then nearly loosened it, except

that Van had decided that discretion was the better part
of disgust.

"Nicky, that's *gold-veined, antique-style* mirror slathered
all over this place!"

"You're right," he consoled. "Your eyes don't go with
this decor. I'll change it. I was planning to anyway." He
rolled over again and wriggled his way up the gelatinously
shifting slick bedding to concentrate on kissing a path
along her skin just above the red satin sheet. "None of
this is the real me," he reassured her between kisses.

Van stared aghast at his face, now clearly wearing the
badges of his assault. She was undecided whether to
laugh or cry—or simply call for help.

"I can't believe I'm here," she finally managed to
say.

"You can't believe which—that you made love in a
room as lowbrow as this, or with me?"

"Neither. Both. I . . . don't know—"

Nicky's forefinger pressed silence to her lips, his face
straining upward to meet hers. Van found her chin
dipping to accommodate him, her lips yearning toward
his own, when the door thirty feet across the red shag
carpeting cracked open.

"Anybody up? Oops! Sorry, Nicky, that's a bad joke.
It's just Darcy. I needed the whirlpool again, and you
said anytime . . . are you in there, Nicky? The penthouse
door was unlocked."

He swore softly against the cleft of Van's breasts,
then lifted his head to answer. "Yeah, I'm here. Go
ahead and use the spa. I'll . . . uh . . . I won't be out
before you leave."

"Roger, Nicky!" Darcy's blithe voice faded as she
progressed back down the spiral staircase.

Nicky rolled off the bed and vanished around one of
many bloated swags of red velvet festooning it. Van
looked warily around in his absence. She'd never seen a
larger or more loathsome bedroom, not even in an Arab
sheik's suite at the Athens hotel.

Nicky reappeared from around the bed curtains, white duck pants his only uniform of the morning. "I'm sorry we got pinned in here by Darcy—"

"How could you forget to lock the door after. . . after those men last night? We could have been killed in . . . in *your* bed."

Van's shudder might have indicated a fear of mortality or of the idea of being found dead in *flagrante delicto* with Nicky Fontana, or simply of being found dead in a place in which she normally wouldn't be found—well . . . dead.

A smile quirked Nicky's slightly blistered mouth. "We didn't sleep that much. And I told you, those hoods were just trying to scare me—"

"Well, they scared *me!*" Van ran her hands up her naked arms, momentarily forgetting the sheet.

Nicky's eyes hooded. "You should scare more often."

She hid her face in her hands. "It was the brandy," Van moaned.

The red satin rippled as Nicky braced one knee on the bed and took her face in his hands. "I don't care what you call it, Evangeline. It was real."

"And what are you calling me now?"

Nicky grinned. "You were right. Vanessa's no name for you. So I thought and thought, and now I know what you're hiding—E*van*geline, like in the poem. E*van*geline von Rhine. It's a ponderous monicker for a wispy girl like you; no wonder you shortened it."

"I did not! I was never an E*van*geline or a *Van*essa or a *Van*ya or whatever ridiculous name you make up for me!"

Before he could answer—and his face wore an expression that indicated he intended to—a diffident knock sounded on the door, inadvertently pushing it even farther open.

"*Now* who?" Van hissed. "Am I to be paraded like this in front of everyone in Las Vegas?"

Nicky ran to keep the door from yawning further ajar. "Yeah?"

A female hand floated through the opening, trailing a pair of royal-blue high-heeled sandals and several damp pieces of women's clothing.

"Ah . . . Nicky. That whirlpool looks as if you held naval maneuvers in it last night—in the war of the sexes, that is. I only picked up the women's clothing. There was an article of men's attire—one single item— that I left for you to pick up, as a matter of principle. Men should learn how to do these things. But your . . . um, guest might appreciate getting these pronto."

"Thanks, Darcy; you're a real sport," Nicky said sarcasticly.

"Sure thing. Twenty minutes should get my leg back in shape, and I'll go. *Ciao.* . . ."

Nicky moved back toward the bed, his arms draped like those of a dress-store clerk.

"Someday I'll strangle that girl—" He watched a large, red-satin lump burrowing toward the center of the circular bed. "Van, baby, don't take it so hard. She doesn't even know who—"

"But she knows *what*! Oh, I could die," came the undercover wail.

Nicky peeled her like a shiny scarlet grape, only to find her face almost redder than the sheets. Van snatched the damp clothing from his arms.

"At least be a gentleman *now* and turn your back while I get dressed!"

His dark head shook mournfully as he sat on the mattress edge. "Damn. I wish I had a cigarette, but I haven't carried them for two days—Hey, does that mean I quit smoking?"

He turned for confirmation of this admirable development, but his over-the shoulder glance met an icy-eyed Van hastily buttoning her wrinkled blue-silk blouse. Nicky snapped back to face the heavy red-velvet curtains veiling the windows.

"She'll be gone in a jiffy," he said. "This doesn't have anything to do with what happened last night."

"It has everything to do with it." Dressed at last, even if not neatly, Van came around the bed to confront him.

Her hair fell little-girl loose, but under those wheat-colored waves her face was grimly set. Nicky read a smidgen of regret in her expression, but he was a born optimist.

"This just goes to show how... inappropriate last night was, Nicky. To us, to our respective positions with the hotel. It can't happen again."

He rose abruptly, but the imperious flash of her open palm, quelling as a traffic cop's, stopped him from speaking.

"Yes, I know it was a stressful evening. We were both scared, hungry, and—"

"Cold?" he interjected bitterly.

"—and carried away. What happened was perfectly natural, under the circumstances. But it doesn't have to become, er, chronic." Every word she chose, trying to be so adult, came out childishly awkward, Van knew. Some raw fear made her talk on, feeling all the while that she was losing her grip on a ladder of silk. "Not while we're working so hard on the hotel. Business is business, and pleasure is—"

"—is nobody's business but ours!"

"Maybe in your world, but not in mine. We'll just pretend it never happened."

Van went to the window to pull back the ponderous velvet. A beacon of daylight spilled in, turning her blouse electric blue and painting her hair the color of melted butter.

She wouldn't live like her father, Van told herself grimly, hiding behind closed doors, imbibing transitory love on the sly. She'd be leaving soon, once the hotel was done and "class" was no longer a critical commodity to Nicky. He was hardly someone to rely upon when it came to enduring emotions—Nicky, who within a week or a month could be telling her the same cold sensible words of farewell.

"I'm not saying I regret it," Van added more softly.

"Thanks."

"But we're both adults and can control our whims. Once the hotel's done, if we should care to ... revive the relationship, I see no harm in an occasional—"

He was beside her ripping the curtains shut. In the heavy shadow his face looked fiercer than it had confronting the thugs in her overlit office the night before.

"You say you don't regret it?" he demanded.

Her self-contained expression melted like flame-licked metal while he watched.

"Not a moment," she whispered, her face tilting to his.

"But you'd walk away from it, like ... that!" His fingers snapped sharply. "Like it was something that didn't matter—some side bet you could afford to lose?"

"Isn't that what men do all the time?" A shadow moved in the room, a shadow from a sand castle Van had smashed long ago. Her voice tautened with control. She'd always been such an adult little girl; it had spared her many disappointments, but not enough. "Really, Nicky, you must learn to separate passion and love. Sometimes you are such a child."

She patted his cheek with icy fingers.

"Yoo-hoo! Anybody home?" Darcy's voice sparkled like sunshine outside the bedroom door. "I'm on my merry way, folks."

They heard the distant slam of the unmarked door that entered the suite.

"All right," Nicky said slowly, as if he were learning the words and the music to a new song for the first time, "we'll do it your way. You might as well go now. The coast's clear."

At the door she paused to look back. "About those men—"

"I'll peel Uncle Mario's brain, find out who's muscling in on who nowadays. It happens all the time in Vegas."

"We should discuss how we'll increase security. There'll be workmen soon, chances for sabotage."

Nicky's hand waved away such dire possibilities. He stood motionless against the lavish red velvet, the lower half of his figure clothed in white, the upper half unclothed bronze. He looked like a severed man, Van thought with an odd pang, as if somebody had cut him in half and he hadn't notice it yet.

"All right," she agreed, her voice choked. "I'll see you in my office later."

Nicky nodded, not moving, oddly frozen for so vital a personality. Van pulled the door shut behind her, shutting out the disturbing scene, shutting out the gaudy bedroom.

Perhaps, she told herself, Nicky was learning to grow up and face the music in a two-faced world. It struck her that she had finally been behind the closed door and that now she was walking away from it, shutting herself out as she had so often been shut out.

A week had passed since Van and Nicky's night together. The architect from Brazil had come and gone, with his minions, and would return soon with final plans for approval. Before long, the Crystal Phoenix wouldn't be a dream anymore or a deserted hulk sulking on the scintillating Strip but a dazzling reality.

Visualizing the hotel in all its promised dazzle, Van walked through the empty lobby and straight into the arms of a dark-haired youth wearing a pale sports ensemble and a big grin.

"Hey, 'scuse me, lady—I didn't see you, for which there is no forgivin' me."

"Shame on you," interjected his clone, who appeared to have popped from behind a pillar. "Are you makin' a pest of yourself again, Ralph? Give the lady some breathin' room and a chance to look at a real man."

"Who're you kidding?" demanded another. I'm senior here, kid. Ernesto Fontana at your service, ma'am. I didn't know Nicky had got so smart at keeping' a good thing under his panama."

"This is not whom you think it is," interjected a fourth man, whose mustache lent a thirtyish dignity to the group. "This isn't Nicky's new lady; it's Evonne van Rhine, the new manager, dummies!"

"Aw, Aldo, it is not!" argued one.

"You've got grapes in the *capo*, Aldo," said another.

"*Sour* grapes," put in the first to greet Van, apparently the second-youngest Fontana brother. This young man bowed to indicate a chair. "Have a seat, miss. Those little feet must get tired from being stood on so long."

"I presume I'm speaking to Fontana Incorporated," Van observed as she sat. If Nicky could be a conundrum, a temptation, an irritant, the Fontana boys, *en masse*, took her breath away.

"Oh, no," Ralph answered eagerly. "This is just a few of us. Dominic isn't here, or Emilio."

"Or Giuseppe," added Aldo.

"Or Armando," said the middle brother.

"So we're less than half the family, but what's to miss? Tony is here." The speaker, evidently the Tony in question, smiled modestly.

"And Rico." Another brother bowed to introduce himself.

"So this is the Crystal Phoenix!" Ernesto, the eldest present, took the measure of the lobby with a blasé face. "It has . . . possibilities." He toyed with the red carnation impaled in the buttonhole of his pale silk-blend Italian suit.

"So this is the famous Miss von Rhine." At least Ralph got it right, Van thought as he sidled up beside her on the extra-wide lounge chair. "Uncle Mario said you were some spicy pepperoni."

"Maybe Nicky's not crazy, after all," Rico conceded with a wink. He leaned near to Van as she leaned away from his encroaching brothers. "Maybe there's more to the hotel business than we thought."

"Well, it's been charming meeting you all—yes, I know you're not *all* of the Fontanas, but I'm sure you're a representative sampling. If you'll excuse me, there really are some things I should be attending to in my office."

"What?" they demanded in disappointed chorus.

"The, uh . . ." Van foundered.

"The details." Nicky had dredged up the dead weight of her lost sentence himself, coming up behind her to perch on the chair back, thereby completely hemming her in with Fontanas. "I said I'd like a couple of you boys to drop by now and then. Why the Family excursion?"

He may have been the youngest, but the others answered with a promptitude that bespoke a certain respect.

"We, uh, just wanted to look over the premises."

"To see what we were guarding," Aldo put in, rolling his eyes romantically at Van.

"If you only wanted a matched pair, Nicky," Ernesto said with fraternal disdain, "you should have asked for Dobermans."

"'Guarding'?" Van twisted to look more directly at Nicky than she had in a week.

"Yeah." He had been toying with the cigarette case, which he'd taken to carrying again, but he dropped it into the side pocket of his light-colored linen blazer. "The boys here are our new security patrol. Less obvious than the normal types and just as discouraging, maybe more so. They're doing me a favor by seeing that nobody messes with me, my hotel, or my classy manager."

On the last words his hands moved lightly to Van's shoulders. She resented the possessiveness of the gesture even as his touch engendered an uncontrollable jolt of adrenaline. Van kept herself still, recognizing that Nicky knew by now how to establish his territory among so large and competitive a brotherhood.

All the smiling faces sobered. "Uncle Mario doesn't know," Ernesto said, making the sentence a statement.

"No," Nicky answered, as if addressing Van only. "I thought it best to keep the Family out of it officially. It's my hotel, my business. But—" He stood, and Van eased back into the chair as she felt the light pressure of his fingers melt away. "—if you guys need some Family seniority to give you bozos permission to visit your little brother—"

"No, Nicky!" "No way, *bambino!*" "No problem!" chorused the brothers.

Van rose and smiled. "It was so nice to meet you all. I won't worry about the hotel with you four—"

"Nine," Aldo corrected. "All nine of us will be dropping by in turn."

She tried not to look dismayed. "With you *nine* gentlemen"—they preened in unison—"on the premises."

"I guarantee, Miss von Rhine," Ernesto announced formally, "that not a strand upon your golden head shall be touched by any of the lower elements in Vegas."

"Very. . . reassuring," Van said in farewell, moving quickly across the vast lobby.

At the office hallway she paused. The Fontana boys had swarmed around Nicky, dispensing mock blows followed by quick, happy hugs. They'd heard of the assault on one of their own and were responding. Van shivered. She felt alone, left out in the cold, and could sense the fraternal warmth radiating across the room as if it were being generated in cruel, deliberate contrast.

As she watched, Nicky turned suddenly from the group. His eyes met hers. Van smiled uncertainly, ashamedly, before turning and walking away.

* * *

"So," asked Van, trying not to sound censorious, "how long have you been . . . in your line of work, Mr. Nostradamus?"

The wizened little man chuckled, a sound like popping corn. "Since Methuselah was knee-high to a palfrey, Nostradamus has had *bets* in his belfry." He nodded sagely. "And you don't have to call me mister, sister; I know I'm just a plain old bookie, cookie."

"But don't your friends call you something . . . uh, for short?"

"The only pet names I ever hear are most unsuitable for the feminine ear," he answered promptly.

Van sat back in the lumpy lobby chair and glanced at her undistinguished but poetic companion.

The doors of the elevator behind them whooshed open. It was Nicky in the still-slightly-bruised flesh, all duded up for a Friday night out on the town. On his arm was none other than the dazzling Roxelle, draped in rhinestones.

An unlit cigarette hung from Nicky's lower lip with the same illusion of levitation as when Van had first laid eyes on him. Miss Roxelle was playing femme fatale to the high-heeled hilt, Van thought uncharitably.

The dancer minced over to Van and Nostradamus, dragging a somewhat sheepish Nicky behind her.

"Nicky's taking me to the Palace Court at Caesars for dinner, isn't that sweet?"

"Tooth-decaying," Van answered.

"Yeah, well . . . the Palace Court is nothin' special," Nicky put in modestly.

Van raised an eyebrow. She had researched every restaurant in Las Vegas and knew the Palace Court as one of the most costly.

"Here's something, Nicky boy, to help you swallow your dinner," Nostradamus offered, rising and peeling a much-worn leather billfold from his pocket. "While you eat steak, my wallet grows thinner."

Nicky only grinned as Nostradamus counted five limp

hundred-dollar bills into his palm and slapped the folded bills carelessly into his jacket pocket.

"I'd like to consult with you in the morning," Van told Nicky. "The architect needs a final go-ahead—"

"Fine, fine!" In matters of business, Nicky was magnanimous. "I'll stop by your office first thing tomorrow."

He hadn't "stopped by" since the night of . . . Van's thoughts balked, refusing to grant it a title. In the meantime Roxelle and Nicky were moving to the lobby doors.

"When they say 'ankling,' that's what they mean," Nostradamus mused, ogling Roxelle's departure. "They won't replace *that* with any machine."

Chapter

Ten

"So I'm here," Nicky said.

He stood in front of Van's desk, looking like a defiant schoolboy, impeccably groomed but radiating an air of truancy.

Van glanced at the flat full moon of Swiss gold on her wrist.

"Yeah, I know it's one o'clock." Nicky's knees suddenly buckled, and he sat hastily on the spare visitor's chair. Seed pearls of sweat glistened on his forehead; the healthy summer bronze of his skin had tarnished to green.

"Are you all right?" Van, concerned, was standing, but Nicky waved her back into her seat.

"Fine. I just had a big night out on the town last night," he explained with a flare of his usual bravado.

"Oh." The word, short as it was, came out pinched, as if it had been marinated in lemon recently. Until then, Van had successfully expunged the distasteful image of Nicky and Roxelle from her mind.

He read her thoughts, then shrugged his surrender to the truth.

"I got in at midnight—some night on the town. I left Roxelle off early and mostly walked the Strip—smoking." His face curdled. "I must have smoked a whole pack—!" His shoulders shuddered as he rubbed his face in his hands. "I think I'm cured." He peeked up between careful fingers. "Of cigarettes."

"Then I imagine the idea of lunch"—Nicky made an

ungentlemanly noise—"doesn't appeal to you, so we might as well tour the hotel."

He nodded docile agreement and followed her into the lobby.

"I want you to keep abrea—current with what's happening," Van said. "After all, it's your hotel."

"I guess." Nicky shoved his hands in his pants pockets and studied the floor as the tip of his cream-leather loafer made idle patterns on it.

Van, observing this uncharacteristic indifference, sighed, bridled, and then straightened.

"We'll begin with the carpeting, since it intrigues you so much. As I mentioned, Montero is one of the most innovative architects in Brazil. He's going along with our glassed-in outer-waterway concept, and his interior designers have honed our approach. The carpet, instead of the commonplace red-and-black that haunts most Las Vegas hotels, will be a custom-woven deep-burgundy-and-navy color, with an Oriental medallion design of a phoenix on a solid ground. The phoenix motif will repeat itself on the hotel linens, the doors to the suites—in fact the peephole will be the phoenix's eye—the towels, bedding, major door hardware, bathroom fixtures, bath mats, and so on."

Nicky nodded. "I get it; 'motifs' are classy, and burgundy-and-navy is the next thing to black-and-red, but . . . nicer somehow."

"Subtler," Van elaborated. "Less predictable. The Crystal Phoenix will draw from the familiar, but transmute it. There will be touches of the Chinese, the contemporary, the commercial. It will offer a kind of architectural alchemy, an oasis of elegant entertainment."

"To the tune of eight million bucks," Nicky noted ruefully.

"Seven and a quarter million bucks," she corrected. "You're still spending seven hundred and fifty thousand to remodel the penthouse, aren't you?"

"Yeah, sure . . ." He spoke as if just remembering the

project. "Why not? Why shouldn't I have that the way I like it?"

"I'm not saying you shouldn't. It's budgeted in." Van frowned and looked down at the Plexiglas clipboard she held pressed against her chest. "Nicky, don't you *care* about the hotel anymore? Have you lost interest?"

"No! It's just that you—Montero, the interior designers—have it under control. Everything's in motion, like a train on a track. The Van von Rhine Line. What's left for Nicky Fontana to worry about except some local muscle? I seem to be—"

"Superfluous?"

He looked at her with a weary, tolerant smile. "I wouldn't have put it that way. I was going to say dead weight. Excess baggage."

She bristled defensively. "You're the man with the money."

"I know. That doesn't seem to be enough, the way it used to be. Look, the hotel's shaping up swell. It's more than I ever dreamed it would be, more than I ever *could* dream it to be. So take the seven hundred and fifty grand and spread it around down here where it'll do some good. I'll fix up my joint from a little dough I got tucked away."

He turned for the elevators.

"What about . . . our tour? Aren't you going to see how the rest of the hotel is planned?"

He paused and glanced back briefly before the stainless steel doors snapped shut on him. "Surprise me."

The pressed cobalt-silk blouse was hanging from the doorknob to her room when Van finally returned to it at eight-thirty that evening after another solitary dinner out.

It startled her, resembling a vivid ghost of itself as it shook subtly in the unseen draft from an air-conditioning vent. She paused and stared at it until a faint sound attracted her attention.

She whirled. A silver-haired man she'd caught sight of around the hotel on several occasions was walking along the hall. Going to his room? She and he nodded at each other, and then he disappeared behind the door of the room adjacent to hers. Amazing, Van thought, that they hadn't run into each other before.

She went into her room, hung up the blouse, and exchanged her work clothes for a nightgown of silver-gray silk. She slid between the white sheets, the familiar feel of hotel-grade cotton and polyester bed linen smooth on her cheek.

Visions of the Crystal Phoenix's revamped guest rooms danced in her head with sugar-plum sweetness: a navy-burgundy-and-cream color scheme, with new amenities in every unit—wall-mounted hair dryers, bathroom-ceiling heat lamps, phones in both bedroom and bath...

One such phone was ringing now with the most undreamlike insistence. Van dredged herself out of the bed linens to pick up the bedside phone. The luminous clock dial read ten forty-five.

"Yes?"

"It's Nicky. Listen. Brother Ralph was prowling the lobby and thought he saw signs of somebody poking around. Are you all right?"

"I *was* all right," she told him sharply. "I was sleeping."

"Your door's locked?"

"Of course! I didn't grow up in hotels for nothing."

"And no one's been lurking around?"

"Nicky, I haven't seen a soul all day except for that stray black cat and the poor old man I catch sight of around the hotel, and he hardly looks like hired muscle."

Nicky's voice tightened. "What old man?"

"I don't know... some silver-haired duffer; stooped. I've noticed him before. Don't you even know who does the dirty work around this place? I supposed he was the gardener or something. He looks as if he'd enjoy outdoor work—something about his sun-seamed face..."

"Van, I have a service handle all that and the pool. And I don't employ—"

"Nicky! Are you there? Is something wrong?" She sat up. Maybe somebody *was* in the hotel. Maybe while Nicky had been worrying about *her*, they'd been stalking *him*. "Nicky!"

"Hey. Calm down." Now his voice thickened and warmed with the old Fontana charm. "I, uh, think I'll run down and check, just to make sure. Don't unlock your door until I get there."

Her hands tightened on the receiver. "I'm not sure I'll unlock it *when* you get here.

Silence, followed by a gusty sigh. "I'm not kidding, Van. Just sit tight. I'll be right there. Don't open the damned door until then, and then open it, no matter what you want to prove to me."

He hung up without a good-bye, leaving Van clinging to a droning dial tone and the realization that she might not be as utterly alone as she had thought she was, which was cold comfort under the circumstances.

The clock was a digital model, its bright red numbers dancing through the normal one-to-ten sequence. She would have preferred watching a second hand spin slowly round and round. It was somehow more comforting to watch time pass in the hairline-thin progress of a gilt wand than to see it jerk from minute to minute in a numerical St. Vitus dance.

She got up and found an aqua terry-cloth robe— street length, strictly for travel and quite unattractive over the long gown—but she was cold, and Nicky Fontana was coming.

She put on slippers and even combed her hair, studying her pale face in the bathroom mirror. Why couldn't danger do the decent thing and raise its ugly head before a lady took off her makeup? Not that Nicky Fontana would care; he seemed intent on proving how little he cared about anything nowadays.

The knock on the door startled her, like anything

expected for too long. She peered through the peephole, remembering the first night he had stood outside her door, the night they toured the Strip.

Nicky exploded into the room as soon as Van unlatched the chain, looking around as if for a phantom lover. "You okay?"

She nodded. "But what—?"

"*Shhhh!*" One hand was on her lips. The other held a gun.

"Nick-y!" she protested.

"Take it easy. Better this than not. And keep your voice down; these walls are rice paper. I told you, nobody's supposed to be around here, period. You've got a prowler."

"Maybe it's some old vagrant who slipped in when no one was looking. There are panhandlers in Las Vegas."

"Yeah. And they're down on the Strip panhandling at this hour. It's their prime shift. Now cut the palaver. You say this guy went in next door?"

"It looked like it."

Nicky flashed a passkey. "I went downstairs and got this."

"That's what took you so long."

He grinned suddenly. "Did you miss me?"

"No! I just sat here doing my nails!"

"And that's what you can do while I go next door. If I don't come back or knock on the wall in a few minutes, call the police."

"Can't you call your brothers first?"

"And look like a fool if it's just an empty room? No thanks."

"You'd die to save face in front of your brothers?"

His hand clamped her forearm. "Nobody's going to die. This old dude sounds like a pushover even Nostradamus could handle. Just sit tight, and I'll be back in a minute or two." He turned for the door.

"I'm going with you. It's my job! And besides, I'll go crazy if I have to sit alone here any longer—wondering."

In a blatant appeal to his macho heritage, she added, "I'm probably safer with you."

He finally nodded. "All right. But stay behind me. And get ready to rabbit back to the room and call the cops if anything goes wrong—with me or without me."

Van nodded doubtful agreement. Nicky eased out of her room and crept down the hall halting at the closed door. She watched him slip the key into the lock, the gun thrust into the back of his belt as he turned the knob. He moved as silently as a second-story man, no doubt an inbred Fontana talent, Van thought rather unfairly. She clung to the cold hallway and waited when Nicky entered the room.

Nicky stepped back into the hall, the gun held carefully yet casually in his hand high on the opening door.

"It's all right. False alarm. Nobody here. Looks like nobody's been here since 1945. Come on in, Van. You won't believe your eyes. This is outa sight!"

Unlike most of Nicky Fontana's assertions, this one promised to be a massive understatement.

Chapter

Eleven

"You ever seen anything *like* this joint?" Nicky demanded.

He set his gun on a mahogany side table beside a lamp whose cream-silk shade, quite dusty, was decoratively laced down one side in perfect imitation of a nineteenth-century corset.

Van moved over the threshold like a sleepwalker, looking at the time-dusted furniture that crouched in every corner of what was obviously the living room of a suite.

"Mahogany, right?" Nicky asked. "Ever see anything *like* it?"

"Only at the Algonquin Hotel on Forty-fifth Street in New York City. This is authentic, original 1940s decor."

"But it's first-class stuff?"

"First class."

Nicky nodded and sank into a skirted overstuffed chintz armchair. "The Joshua Tree was built around 1945," he said, "in the postwar building boom Bugsy Siegel started that made Vegas into the hot town it is today."

"This is incredible." Van moved through the room, dusting her fingertips over faded upholstery and along the grimy slats of painted wood venetian blinds. Above the cumbersome blinds loomed upholstered satin valances with their corners curled into shapes resembling the upswept coils of pomaded hair on the glamour girls in 1940 films. "The color scheme alone is priceless—"

"Yeah, what do they call that shade of green?" Nicky

pointed at the wall paper, a black bamboo design etched on a background of pure...

"Chartreuse," Van answered promptly.

"When I was a kid, I used to call it slime-green. Anyway, when I first came in, I poked my nose and the Beretta's—into every nook, cranny, and closet in this suite. There's no seedy old gent to be seen. Just more of this funky furniture."

"Obviously, the suite was decorated originally for a resident guest. She—or he—must have lived here since the Joshua Tree opened."

"Hey!" Nicky's fingers snapped smartly as he lurched forward in the froufrou-laden chair. "I bet this was Jersey Joe's setup! He was a small-time Howard Hughes, sort of. Anyway, he kept to himself and lived at the Joshua Tree. The word was he'd been rich once, only nobody knew how or why. I think he croaked"—Van stared at him uncomprehendingly— "the old coot kicked off about the time the hotel changed hands eight years ago."

"Charming story." Van moved into the adjoining bedroom. "'Jersey Joe' must have had some...dough... because this stuff wasn't cheap, even then. Will you look at the satin spreads on the twin beds? Jersey Joe must have had a Jersey Jenny in his life once."

"A lot of characters hung out around Vegas back then—you know, colorful types."

Van turned to regard Nicky, who had come to stand in the doorway and looked as colorful as could be in a turquoise knit sportshirt.

Suddenly a horrendous *thump* came from the living room. "The *gun's* on the table!" he whispered, turning to face whoever lurked behind him.

Van ran for the doorway, knowing she shouldn't have.

They confronted an empty room. No visible trace of what had caused the harsh noise remained, not even a swaying blind or a swinging door.

"Something must have moved," Van declared.

"Some*one*," Nicky corrected grimly, arming himself
again.

But he could find nothing to aim at but emptiness
and faded furniture. He finally lowered the gun, shaking his head.

Van opened the center drawer of a Sheraton desk
against one wall. "Was Jersey Joe's last name Jackson?"

"That's it!" Nicky ran to the desk and hung over her,
his closeness pressing the rough terry-cloth robe to her
shoulder blades.

"That must be the old dude's bankbook. Hezekiah
Joseph Jackson . . . no wonder they called him Jersey
Joe. Man, his account was flat as Irontop Mesa when he
blew out. Not a peso in it! They must have buried him
on the county and forgot all this. Crazy, isn't it?"

"Not so crazy. There's the thump."

Nicky's eyes followed Van's pointing finger to the wall
behind the desk. A large canvas of some kind leaned
behind it. On the wallpaper above the green-shaded
desk lamp, a large rectangle outlined an acidic blotch of
unfaded chartreuse.

"Off the wall!" Nicky declared. "It let loose and fell
off the wall after all this time." He groaned while
leaning down to wrestle the canvas free. "Hey, it's a
blown-up photo. You want to see what Las Vegas looked
like before the war?" Nicky stretched to hook the work
on its rusted hangers and stepped back.

"Once a wasteland, always a wasteland," Van noted,
studying the black-and-white aerial photo of what seemed
an endless desert undistinguished by signs of any living
creature other than a wild burro and a blur of rocks that
assumed the shape of a camel. "That's a strange, office-
like thing to hand in a place decorated like this."

"Some people like the desert," Nicky said pointedly.
"Some people like to see the stars and sniff the sagebrush. If you came to Vegas back in the thirties, before
air-conditioning, you had to like the desert, believe
me!"

"I believe you." Van looked around again with a cool, professional eye. "I don't know what we'll do with this suite; maybe simply lock it up and forget it. I could have sworn—"

"Look." Nicky took her by the aqua-terry-cloth shoulders and kneaded them as if reaching for the muscles beneath. "You've been working hard lately, and living like a hermit in that suite next door. The hotel's semideserted except for all these characters around the place who have the mistaken idea that I won't mind if they come and go as they please. So it's my fault. This isn't a normal place, Van, and won't be again until it's redone and filled with people and singing slot machines and live music and laughter and Lady Luck."

His voice was almost hypnotic. "Maybe that's why we get on each other's nerves," he continued.

Nicky Fontana in a state of sweet reason grated on her. She tried to shrug away his hands. "That's not why! It has nothing to do with this hotel or my fatigue or your intentions."

"What has it got to do with?"

"Us!"

Nicky's massaging hands dropped from her shoulders. "I didn't think there *was* an 'us,' just an 'indiscretion.'"

"There is and you know it!" Van sat on the sofa. "I have *tried* to ignore it!"

"What're you ignoring so hard? Me?"

"Not you. I don't blame you. You can't help being . . . I blame—*it*."

"It." Nicky sat beside her, laying the gun on the low glass-topped coffee table butting against their knees.

She felt confused, he realized, and afraid of getting hurt, like someone bumping around in a strange room in the dark. That was exactly what they both were doing, he understood suddenly. They were cracking their shins on each other and cursing the darkness.

"Just forget it," she was saying. "You're right.

"I'm exaggerating—"

"No, you're not. This place is bad for you. I'm bad for you."

"No!" She looked more horrified than when the photograph had fallen moments before. Then her voice gentled. "No . . . you're not bad for me—"

"Then the hotel is!" His voice was so rough, it surprised him. "Why?"

When she answered, she stared straight ahead as if on a witness stand. "I grew up in hotels. All I know is hotels. I thought that's all I could do . . . something with hotels. Maybe I was wrong, because I wasn't happy in hotels."

"Why not?" Nicky almost whispered now.

"Oh, I suppose when I was a child, it was my father. He wasn't an affectionate man, at least not to children, and we lived in such an adult world. And then, when I got older—"

She stopped, her fingers rolling the terry-cloth robe into a wad on her knees.

"So what about me bothers you!" Nicky persisted.

"Everything! You're so carefree and optimistic and engaging and irresponsible—"

"Hey, I may play the good-time Charlie, but this hotel is a big responsibility; I put more work into it than shows. How do you think I got the consortium together to buy the building in the first place—all legit Vegas business types? That's why I got a college degree in business administration. I'm responsible to them for the good use of more dough than Mama Tinucci ever wrapped around a pepperoni in her wildest dreams.

"So I don't know chartreuse from puce. Nobody's going to scare me off this hotel—not hoodlums and not a classy ice cube."

"I'm not an ice cube! And besides, how could I, a poor little orphan, scare a big-time Vegas operator like you away from the Crystal Phoenix? Why would you even think that?"

"Because you damn near have since . . . that night."

Her face shifted through several expressions he had seen before: shock, denial, icy pride. It finally settled on one he had never seen before. He instantly christened it Haute Surprise.

"It was that bad?"

Nicky brought his face so close it almost touched hers, a trick his Uncle Mario performed when he wanted to make sure that someone understood him perfectly.

"It was that *good.*"

"Oh." She flushed and suddenly released the furrows of mangled fabric on her knees. "Then what's the problem?"

"You!" Nicky got up to pace. "You just turned off, like one of those damn peacock faucets in my damn overdecorated bathroom! You made me feel like something in bad taste. Like you thought I wasn't worth bothering about. Maybe a kick to go slumming with, but nobody to get too close to. Who cares what the bedroom scenery's like when you're making love?"

"I'm sorry! I was surprised, that's all. I hadn't seen where I was until I woke up, and I certainly didn't expect to wake up there. Is that why you seem uninterested in the hotel remodeling now. It reminds you of me?"

"It seems cold, calculated, expensive. If that reminds me of you, then that's it." Nicky turned his back on the room, studying the almost abstract black-and-white monotony of photograph-frozen desert.

"I'm not that way. I've got a good head for business, and I like to keep my feelings under control, but—"

"Why?" Nicky asked.

"Well, it makes for a smoother-functioning world. Mature people can't get things done without managing their feelings."

"You call that mature? I call that having no fun. Van—oh, what's the use?" Nicky strode to the open door.

"And"—something in her voice stopped him—"and people can't use you if you control your feelings. They can only hurt you if you thrust your feelings right out there in plain view to be seen and mauled . . . and walked out on."

"I know."

She came up behind him. "Nicky. I didn't do that to you." He was silent. "I couldn't have. You have nothing to lose."

He wheeled, then leaned against the doorjamb, deceptively relaxed, his head tilted back to rest on the frame.

"Okay. I started it. It's my nature. Maybe I'm not mature. I act on what I feel. I knew you were—well, not my type, but I went for it anyway. So I started it. But you finished it. 'Very nice, Mr. Fontana. Quite an amusing evening, although the ambience was too-too tacky. We must do it again sometime, but not too soon or too often. Wouldn't want these outings to become habit-forming or anything.'"

"I gave you your freedom! Isn't that what men want— women who don't tie them down?"

"Van . . ." He ran impatient hands down her arms, stared as deep into the defensive cobalt shoals of her eyes as he could get. He enunciated every word. "I don't want to know what you *think* men want. I want to know what *you* want. I want to know if you want me!"

She swallowed. He could see tears sheening her eyes. "That's a very impolite thing to ask a lady."

"I'm not a gentleman."

She smiled suddenly. "Yes, you are; you just don't know it."

"Don't you care if we never get any closer than this again? Don't you care if we turn this hotel into a palace and we're the loneliest people in it?"

"Lonely?" She wanted to deny the word, Nicky thought, to deny his right to use the word. "How can *you* talk about loneliness? You have that huge family who adores you. You have bookies and vagrants and chorus girls in your hip-pocket. You have money and security and enough confidence to sell the Brooklyn Bridge to . . . to the Kremlin! Don't pretend you need me—"

Nicky's hands tightened. "What if I did? What if I did need you—and there was nobody there? If there was just another vacant room?"

Van glanced down at his grip—half custodial, half homicidal. Nicky fanned his hands free as if to prove he didn't need to touch her.

She turned back to the sofa, sitting in the exact middle of the long cushions, making herself approachable and absolutely unapproachable at the same time.

It was what was driving him crazy, Nicky reflected, the way she drew him and repelled him, the way his heart went out to her and then hit hard on the invisible barrier of her tightly closed emotional front door.

She folded her hands on her lap, company-manners style. "I don't want to . . . impede . . . anyone by becoming overly dependent, by making a scene. Would you be happier if I camped on your front doorstep, if I challenged your girlfriends to mud-wrestling matches in Caesars Palace? If I lost all my dignity?"

"I like your dignity. And I like you when you lose your dignity," he added mischievously, unable to resist.

This time she didn't flush. She didn't even answer.

"I'm not your father, Van," Nicky went on seriously. "You don't have to stay out of my way. You don't have to 'spare me' yourself."

Her chin trembled infinitesimally. All the warmth in Nicky strained to leap to her side and enfold her in his empathetic arms. Poor little orphan. Her sarcastic self-analysis had been too astute. She was indeed an orphan, consigned to hotel hirelings and shadowy back halls by a father too awkward to do more than tolerate a kid, he thought bitterly, and then knew he could never understand such rejection. Nicky held himself back, waiting.

"But it isn't just my father. There was a man. I was just nineteen; we were in Munich at an ultra-modern hotel there. My father preferred a more traditional hotel, but he was, after all, German and thought he could feel at home there. Anyway, Gerd was his assistant manager. He paid attention to me, which my father didn't notice—"

Nicky let an impolite sound escape.

"Gerd was very logical, very ambitious. Somehow he managed to charm me. He took me up to the rooftop one night, with a magnum of champagne—"

"Brandy's better," Nicky said sardonically.

She looked up, startled.

"For rooftop seductions. Go on."

His self-deprecating humor had helped. She met his eyes as she talked now and got right to the ugly heart of the matter.

"It was champagne—that time. Gerd, 'plied' me with it, I think is the expression. I was a child still. He seduced me. I thought I loved him. Then I found out who he really was courting when I overheard some of the maids gossiping. The hotel. My father. He wanted to become manager when my father moved on—as Gerd knew he would—as my father always did. Gerd would have married me, I think."

She looked down at her twined, ring-bare hands. Nicky realized he'd never seen so much as a friendship ring on her little pinkie.

"But I found out. So when my father left, as he always did, he took me with him, as he always did. Gerd became manager anyway. I had been just so much . . . overkill."

"Gerd was a creep," Nicky said flatly.

Van laughed. "Among other things."

"It could have been worse," he consoled. "You could have married the bastard."

"'Bastard.'" Her lips tasted the word as she said it. "I like that. I never thought of him that way."

"It always helps to have somebody else call 'em bastards for you," Nicky explained casually. "So what has all this to do with me?"

"I just wanted you to know that it's all right."

"That what's all right?"

"The . . . the other night. It was just something that happened. I don't expect anything more out of it. I got over that. I'm a big girl now. I don't blame you, and you shouldn't blame me. It doesn't have to lead to anything or pretend to be anything more than it was."

Nicky squatted across from her, staring at her gravely over the cocktail table. "What was it?"

"A mutual . . . sensual . . . encounter, I suppose. I don't regret it, I'm even flattered—"

"Well, I'm not!" Nicky thundered. His dark eyes narrowed. "How dare you, Van von Rhine? Where do you get off, thinking of me as a casual lay? As somebody you can turn on and off. One-night stands aren't my style."

Van's mouth opened as wide as her eyes. She looked like a cartoon character drawn in a state of mesmerized shock.

"I—I'm being very reasonable. You should be grateful," she sputtered. "What about those chorus girls you have running in and out of here day and night?"

"Darcy's a pal. I went to high school with her, for Chrissake! And Roxelle—well, she's a lot of fun, a very funny girl. I like her. It wasn't until you came along that I started seeing that maybe I was interested in something different, something more. I got aspirations, Van, give me credit for that."

She looked down at her tightly folded fingers. "I'm facade, Nicky—a European education, a certain sense of instilled style. You call it class, but that's not much to aspire to. You've got more class than everyone listed in Debrett's *Peerage* put into one big blue-blooded ball."

Nicky's hands reached out to cover hers. He rose, drawing her up with him and steering her around the furniture into his arms. "Now," Nicky said sternly, "I don't think you should stay alone tonight, after this scare, and I certainly don't want to. So we can go back up to my place, or next door to yours. If you say so, I won't lay a glove on you. If you don't, you can expect first-class fingering and lots of it. I don't apologize for that, and you don't apologize if I happen to decide I like you and we should do this more often."

She was ready to cling to him, but still reluctant enough to argue. "Nicky, this complicates everything—"

"Not everything, just our crummy little corner of the world. We can handle it," he promised, bending to kiss her wet eyelashes.

Her arms convulsively clasped his body, her upturned lips brushing the rough side of his shaven cheek.

"Nicky, you're impossible," she whispered.

He moved finally to take from her lips the wordless message he trusted more than talk. The photograph behind them crashed to the floor, and they turned, a bit late but still startled, to face it.

"I'll hang the damn thing up so good it'll stay there until doomsday." Nicky moved toward it.

"No!"

He paused, eyebrows raised. "No?"

"Leave it; I'll have it moved to my office in the morning."

Nicky looked even more confused.

"As a souvenir," Van explained. "Of tonight. Unless you think," she added provocatively, "that it won't be worth remembering."

"Tell me," Nicky begged, drawing featherweight fingers along Van's shoulder.

"No." She giggled girlishly. "No way."

"Tell me," he insisted softly. Then his eyes spoke for him. "Trust me."

She sobered instantly. "It's . . . it's—"

"Come on, spit it out, or I'll resort to torture." His fingers drummed lightly along her bare sides.

"That's not torture, Nicky. If you want to talk real torture . . ." Exploring fingers spider-walked delicately from his hips into the shallow valley of his loins.

"I give up," Nicky swore ardently. "It's *killing* me. But tell me your real name before I die."

"I thought the *victim* was supposed to confess?"

"Yeah, you're a little rule keeper, aren't you?" Nicky responded with deeper kisses and farther-ranging touches until Van's delight made her warm body shiver beside his. "Warning's fair; I break rules. And I ferret out names. Tell me."

"You'll laugh."

"Not . . . doing this, I won't."

"Oh. Oh, oh, oh, Nicky! Vanilla!"

"Huh?"

"No, don't stop. Oh, that's wonderful. *Vanilla*. That's it. My name."

He stopped. "It's a pudding!"

"And an ice cream and a color and the bean of a South American orchid—and my name."

Nicky rolled onto his side to take a new look at her. "Where'd you get it?"

"From my mother. Nanny said she was American and whimsical. Nanny was British, and of course neither approved of being American or whimsical."

"Va-nill-a." Nicky let the word loll lazily on his tongue. "I like it. But is it—-tasteful?" he teased.

"Absolutely not! That's why I never use it."

"Never say never, Vanilla." Nicky proceeded to lick his way over the seldom seen parts of her anatomy. "*Umm*, just right—smooth and creamy."

"I'm sure that's not what my mother had in mind."

"Who knows what she had in mind? I don't think she would have wanted you to be Van von Rhine."

"I don't know what she wanted for me. Sometimes I hardly know what *I* want for me."

Nicky sat up in the tangled sheets. They were in Van's bedroom, where they had elected to go more from urgency than choice. The fright that had reunited them had been forgotten. Jersey Joe Jackson had been permanently installed in their minds as a bizarre, benign fairy godfather in absentia. If he hadn't been a creature of his times and subscribed to twin beds, they might have mussed the long-ago-made-up linens in the room next door.

"I like it here now," Van said, staring at the softy lit ceiling where the bright shadows of Las Vegas's neon fireworks danced. "The room didn't feel . . . loved in—before."

She prepared to blush in the dusky light, but Nicky was there before the boldness of the new thought could sink in. He seemed endlessly capable of blending sex and affection, eroticism and fondness.

Van felt embraced on every level when she made love with Nicky. She curled her fingers into the sheared softness of his hair and murmured her appreciation of his amorous forays until her inner fires, temporarily banked, flared to join the melting power of his touch.

They came together like fire and ice. Van felt herself catch flame in the searing energy of their lovemaking, felt her inhibitions peel away until only her innermost core was burning, burning.

Interlude

Midnight Louie Examines His Situation

I do not have to spell it out for anyone who has spent any time and money in Vegas whatsoever. They are good days indeed when a new establishment is prettying up to open and the dice always seem to be landing seven-up all along the Strip and downtown.

Naturally the whole town is atwitter over the new Crystal Phoenix, given Mr. Nicky Fontana's dark-horse mystique among Vegas front-runners and the even more mysterious shenanigans of an architectural and managerial nature going on daily in the ex-Joshua Tree. Las Vegans love long odds.

The old place is crowded now with construction workers, mirror installers, crystal hangers, electrical engineers, and neon artists, who are the most unusual of the lot. Not much salvage is available anymore from the old days, but luckily there are many new pickings for the likes of Midnight Louie.

It is indeed a pleasure to spend one's time around and about the Crystal Phoenix during reconstruction. With Mr. Nicky Fontana and the lady with the Lake Mead eyes all is sunshine, as I hear every day while making my discreet rounds.

"Oh, Nicky," says she. "Do take a quick look at these new plans to see if you approve!"

And Mr. Nicky Fontana, he drops whatever he is doing, which nowadays is likely to be analyzing budget projections on computer printouts rather than eyeing racing forms or overseeing the architects instead of

*racing around Vegas in his 'Vette with the T-tops down,
so Mr. Nicky Fontana, he rushes over and says like
this:*

*"Oh, yes, Van, what is it I can do for you? Or would
you like to indulge in a small intermission while we
ankle over to the Dunes for luncheon?"*

*I tell you, it is enough to make an old Vegas hand
more than somewhat queasy, were he not sentimental at
heart.*

*Now it is known for a fact that although Miss Van
von Rhine continues to inhabit the suite numbered
seven-eleven, Mr. Nicky Fontana finds it necessary to
visit her frequently for late-night emergency sessions,
strictly having to do with hotel business of course.
Miss Van von Rhine's dainty high heels no longer
make the journey up in Mr. Nicky Fontana's private
elevator.*

*But this may be to squash uneducated talk, as it is
also true that Mr. Nicky Fontana's ladyfriends suddenly
are making themselves scarce, as is the esteemed
Nostradamus and other Las Vegas landmarks.*

*Some may challenge the insights of a mere hanger-on
such as myself into the intimate domestic arrangements
of highfalutin' folks like the honchos of a brand-new
Vegas hostelry. But such shortsighted individuals overlook a lifetime's experience of getting around quietly,
keeping my ears perked, my mouth shut, and my tail
well out of the way of anyone's size thirteens.*

*I conclude it is plain that prime opportunity awaits
an all-around handy guy like myself at the Crystal
Phoenix. Although no one hears one syllable about who
is behind the muscle trying to move in on Mr. Nicky
Fontana, the three beach boys do not show up again, no
doubt deterred by my vigilant presence, as well as
frequent inspection visits from the brothers Fontana in
full Family gear, which is to say packing sufficient iron
to sink the QE Two and its lifeboats.*

So events are moving along in a spirit an optimist

would call peachy-keen, and I am all set to put my professional services at the disposal of the Crystal Phoenix for good and all when the blond doll in the Charles Jourdan pumps sashays in with an eelskin briefcase one Monday morning and makes straight for Mr. Nicky Fontana's penthouse in the clear view of six carpetlayers, twelve mirror installers, one electrician, a vagrant who got mislaid with the carpeting, myself— and Miss Vanilla von Rhine.

Chapter

Twelve

Van stared at the closed stainless-steel elevator doors, absently sticking a pencil behind her ear and letting her armful of architectural plans droop.

Beside her, a momentarily ignored Walter Maxwell, fedora in hand, was turning slowly under the newly installed ceiling to admire glittering swags of crystal ruffled like an Austrian sheer into a solid canopy of icy bright light.

"Not bad," he said. Van looked at him sharply, then back to the elevator doors. "The lights, I mean," Maxwell modified rapidly.

"How did she get a key to the penthouse elevator?" Van asked, more puzzled than perturbed.

"The . . . uh, young lady?" Maxwell cleared his throat, a helpful stalling technique for lawyers caught flat-footed, especially those who lived in Las Vegas. "Funny, I thought she was you when I first got here. I followed her in, in fact."

"Me?"

"She looks like you. From behind, I mean. Blond, and a certain classy way of walking—"

Van's face darkened on each blurted phrase, turning especially dire at the word "classy." But her voice remained cordial. "Come to my office, Mr. Maxwell; I'll show you the rest of the plans for the Crystal Phoenix. You haven't seen anything yet!"

The final phrase, and the enthusiasm, reminded Maxwell of Nicky Fontana if the diction didn't. "Nicky mentioned a roof of colored water too?"

"That's for the Crystal Promenade. I'm hoping the hotel gets some publicity on that; it's the first non-residential application of the technique I know of."

Maxwell took in Van's plain but paper-swamped office with encouraging wonder. "I don't know how you did it, Miss von Rhine, but it looks like the Phoenix is going to come roaring right up from the ashes with a bang."

"Is that what they're calling it already—just the Phoenix?"

"A shame, since the whole monicker's so classy. But it's like Caesars, you know. Everybody and everything's gotta have a nickname in this town."

"What's yours?"

"Maxie."

Van extended an elegant hand. "Mine's . . . Vanilla. Have a chair, Maxie."

"Thanks, but—" Maxwell, in lifting tented architectural plans from a chair, had found an oversized black cat opening one baleful eye of unforgiving jade and elected to remain standing.

"There's no need for formality between us, Maxie. You've been playing project matchmaker since the beginning. Why, if it weren't for you, this hotel would still be a . . . a paper phoenix." She rattled plans under his disavowing nose.

"Matchmaker? Me?" Maxwell blanched and clutched his hat to his stomach, which had been troubling him of late.

Maybe he hadn't come by the Crystal Phoenix often enough, but something had changed. For one thing, Van . . . Vanilla von Rhine's face was showing a wicked little dimple whose existence he'd had no earthly reason to suspect before.

"Is it true?" he blurted. "What they say? That you and Nicky are—"

"Are what, Maxie?"

"Uh, making this a real partnership deal? I hear Nicky's told his uncle Mario that you are single-handedly turning the old hotel into the finest flophouse—I mean accommodations—west of New Orleans. Um, all these plans look splendid, er, Vanilla. Splendid. I'll stop in again soon, when I can. Say I said hello to Nicky."

"Hello, Nicky," Van echoed obediently, her face lighting up like the crystal ceiling. She was looking behind him.

"Hi, Maxie!"

And there was Nicky Fontana, holding up the doorframe and claiming his territory, as usual. He smiled at Van and thumped Maxwell heartily on the back as he passed him to evict the black cat with firm hands and sit in the chair. "How goes it?"

Coughing discreetly, Maxwell edged for the door. "Fine. I'm fine," he assured them. "The hotel looks fine. And you both look...*fine*! 'Bye." He vanished behind the closing door.

Van burst out laughing.

"What did you do to the poor guy?" Nicky wondered.

"I asked him to call me Vanilla."

"Hey, that's my perogative!"

"Only in certain private places. Publicly, using the name might lend me a dash of Las Vegas flash."

Nicky leaned across the paper-piled desk, crushing stiff plans noisily, to cradle her chin in the fork of his hand.

"But then if we get married, you'll be Vanilla Fontana. It sounds like an ice-cream sundae."

"We haven't said anything about getting married." Her face had tightened to the old look. Nicky diagnosed it as cold feet overriding a hot heart.

He shrugged, leaned out of his chair to kiss her lips lightly, and lounged back among the crackling plans. "There are twenty-one wedding chapels in the naked town; who knows? We might get the irresistible urge to sample one."

"Now *that* sounds like Baskin-Robbins," retorted Van,

changing the subject. "And besides"—an edge to her voice made Nicky look up sharply from consoling the displaced cat with rhythmic caresses—"you can't go anywhere now. You have company upstairs."

Nicky's hand slapped his forehead. "I forgot! The penthouse decorator awaits! I'm jazzing up the old joint. You did use the seven hundred and fifty thou down here?"

"No good hotel manager refuses money."

"Don't look so guilty; you're right. 'A penthouse is a status symbol for certain insecure guests whose egos need boosting.' Better the big dough be lavished on the paying customers."

"Where did you hear that penthouse line?" Van's face had whitened to the color of candlewax.

"Max-ie." Nicky nodded and grinned at the closed door. "After all, he is the Family lawyer. He's gotta report disloyal talk." Standing, Nicky stretched his long, limber body as unselfconsciously as the mirroring feline uncoiling at his feet. "That's what I pay him for—snitching."

"And you pay *me* to think of things like . . . oh, what a waste of time and money penthouses are."

"Yeah. So I won't waste much dough on it, I promise." Nicky winked and ducked out the door.

"He will be the despair of me," Van told the cat in heightened exasperation. Her tones grew silken. "Did the mean man take your chair?"

But despite Van's attempt to restore it to its habitual seat, the cat eeled from her custody, unwilling to accept favors where it expected to rule.

Van, hands on hips, sighed at what amounted to the third defection from her office in as many minutes. For some reason, the figure of the mysterious blond visitor to Nicky's lodgings strode into her mind on efficient midheight heels. An attractive blonde freelance "decorator."

Her fist hit the desk, rustling the papers madly.

Damn it, she'd put too much of herself into the Crystal
Phoenix, into everything and everybody that had anything to do with the Crystal Phoenix, to let anyone stop
her now—even "outside muscle" of the distinctly feminine variety.

"You're tense," Nicky observed.

Van sat on the edge of her bed, still dressed for
dinner in an ivory-silk pantsuit.

Nicky pressed against her while his sure fingers
massaged her temples, the bed creaking companionably
as he rested one knee behind her.

"Making a hotel over is as tough as pulling payoffs out
of Nostradamus," he mused in a voice smoother than
fettuccine Alfredo. "It's a good thing I thought this
project would be fun."

"You must be having fun redoing the penthouse," Van
said suddenly.

The silken circling motion of Nicky's fingers stopped
cold. "I have more fun doing this," he said. Suddenly
he rolled backward on the bed, one arm hooking her
midriff to sweep her atop him. Nicky, on his back, was
engaged in arranging Van as if she were a pet cat. His
fingers combed her hair loose, he pinned her evasive
hands to his chest. Then his palms stroked the length of
her back and legs as far as they could reach, rippling
the candleglow-soft sheen of silk covering her.

"You're very distracting," she said, her voice suddenly husky.

Nicky's knowing eyes darkened, as if the pupils had
drowned instantly in their own spreading satisfaction.

"You deserve distraction," he said, his fingers seeking
the silk of her skin beneath the loose garments. "Its
a tough job, but somebody's got to do it. And you get
all the hard work—"

"But isn't it worth it?"

Caresses paused as they measured each other's eyes.
That evening had marked the debut of the new mar-

quee neon. Nicky and Van had celebrated by dining atop the Landmark Hotel tower for an unrivaled view of the Strip's nightly light show.

Waiting for the prearranged moment when the Crystal Phoenix marquee joined the fireworks, Nicky had held Van's hand across the snowy table linen. While they watched, a new ring of light exploded into life around the black obscurity of an otherwise dark building. It felt like attending the birth of a star.

Van's eyes had sprung tears, and Nicky's hand had nearly crushed hers within a fistlike grip.

"The best Strip-tease I ever saw," he joked. "Look, here comes the sign—"

Not far from the Flamingo, an ice-blue phoenix unfurled triumphant neon wings and sent magenta ripples running rings around the darkness under a cascade of pulsing whitewater lights meant to represent a fountain.

"It's gorgeous!" Nicky breathed as he watched through the windows, still holding her hand tight.

"That's what you always said it would be, even that first day."

"Did I? I must have been . . . obnoxious."

"Unremittingly. But you were right."

"I picked the right manager."

Van had stirred in her chair, the spell broken. Far away, the lights melded into the speeding blur that rings the riders on a carnival carousel.

Now she lay in his arms in her hotel bedroom, still vaguely disturbed even as she aided and abetted his amorous attentions. Someday soon, she told herself, the hotel would be done. And so would this.

Nicky's searching mouth fastened on hers, but even as Van mentally cataloged her objections to the futility of passion without the promise of a future, Nicky suddenly wrenched away.

He rolled off the opposite side of the bed and went to stand at the uncurtained window.

"What's the matter?" she asked.

"Your heart's not in it," he answered. "It's like trying to kiss the surf. Every time you're about to drown in your own tide, you ebb back all the way to China."

"How can you be so sure?" Van asked, miffed. He made her sound as mechanical as Hoover Dam.

He turned from the rectangle of night, the details of his form equally black against it.

"Because I love you, Van. That makes you easier to read than Nostradamus's pan when he owes me dough."

She sat up, cautiously. "Maybe love makes it easier to *mis*read people."

"Not me." He sounded very sure of himself. "Doesn't it mean anything to you that I said I love you? I don't do it every day."

"Oh, Nicky... you have been loved by everybody and everything since you were bounced on your uncle Mario's knee. It's sweet that you include me in this expansive company—"

"It's not 'sweet'!" The words exploded on a wave of raw feeling, washing over Van with a stinging, hot intensity. "It's hell." Nicky jammed his hands into his pockets and circled Van, careful to keep a precise distance between them that only his voice penetrated.

"I don't say that stuff that often, Van. Yeah, you're right. I've had more than my share of love—sometimes so much it damn near smothered me, and what could I do? They loved me. Is that what I'm doing now, Van? Smothering you?

"I get the feeling you want to keep me just so far away—maybe at the ends of your pretty, pale fingernails. I can feel your fingers brushing me, all the time, just the faintest touch. The brush-off. The arm's-length treatment." He paused in his restless circling. "That's not good enough. I'm not the arm's-length type."

"And if I am?"

He stood even stiller. "I'll have to put up with it, I guess. But I'm sorry for you."

Her voice came softly. "It's . . . more strain than we realize, seeing dreams come true. The hotel—"

"Damn the hotel," he broke in, but she went on.

"The work, the worry. The paranoia, knowing there are forces that wish one would fall, that might make one fail—"

"'One'—hell! Me! Us! The Fontana Family. It's called muscle, Van, and it's ugly and real, and I can fight that. I can't fight the kind of muscle you use. You flex it like a pro. I think it's just not caring enough."

"Then maybe you won't have to love me anymore," she suggested quietly.

He thought it over. "No." Nicky went to the door. "No, that won't happen."

She followed him. "Nicky, I don't want to hurt you. You're the nicest . . ."

His laugh was rueful. "'Nice' is not enough, babe. 'Not wanting to hurt' isn't good enough when your words are running the razor down my veins. *You're* not enough—have you ever said you loved anybody?"

"Of course I have!"

"I don't mean *did* you ever love anybody. Sure, you did. You loved Daddy until he died and probably a few kindly nannies and maybe some stray cat, but did you ever *say* it?"

"It's different for you!" At last her voice sawed cleanly through raw emotion. "It's easy for you! You belong to a clan, for God's sake, Nicky! Your grandmother leaves you money, your uncle would kill for you, your brothers will fight for you, your dozens of friends will never leave you lonely. It's so easy to love when you've *been* loved. It's so easy to say it when you take it for granted!"

Nicky's hands on her elbows swept her into the corner behind the door, into the darkest part of the room. Only his voice lit the shadows, white hot.

"You ever wonder what happened to my papa, Van? Or why uncle Mario is head of the Family when he was my papa's younger brother? Or why my mama lives in California, like my grandma did before she died—why I lived and went to school there?

"Papa *died*, Van, just like yours. Maybe he was a warmer man than your father, maybe I loved him more than you loved yours—I don't know. But he's just as cold and dead now. He died in a hotel. In a restaurant. Over a plate of Mama-Tinucci-brand pasta. Lead poisoning's what they used to call it. The police called it a Gangland Killing.

"The killers sprayed the place with bullets and spaghetti sauce and blood. Papa pushed me under the table at the first shot. It was my birthday; that's why we were there. That's why they knew he would be there—all alone in Mama Tinucci's brand-new restaurant. With just me, no muscle."

Only the sound of Van's horrified sobs shattered the dark now, but Nicky didn't seem to hear them.

"That's why we went to California. I was twelve; my mama and grandmama said that they'd had enough of it, that I needed a . . . vacation from Fontanas. I didn't come back until after college, until after Mama Tinucci was gone, and then only because I had to." His voice made a wrenching attempt at lightness. "I guess you can take the boy out of Las Vegas, but you can't take Las Vegas out of the boy."

Shock had made Van breathless. "That's why . . . why your grandmother left you her money, why your family didn't want you to rebuild the Crystal Phoenix. That's why they all rallied around at the first sign of danger! They feel they must protect you after that."

"Yeah, but they can't." Nicky's voice had roughened again. "They can't protect me from you."

She put her hands to his shoulders, to the lapels of his silk-weave sport coat, almost expecting to feel a spaghetti slick on the immaculate cloth, to see bullets erupting in lava-red spumes from the dark, to smell powder and spaghetti sauce, and to touch fresh blood blossoming like a red carnation in his buttonhole.

Nicky spun her around again, pushing himself into
the corner now and bringing her with him, pressing her
to him as if they were two children hiding, so close
their ribs dovetailed.

Van felt herself sucked into the fierce maelstrom of
his emotion. Breathless, she felt the endless length of
his body truly merge with hers. Limp, she sensed the
nearing vacuum of his mouth, felt herself about to be
siphoned into the still eye of his storm of love and pain.

"No," she protested to the unhearing elements that
claimed her, the least of which was love. Nicky's hunger
found her, took the "no" from her mouth, and replaced
it with the life-affirming "yes" written on his lips,
carved into the steel bones of his determination.

Such a man would force a phoenix from the ashes,
Van thought as her senses and emotions entwined inex-
tricably, as Nicky's kiss sought the innermost uncertain
parts of her and consummated the union of their
weaknesses as completely as their workaday alliance
had united their separate strengths.

Dizzy, still swathed in the dim room's darkness, Van
pulled away for a determined moment.

And Nicky, quelled at last by the violent embrace
he'd begun, read revulsion in her withdrawal. He apol-
ogized as best as he could, as delicately, his voice
almost inaudibly husky. "I said before this wasn't my
style. Maybe I was wrong."

She shrugged under his hands slightly, in a cold,
heedless way that further chilled his cooling blood.

"Nicky..." Hands as soft as corn silk found his face.
"I—I'm afraid I might... love you too."

Shock silenced them both. Neither moved, although
their breathing came in tandem after a while, and that
close-quarters motion, so slight, began to stoke powerful subterranean fires. After an even longer while, she
spoke again. "I'm sorry if that scares you. That's not my
style."

"What is your style?"

"I don't know."

"Then let's find out."

"My father died of love," she told him later, much later, while they lay under the white firmament of sprayed-on plaster and watched faint rainbows of reflected neon dance like the aurora borealis over the ceiling.

"How?"

"In a hotel—like this but not like this. Behind a closed door that I wasn't supposed to notice. Doing something that little girls aren't supposed to know their elders do. Except I don't think it was love; it was necessity."

"Maybe you're wrong." Nicky's hands warmed her from the limpid dark. "Sometimes we underestimate our parents' capacity to love. Maybe he just couldn't show it."

"I don't know. I only know I don't want to be left out like that again, to be behind the door someone closes in my face—"

"Life is full of closed doors, Van, and closing doors. Nobody can protect you from that. Not even the censor in your soul."

She turned to him, the sheets rustling conspiratorily. "And nothing can guarantee that you will be taken seriously, Nicky. Not even the most vaulting of ambitions."

"Just you." Nicky's fingers tunneled into her hair to hold her face still. "Just you take me seriously, Vanilla mine. I mean what I say."

He put his face alongside hers and said what he meant: "I love you."

The words rose above the homely hum of the air conditioner: "Trust me."

Chapter

Thirteen

The crystal phoenix itself arrived in time for Christmas.

Like a treetop angel, it descended on McCarran Airport from above. It came upon a midday clear, embedded in a rough but sturdy crate, marked Fragile.

"Jeez, I'm snowed under up here, Van," Nicky complained when she rang the penthouse to tell him of the arrival. "I didn't know redeocrating could be so much work. Look, I'll get down as soon as I can. In a minute."

So Van paced alone in the lobby, waiting for the centerpiece of the Crystal Phoenix to rest upon its appointed nest.

A circle of rich navy carpeting, duly stamped with the gold-phoenix signature medallion, had been vacuumed to pristine plushness. A custom Plexiglas pillar eighteen inches in diameter marked the lobby's center, gleaming like a plinth of polar ice, its empty top surface bald of its crowning glory.

Two glaziers toted in the crate while Maxie and a kibitzing Nostradamus trailed them like nervous courtiers. The bookie was muttering rhymes like prayers.

"I haven't been so edgy since Ali fought Frazier. My money's on the crystal, but not the glazier—"

At that instant one of the glaziers stepped on a piece of unclaimed pipe and slipped. Workmen froze. Van clutched her heart, or where she thought it should be, and found not even a feeble blip.

The glazier caught himself, hurled himself forward a

few fast steps, his fellow toter stumbling with him, then straightened and moved on to sighs of relief so universal that it sounded as if the sea had invaded Las Vegas.

Near the pedestal the workmen stopped, drawing screwdrivers from their hip-slung tool holsters to disassemble the crate. Clumsy wooden sides were gently lowered. Van hovered near to watch the inner packaging peeled away.

At last it stood under the myriad crystal droplets of the ceiling, catching light, shattering it, dashing it to smithereens on the reflective surfaces all around—the crystal phoenix Van had commissioned from the great French house of Lalique.

It was magnificent—sheer winged ice rising from the glassmaker's fires, a thing of clarity and crystalline perfection—legend personified. Van stared at it, remembering the late-working evening Nicky had found and frowned over the bill.

"Forty grand? For a glass knickknack? This Lalique joint has taken you to the cleaners—"

She had hushed him with a quick kiss. "It's 'Lah-leek,'' darling, not 'Lall-i-cue.' And pieces like this are commissioned as gifts to kings, queens, and popes. Maybe you're right, though. Maybe it's too good for the Crystal Phoenix."

"Hey!" The bill was swiftly flipped over to make way for the next. "Nothing's too good for a class act like the CP. Or me," he said, concentrating on billing and cooing instead of bill-reviewing, the phoenix forgotten.

Now the bird stood here, caged in glass, its unfurled wings skeining the air for slivers of silver light. The glaziers, hands gloved in flannel, lifted it atop its pedestal.

A hushed clapping sounded from all the happenstance occupants of the lobby, from friends and workers who had stopped to watch the informal installation ceremony.

Van wished Nicky were here, that he had made it

down in time, and then, suddenly, she was glad he hadn't.

A shattering of glass rang like wind chimes too quickly silenced.

Another burst of breaking glass exploded.

And another

The applause ended as spontaneously as it had begun. The impromptu audience stood as frozen as the phoenix, staring at the fragile artwork and puzzled to find it still poised on its pillar of light-iced Plexiglas.

The crashing-glass sounds had come from the huge lobby's fringes.

A man in denim coveralls, bare arms and chest muscle-knotted, kicked a wooden box from his path as he came forward. Shattered glass jingled as loud as payoff coins in a slot machine drop. He cradled another box like a babe in arms. Stopping, his arms dropped. The box hit carpeting, the impact muted but its contents chiming brittle news of their destruction.

"Stop that!" Van instinctively stepped in front of the phoenix.

Another workman advanced, his hand heavy with a tool. He passed under an aluminum twelve-foot ladder, shoving it behind him as if it were a door that needed closing. It toppled hollowly. The man paused, lifted his implement to the ceiling. Crystals shattered to the pumping sound of explosion after explosion as bullets spat into their glittering midst.

More men were advancing—workmen by dress, thugs by vocation. Van recognized three hard faces from the night she had found strangers confronting Nicky in her office. They were six men now, planted here to do battle at just this psychologically destructive moment. Here to destroy.

One spoke. "Too bad Nicky Fontana isn't here. It's like a Fontana to let a woman take his medicine for him. Tell Nicky Fontana that we object to turning a nice deserted place like the Joshua Tree into a junky Christmas tree.

"Tell Nicky Fontana if he don't forget this hotel, we'll put out *his* lights next time."

They brandished crowbars, pipes, and two-by-fours. Van guessed the gun had emptied itself on the ceiling. They came in a line.

"Outa the way, honey. We'll clip the wings on that pretty glass bird of yours first, then smash the rest."

"No."

They paused in sheer surprise.

"This is *my* hotel," Van continued, her voice crystal cold. "I redesigned it. I worked on it until I couldn't see straight. I planned for every bar of soap in every guest room. I'm not going to make it easy for you."

"We don't have to make it easy for you either, honey." The speaker's lips wore the same curl of uncaring scorn as the rest. "You get in our way—"

"I *am* in your way!" she thundered back. "People like me have always been in the way of people like you— barbarians who'll take the shortest, crudest path to what they want."

"Callin' us names won't stop us. We want the bird and a lot more. You won't stop us, not a puny little thing like you. You'll be mincemeat."

"If it's mincemeat you crave, try over here," came a dry familiar voice. "When I'm through with you guys, you won't fill a flea's ear."

Van glanced over her shoulder. Nostradamus stood behind her, his everpresent racing form hung hankie-style over something in his hand that made a remarkably straight crease in the paper.

Next to the little bookie was Walter Maxwell, armed only by his baldness and a grim expression. Between the two men's braced legs, the big black cat stalked, lashing its tail and growling in a low, mean minor key.

At the lobby's far-flung edges, workers discarded a pall of self-interest, picked up hammers and screwdrivers, and edged forward, ringing in the people gathered around the phoenix. A crowd stood behind her, friends and strangers, including the nondescript men who had staked out a claim on the lobby of the Crystal Phoenix long before it had held a future. She even thought she glimpsed a tall, silver-haired figure at the back, but she didn't dare keep her attention off the men before her. When she looked at them again, their faces looked stupid with surprise. They hefted their makeshift weapons with no heart.

"Tell Nicky Fontana—" the leader began again.

"Tell him yourself," came a voice from behind everybody.

Nicky stepped from the elevator. The doors stayed open, as if they'd been set that way, as if they'd been that way for a long time. He held a gun but didn't bother to aim it.

"She's right," he told the thugs as he joined Van beside the crystal phoenix. "It's her hotel. And their hotel." He waved at the people behind him. "And their hotel." Nicky indicated the glowering workmen. "Everybody's worked too damn hard to let some snot-nosed hoods wreck so much as a light bulb in this place.

"So you boys better climb that unlucky ladder you walked under and screw in the new bulbs the workers will pass up. Your aim was lousy; you hardly broke any Austrian crystal pendants—we can order new ones in no time. And then you'll leave. If you ever come back—in any shape or form—the new security force'll chop you up and feed you to the sushi chef. Got it? Then up that scaffolding, pronto!"

Nicky smiled modestly as a second round of applause burst forth.

"Back to work," he threatened congenially. "It may be your hotel, but I'm boss." He caught Van around the waist. "So's she." He leaned near to whisper, "You want to be security chief, baby? I can use a man like you.

But you gotta wear Bermuda shorts, like those jungle johnnys, so the clientele can see your legs—"

Van stopped him with a genteel kick in the shins, undetectable to the casual observer, then turned to make sure the phoenix stood unharmed. But her arms clung tightly to his torso, and Nicky, feeling her adrenaline-revved body close to his, thought about converting fear to something more enjoyable.

"Isn't it gorgeous, Nicky?" Van was asking in a slightly shaking voice. "Quick, can you glaziers bolt on the Plexiglas cover before I have a heart attack?"

Van snuggled close to Nicky. "You know what *really* scared me?" she whispered. "I thought I saw the silver-haired man from upstairs lining up on my side! It was eerie."

He hugged her, laughing. "Ghosts, Vanilla baby, make good allies so long as you don't believe in 'em. I tell you, he doesn't exist."

Loath to argue, she watched from the safety of his arms as a secure transparent box of plastic swallowed the crystal phoenix. "Oh, Nicky, isn't it the best thing you ever saw?"

"Not quite," he said under his breath, and when she turned to correct him, kissed her. "And it isn't worth getting made into chopped liver for, either. But it *is* worth forty grand. So I guess it *is* an endangered species."

Chapter

Fourteen

Rich burgundy carpet clung to the driveway curves like a velvet bodysuit. Long-stemmed silver champagne stands holding calla lilies stood floral guard on either side of the black-glass entry doors. Arc lights restlessly probed the sky above the Crystal Phoenix while the hotel, draped in as many light bulbs as a movie goddess's wardrobe has sequins, put on the ritz for its opening.

Everyone was invited and everyone came. Media, Beautiful People, tourists, high rollers from the East, low rollers from the budget tours of West Los Angeles, local beauties, beggars, bookies, and a visiting Arab pasha or two.

Gentlemen wearing light suits with dark shirts and white ties prowled unhampered. Ladies and gentlemen wearing the smart navy security uniforms of the Crystal Phoenix discreetly kept eyes and walkie-talkie ears on the aforesaid gentlemen.

Guests in every degree of dress ranging from fringe-and-rhinestone Western to black tie milled around the computerized carousels of video poker and pumped courtesy coins into the greedy guts of spanking-new slot machines.

Carnival-colored chips slid rapidly across navy Ultra-suede, exchanging hands from house to guest and more often vice versa, at tables strung along the long crystal-lit casinos. Gold-capped fingernails as long as their owners' fashionably dangling earrings tapped impatiently on soft Ultrasuede rim cushions while cards or dice fell into disfavor.

Along Slot-Machine Row, abandoned lowball glasses kept company with empty paper cups bearing the hotel's phoenix emblem in gold on burgundy. Similar paper cups, overflowing with coins, slid across the pink-marble surface of the change booths and into relentlessly efficient machines that swallowed them en masse and then burped out an instant and accurate accounting.

New twenty-, fifty-, and hundred-dollar bills slipped into the hands of lucky winners. Losers slipped fresh fives, tens, and dollar bills under the metal grill in exchange for smaller coinage and hopefully better luck.

Around the crystal phoenix sculpture itself, center stage opposite the entry doors, gathered a motley assemblage.

The nine Fontana boys wore angelic off-white from toe to tie. Mama Fontana, in town for the occasion, accessorized a California tan with black-charmeuse evening pants and a gold crocheted top. She was tall, enviably slim and not at all what anyone who had not met her expected.

Uncle Mario seemed subdued in undertaker's black, with one red carnation impaling his lapel. Walter Maxwell, surprisingly, wore black tie and looked morosely self-satisfied. Nostradamus had produced a vintage pinstriped suit. In its buttonhole bloomed a yellow calla lily, suspiciously reminiscent of the variety displayed in bunches outside the front doors.

Van, nervous as a bride, tried to keep her hands off the sides of her white-satin gown, which began with a halter top twisted with pearls and flared to a trumpet skirt at the floor.

Her hair, for once, was not twisted up but allowed to duplicate the shining lines of her gown by fanning to her shoulders. At her wrist, because there was no possible perch for anything on her skimpy gown, bloomed a corsage of ruby-red roses interspersed with sprays of fragile lilies of the valley, a gift from Nicky Fontana.

Nicky himself was nowhere to be seen, having been summoned to attend to twenty major undisclosed crises occurring simultaneously offscene.

"Do you think it's going well?" Van asked for the thirteenth time, turning to the nearest available ear.

The ear was homely in the extreme but grew on a sympathetic face.

"I'll lay ten to one for a lobster dinner; this little joint's gonna be a big winner."

Nostradamus beamed just in time for the photographer from the Las Vegas *Review-Journal* to shoot Van and the bookie in unlikely camaraderie.

"Your name, sir?" the ignorant photographer barked, notepad in hand. He knew who Van von Rhine was, having already taken a formal shot of her and "hotelier" Nicky Fontana under the feverishly blinking phoenix marquee outside.

"Egbert," Nostradamus said meticulously. "E-g-b-e-r-t. Teague. T-e-a-g-u-e."

The photographer dutifully noted it.

Van stared at them both.

Nostradamus winked.

At their feet, something shifted. The black cat, now formally the hotel mascot and so pictured with Van in the Crystal Promenade for a Sunday feature story, wove through their legs, imparting static to Van's gown and thus encouraging the satin to cling even more than it inclined to.

"Nicky wants you."

Van jumped. Behind her towered show-girl Darcy in a long prom-pink gown with wrist-length sleeves.

"He called from the penthouse, Van. Something's up, I guess. Anyway, he said he needed you upstairs."

Van froze guiltily. "Oh, no . . . I hope he didn't blunder into—it's supposed to be a surprise!"

Darcy shrugged monkishly cowled shoulders. "Maybe he's got one for *you*."

Van was already racing into the elevator.

At the top, the doors split open on Nicky, looking like Prince Charming in satin-striped black trousers and a cobalt-blue dinner jacket over a ruffle-fronted formal shirt. Van wondered wildly if St. Jude's good will could broadcast through all that starch.

"There was something you wanted to show me?"

"Yeah." Nicky's hand glided to her bare back to guide her along the hall.

Van planted high white-satin heels. "Let's not play games, Nicky. If you found it, you found it. Come on, I'll show you."

Nicky raised a jet-black eyebrow as Van brushed by him. Instead of entering the penthouse, she strode down the long hall to a new door cut through to the roof's remodeled guest whirlpool area.

The scaffold-mounted sheet plastic that separated Nicky's private deck from the much larger public area flapped in a soft night breeze. Below them, prime-time Vegas glittered, a rhinestone spiderweb. At their left, thrusting into the night like the prow of a dark crystal ship, rose a massive carousel shape of tinted glass and steel.

"I called the electrician before I came up," Van fussed. "At least the lighting's functional. The rest isn't quite done. Wait a bit," she advised. "It'll come on in a second."

Nicky, who had been studying the wind-sculptured liens of her gown, obediently stared at the alien construction.

"What the hell is this?"

"It's where your extra seven hundred and fifty thousand dollars went, Nicky. It's—there, here come the lights!"

Around the construction's circular top two strips of rippling neon illuminated a Times-Square-style header. Then came the news broadcast to anyone with eyes in Vegas: NICKY FONTANA'S CRYSTAL CAROUSEL NOW OPEN. Each letter scintillated like gold dust.

"You said, 'Surprise me,'" Van observed in the silence. "And I did take your name off the hotel." She held her breath.

He watched the illuminated letters circle for perhaps three cycles, then cleared his throat. "Um, isn't this a teensy bit . . . flashy?" Nicky asked delicately.

She turned on him, her mouth agape in outrage—it was what he'd been waiting for. He captured her lips in a kiss of the distinctly flashy variety.

"It's gorgeous, Van," Nicky approved happily when they finally separated to catch their breath.

"It's got a great view of the lights," she said eagerly. "Three hundred and sixty degrees of view; the glass is smoked. We'll book the best lounge acts, aimed at an intimate audience. It'll be the classiest place in Vegas, you just watch, Nicky!"

"Vanilla, baby, you don't have to sell it to me. How'd you manage to slip it past me?"

"I punched a public elevator through at the end of your penthouse hall. You thought they were simply working on the expanded whirlpool deck for the guests. . . ."

"Oh, yeah, this maze." Nicky took her hand and led her down redwood steps past secluded spas bubbling solitarily into the night. "I approve. I approve of everything you do," he added, looking back through seductively half-mast lashes. "Now I've got a surprise for *you*."

He was leading her back to the penthouse. Van balked again, this time before the plastic-curtained scaffolding.

"Nicky, it's unlucky to go under there. Maybe another time." Her fingers twisted in his.

"Now," he insisted. "What are you afraid of?"

"Nothing!" she said too quickly.

Nicky drew aside the wind-battered plastic and escorted Van under the scaffolding. In its rough privacy he collected another, softer kiss, then led her past his own vacant whirlpool and deck to the glass doors.

"Nicky, I . . . I have to be honest." Glimpses of purple

flocked wallpaper and varicose-veined mirror tiles collided in Van's brain.

"Of course you do," he soothed. "Don't be nervous, Vanilla. This is one closed door you'll be glad you opened."

He swept back the sliding glass door, then turned to shut it, encasing them in silence and moonlit dusk. "Close your eyes," he ordered in a tone so silken, she couldn't refuse.

Van's eyes squeezed shut. She heard Nicky's clothes rustle and the click of a switch, then felt bright light dancing on her lids. Her eyes winced further shut.

"Open them." Nicky's arm tightened around her nearly naked waist. His warm breath, riffling her hair, and the sharp scent of his soap enveloped her in heady intimacy. If only she could hide her true reaction to his ghastly new decor. . . .

"Open them." It was an order now, and she did.

Van looked left, then right. Her mouth opened to match her eyes. She looked up, then down. She looked at Nicky, then back at the room.

"We're in the . . . bedroom."

"I moved the master bedroom down next to the living room. Who needs to waste time climbing all those spiral stairs? Now the home office is up there, with the library and the game room. Guess who gets which?"

"I . . . I can't guess anything." Van moved away, sinking into wall-to-wall cream-colored wool carpeting. The anticipated king-size bed was there, unexpectedly dressed in tasteful Porthault bed linens. An ivory lacquer headboard and dresser furnished the room; an oversized mirror discreetly dominated one wall. Even the walls were soft, upholstered in off-white grasscloth.

"You had the entire place redone—like this?"

"I had a little help." Nicky grinned. "From some snooty interior designer likely to have insight into how a first-class blonde with a bun would like things done."

"But the flocked wallpapers and phony corks, the

ghastly veined mirror squares in those boxes the hoodlums broke!"

"Decoys," Nicky admitted smugly. "I knew you'd
peek. This here's the real McCoy."

"For me? You did all this—for me?"

He came over, turned her to face the mirror, then
wrapped his arms around her so tightly, she felt like
white-satin wallpaper plastered to his body.

"For us." Nicky nuzzled her neck. "To live in and to
run the hotel from and be"—this part scared him,
Nicky thought with sudden panic, but if ugly thugs with
tire-size biceps couldn't stop him, neither could dainty
little dolls with impeccable taste—"and to be married
in."

"B-be married in?"

"Okay, we'll get married someplace else—but to live
in *after* we're married, which should be damn soon.
Unless you don't like this." His forehead corrugated
anxiously. "Unless it's not . . . classy enough."

Van squirmed around to face him.

"You . . . want me to stay? I would—without a wedding ring or a redecorating job! I've been thinking, and
I finally . . . decided not to be afraid, Nicky. Not about
anything, and most of all, not about loving you." The
vivid blue of her eyes softened in a haze of tears. "I do
love you, Nicky. I'm sorry I was so hard to love sometimes, but you never gave up on me. You've had the
real class, all along. You don't need to make anything
over for me. Nicky, I'd live in Liberace's limousine to
be with you!"

He never could stand tears, so Nicky closed his eyes
and kissed Van until she cried, "Godfather!" She didn't,
for a very long time, but finally pulled back a little in
his arms, breathless and radiant.

"Can't you do *anything* wrong?" she teased. "Seriously,
Nicky, this . . . this room is first class! Posh to the port-
holes. But—" She pulled away and ambled coquettishly
to the bed, trailing the fragile scent of lilies of the

valley. Her fingertips skimmed the luxurious linen. "I might . . . um, miss . . . some of your more decadent old flashy comforts a teensy bit."

Nicky grinned his triumph in a tackily open manner. "Hit those headboard console buttons, Vanilla baby."

Walking under the scaffolding had been lucky after all. She'd hit pay dirt on her first try. The ceiling over the bed peeled back with a discreet mechanical hum. Van looked up to see herself looking down.

"Play it again, Van."

She did. The mirrors slid away to reveal the midnight celestial floor show as the featured stars paraded in the skies over Las Vegas. Then everything slid away, and Van was enfolded in Nicky's arms for the first of what promised to be a series of absolutely top-drawer sensual encounters of the soon-to-be-marital kind.

In fact, as the guests attempt to turn the former Miss Vanilla von Rhine and Mr. Nicky Fontana into rice pudding, I am taking a small recreational dip in the hotel carp pond, luckily unobserved except for a few squealing pigeons overhead.

Unluckily, I am interrupted by Nostradamus, who slips away from the bridal festivities to smoke a stogie in the courtyard and discerns me in the act of disposing of a tail fin.

He leans down to blow a cloud of blue smoke directly in my kisser whiskers. I sense one of his more repellent bits of doggerel coming on. Nostradamus and I go way back.

> "Well, who do I find with his paw in the pail,
> But Midnight Louie at the end of this tale."

With which he gives my posterior appendage an undignified yank. I look up at the little bookie and wink one baby green peeper. After all, nobody in his right mind is going to squeal on a swell fellow like yours truly—especially now that I am the house fuzz.

Epilogue or

Midnight Louie Has Another Word

For the Prince and the Princess, things turn out with a modicum of bliss. They get hitched in the Crystal Promenade at the biggest bash this town ever sees except for the opening of the Crystal Phoenix a month previous. Every limo in Vegas is present, with the exception of those belonging to shady characters who might wish the Crystal Phoenix ill.

Miss Darcy McGill is maid of honor, and if you think Miss Vanilla von Rhine makes a nice-looking little doll in her street clothes, you should eyeball her in seventy yards of imported Spanish lace on Macho Mario Fontana's arm as they come down the aisle. Macho Mario seems reluctant to give the bride away. Mr. Nicky Fontana, of course, is the cat's pajamas in his tails. Nostradamus is best man, and all the Fontana boys are ushers.

You may detect a certain notable absence among the official bridal party, namely myself. Well, the truth is—and do I tell you anything but the truth, the whole truth, and nothing but the truth?—the truth is that I am already on duty patrolling the grounds in my new capacity as undercover house dick for the Crystal Phoenix, the grandest little hotel to hit the Las Vegas Strip.

The Show Girl
and the Prof

Chapter

One

"'Visitors aren't allowed backstage,' she pointed out, dabbing her chin with a makeup sponge.

"The Arab prince stood behind her, glowering seductively. The snowy whiteness of his traditional head-dress haloed a swarthy face. She leaned closer to the mirror, its edges haphazardly framed with snapshots, postcards, and notes written in lipstick. She knew why the Emir of Shambar's son was in her dressing room, even though he shouldn't have been. Rules meant nothing to a prince used to lawless Arabian nights and hot, shifting desert sands.

"'I bribed the guard,' he confessed. His nimble fingers produced what appeared to be a one-dollar bill tailed by a tight train of three zeroes.

"Her eyes, a soft hazel but as fierce in their way as the Arab's darker ones, met his in the mirror.

"'You paid too much. Usually a fifty will do it.'

"He shrugged, a gesture that emphasized the voluminous robes draping his figure. 'It matters not. What does matter is that it is necessary for you to call me Highness.'

"She pushed back her chair, and rose slowly. Her body seemed to uncoil forever in stages of calculated grace—after all, she was a dancer and nearly six feet tall without shoes.

"The top of his head came to her collar bone. Smiling, she complied dutifully with his custom.

157

"'Yes, *High*ness.' But she had put a certain emphasis on the title that even a prince couldn't afford to overlook.

"Throwing the thousand-dollar bill onto the cluttered dressing table, the Emir of Shambar's son drew his desert robes around himself.

"'I have not finished with you,' he threatened as he exited through the door.

"But Sirene merely sat again, more slowly than she had risen, and turned back to her mirror. She plucked up the discarded thousand-dollar bill and thrust the money deep into the fragile custody of her flesh-colored net-and-rhinestone bra.

"*This,* she vowed to herself, *is as close a you'll ever get . . . Highness.*"

"Well." Professor Stevenson Eliot Austen stopped reading and cleared his throat, in that order.

His creative writing class sat rapt, chins braced on fists, eyes wide. The mesmerizing Austen baritone could make a yawn sound impressive, but for once his subject matter was equally exciting.

"An admirable attempt," the professor began his evaluation, rattling the pages from which he'd read. "It shows, uh . . . vivid word choices and endless imagination. It also glamorizes the seedier aspects of our city, and on that I would mark it down. Las Vegas as a fleshpot is a cliché, Miss—er. . . Miss McGill."

It wasn't hard to tell who Miss McGill was. A long-limbed, pink-faced young woman in the very back row of ranked seats was even now shrinking onto her tailbone in a futile attempt to escape notice.

Professor Austen adjusted his black-framed glasses on his every-so-slightly aquiline nose, folded his sweater-clad arms, and waited patiently for the author to declare herself.

At last a long, narrow arm snaked slowly upward at the rear. Austen nodded satisfaction. "I see Miss McGill anticipated my reaction and took care to situate herself well out of my view."

The class laughed knowingly. This early in the first semester, class spirit was nonexistent, but would-be writers always appreciated the professor's arid brand of humor.

He abruptly shifted his weight off the desk corner and replaced the paper on a scanty pile, then turned a mock-severe frown on the complacent students. "This is a *creative* writing class. Miss McGill merits an A for creativity—if a D-plus for content. Please, Miss McGill," he cajoled, "try to find some inspiration in Las Vegas besides the tawdry second-hand daydreams purveyed by the Strip and Glitter Gulch. You obviously don't have the slightest experience of what you're writing about. The 'Emir of Shambar's son' indeed."

"Excuse me, Professor, but—"

Austen glanced up from selecting a new paper for presentation. "Well, stand up, then, so we can hear you. Don't be shy."

After a pause, she stood. She was nearly as tall as her unlikely fictional heroine, a fact not lost on the man at the desk far below. Unlike the scintillating Sirene, however, the woman in his classroom was fully clad—in faded blue jeans and a loose, long-sleeved sweatshirt. A pale face clear of makeup seemed to put her age somewhere in the very tender twenties.

"You wanted to say something, Miss McGill?"

Her low voice carried well despite a tremor of shyness—or rebellion. "Only to say, Professor, that seventy percent of the people in Las Vegas feed their families and build their churches on the money from the casinos. And *they're* considered respectable citizens. So why isn't the industry that's the very heart of Las Vegas, both economically and sociologically?"

"Grammar is not my subject, but 'respectable' is not a synonym for 'worthwhile,' Miss McGill," he pointed out.

"Nor is it synonymous with good literature," she shot back, blushing fiercely when everyone turned to stare at her. "Look at Damon Runyon! He wrote about the people on Broadway in the twenties and thirties . . . about gamblers, petty criminals, and chorus girls—"

Austen's eyebrows had risen with new respect at this unexpectedly spirited attack. "Yes, yes, Miss McGill. But that's light entertainment, not serious fiction. Or do you consider your story serious fiction?" He smiled polite disbelief.

"N-no, I would never claim—"

"But I'm being unfair, a tendency among college instructors, I'm told." He smiled charmingly at his students in general before returning his attention to her, to end the disruption.

"It's obvious you're serious about your writing," he said more gently. "Perhaps that's the best definition of serious fiction. But you need to find a larger subject matter to be serious about."

"What?" she demanded. "Death and taxes? War and revolution?"

Austen removed his glasses, baring amused gray eyes. "Those subjects sufficed for Tolstoy. Perhaps you should apply yourself to taxes; not much of a literary nature has been written about them." He glanced at the big round schoolhouse clock on the wall.

"The important thing, class, is that Miss McGill *wrote*. She did not waylay me before class to beg off because she hadn't had time; she did not merely re-phrase some claptrap she'd read before. She wrote an original short story. And that's where we all must begin.

"So before you snicker, examine your own consciences," he instructed. "I'll be reading *your* literary attempts next. Turn off the MTV for an hour and see what you can dream up if you stop being mere passive consumers."

Austen concentrated on restacking his papers as his students left the room. When he looked up she was standing before him, the long-legged one, as vigilant yet oddly relaxed as a gazelle frozen on an African savanna, her bright hazel eyes watching him. He was startled, seldom finding female students at his own eye level.

"Yes, Miss McGill? I hope I didn't embarrass you just now. A writer's ego can be fragile—"

"Oh, you probably did, Professor," she admitted wryly, clutching her notebooks more tightly to her chest.

He glanced down before he could help it. The unblushingly concrete description of Sirene's purely fictional charms made him curious about the author's endowments. Did she write from envy or experience? Surely not experience, something inside him told him, something fiercely insistent, something almost protective.

"—it isn't your fault if my ego ends up on the chopping block," she was saying generously.

He whipped off his glasses to stare forbiddingly at her, then jammed them back on. "That's very kind of you, Miss McGill—to excuse me. Usually I do the excusing."

She smiled again, undeterred by his John Houseman act, then speared the top of her paper with one long forefinger. "I thought I had typed my name on there."

"You did..." He snatched up the pages. "It's right here, Miss McGill."

"Darcy, it says first," she interrupted. "If you keep calling me 'Miss McGill,' I'll think you dislike *me* as much as you do my writing."

"Not your writing; that shows definite promise. It's the subject matter. But if your heart's set on chronicling the sins of Las Vegas, well then, I imagine there are enough sins committed in this benighted city to keep you busy for some time," he added dryly.

"You imagine? Haven't you ever experienced Las Vegas nightlife in the flesh?"

Surely her word choice was accidental, he thought.

She couldn't be *teasing* him! Students never teased Professor Stevenson Austen.

"It's quite possible, Miss McGill," he said, sticking to the formalities she had challenged, "to live an entire lifetime in this city and completely avoid the excesses of the Strip or downtown."

"Darcy," she insisted with a warmth that belied her earlier shyness.

"The 'miss' is no term of dismissal." His answering smile exposed a good-humored dimple at one corner of his mouth. "It's simply unwise for me to address students on a social level. Now I've got another class elsewhere, so—Look, Miss McGill." He stopped at the door, jamming his glasses into a sweater pocket and regarding her with misty close-up focus.

"If you like writing about chorus queens and sheiks of Araby, go to it. Don't let some stodgy old English professor talk you out of it. But don't expect him to applaud you, either."

"You're not old, Professor." Her eyes were as wide open as the African plains. "Why on earth would you refer to yourself that way?"

All the adoring female faces that had sat the front rows of his classes since he had left graduate school flashed before his eyes. A red-blooded, twenty-three-year-old male dropped into a school of lady minnows all too eager to nibble on forbidden fruit had to hide behind something. He noticed with annoyance that she hadn't disagreed with the "stodgy" part of his self-description.

"I'm old enough to have earned a Ph.D.," he said sternly and rather stodgily, reminding himself that even at the ripe old age of thirty-two maintaining an unreachable facade could sometimes be damned hard work. "That contributes to aging before one's time. And speaking of time..."

He was squinting pointedly at the functional Timex on his wrist, moving his arm closer and farther by turns. Impulsively, Darcy McGill caught it in her loose, commanding grasp as efficiently as a nurse taking a pulse.

"Three-fifty-nine, Professor, time for your next class, The Twentieth-Century English Novel."

Darcy heard her own words coming out in just the casually flip tones she wanted, but she didn't release his wrist. Her easy, unplanned gesture seemed much too hard to undo. Her heart was surging strangely, her fingers tingling from stolen sensations—the rasp of the tiny hairs topping his wrist, the surprising patch of satin-smooth skin beneath it.

Their look held, the small shock of physical contact growing into something far less physical and even more shocking. It finally made her drop his hand like a hot coal.

"Oh, say. . . time for me to run, Professor! I'm late for a very important date." Recovering her poise, she laughed into his eyes and winked mischievously. " 'Bye now."

Professor Austen watched Darcy McGill dart down the hall as if *he* had been guilty of keeping her. She made him want to forget his carefully nurtured dignity and run after her and—

"A . . . lovely woman," he noted to himself, then looked around to make sure no one had seen him.

Darcy McGill slammed her books down on Van von Rhine's desk.

"Can I dump these here? I want to come up and read in peace and quiet during break—"

"Just collect them when you're done," said the dainty blond woman behind the massive desk overrun with paperwork. "I'll leave the door open. How are things at the University of Nevada at Las Vegas these days?"

"Oh, ducky!" Darcy hurled herself into a chair. "I love creative writing, but the classwork is more personal than I thought it would be. Today the instructor read my assignment—aloud—in front of the whole class."

"Instructors generally read things to their classes," Van said.

"Maybe Nicky's right," Darcy went on grimly. "You can learn as much from life as you can in a classroom."

"Of course Nicky's right," Van agreed. "He's my husband—and he has a college degree."

Darcy's tennis shoe kicked idly at the desk, dislodging a large black cat from under the kneehole. "Point taken. If hell-raising Nicky Fontana can be the first in his somewhat larcenous Family to get a sheepskin, I guess I can pin one on my dressing-room door."

"You don't have a dressing-room door. Aren't you sharing the storage area with the other three queens?"

"Yes, and Nicky keeps promising more space, so we can all have private niches."

"The show's going better than we thought, which doesn't leave time for a revamp. I guess Danny Dove knows what he's doing, at least in the matter of revues. We never wanted the Crystal Phoenix to be a big show hotel, it's not in the size league of the Goliath or Caesars."

"It's big enough, Van, to allow you two to polish your nails on your respective lapels—oh, yikes! Fingernails! I better get down and start donning my armaments. Why are you working so late, anyway? Nicky won't be crazy about that."

"Nicky needs to have his machismo challenged regularly." Van said, rising to see Darcy to the door.

In the process one stiletto of her Italian heels pinned a swatch of black fur to the floor. Something roared like an affronted jackhammer.

"Oh, Louie, I'm sorry." Van bent to caress the gigantic cat at her feet, then stepped elaborately over him. "He's such a lump of coal; always underfoot. Or maybe I'm just clumsy."

"Clumsy?" Darcy paused to survey Van's petite figure. "You're a china shepherdess. You should galumph through life like me, five feet eleven and growing."

"Being tall's an advantage on a Las Vegas stage, Darcy. Girls the country over would kill to be in your tap shoes."

"Especially at the Crystal Phoenix, where the haute high rollers all come. You've done a great job managing the place, Van. If Nicky hadn't married you, I bet his uncle Mario would have, just to get such prime talent in the 'Family.' I have to admit they sure can see me from the back row, or *in* the back row. I gotta go, or it'll be curtains, and I won't be ready."

Darcy dashed through the hotel service areas, down the stairs and finally through twelve-feet-high double doors to the storage area she shared with three other dancers and sat down at her spot.

Dusty makeup lights framed the memorabilia stuck into the mirror frame like prom cards into a high school girl's bureau mirror.

Since she had been ten, Darcy had haunted dance studios and practiced pliés until she thought her knees would snap off. She was inured to knotted muscles and sweat-soaked leotards. She had dreamed her California girlhood away on toe shoes and her own reflection in walls of wavy mirror. She had always wanted to be a professional dancer. And now she was.

Darcy smiled at the odd way dreams have of ending and stuck more bobby pins into her free-flowing ponytail.

In minutes the lotion-spattered mirror before her reflected a smooth expanse of pancake makeup emphasized with the exaggerated, painted-on features meant to be seen on stage—soot-lined eyes, arched black eyebrows, blue-shadowed lids, lips glossed redder than a candied apple. Topping it off were jet-black false eyelashes long and stiff enough to do double duty as chimney sweepers' brooms.

She looked exactly as she had described Sirene. *Fictional indeed,* she fumed. *Write about what you know. Mularkey!* She *had* written about what she knew, and Professor Austen hadn't believed her. He seemed

determined to see her as some nice tall girl at the back
of his classroom when Darcy secretly longed for a much
flashier place, front and center, in his attentions.

Her mind painted his features over hers in the
mirror. She knew them by heart—stream-cool gray eyes
that could warm in a second, a slow smile that was the
velvet glove worn over his steely professional classroom
demeanor. There was a slight formality to Professor
Austen that Darcy longed to shatter. She'd love to see
Stevenson Eliot Austen with his hair rumpled, his rep
tie loosened, his feelings unbuttoned all the way to
his—Reality intervened.

Darcy stood frozen at the front of the classroom,
books clutched to her chest, flattening her bosom to
pancake dimensions, and stared deeply into Professor
Austen's sincere gray eyes. She swallowed, hard.

"After your next class? To talk?"

"I wasn't inviting you to an execution, Miss McGill."
Austen paused in arranging the books upon his desk in
their usual fastidious order. "Would waiting around
campus for an hour cause a problem?"

"No. Yes! I have to be somewhere by six—"

"This won't take long—ten minutes, maybe? We can
meet here. No one's using the lecture hall, and you
could kill time by writing in your journal."

Darcy walked as one condemned to her usual seat.
When everyone drained from the room at the end of
class, she remained high and dry in her seat, alone.

She watched the big round clock on the wall and the
way the serrated palm leaves outside the window fanned
the blue afternoon blaze of desert sky. She wrote that
observation down, then another and another.

"I hope I'm not interrupting you."

Had time gone that quickly? Darcy looked up, then
down. Austen stood in the doorway, his arms empty of
books for once, empty of everything but a slim furl of
papers—hers.

"No, I just finished." She scrambled to put her papers away, grabbed her purse, and began descending the aisle stairs while he watched. They seemed eight hundred feet long, and the risers felt impossibly narrow. Maybe one of her low heels would catch on one and hurl her down, into his arms—

But nothing happened, except that she arrived at floor level and eye to eye with Professor Austen, who seemed particularly intimidating today.

"Don't look so panic-stricken, Miss McGill. I only want a few words with you. Have a chair." She sat in the molded plastic model he pulled up to his desk.

"I see you took my advice to keep your subject matter if you felt like it." Austen was skimming the tops of several assignments. "And your writing is sharpening. In fact, they make quite an amusing set, these adventures of the sumptuous Sirene." He paused.

"Miss McGill, I hope you won't take this in the wrong way—you're a talented writer with an astute eye for detail—but I'd be derelict if I didn't—"

"Didn't what?"

"Advise you to give up these imaginative excursions into the sleazy side of life in Las Vegas!" he urged. "What can you know of it, anyway?"

"I've lived here since high school, I—"

"Living in Las Vegas gives no insight into life in the fast lane," he objected. "There are two cities here—the ordinary, quiet, churchgoing community that would exist quite nicely without the gaudy goings-on that occur on the bright side of town. Then there's 'Las Vegas'—the flashy, no-holds-barred city that panders to greed and ignorance, that glamorizes gamblers and chorus girls, high rollers and hookers—really, these are not admirable people, Miss McGill. I hate to see a talented young woman like yourself losing her head in candy-floss dreams of an unreal world."

"I'm not that young! And I guess I can lose my head

if I want to." Darcy felt stunned and a bit angry to hear her hero unknowingly dismiss her very way of life.

"You're young enough to know nothing of the world that attracts you," Austen continued with calm, infuriating certainty. "A cardinal rule of writing is to write what you know—"

"I am!" Darcy burst out.

He actually reared back, as if to see her more clearly.

"I know about everything I put in those papers! I *was* writing from life!"

"Not *your* life?"

His eyes were shocked now. Darcy felt an abrupt surge of guilt and, oddly enough, protectiveness. All his regard for her "talent" would shatter if he knew she made her living as a chorus girl. He must treasure some illusion of the sweet, unpretentious Darcy he saw in class every week.

"Oh, not my life, really," she denied automatically. "No, it's . . . my . . . my sister's!"

"Oh." He looked so relieved that her wild story seemed justified. "Your *sister* is one of these"—he paged rapidly through the papers, finding the quote—"these 'hard-working hoofers with hearts as soft as the cherished pink satin tutus they wore at nine.'?"

Darcy gulped. "Perhaps I exaggerate a bit. Poetic license, you know. But, but Sirene is my sister, yes."

"Your parents named you Darcy and her Sirene?"

"Noooo." Darcy's imagination cast around frantically for something to cling to—the invention that gave her writing such liveliness. "My parents named her—Irene! But when she went on the stage, she added, the *s* . . . so she would stand out."

"I should think that a woman six feet tall would have no problem doing that in a normal occupation and with her right name." He glanced quickly at Darcy, and his dry manner softened. "I'm sorry, I don't mean to imply that being a tall woman is—"

"It is!" Darcy said tersely.

He cleared his throat. "Tell me about your sister. I may put down her profession, but you obviously look up to her."

"Or would if I could." Darcy grinned wickedly. "But we are *exactly* the same height. In fact, we're, uh, twins. Fraternal twins. Sirene is older by five minutes."

"I see." He leaned back in his swivel chair. "And you went to school together?"

"Of course." Darcy's improvisational mind was beginning to believe her own story as she sketched it. It was a challenge, a class writing exercise more than a lie, she told herself, like composing an entire Sirene story on the spur of the moment.

"Oh, you should have seen Sirene in high school!" Darcy rambled on. "She was captain of the cheerleading squad, and always got the best solos at the dance recitals."

"You didn't dance yourself?"

"Who me? Heavens no! I was the bookish type. Very sedate. And a little nearsighted. I couldn't make it across the classroom to dust the erasers for the teachers without tripping. I was born with three left feet. But Sirene—"

"Yes, I think I have quite a complete picture of Sirene right here," he said, patting the papers. "It's you I'm interested in."

"You are?" Darcy gazed into his gray eyes, feeling dazed.

"Of course I'm interested in you. You're far too modest. You're a promising writer, but isn't that sense of humor you volley about like tennis ball simply camouflage for a more serious side of Darcy McGill? Write your tales of the chorus line if you like, since they're based on reality, though a somewhat skewed one. But I still think you should look beyond that."

"All right."

She stood with a glint in her eyes. Somewhere in that

stodgy, professorial speech she saw that her hero wore more than reading glasses. He had blinders on as big as a billboard. As long as he peered at the world through thick prejudice-tinted lenses, he'd never see or appreciate Darcy as a complete person—chorus girl *and* nice girl, dancer *and* writer. He couldn't even accept her *writing* about backstage life. What made him think that he was so right and she was so wrong? Her Irish temper was up and racing its motor. Talk about sterotypes! How she'd love to teach Professor Austen that the life of a Las Vegas show girl was not the hollow, clichéd existence he assumed it to be.

"I hope you don't have to spend all your weekends reading our little class exercises, Professor," Darcy remarked, probing.

"No way." He smiled amiably, almost rakishly. "In fact, I'm partying tonight."

"Oh. Well, I'm going to kick up my heels tonight myself," she put in airily.

"Good! Glad to hear it!" His face warmed with the first expression of personal interest Darcy had detected. "That's the spirit. Can't sit in a corner and write all the time, you know."

"I'll think about what you said, Professor—about being serious." Darcy allowed herself the luxury of cataloging the fascinating fogscape of his eyes: *Inner quicksilver shifting through a range of stormy sea changes— wise/foolish, kind/cruel, electric/insulating. . . .*

"Good." He stared at her a moment as if he too were penning mental sketches of her eyes. Then he blinked and pulled the glasses from his breast pocket, donning them like a transparent shield. "By all means, consider being serious, Miss McGill. Good-bye, then, and have a good weekend. Don't stay up too late," he joked, beginning to back away.

"No," she answered, grinning stupidly and feeling like an accomplished liar. "I won't."

Darcy set off down the long hall, dreading the still-fiery Las Vegas heat and the clogged rush-hour traffic, even if the distance between the university's halls of ivy and the Strip's halls of hilarity was only a few blocks.

Chapter

Two

"Ooh-la-la, honey! You're late."

One of the gigantic dressing-room doors stood ajar a crack, and in the crack floated a face.

"Hi, Midge. You're later." Darcy turned in her chair to greet the woman still poised in the doorway. "Sit down and stay awhile."

"Funny." Midge sprang her lean, mean, blue-jeaned body into the next chair. "You're always here first—even when you're late."

"Just fast on my feet," Darcy sang back, executing a series of tap steps with her tennis shoes, still sitting.

Darcy grinned at Midge before bending to pull off her shoes. Two more opposite-looking women would be hard to find in a radius of four hundred miles. Midge was lean where Darcy was lithe, angular where she was simply supple, and almost twice her age, although no one dared inquire exactly what that might be. Yet the face Midge expertly erected in stage makeup blurred their differences. By the time Darcy straightened and began hunting up the wig for her first number, the Midge in the mirror seemed her spitting image.

"The professor kept me after class," Darcy admitted while dressing.

"But it's working out okay?" A new speaker had just rushed through the doors, a redheaded woman—long, tall, and handsome—Jo. "Lordy, we all better move our behinds."

Midge squinted critically at Darcy's glue-glazed nails.

"If those things don't set by showtime, they'll go flying off during your costume changes like old piano ivories."

"A stodgy old academic type is worth risking your genuine false Coquette-of-Hollywood nails—with batch-blended glitter? Some people have warped values," Jo lectured.

Darcy paused to consider while her faux nails and original-issue fingertips dried—hopefully—till death or Nail Undo did them part.

"He's not really stodgy, but funny in a dry sort of way. And not old at all. Thirty-something."

"Single?" Trish, a big-boned blonde, bounded into the dressing room last, her voice humming with brash interest.

Darcy squirmed but continued painting half-moons of blusher under her cheekbones. "That's not what I'm at UNLV to learn." She whisked a carrot-colored wig off its Styrofoam wig block, which some idle chorus boy or girl had painted with Technicolor features, and pulled the wig over her flattened hair. "Hey, they stayed on!" she hooted triumphantly, flashing ten red talons.

Several minutes later, Jo, Midge, Darcy, and Trish joined the stream of dancers clattering up the backstage steps. Darcy was last to hurtle up to the mirrored offstage door that offered an eleventh-hour costume check to every racing dancer who pounded past it.

She looked uncannily like all the rest—an elongated figure of unclad female beauty, a rhinestoned G-string sparkling at the junction of sleek thighs, with rhinestones draping her bikini bodice and entwining every extremity. If only "stodgy" old Professor Austen could see her now!

Darcy winked at her glittering reflection and rammed palms-first into the door, pushing through the cluttered dark backstage and onto the sun-bright dazzle of the stage beyond.

Maribu-feather snowflakes floated in spotlight beams. A hundred begemmed bodies on the hoof drummed up

a racket that never floated past the footlights over the
prerecorded chorus.

"Turn in our notebooks?"

Darcy sat stunned in her seat that afternoon, watching
her classmates fish the objects under discussion from
inside knapsacks and tote bags.

"I—I didn't know he was going to *c-collect* and *read*
them," Darcy stuttered to the would-be playwright
next to her.

He shrugged. "All the better. Old Austen will get a
sample of your writing with your hair down."

"He's not old!" she snapped without thinking.

"Hey, it's just a figure of speech. What's the big deal?"

"Nothing," Darcy said, lingering in her seat while all
the others filed out. Each one deposited a notebook on
the growing number atop the professor's desk. Darcy
watched the pile rise as if mesmerized by a spreading
mushroom cloud of doom.

Finally, Austen looked up at her, at the green notebook clutched in her frozen hands that she wished she
had left in a locked drawer. Everyone else was gone.
They were alone, utterly alone.

"Saving the best for last?" he joked. But he sounded like
he was looking forward to reading her off-the-cuff scribblings, as if he thought she was the best writer in the class.

Darcy got up and slunk down the stairs, her toes
stuttering on the risers so that she almost slipped a
couple times. For heaven's sake, where was the surefooted chorus girl when she needed her? Where was
Sirene, who knew how to handle everything, including
handing your secret heart right into the palm of the
man it quivered for?

"Are you sick, Miss McGill?"

"No. Yes! I mean, not physically." He was looking so
damned concerned. And well he should be. If he read
what she'd doodled in her notebook.

"Are you sure you're not ill?"

She nodded mutely, clutching her notebook to her breasts.

"I'm looking forward to seeing your journal," he said.

"You can't!" she said.

"Why not?"

"I'm . . . it's not ready."

"The whole point is for me to see your unpolished work. I'm not going to mark you down on spelling and grammar or even writing style. I just want to see where your unconscious takes you, how you express yourself when you think no one is looking."

"You can't!" she repeated.

He straightened. "I'm sorry. You have to turn it in. It's required."

"But . . . Monday then." She could write all weekend, create a whole new notebook.

"Everyone else has turned in his or her work today. Why should I make an exception in your case?" He was being divinely reasonable.

"I didn't know that I had to turn it over," Darcy wailed. "You see, I can't."

"You mean you won't."

"I mean I can't," she answered, her eyes pleading. "I would if I could, but . . ."

His eyes narrowed. "Is it something to do with Sirene?"

"Huh?"

"With your sister Sirene?"

"Oh. With her. Well, yes, actually," she said, playing for time to think. She so hated to disappoint him, but she could never show her face in his class again if he actually read—Darcy shuddered.

"Good God, you really *are* upset. Sit down and tell me why. I won't bite."

His hand pressed her shoulder until she sank onto the chair nearby. He perched on the corner of his desk. With a combination of numb lust and writerly observation,

Darcy watched the fabric of his pants pleat across the long muscles of his thigh.

"It's just that I've never voluntarily shown anyone!" she confessed. That was the whole truth.

"You've sat here and heard me read your rather risqué tales of Sirene to the class," he pointed out. "For crying out loud—"

"But that was finished work."

"I know your notebook efforts might be crude or embarrassing—"

"No, you don't," she muttered. "You don't understand. I *lock* this notebook *up* where I work. I can't let anyone see it."

"You lock it up?" He stared into her eyes, searching for truth, and found it. "You really are sensitive. What does Sirene have to do with it?"

"Sirene?" *Damn Sirene!* she wished heartily. *Damn all inventions that turn into monsters that turn on their creators.* "Sirene peeked once."

"At your writing."

Darcy nodded, seeing the scene in her mind now, seeing shy young Darcy—which she had been—and a bolder, brassier version peering over that over Darcy's shoulder. For a second it looked uncannily like . . . herself.

"I was—we were—twelve."

"And you kept a journal?"

"Oh, I've always wanted to write," she confessed with absolute honestly. The answering smile in his eyes branded itself on the deepest darkest depths of hers.

"And Sirene violated your journal?" he prompted.

Darcy nodded grateful agreement, happy to have him draw conclusions so she wouldn't have to stretch the truth any further.

"And you can't stand anyone reading your private journals since then, is that it?"

Darcy sighed happily and nodded, staring into his understanding eyes.

He stared back. Somehow his hand had returned to

her shoulder. It felt warm and not heavy at all. Darcy smiled idiotically.

"Do you feel better now, for having told me?" he asked, his voice deep but hushed a bit so that it vibrated.

She could have purred. "Yes, much better. Awfully much better."

"I guess"—his hand tightened on her shoulder, then abandoned it as he stood and turned away—"I guess I can make an exception, given the circumstances. Violating a child's privacy can be quite traumatic, even if it's by a sibling."

"A what?" she asked, still happily dazed.

He wheeled to face her again. Darcy was shocked to read anger in his face, an expression she'd never seen there before.

"By your sister, your damnable sister Sirene! Darcy— Miss McGill, I wish you'd sit back and take another look at your sister, at your relationship. I don't think she's the best influence on you. You really are a bit oversensitive about this—" His fingers paused momentarily on the green notebook cover in her lap, and she jerked as if scalded, whether from what he touched or where it lay when he touched it she couldn't tell.

"You see?" He shook his head. "Just try to relax about it. Maybe you could start a journal you know is going to be turned in. Maybe you'll get around your hang-up that way. It's not healthy to be so . . . secretive . . . about your writing. Just go home this weekend, try to write something you can show me, and don't worry about it."

"You won't flunk me?"

"No." He laughed.

"You won't hate me?"

"Of course not. My star pupil? I'd have to be crazy. Anyone would have to be crazy to hate you. You've really got to work on a better self-image. What you have to say is important. But you know that, deep down, don't you? That's why you're here in my class."

She stood, the notebook sandwiched between her arms and chest. "That's why I'm here in your class," she repeated.

"Good." He smiled and put on his glasses, then looked at the piled notebooks and sighed. "I've got a weekend of deciphering illegible student chicken-scratchings. I wish yours were among them. It would have given me something to look forward to."

"I—I wish it was too," she said. "I really do!" And, mortified by her adolescent behavior, she fled the classroom.

Interlude

An Interjection from
an Old Acquaintance

I cannot fault so sweet a little doll as Miss Darcy McGill, although she is no little doll in person, as most hoofers in this town start at five feet seven. The best average between five-ten and six-one, much like quarterbacks.

Being more than somewhat small in stature myself, comparatively speaking, you can see that a guy like me is handicapped. You can also apprehend that many guys in Vegas come up somewhat short when it comes down to escorting a genuine show girl about town and not looking like a dachshund out for a stroll with an afghan—the canine, that is, not the comforter.

Sad to say, the hardworking chorus girl, who asks nothing more of life than a little glitter and good glue, is often left at loose ends socially, unless she is unlucky enough to be courted by the bozos who believe that a fat wallet is enough to make up for thinning self-esteem.

So I am very sympathetic to these terpsichorean dolls, who hoof their little hearts out for what amounts to decent pay but not enough to write home about, much less send. Although most tourists regard them as glamorous, Midnight Louie has pounded enough neon-soaked pavements in this town to know that most of these elongated little dolls are ladies whose dreams took a detour, and instead of essaying Swan Lake at the ballet, they are shedding swansdown from costumes that leave little to the imagination but pneumonia.

Still, it is a living, and I am hardly one to quibble. These dolls and myself are soul mates of a sort, being largely unappreciated in our own times, and I make sure to favor them all with frequent dressing-room visitations. I am especially welcome in the four queens' quarters, know as the Forbidden Zone among the other chorusters.

Miss Midge Mancini keeps a wire brush—originally intended for suede shoes, I believe—with which to polish the more hirsute portions of my anatomy. The Misses Trish Reilly and Jo Hastings manage to import caviar of an adequate grade and the occasional tin of sardines for the jolly little preshow parties we five share.

And Miss Darcy McGill, who has a heart of solid platinum, provides me with a red-velvet pillow near the warm rays of her makeup lights and leaves me occasional reading material for the long hours I must while away guarding the below-stage area while everybody else is tapping and rapping in the spotlights upstairs.

It is a lonely and arduous life I lead, but somebody has to do it.

Chapter

Three

"Dar-cy's got a vis-i-tor, Dar-cy's got a vis-i-tor..."

Jo mischievously pranced behind Darcy's chair. Her childish singsong sounded incongruous coming from a woman posing as the black-satin queen of clubs and wearing as little clothing as the trey of spades has spots. She doffed her heavy headdress of fountaining jet plumes to crown Darcy with its splendor.

"Guess who is it?" Jo asked coyly.

Darcy froze in unbuckling her red-satin T-straps. "Not the Son of the Sheik? Say it isn't so."

"It isn't." Jo tantalizingly produced a note of yellow paper from the cleft of her bosom, drawing it up between two inverted and barely concealing black-satin hearts. "Not unless His Royal Lowness has changed his name to Steven Eliot."

Darcy frowned, mystified.

Jo leaned closer. "Um...Austen, I guess, is the last name. I'm afraid the writing smudged from my"—Jo performed a burlesque-style bump that begged for a drum roll—"body heat," she finished in a foghorn whisper.

Darcy snatched for the tiny notepaper, but Jo slapped its glued edge to the litter surrounding Darcy's mirror and retrieved her headdress.

"Cut out the cute and move your fanny, Jo," Midge intervened gruffly. "I'm sure Darcy would rather receive her guest privately."

Darcy, sitting frozen amid the usual postshow chaos caused by assorted chorines changing into street clothes and skedaddling, was sure the exact opposite was true. She leaned toward the mirror-posted note, squinting at the fuzzy lead marks indicative of a pencil in urgent need of sharpening.

But she could learn no more than the three little words that Jo had revealed originally. *Steven*. *Eliot*. *Austen*.

Steven? Ohmigod! He must think he was calling on the notorious Sirene and didn't want to intimidate her by using the full Stevenson.

"Who *is* this guy?" Trish already had eeled into stirrup slacks as formfitting as her tights, then tied on a red-print bandanna that clashed gloriously with her Titian hair.

"Nobody!" Darcy assured her so quickly that even Steven Eliot Austen would have objected had he been present.

"Oh." Trish nodded knowingly. "No money, huh? Well, dump him quick. I gotta run—grocery shopping."

Two A.M. was prime time for busy show girls. Las Vegas food markets stayed open like casinos, around the clock.

In the dressing room, Jo remained behind, pausing behind Darcy's chair on her way out. "And be prepared to tell Auntie Jo *all* tomorrow night before the show—"

On that ominous advice, she left the dressing room. Darcy was alone, except for a drowsing black cat artfully curled on a crimson-velvet pillow.

"Oh, Louie—what should I do?" Darcy wailed.

Darcy raced for the hall, her heels ringing maniacally on the concrete. Near the pay phone with its scribbled corona of graffiti, Darcy punched Jake the doorman's extension into the house phone.

"Jake? This is . . . Miss McGill. Send Mr. Austen down, with good directions, please."

"Oh, going formal, are we? Very good, madame," Jake replied with just enough sarcasm for only Darcy to detect.

She clattered back to her dressing room to unpin her

long brown hair. Daytime, and on campus, she wore it in a ponytail. But Steven was coming—now at least she knew what he called himself outside class. Darcy whimpered, then steeled herself. Think. Why was he here? Because he must care. About Darcy. She made herself concentrate on one thing at a time. Steven. No, her hair. Or. . . Sirene's hair. Of course, Steven must see what he expected to see. Sirene. Steven and Sirene. And Darcy? Forget Darcy, she told herself savagely. At least she would see Steven, talk to Steven, even if he didn't recognize her. And he wouldn't, not if it were in her power to spare him disillusionment.

So, her hair. For shows, she pinned it any which way, to go under her wigs. Now, she needed an updo that would suit the sophisticated Sirene. Playing with recalcitrant locks of fine brown hair occupied her frantic mind and fingers until an unmistakable shadow filled the doorway.

"Excuse me. Miss McGill?"

Darcy spun around as if wildly surprised. And she was—to hear him address Darcy and yet not address Darcy.

"I'm afraid we haven't met," she blurted, eager to establish that the seminaked female he was seeing couldn't possibly be anyone from class. She had to spare him—and herself—that revelation at all costs, she told herself desperately. Otherwise, she could never face him again, and that was more than she was willing to give up.

He crossed the threshold as if stepping over a live power line. His shoes were so polished, they looked wet, but he was still wearing the tweedy jacket, with a button-down shirt and a gray-wool tie.

"I'm, uh, an instructor of your sister's." It occurred to him she might have more than one. "Your twin sister, that is. Darcy."

"That's all there is," Darcy answered brightly, her mind still spinning to weave some way out of this awful situation. The fewer members of this make-believe family, the better, she told herself. "You, you must be from the university campus. I never get over there, but it looks pretty with all those trees and things."

"Yes, yes." He sidled into the room, his eyes roaming over the accumulated cosmetics and costuming. "Lots of trees." His gaze rested on Midge's rhinestone bikini, hung graphically from her now-dark makeup lights. "Er, Miss McGill . . ."

"Sirene to you," she insisted nervously. The more convincing Sirene was, the better for Darcy. And Steven. "Steve, is it?" The intimate form of his name slipped more sweetly off her lips than it had a right to. "Any friend of Darcy's is a friend of mine."

"I'm not precisely a friend. I'm an instructor," he said, smiling. "But I am interested in her education. She shows remarkable writing talent."

"Oh." Darcy thrilled to hear him praise her in someone else's presence. In Sirene's, she reminded herself brutally. "Yeah, that's Darcy," came out carelessly, a tone below Darcy's normal speaking voice. "Always scribbling things down. She even gets fancy with the grocery list. I mean, you'd think she could write down 'peas,' but no, it's gotta be 'Green Giant frozen LeSeuer baby peas,' you know? It doesn't surprise me she's good at English."

He smiled, and her heart plummeted. "Creative writing and English are hardly the same thing, Miss McGill."

"No, but they're peas in a pod, right, Professor?" she quipped. "Kinda like Darcy and me. Twins." Darcy/Sirene was slipping into firm character now. All she needed was a wad of chewing gum. It was kind of fun—even a bit liberating—to pretend to be somebody else, somebody sure of herself who didn't have to hide how she felt all the time. Someone who had never been shy. "So what can I do for you?" Sirene inquired

genially, rising to lean her bare hips against the dressing table.

The gray eyes followed her motion with barely
concealed interest. "If I've come at a bad time, I can
call again, at your convenience. But I didn't want Darcy
to know and didn't know what hours you kept—"

Sirene's self-mocking laugh interrupted him and surprised the heck out of Darcy. "It ain't bankers' hours,
Doc—or aren't you one?"

"No, I have a Ph.D."

"Well, have a seat too." She pulled out the light chair
from Midge's table.

He eyed the seat's faint dusting of silver glitter
interspersed with a vagrant Maribu feather, then sat
with grim resolve.

"Did you see the show?" Darcy whisked her chair
around so the back faced him, but Sirene straddled it
limberly, her arms resting along the curved top.

Austen's chair's legs groaned across the concrete as
his settling-in motions bucked it and himself back a bit.

"Yes." He raised the folder he had been clutching.
Darcy, who was used to seeing him accompanied by
books and papers, recognized the menu-size show program. "This was my first Las Vegas show, actually."

"How long have you lived here?" she asked.

"All my life, but—"

"Oh, I know. You're one of these hoity-toity intellec-
tuals who think the only dancing that's arty is done in
toe shoes by girls who look like they're wearing tulle
dusters for skirts."

"On the contrary, I think some modern dance, Denis
Shawn, for instance, is—"

Red-satin shoes tapped him into silence. Sirene was
about to give him what-for, and Darcy secretly approved. She was only telling the truth in Sirene's
inimitable way, well cataloged in the stories Darcy had
penned for class.

"Well, let me tell you, Doc, that toe-shoe routine

can damage a girl's anatomy, plus you have to starve
yourself half to death. This Vegas footwork takes as
much skill, and some of the costumes we wear are a
damn-sight heavier than tulle."

He studied the length of her splayed white legs.
Sitting as she was, with most of what there was of her
costume obscured, she looked as if she were clothed
only in the shadows cast by the curved latticework of
her chair.

"Your anatomy looks quite undamaged and relatively
unstarved, if I may say so, Miss McGill."

"Sirene!" she insisted sharply. "And thank you." To
separate Sirene further from Darcy, she forced herself
to preen sexily, arching her back and lifting a hand to
the gleaming hair coiled cobralike atop her head.

Professor Austen's eyes did not move to her head.

"What I'm here for," he began again in much the
same dignified tone with which he opened the first class
of the semester, "is to discuss your sister—her writing,
actually, but that begins with her, and it's she I'm
concerned about."

"Yeah?"

Sirene spun her chair back to the mirror and began
patting her face with a powder puff. Her profile seemed
to put him at ease.

"Yeah," he answered a bit aggressively, anger edging
into his voice. "You don't seem to realize that your
example—your somewhat flamboyant lifestyle, that is—
is having a detrimental effect on Darcy."

"No kidding?" Sirene spun around again to pinion his
cautious eyes with a see-through gaze. " 'Detrimental.'
Is that like dandruff?"

He ignored her response and pointed triumphantly at
her face, as if relieved. "I see it now! Your eyes are
blue. That's the difference!"

Darcy was shocked. He *believed* in Sirene so completely
that he had misinterpreted the color of her eyes. He
was, as usual, seeing only what he wanted to see. The

insight dismayed her, trapped her, made something in her surrender. Maybe... maybe Steven would like Sirene better than Darcy. Maybe she should really *be* Sirene. It was no sooner thought than some imp in Darcy drew Sirene even more firmly into the scene.

"What color are Darcy's eyes?" she asked, lowering her heavily blue-shadowed lids modestly.

"Hazel," he answered promptly. "A remarkably clean, sharp hazel, bright as water-polished agates."

Inside Sirene, Darcy melted like hot fudge. She desperately wanted to claw her way out and receive the compliment in person.

"My, you *are* a writing professor. You go on just like Darcy," Sirene cooed admiringly. Darcy stood up abruptly, shocked by what she had said. She intended to banish Sirene before she did or said something unforgivable and confessed everything.

Steven's eyes followed the uncoiling of her body with an appreciative masculine glimmer she knew Darcy would never catch in his expression. Oooh, men were so blatant! His open look sent hot shivers down her spine to her tap shoes. He was so damned attractive. And for once, Darcy didn't feel at all shy. . . .

Maybe Sirene was a side of Darcy that needed to peek out now and again. Maybe Darcy had a right to defend her profession and her lifestyle against his ingrained prejudices any way she chose. Maybe Professor Austen needed to be taught a lesson.

So Sirene still stood there, looking, in all her feathered satin-and-pearl glory, like a figure from an Erte print. The professor, recognizing a new boldness in what he perceived as sufficiently bold already, leaned back as if from a fire.

But the shockingly small bits of red satin advanced recklessly as Sirene, fully in control now, gyrated toward him.

"What color are *your* eyes?" she inquired softly.

He stared at her, a surge of honest lust dueling with

his carefully nurtured better instincts. He was here to help Darcy, not to seduce her sister, he reminded himself, attractive as that sister was.

She must have read the conflict between desire and decorum in his eyes. Suddenly, Sirene kicked a leg over his head and straddled him as if he were a chair, her long legs parting to support her weight on his lap. A red-nailed hand moved to his temple, then wrenched his glasses away.

"Wait a minute! I need those to see!" he protested.

He reached after them but her arm—long, white, and gracefully in command—planted them well out of reach on the dressing table. Professor Stevenson Eliot Austen felt the balance of power they teetered upon deposit him on the ground with a jolt.

"Gray," she answered herself softly, gazing deep into his eyes. "I don't have any fancy words for them, but it's a very nice gray."

Something in her tone touched him, held him helpless. He'd have thought sincerity to be alien to someone like Sirene. Perhaps Darcy was right, and he had misjudged Las Vegas chorus girls. After all, Darcy admired her sister, accepted her. Perhaps he should try to.

Sirene's nimble forefinger traced a light path down the middle of his face, from hairline to nose to the channel above his lips. It skipped his mouth and came to rest, pointedly, in the small depression in his chin that his mother had called a dimple when he was a baby and that he had avoided calling attention to ever since.

"You know, Professor, you're really quite a nice-looking man. If you'd just relax; you know, get the wind and the rain in your hair, loosen your tie."

Devilishly agile fingers were fussing at the knot under his Adam's apple, which was engaged in the urgent task of bobbing for saliva or breath or both.

"Now see here, Sirene—"

"Oh, I do see," she answered, her voice lowering as

her hands slipped inside the jacket and began smoothing his shirt to his torso. "You're in good shape. Racketball?"

"Tennis," he corrected automatically, staring into the red-white-and-blue features that hovered over his with narcotic effect.

"Ummm, tennis." Darcy had an irresistible vision of Steven in tennis whites, neat and attractive. "I just love tennis," Sirene gurgled breathlessly. "All that lunging— and glistening sweat."

Sirene's face was on a collision course with Steven's. He stiffened the reins of his control as her lips—red, full, and sinfully glossed—moved along his.

She didn't so much kiss him as take his lower lip between the softness of hers and nibble her way from one side to the other. Something warm flicked intermittently against his inner upper lip. Incongruous chills shivered through his lower body. Her hands, spread upon his face, drove gently prodding nailtips into his temples.

"You have a delicious mouth," she was murmuring, now rapt in performing the same excercise on his upper lip. "I love to watch your lips when you talk. Has anyone ever told you that?"

"Ummf, no. I can't say they... er, Miss McGill, you have pushed me into a corner."

"Awwww." Her regret sounded distinctly like the falling of crocodile tears. Her thumbs framed his mouth, the nails digging every so gently into his cheeks. She eased back for a moment so he could attempt to focus on what was happening, on her face. For a mad moment he saw hazel superimposed on blatant blue. Before he could separate reality from surprising fantasy, she swooped toward him again. She kissed him thoroughly.

He grasped her arms tightly, hesitated, then repelled her with the same strength it took to ram a low serve over the net. She was stronger than he had thought. It was as much her willingness as his insistence that finally loosened her grip.

He opened his eyes, closed against the recent overwhelming assault, cautiously. This was worse. His grasp on her arms had forced her breasts into a condition of cleavage usually confined to racy men's magazines, and he had pushed her away only enough to present this rather obvious display right under his nose, metaphorically speaking.

"Please, Miss—" He couldn't call her that, he thought vaguely, not after this. "Please, Sirene. I came here to talk about your sister. Now." He assumed a fierce tone, as if dealing with a classroom disciplinary problem. "Give me back my glasses."

She looked down at him, her hazel/blue eyes, limpid, her mouth pouting sensual satisfaction, then plunked the glasses sulkily into his open palm.

"Now get up."

She did it by simply straightening her endlessly long legs, so that she straddled him like the unfortunate statue of Goliath outside the even more unfortunate hotel of that name. Hands on naked hips, she tilted her head and stared down at him.

"Now, step back."

She complied, smiling. "Is this a game? Kind of like Steven Says?"

Any straw in a storm, he thought, berating himself for mixing metaphors. "Yes, a game. Steven says change into your street clothes."

"Okay." Her compliant hands went to the slender ropes of pearls swagging her hips.

"Steven says wait! Change when I'm gone. I'll be outside."

Outside, Steven paced, studying expanses of mint-green walls interrupted by gray-steel circuit boxes as if their homeliness conferred an aesthetic satisfaction beyond price.

Steven pushed up his jacket sleeve to read the Timex's plain face. Two o'clock. In the morning. He must be dreaming. Why on earth had he left a perfectly pleas-

ant, decorous faculty party early to come to this, this—
he glanced around—this bunker of iniquity, this sequined sepulcher, this web for the unwary?

Spinning to make yet another pointless stalk in a new
direction, Steven found himself nose-to-nose with a
posted note. Not a note, a quatrain, the academic in
him corrected. Three quatrains, in fact. He read them,
merely because presented with written words—whether
by W. H. Auden or the promoters of a breakfast cereal—
Stevenson Eliot Austen read them.

He was smiling by the time he finished. Their home-
spun humor banished disturbing visions of temptresses
in clinging costumes. Even the awesome Sirene was
merely making a living doing a six-day-a-week grind far
more arduous than it was glamorous. Once removed
from this rather bizarre background, he was sure she
would sit back sensibly and listen to his advice about
her shy twin. Then she would do all within her power
to liberate Darcy from a stifling sister worship and put
her on the road to academic purity of purpose.

Satisfied with his conclusions, Steven stopped pacing, readjusted his much put-upon glasses, and contemplated a serene future.

Inside the dressing room, a desperate Darcy was
tearing open locker after locker. Her own held jeans
and a sweater, a pair of battered suede boots, an
umbrella, and a broken package of sadly decaying Hostess Twinkies.

Jo's wasn't much better. Midge's locker was papered
with photographs of her kids and her dogs. The middle
locker was jammed with all their junk, which it proceeded
to disgorge en masse onto Darcy's tender insteps.

"Ouch! Back, back, I say!" She kicked the flotsam
behind the closing door as she jammed it shut.

Trish's locker was Darcy's last hope. She cracked it
open cautiously, then sighed vast relief and swung wide
the paint-chipped door.

Pristine, hanging quietly as if secreted there by a fairy godmother for a rainy midnight, dangled a single tongue of flame-red silk. Beneath it, neatly paired, rested red-leather spike heels.

"The answer to a maiden's prayer," Darcy whispered. She extracted the dress and plastered it against herself. "Well, not exactly a maiden, I guess, but . . . it'll do."

She quickly slipped into the dress, which Trish kept primed for sudden hot dates with suddenly hot high rollers. Its short petal-shaped sleeves matched the petal-cut skirt that slit open on her inner thighs when she walked. The crossover bodice permitted no bra; the slit skirt allowed for no slip.

Darcy mounted the steep heels and checked the mirror. The ensemble was made for Sirene, and it would never have done to let Professor Austen see Sirene in Darcy's denims. An emotion, perhaps shame, knocked discreetly in Darcy's silk-draped breast. Something stronger shoved it rudely aside as she surveyed herself in the mirror. She smiled tigressly at herself and darted to the door to sweep it wide.

"I'm ready, Professor!"

"Yes, so I see." He peered into the room as if expecting witnesses to pop out from under the hanging feathers. "I was, uh, just reading the verse on your door."

Sirene's face, stripped of its queen-of-hearts excesses but still made up well beyond street wear, stayed as blank as it was meant to look on stage.

"The, um, 'Final Warning.' "

"Oh, that. Darcy scribbled that one day when I complained how everyone was stampeding through this dressing room like it was the men's room of the *Titanic*."

"I'm sure that a show girl relishes her privacy as much as the next woman," he conceded. "That's a most attractive outfit." He spoke by way of uneasy conversation, but his eyes said more.

"Thanks, Doc." She turned quickly to the mirror.

"I was reading the program and noticed your name is listed oddly. . . ."

Sirene's pliant form froze.

"It says 'R.C. McGill.'"

"Um, that's my *real* name," she was able to answer with prompt honesty. "Sirene's a stage name."

"So your sister told me." He frowned, an expression that sat his ruggedly refined features even better without the glasses to filter its effectiveness. "But I distinctly remember her saying your real name was Irene."

"Yes!" Sirene spun from the mirror to face him. *Damn that blabbermouth Darcy!* "Ramona Catherine . . . Irene. Irene is my confirmation name." That was a lie, but a person can confirm a name on herself, can't she? Darcy didn't know, but had a feeling she just had.

The professor's sober face brightened. "Confirmation. Glad to hear it."

"Well," Sirene noted coyly, "there are more churches in Las Vegas than bawdy houses, did you know that, Professor?"

"No, but it's somehow reassuring, Miss McGill. Now. I suggest we go somewhere quiet where we can discuss your sister, which is what I came here to do."

"What's to say about Darcy? She's as simple as pie. Oh, all right. I know she's your precious student." Sirene elaborately outlined her already red mouth with a swath of Crimson Pirate borrowed from Trish's stash while the professor watched respectfully.

"What d'you say about going to my place?" Sirene suggested, popping up from her chair like an inordinately pleased jack-in-the-box.

"Ah . . ."

"*Our* place," she reminded him. "Darcy's and mine. There's nowhere quiet in Vegas unless it's private."

"Yes, I can see that, but won't your sister be home?"

"Oh, that." Sirene's supple hand dismissed the idea in a flash of comet-red fingernails. "She's at a party tonight that's way out in the valley. Darcy'll sleep over."

Steven frowned. "Is she accustomed to doing that sort of thing?"

"Sure. Oh, say, professor. Don't look so worried." Sirene took his chin in her fingers and shook it admonishingly, her scarlet lips puckered within kissing distance of his.

"The crowd she hangs out with is like, harmless. They're all pals, one big happy family. Don't you worry. *Darcy* would never do anything"—Sirene frowned prettily, for once lost for words—"risky?"

He reclaimed his chin by unclamping her long fingers, one by one. "I think you mean 'risqué,' Sirene. And I'm relieved to hear it. So if you'll lead me to your car, I'll find mine and escort you home."

"It's too bad we've both got cars," Sirene reflected, insinuating a bare arm through his.

"Most unfortunate," Steven said dryly, untangling their limbs. "Look here, Miss McGill, I mean business, and I don't want you to get any ideas otherwise."

"Of course not. Not in a million years," she purred, preceding him through the dressing-room door. She looked over a silken shoulder. "Just follow me."

Chapter

Four

"And to think I could have been quietly playing Japanese Go at the Humanities Department head's house tonight," Steven muttered to himself in front of the plain apartment door.

Sirene, leaning on his arm as her elevated heels seemed to require, delved for the key in a purse that struck him as familiar. She caught him staring at it and promptly lurched against his side, hip-to-hip, the sudden motion unleashing a great deal of what TV marketing experts call Jiggle.

"Please contain yourself, Miss McGill," he urged, eyeing askance new depths of décolletage.

Unwittingly, his form of address unleashed another pet peeve of Darcy's, which in turn prodded Sirene's wildest instincts into even further control.

"'Miss McGill,'" she pouted wickedly, opening the door on total darkness, "sounds like an old-maid English teacher. You *were* calling me Sirene."

He was glancing worriedly into the darkness. "You're sure that—"

"Darcy won't be back till high noon tomorrow, Steven," she reassured him with what in fact was becoming the truth. Darcy would never have had these pulse-pounding moments alone with Steven had Sirene not wriggled so beguilingly out of her subconscious. "We can have a nice tat-a-tat. I promise."

"That's 'tête-à-tête.' Um, are there any *lights* in this room?"

"Scads. One over there, I think."

"Where?"

"On the wall behind me."

"Oh."

"Ooooh . . . Steven!"

"Sorry." But he didn't sound it, and his hand lingered on the silk-clad softness of her midriff. "I, ah, mistook you for the wall. There. That's better."

The sudden brightness found Steven pressing Sirene between himself and the wall in question—how, he could not exactly say. She fit against him perfectly. He wondered why he'd never realized how delightfully a man and woman of similar heights dovetailed. Like most tall men, he'd instinctively dated petite women. But as Sirene's hipbones meshed with his pelvis and her lush breasts accommodated the pressure of his chest, he began to reconsider his preferences—hotly.

But he had nothing in common with this woman, he realized, suddenly horrified, no attraction beyond the physical. And he was here for a much nobler purpose than self-gratification. Releasing her, he stepped instantly away to survey the room. Brick-and-board bookcases, sparse rattan furniture, and profuse hanging plants proclaimed it the usual student digs. A series of expensively framed prints enlivened the walls above the unpretentious furnishings.

"Very nice," he approved and then frowned, suddenly remembering Sirene's apparently garish tastes.

"Darcy did the decor," she said hastily. "This isn't the kind of thing I go for. It's a little dull."

"Indeed. I think you've put your finger on the root of the problem, Sirene."

"I have?" She vanished behind the kitchen partition but popped her head out a moment later, along with an arm brandishing a bottle of Scotch. "Drink?"

"No!" Settled on the small wicker sofa, he reached into his jacket pocket for his pipe, remembered he had left it in his car, studied the area for alternative props, and finding none, reconsidered. "Well . . . yes."

Sirene shuddered with delight. "I love you eggheads. You make everything sound so important. Straight up or with the rattle of dice?"

It took him a few seconds to interpret her colorful phrase. "With ice cubes, please."

She emerged with lowball glasses moments later and handed him one piled with ice cubes. "I thought for sure you'd take it without ice, like the Limeys do. You look English; you dress English."

"My dear Sirene, I merely teach it."

She draped herself into the chair opposite—a coolie-hat-shaped circle of rattan braced by three spindly wrought-iron legs. The bracing effect of Sirene's sinfully long legs, crossed and bare to where angels dare not tread and devils often long to was not lost on Steven, who took an even more bracing swallow of Scotch.

"So tell me about yourself," she invited, sounding genuinely interested. "Did you always want to be an English professor?"

"God forbid!" He smiled at his own intensity, then, oddly enough, relaxed. Steven always guarded his deepest aspirations from his fellow instructors. An academic atmosphere seemed to grade every nuance of ambition. But of course Sirene was light years removed from all that. Sirene wouldn't . . . couldn't . . . judge him. He found himself telling the whole truth, even to himself.

"I wanted to be a writer," he said. "Then, failing that, I would have settled for simply being a critic and crucifying those who did manage to be writers. But such a noble career was not to be. I decided to teach."

"What kind of books did you want to write?

He cleared his throat. "It's called literary fiction."

"Sounds serious."

"Very serious, indeed. It's so serious, in fact, that very few writers actually do it."

Sirene nodded gravely, sipping her drink. "I thought all fiction was literary?"

"Well, yes. But some is more literary than others."

"What Darcy does isn't literary?"

"Not in the serious sense."

Sirene nodded even more sagely. "So you want her to give up doing what she wants to do, so she can do what you gave up on doing a long time ago, is that it?"

"Uh . . . no! Your logic is convoluted, Sirene."

Her smile widened. "Yeah. Guys have told me I'm convoluted before."

Rage roared through Steven at the idea of "guys" telling the woman before him anything. He tore his eyes from the delicious convolutions of her form, set his drink on a pile of magazines, and stood to pace out his frustration.

"You seem to be deliberately dodging the point, Sirene. Doesn't Darcy mean anything to you? You share an apartment with her, after all. Don't you see what the very fact of your existence, the mode of your existence, is doing to her self-esteem?" And his self-control, he might have added.

She waited until his pacing brought him abreast of her and then rose fluidly in front of him, nearly touching him. Their heights were dead even.

"You're really tall aren't you? Quite the Amazon. Darcy never seemed—"

"Darcy and I are exactly the same height, Professor. Exactly. Maybe you never looked as hard at Darcy as you're looking at me right now."

"Still . . . you seem taller. As tall as me. I mean—*I*!"

"Aw, grammar giving you trouble?" she cooed, unable to resist leaning close enough to press against him from knee to chest. Her hands smoothed his ruffled tweed shoulders. "I'd say I'm exactly as tall as you. Even Steven."

"It's the shoes!" He looked down, hoping to spot the

footwear in question, but saw only the inciteful length of their mated bodies.

She lurched suddenly and dropped three inches. "Is this better? Are you feeling less threatened now?" Sirene's uptilted face drew his down.

"That's exactly it!" His hands grasped her arms, encountered firm warm flesh, lingered, then thrust her away. "You threaten Darcy."

"Me? Threaten Darcy? Listen, mister, I take good care of the kid. I clue her in to all sorts of things. You'd be surprised what she learns from me."

"But Darcy's no kid, Sirene. Somehow, your mere five minutes' earlier entry into the world gave you an edge, an edge you've been using against Darcy, unknowingly. How old are you?" he bellowed from a position on the other side of the sofa.

Lashes long as caterpillars blinked. "Twenty-eight."

"How blind I've been! Of course, she's an *adult-ed student*, not just an undergraduate. You see, she's so afraid of competing with you that she passes for a girl instead of a woman."

"Darcy? Afraid of me?" Sirene slipped away long enough for Darcy to realize that Steven was coming up with some far-out psychological fairy tale ... *why?*

Her bewilderment freed him to come around the furniture again.

"I'm afraid so. The only pieces she's turned in for class assignments all revolve around her 'sister, Sirene.' You wouldn't believe the imaginative nonsense she weaves, about you being wooed by the sons of wealthy Arab sheiks and, oh—incredible things."

"Incredible, huh?" Sirene's bare foot was tapping indignantly, her arms crossed, raising a formidable swell of décolletage.

Steven elected to ignore all that, including the slightly miffed tone in Sirene's voice. He felt himself on the verge of a breakthrough—that moment when a less agile intelligence is finally led to the inevitable conclusion that he, the instructor, had seen all along.

"Don't you see? Your glamorous lifestyle—the clothes, the men, even if most of them are figments of Darcy's imagination—your rather ostentatious occupation. Even your . . . um, generous proportions—all things Darcy has no hope of having. You've intimidated her, Sirene, into becoming a mousy little scholar who pours the dreams she should be living into stories—fantasies—about you."

"Mousy? Little? Darcy?" True incredulity underlined Sirene's words.

"Well, not literally. But figuratively speaking, Darcy can't hold a candle to you in your nightly strut through the spotlights." Steven was on a roll, insight and his dramatic instincts blending to etch a scenario that resolved all his own inner doubts. "She's trapped in your glamorous shadow, Sirene, condemned to come second always, expected to be a good sport and laugh at herself and write you a piece of verse if you need it."

He knew the warm satisfaction of having convinced her, for Sirene turned suddenly away from him, her fingers fanned atop the coolie-hat chair, her shoulders trembling a little.

"I didn't know I was such a—a bad influence," she gasped. The Darcy inside her was drowning in disbelief. Steven's need to make Darcy into what he wanted her to be—an innocent, dabbling in fantasy—drove her nearly to audible laughter.

Steven watched Sirene carefully. He considered himself as incompetent to deal with female tears as the next man, but there was no doubt that he had caused these and should do something about them.

He approached her gingerly from behind, employing the wise, tolerant tone he applied to distraught D students.

"Now, now." He patted her shoulder, encouraged to find his feelings remaining strictly platonic for the moment. "It's not as bad as that. Knowing the problem means you're halfway to solving it."

"Oh, but it *is* bad!" She whirled like a crimson dust devil, throwing herself against him and burying her face in his tie to disguise her despairing amusement.

He cast his arms around her to keep them both from toppling.

"It's terrible," she wailed, speaking the exact truth. "I can't help being what I am. I can't believe I make Darcy feel inferior. I never dreamed—"

"There, there." He patted her heaving shoulder again and was rewarded by a slight subsiding. Darcy burrowed into him with a gratified whimper, her temple pressing his cheek. Even under false pretenses, being in Steven's arms at last was divine, she thought. She loved the diffidently warm and gentle way he was handling Sirene. She couldn't end the illusion and confess her role-playing now if her life had depended on it, because, in a strange way, what was happening between Sirene and Steven was as honest and genuine as the real-life relationship Darcy had wanted for herself.

Steven's deep voice was rumbling comfortingly under her ear. "I know that you never suspected your influence on Darcy."

She murmured agreement, lost in his embrace. She'd never suspected the existence of someone like Sirene within herself, someone daring enough to take what she wanted when it was right in front of her.

Then Steven proceeded to put his foot squarely into his mouth and, indirectly, her ear. "And things could be worse," he continued. "Darcy could have reacted to her inferiority complex by trying to imitate you rather than simply idealizing you."

"That would be worse?" Sirene hiccuped. Anger swept away her inner content. Would Steven never give up his prejudices? A hard answer came from Sirene. Perhaps only if she—Sirene—continued to give him a tough course of remedial education.

"Much worse," he said complacently.

"What's so bad about it?"

"Oh, not that the way you are isn't perfectly splendid for you, Sirene. But it's not right for Darcy."

"Or you," came her smothered voice, followed by further eruptions of an emotional nature under the silky lava of her dress, this time tears of real frustration.

"That's not true! I like you a lot. You're obviously a very lovely woman. I don't need my glasses to see that. But—"

"Yes?"

"Won't all that makeup run?"

"It's waterproof," she retorted. She wanted to shake him. She wanted to kiss him. Most of all, she wanted to make him see that a woman could combine goodness and glamour in the same package. "So you think I'm pretty?" she probed.

How on earth had the conversation turned to this topic, Steven wondered, but he manfully attempted to deal with it.

"More than pretty," he said as if cajoling a child. "You're—"

"Attractive?"

"I'd say... stunning."

"*And*—?"

"And talented and glamorous..."

She looked up, her face surprisingly dry, the makeup unblurred and her expression so luminously expectant, it shook him.

Steven's fingers circled on the silk of her back. A scent of Oriental subtlety wove around him. He couldn't remember when he'd last known a woman who wore perfume—or had been close enough to one who did to appreciate it.

"And, and..." He fought for words to talk him out of the entrapment of his own desires. Sirene's ardent eyes stared unblinkingly at him. He couldn't say what color they were; other senses than sight were surging to the forefront of his awareness—touch, taste, smell.

"And exciting," he conceded.

She shimmied with pleasure. Steven felt his hands slide slowly down her back to her hips.

"Soft," his mouth said, drugged by the way the word felt on his lips. She seemed to melt into his bones. "Seductive." Her face strained toward his.

The vibration of the words on his lips was branding his soul. "Sexy." Her crazy eyelashes were lowering like tangled curtains over her eyes so he could finally do what he'd been wanting to do all night.

He leaned his head down the little it took and matched his lips to hers with unleashed boldness. This time *he* let the kiss ebb and flow, let it cool and catch fire, soften and turn to burning steel.

Sirene aided and abetted him with her own brand of active surrender. Cool hands slipped the glasses off his face and conveyed them somewhere into the smoky ether swirling around them. A leg flexed at the knee, then raised so that the inside of her thigh stroked sinuously along his outer thigh. Only a dancer could execute such erotically subtle moves, he thought. Nimble fingers were tugging at his tie in earnest now. The buttons on his shirt strained apart as teasing fingernails strolled across his chest and burrowed into the thick body hair.

He found the single hook at her side, the one that held her dress on, and released it, thrusting his hands inside the separating red-silk curtain. A silken body and pungent warmth greeted his fingers.

Their first kiss grew fiercer. Finally they parted, and both stepped back a bit.

"Sirene, I . . . this isn't a game. I may be an intellectual type, but I'm a man, and I want you."

"I may be an empty-headed hoofer, but I'm a woman, and I want you," she answered with wry, mirroring honesty.

She took his hand and turned to lead him to the
bedroom.

"My glasses—"

"I'll give them back. In the morning."

At the door, which stood ajar, its narrow bar of
darkness hinting at delicious secrets-to-be, he threw
one last bone to the mongrel of his conscience.

"Darcy . . ."

Sirene smiled tenderly. "She won't be back until long
past dawn, lover. And by then, you'll be long gone."

Interlude

The Twelve O'clock Scholar Speaks His Piece

I consider myself a self-educated individual. Some quite notable dudes never acquired a sheepskin in their lifetimes, including Mr. Abraham Lincoln, late of Illinois.

You could say I am street savvy, or that I earn my degrees in the School of Hard Salami. Everything I am I owe to keeping my peepers primed, my ears pricked, and my mouth sealed tighter than a Sunday-school teacher's knees on Saturday night.

I am not the most delicate of guys; many a rough exterior hides a heart of gold. Yet I am a reasonable little dude and spend most of my time now crossing my feet and musing on life's odd ins and outs. I am quietly engaged in this very pursuit one Saturday morning, warming the plump red-velvet pillow that Miss Darcy McGill keeps fluffed and lint-free for me on her dressing table, when who should burst in but the same Miss Darcy McGill. She casts herself upon my bosom and bursts into excessively wet tears as well as enough wails to summon the paramedics.

"Oh, Louie," says she, just plain Louie being my monicker among my intimates. "Oh, Louie, what have I done! What will I do? It is wonderful! It is terrible! My life is ruined. What will happen to Steven if the university regents find out? How can I go back to class? What will I do if he comes here again?" and on and on in like vein, as little dolls—

207

even if they are big dolls—can do when they are sufficiently stimulated.

I am not a man of the world for nothing. I allow her to dampen my whiskers unabated for some time, then look at her wisely. I learn long ago that when a distraught doll throws herself upon your shoulder, the wisest thing is to listen and let her talk herself into her own solution.

"Oh, Louie," Miss Darcy McGill is sobbing, her long red fingernails clutching rhythmically at my sides, which is a cute habit when I do it, but a little hard on the old hide, if you know what I mean.

I am more than somewhat surprised that this little big doll is wearing these shives at eight-thirty in the A.M. when she is not scheduled to appear on stage for almost twelve hours yet.

Also, I notice that she still has on the makeup she wears the night before and that it is sadly the worse for wear and is being helped in no way by the waterworks sluicing down her once-piquant features.

So I mull it over and conclude that the dude who visited her in this very dressing room last night must be the cause of these histrionics, though he is a somewhat dignified dude whom one ordinarily would not suspect of churning up a delicate young lady like Miss Darcy McGill into chopped liver.

It strikes me that Mr. Steven Eliot Austen may be something of a bounder. As I take a dim view of anyone breaking the hearts of the little dolls with whom I surround myself, and as Miss Darcy McGill is queen of hearts in the Crystal Phoenix Royal Suite Revue, I fear that I myself will have to step in and take action.

But for now, I murmur sweet nothings some auditors of which are pleased to describe as a sort of purr, being that my tone is somewhat rough from the time Butch the Bowser is chasing me down Tropicana Avenue and I dive under a broken board in a parking-lot fence but get a nail in the voice box.

So for now, I soak up the sorrow, and I listen and look wise, which is not an unsuitable appearance to cultivate on any occasion, and you can quote me on that.

Chapter

Five

"Sirene leaned thoughtfully against her cluttered dressing-table edge. Ladder-long legs stretched into the small room's center and were delicately crossed at the ankles.

"Standing at her feet, quite literally, was a man in a dark green suit who looked like it had been on him longer than his chronic five-o'clock shadow. It bagged where he sagged.

"'I'm on a roll, Sirene,' he was saying. 'Come on, what've you got better to do after the show than hit the craps tables? They'll be gathering around the green-felt riverbank when I roll, baby. Whadaya say?'"

Professor Stevenson Eliot Austen's piercing gray eyes clung to the pages before him. Once again, Darcy McGill's work was on the critiquing block, but this time he could barely read the earthy prose. Darcy's writing was all too effective, but his judgment was going AWOL.

Steven pushed his glasses lower on the bridge of his nose. He didn't *want* to find out if Sirene would go out with the low-life gambler. He didn't want to think of Sirene living the flashy life of a chorus queen when all he could see was her lush, languorous length in his arms. And when he glimpsed Darcy's clean-scrubbed innocent face at the back of the classroom, he didn't want to think of Sirene at all.

So of course he had thought of nothing but Sirene for

the past—he checked his watch—five days and twelve hours.

He snapped his lenses back to his face and confronted his class, which was waiting eagerly for the rest.

"It goes on," he said, "in like vein. I doubt we need to read at length. You all are familiar with Miss McGill's Las Vegas fables."

The author in question slouched in her usual rear seat. Steven had seen her enter and had tried to pretend that he had not, as he had done every other day this week, which was how often the creative writing class met—Monday, Wednesday, and today, Friday.

A hand in the front row rose tentatively.

"Yes, Mrs. Warren, you had a question or comment?"

"Question," chirped the woman, who was attending college on the empty-nest plan. "What happens, Professor? Does Sirene go out with the compulsive gambler? And isn't the sheik's son due back from Shambar any day now?"

Steven winced. He'd forgotten; yet *another* suitor of Sirene's. My God, someday *he* could show up in one of Darcy's tales! He managed to quirk a sick smile in the direction of the top row.

"There, you see, Miss McGill? The first reward granted the beginning writer—an avid reader. If you like, class, Miss McGill can copy her assignments before class and distribute installments."

To his chagrin, heads nodded eagerly all across the rows—except the shiny brown head he could barely see. He had perched, as usual, on the desk edge while he read. Now he leaned, Tower-of-Pisa style, to his right but found his quarry hidden by the naturally curly mane of "Spider" Phlugg, a student by day and electric-bongo player by night.

Casually shifting his books, Steven leaned left. No matter how he positioned himself, Darcy McGill was always obscured from his view. He began to think it deliberate, and, miffed, leaned further. Balance lost the bet. Only the quick planting of a foot saved him from taking an embarrassing fall in front of his class.

Steven glowered behind the severe black frames of his glasses. "Class is over, but Miss McGill can stay for a private critique," he announced firmly.

By twos and threes, they left, fifteen ardent souls determined to master English prose. One stayed behind, exactly where she was.

Steven purposefully climbed the stairs to her seat and sat on the adjacent desk. He cast the most recent of the adventures of Miss Sirene McGill to the desktop.

"You're sticking with your Sirene stories."

"Yes." She didn't look up. "I like them."

"Well, you have company. Apparently so does everyone in the class."

"Not you?" She glanced up; one quick clean look from doe-shy hazel eyes.

"Does it matter? I'm only the instructor," he jested.

"Yes," she said breathily, as if speaking before she had found air for it. "You are the instructor."

He studied her. Where Sirene was bare and polished by all the art the stage could assemble, her sister was a matte finish of washed denim, soft-woven sweaters, and unglossed facial features. Only her hair and eyes shone, natural as rainwater.

Sirene in all her artifice was a divine experience, he had to admit that. No woman had ever loved him with the intensity and tenderness that hid beneath that painted exterior. Yet to look unknowing Darcy, her sweet-faced sister, in the eyes and remember his shameless expedition into pure carnal ecstasy . . . Steven cringed at the idea of Darcy hearing news of an affair between her sister and himself.

He sighed and tried to do his job. "Does your sister know how thoroughly you embellish her life?"

"Oh, I don't embellish it. Not much, anyway."

A surge of jealousy revved Steven's blood pressure.

"Surely you exaggerate. She really doesn't have all these men coming around?"

A rapid flash of eye contact darted from under Darcy's drawn curtains of hair. Did Steven really think her so unattractive that he doubted that men would pursue her in any guise?

"All these men, from all walks of life, even—" she began.

"Yes?"

"—even doctors and lawyers," she finished impishly, knowing his concern. "No Indian chiefs—yet."

"I'm relieved to hear it. But surely she doesn't, er, go out with all those men?"

"I think you mean . . ." Her voice sank to a whisper. "Go to bed with."

He stood, caught and not liking it. What would Darcy think of him if she knew he was among her sister's many conquests, no better than a tipster or a playboy? He must protect her, protect himself, even if it meant . . . well, a lie or two.

"I'm perfectly capable of saying what I mean. I'm not inquiring into your sister's morals, Miss McGill. That is none of my business and, I would imagine, none of yours. It's simply that since you say she's a real person—"

"Oh, she is! Even show girls are real persons."

He squinted at her downcast features, detecting irony or some other savage twist behind the innocent face value of her words.

"You know what I mean, Miss McGill," he finally said gently. "When you write about a real person, you invade his or her privacy. How would you like it if I took you for my heroine, and speculated on your social life in print?"

"I'd say you'd have a dull story." Her eyes were twinkling up at him, but he read self-dismissal in them and became the Student's Defender once more.

"There! That's it. There you go putting yourself down

again! Your sister Sirene may lead a more glamorous life than you do, she may be a dazzlingly attractive, vital woman—"

"How do you know?"

He stared into the eyes that now had no difficulty meeting his. Guilt made his own eyes veer away as he detoured from the truth. "Why, uh—I'm assuming, naturally, that she resembles you. She is your twin, after all. And then, all these ... men ... seem endlessly attracted to her."

Darcy's expression softened. She spoke slowly, gently, as if she were the teacher and he a particularly dense student. "Oh, Professor Austen. Men are always attracted to show girls, not mousy little scholars; it goes with the territory. You get used to it."

One of her phrases sounded familiar, but this conversation gave him no heart to search for a literary source. "You mean *you* get used to Sirene getting all the attention, don't you?"

A guilty look flashed across a face not made for that emotion. Then the imp reappeared. "Are you trying to psychoanalyze me, Professor?"

He backed off. He had no right to probe, not after what he had done—confirmed Sirene's superiority in Darcy's eyes by falling for her so-obvious charms. "No. Of course not. I wonder, though. What *is* your occupation? Off-campus, that is."

Her long forefinger balanced on a short pale nail that traced a fleeting pattern on the desk top.

"I, ah, work for a hotel. Behind the scenes. You'd be amazed how many people work behind the scenes."

"Quite a little Cinderella, aren't you, evading the spotlight?"

She looked up from the half-truth she half-hoped he would challenge. His head was cocked in an attitude of quiet concern, an expression on his face that even Sirene had not yet seen—and Sirene, Darcy recalled with delicious mortification, had seen expressions no person had a right to remember in public.

"I'm not 'little,'" she said, pushing herself upright as Exhibit A.

He stood with her, looking appealingly perplexed, his lips parted as if to say something Darcy might want to hear very badly.

"Darcy," he began, with something impulsive in his tone that equally thrilled and frightened her. "Don't—"

"Hey, got to run! If you're not worried about getting to your next class in time, I am. 'Bye, Professor."

She spun around and clattered down the aisle, long brown hair curling like spindrift in her wake. He watched her exit, troubled. The story on her desk remained, its type celebrating Sirene's endlessly long white legs delicately cross at the ankles. Steven swallowed in dry-throated remembrance. Remembrance and anticipation.

"*Who's* here again?"

"*He* is."

"Not the—" Darcy wrenched her chair around to face Midge. "Not—?"

"The professor?" Jo inquired, her eyes open wider than seemed humanly possible.

"Right."

"I won't see him!" Darcy turned back to the mirror, pulling her hair lock-by-lock from the bandeau that held it from her face under the various wigs she wore each night.

"Okay." Midge ambled with elaborate unconcern back to her dressing table. "But Jake must consider him a regular already; he was telling the professor to go right on down, now that he knew the way."

"Oh, expletive deleted!" Darcy's makeup sponge hit her mirror image right in the crimson, lip-glossed kisser. "The least you guys could do is beat it!"

"But we want to *see* him," Trish purred, rising to poise a cocked leg in fishnet hose—an effect that reminded

Darcy of a diamondback rattler—on the seat of her chair. "I've never met a man with a master's degree before."

"A doctor's degree," Darcy corrected glumly.

"A doctor's degree! Oh, that sounds so elevated. I'm not leaving either." Jo planted her barely covered sequined bottom on her dressing table. "He should be along any second anyway."

"All right!" Darcy jumped up, beset by fear and excitement in equal doses. "Just remember not to call me by my first name! I don't want him to confuse my student role with"—she gestured wildly at the carnival atmosphere—"all this. It would be unlucky," she added forcefully. If there was anything theater people respected around dressing rooms, it was superstition.

"What about Midnight Louie?" Midge was running long nails through the silky profusion of the cat's neck ruff as he reclined on Darcy's pillow for the night. "He's black as a casino bottom line, and that's supposed to be unlucky. He practically lives here—"

"Louie never crosses our paths," Jo asserted dismissingly. "He's always following us, looking for a handout, aren't you, boy?" She produced a limp sardine from an open tin and draped it over the cat's extended forepaws.

They all watched fondly as the animal regarded the offering with the initial regal disdain of cats, then lowered his muzzle and dispatched it with quick efficiency. In that momentary lull, all emergencies forgotten, Professor Stevenson Eliot Austen arrived at the crack of their door.

He cleared his throat, not really intending to be heard.

They turned together at the sound, as if choreographed—four tall, feathered, and sequined women, more decorated than dressed—two in black, two in red.

The effect would have overwhelmed a Chevalier. A

mere Austen froze like a hare spotted midmeadow by four foxes.

"So this is . . . England," Jo declaimed, her eyes misty enough to melt. She sashayed over to him, rear black-satin bows wagging, and twined a rhinestone-ringed arm through his. "I just love knights and armor and chivalry and reading about all that stuff."

"Good for you," Steven said, glancing down at her possessive hand on his forearm and seeing past it to less commonly displayed charms. He gently disentangled himself and gave her hand a consoling pat as he returned it to her.

"Miss . . . McGill?" He looked from one red queen to the other, unable to guess who was who beneath the makeup. It horrified him that a woman who had hit him as hard as Sirene should not be immediately recognizable in any circumstances. He'd expected to hear a corny chorus of violins when he saw her again.

Darcy stepped forward with an apologetic smile that didn't really fit Sirene. "I'm afraid you're a sensation; we've never had an English professor backstage before."

"No indeedy." Irrepressible Trish dashed forward to stand guard on Steven's other side, her hand insinuating itself around his elbow. "Say something in literature," she sighed.

"Ah . . ." Steven capitulated and thrust both hands in his jacket pockets, a gesture that had the advantage of avoiding this barrage of feminine attention without insulting anyone.

Darcy felt for him, drawn onto alien ground only because of her, she really did.

"Why don't you wait outside for a couple of minutes, Steven?" Darcy said sharply. "I'll change and be right out."

Steven smiled. "Good idea. I'll, uh, see you later. Nice meeting you . . . ladies."

He nodded genially all around and slipped through

the door. His head popped back a moment later. He smiled nervously and pulled it shut behind him.

"Oh, he's darling! I adore shy men." Trish threw herself back into her chair before looking severely at Darcy. "But you can't have my red dress again."

"Thanks," Darcy said sardonically, jerking open her locker. Her own "emergency-date" dress hung there now, a soft column of magenta silk. Below poised two bronze-leather high-heeled sandals. She tore off her heavily beaded costume and hung it on its proper pegs.

"The professor's such a change of pace for us," Midge said. "Why do you suppose he keeps showing up like this? Can't he just call and ask for a date?"

"It's not a date!" Darcy burst out.

Midge's brown eyes were dubious.

"We have things to talk about, that's all."

" 'It's not a date,' " Jo mimicked impishly. "Look at the girl in that new dress! I'd hate to see what you wear on a *real* date."

"Oh just keep quiet." Darcy hurled herself into her chair to begin pinning up her hair to match last week's style. "It's not what you think. You just don't understand!"

Her fingers shook. *Now what?* her excited, anxious mind wondered. Why was he here, and how long could she maintain the persona of Sirene now that she was caught between two worlds? Did she even want to?

"Good luck, kid." Jo's hand on her shoulder made Darcy pause in her inner rush to utter panic.

"Yeah," Trish seconded. "Whatever's up, have a good time. Or a bad time, if that's what you want. Only find out what kind of cologne he wears. I know two hundred thousand crap players who could use a little finesse."

"Good luck," Midge wished her softly from the silent side of the room.

Darcy took a deep breath. In the many mirrors that fractured the costume-crammed space into a dozen glitter-dusted pieces, Sirene gazed back at her. Her crimson fingernails shone jewel-bright against the interesting clash of the magenta dress. She looked gorgeous and exotic and utterly unlike Darcy.

Of course Steven Austen believed in Sirene. Darcy herself, her writing, and, now, acting talent had forced him to.

She ducked out the door with a final "Goodnight" to the gang.

He was pushing off the slightly soiled wall he'd been leaning against, his hands safely in his pockets, as if he thought she planned to encumber him.

She didn't move or speak, but stood in little-girl recital position—feet neatly together, hands crossed on the small bronze evening purse before her. She even forgot that a demure posture could hardly mask the predatory glamour of Sirene.

"I wanted to talk to you again," Steven said slowly, coming toward her.

"About my sister, Darcy?"

He paused, in speech and motion. Then he removed his glasses so that she could see right into the bottomless silver-gray well of his eyes.

"About you, Sirene."

Darcy felt shock stiffen her shoulders.

"If we could go somewhere private . . ." He smiled. "I know, there's no place 'private' in Vegas. I was thinking of someplace outside Vegas. My house, on the desert. I think you'd like to see it. If you can stay up that late."

She shrugged, not trusting herself to speak, and walked over to him, then walked with him down the long empty corridors to the stairs.

"You're sure it's not too late?" he asked in that deep, thoughtful voice that had first sent shivers burrowing under her sweater in class.

"No," she said. "Dancers need to stay up after a show, to let the adrenaline ebb."

But it *was* too late, Darcy thought, knowing that tears shouldn't be stinging Sirene's false-lash-framed

eyes, that her painted talons should be digging into
Steven's arm instead of keeping to themselves.

Damn that pushy glamorpuss, Sirene! Darcy thought,
already spinning plots that would dramatically bury
Sirene forever. Maybe a car wreck in the desert. Or
perhaps a mysterious disappearance.

Darn that Sirene, anyway, Darcy wailed to herself.
She'd done it. Sirene had all too successfully seduced
Darcy's dream lover, and she hadn't even had to exist to
do it.

Chapter

Six

The desert at night shifted in fluid ripples all the way to the horizon where it beached itself on an endless, ink-black strand of sky. Ribbons of road undulated over the drifts, caught only for short spaces in the artificial roving moonlight of the headlights.

Darcy, in the pasenger seat of Steven's silver sedan, twisted back once to see Las Vegas shrinking in the rear window frame, it's carnival blare of lights fading to a fairyland twinkle.

"You miss the bright lights already?" Steven asked without looking away from the road unraveling in his headlight beams.

Darcy squirmed around to face forward again, forgetting that she was Sirene and that the rasp of shifting silk would draw his eyes. She propped her feet against the floorboard and made a momentary bridge of her body, jerking her skirt down to a decorous position.

The car offered plenty of legroom at least. Darcy eased back. "No, I don't miss it," she finally answered. "I just never saw it from here at night. Is your house far?"

"Not very."

The dashboard lit his profile, casting angular shadows where she hadn't seen them before. He wore his glasses for driving, of course, and reminded her momentarily of Indiana Jones before he traded in his professorial props for a fedora and a bullwhip. The idea that Stevenson

Eliot Austen also harbored a second secretly swash-buckling personality made her smile.

"What's so amusing?"

"Nothing. Only I didn't expect you to drive a Honda Accord."

"You surely didn't expect a Ferrari?"

"No..."

"It's the only car that will run uphill with the air-conditioning on full without losing power. It's perfect for this climate and location."

"Do you always choose things for such practical reasons?"

"Usually." He looked in her direction again, curiously. "You seem pensive."

Darcy figuratively kicked herself. Of course she seemed different! She'd been sitting here like a normal woman, relaxing in the presence of a man she knew, admired, and liked more than a little. She'd forgotten that the indefatigable Sirene was always "on."

"What's 'pensive' mean?" she asked perkily, sitting to attention with an inciting squirm of silk.

"Melancholy, out of humor. You know where the idea of bodily 'humors' originates, don't you? Medieval philosophers thought that the body had four internal states that expressed themselves in four personality types. The melancholy humor was just one. Alexander Pope wrote 'Il Penseroso,' a long poem, about it. 'Penseroso' is Italian. 'Penseroso'... pensive, see?"

A silence pervaded the car.

"No." Darcy shifted again, this time lifting her skirt a few intriguing inches. "Can't you put it in words of one syllable?"

"'Pensive' means 'sad,'" he said shortly.

"Oh. No, I'm not sad, just tired from kicking my can all over the Crystal Phoenix stage tonight." She leaned her head back and inhaled deeply. "I love it when the air-conditioning's not on; I think I can smell the sagebrush."

His teeth flashed pirate-white in the dim car, but his

glasses winked only a white reflection, like a lighthouse signal, as he glanced her way again.

"Quite a romantic, aren't you?"

"Aren't *you?*"

His hands moved to grip the steering wheel, as if reminded of a need for control. "Not usually," he said with a certain grimness Darcy longed to explore. Sirene, of course, simply exploited it.

"Now *you* sound pensive." She wriggled over on the softly upholstered seat to bridge the gap created by the bucket seats and spread her fingers on the steel-hard male thigh muscles she could sense through his pants. "Is that why you wanted to see me, Doc? To cheer you up?"

"No. Sirene—" Impatience throbbed in his voice, then stilled as he turned to look at her. She'd arranged her face so it tilted, almost resting, against the shoulder seam of his jacket. "Not . . . not while I'm driving."

She writhed her way back, leaving the light farewell tracks of her nails on his leg. "I've got to get close sometime," she warned.

"You're like your sister," he noted.

"Oh, really?" Sirene sounded mildly dubious, but Darcy's heart pounded into panic. Had he guessed? "How?"

"Always poking your nose into other people's business, as she does in those stories about you. Don't they bother you?"

"She has to write about something, and I'm handy. Nope, I guess it doesn't upset me. I mean, if she were making stuff up about me, it'd be different. But everything she writes is the truth."

Steven winced as he spun the wheel. Ahead of them, the headlights scythed a wide path of light, revealing a curving private driveway between tall hedges of oleander. In a few moments Steven swung the car into a driveway, punched out the lights, and turned off the ignition.

"Home, sweet home," he announced and got out of the car.

For once, Sirene was speechless.

"Watch out for snakes," he warned, opening her car door. They glanced down together. The dome light illuminated long white legs emerging from a crumpled swatch of magenta-silk skirt and a patch of gray-gravel driveway planted with impossibly high-heeled bronze sandals on high-arched insteps. "On the other hand, I don't think they could reach that high."

"Snakes? What kind?"

"Mojave, sidewinder, and speckled rattlers. But don't worry; there are no diamondback or garter snakes. You don't wander far from the city lights much, do you?"

She shuddered. "No, thank heavens."

His hand levered her out of the seat; she was almost in his arms before her equilibrium returned. Interweaving scents of vintage pipe tobacco and fresh cologne mingled headily.

"It's quiet out here," she said. "Doesn't it give you the willies?"

"On the contrary." His hand on her elbow lightly guided her up the single step to the front door. "It gives me solitude."

Darcy was relieved to hear her heels echo on entry-hall quarry tile as they moved inside and she clicked back into snake-free territory and the comforts of civilization. Steven's turn of a switch made several lamps scattered throughout the main room explode into cheery light at once. She got an overall impression of wood and warmth.

"Why did you bring me here?"

He stood in the shadowy part of the room, near the dark entryway. "You haven't guessed, and you still came? Why?"

"I don't know." She let her purse dangle idly, twisting it against her leg by its golden strap. "I thought you did."

"Listen, Sirene, I do want to talk to you, seriously. About, ah, last week."

"All of last week? Or a specific day?"

"About . . . Friday. Night." Steven patted his pockets automatically and somewhat absent-mindedly, then looked to the mantel across the room. He ambled over to dislodge a pipe from its rack and turned back to her with a disarming smile. "You know."

"No. I don't know."

Sirene dropped her dainty gilt purse on the cushy brown-leather sofa that fronted the fireplace. A plaid-wool blanket lay folded over the top, trailing fringe. Smoke-aged knotty pine, buffed to a Golden Retriever sheen, paneled the walls.

"All these yours, Doc?" Sirene's bedaggered nails walked over the ridges of books on the shelves of built-in knotty-pine cases.

"My name's Steven. And yes, except for the ones that are borrowed."

He sounded distracted. Darcy figured it was Sirene's loose-hipped stroll along the bookcases. When she turned, he was still patting his fingers across the manteltop and looking nowhere but there.

"Here." She ankled back to her purse, bent, pulled out a gilt-embossed book of Crystal Phoenix matches, and walked over to him. "Here's the kind of book you need now."

As she struck, the match instantly flared into strong flame. He stared over its dancing diamond of light into her eyes. She could see the match flame—and herself—reflected in perfect miniature in his lenses.

Reaching for her hand, he guided it to the pipe bowl, then inhaled with curt intensity to stoke the dormant tobacco. There was something covertly sexual about their mute cooperation, something that would have been a big hit in a 1940s *film noir*, she thought. Darcy stood as if hypnotized, letting him hold her hand to the pipe even as the flame licked at her highly flammable false nails, even as the heat intensified on her fingertips.

The tobacco took, and he jerked the bowl away, moving the pipe from his lips and bringing her hand closer to blow the flame fiercely against her for a microsecond before it winked out.

"No harm done?" he asked. He puffed on the pipe; a scent like cinnamon-sprinkled vanilla swaddled her head.

"No." She tossed the matchbook to the mantel. "What *about* Friday? Night."

"I wanted to explain."

"Explain what?"

"That it won't happen again."

Sirene's hands went pugnaciously to her hips before Darcy could restrain them. "You brought me all the way out here to tell me that you *don't* want to sleep with me?"

"No! That is, it's not a matter of 'want,' it's a matter of 'shouldn't.' I didn't mean to, the last time . . . or rather, er, the first time, which will *be* the last time—"

"You do a mean 'didn't mean to,' then, Doc."

"It was a mistake."

"I'll say!"

Sirene turned huffily to stare down at the logs stacked in the hearth. Like herself, they needed only a match to set them off. What on earth did the man want now? Darcy wondered, sharing some of her doppelganger's spontaneous ire. He apparently planned to renounce her body. What was he after—her soul?"

The lightest of touches, tentative as a cobweb, stirred the silk on her shoulder. She turned, her eyes as ablaze as her dress.

"Do you mean to say that you brought me out here on false pretenses, Professor?"

He looked as if a sidewinder had slipped in with them and he'd just noticed it.

"Now, see here, I'm merely taking an interest in your

honor, since you seem loath to do it yourself. You should be flattered."

" 'Flattered'?"

"Flattered that I'm interested in something, ah, other than"—the hand holding the pipe made a different gesture indicating the length of Sirene's silk-sheened torso—"than your more obvious attractions."

"Like what?"

"Less material aspects, like—"

If he said "soul," Darcy was going to let Sirene belt him one.

"Like . . . your mind," Steven finished in high moral certitude.

"So what's wrong with it?"

"It's primitive. Charming," he hastened to answer the growing glint in her eye. "But primitive."

"You thought primitive was plenty okey-dokey last Friday. Night."

"Sirene, you must understand." He paced, ignoring the pipe but cradling it in one palm like a worry stone. He turned back to her dramatically. "I was out of my mind last Friday night!"

"Gee, thanks. You mean you're one of those Heckyl-and-Jeckyl guys? All hot to trot one day and ice a la carte the next?"

Steven stood dazed by the mantel, setting his smoldering pipe back in its rack. "You mean Heckyl and Hyde," he repeated mechanically. "I mean, *Jekyll* and Hyde! You confuse the hell out of me, Sirene, but I assure you I'm no split personality. The man I'm named after, Robert Louis Stevenson, wrote the book on it, for heaven's sake!" Steven's hands settled persuasively on her shoulders. "Look here, Sirene, you can't go through life on a purely material level."

"It's worked so far. What's the problem, Professor? Haven't you ever had any girlfriends?"

"No!" He hastened to correct that hasty impression.

"I've had . . . a few. . . mature relationships, but nothing like, nothing like—"

"Friday. Night." Her lips had tightened in a half-mocking smile. She saw his eyelashes flutter as his gaze focused on her mouth.

"No," he agreed. "I lost my head. I've never met anyone like you," Steven admitted. "Sirene?"

"Hmmm?" The weight of his hands was driving the silk sideways on one shoulder. She felt his hand warm more and more of her skin before he did. The pinpointed sensation was so seductive, she swayed toward him. His hands tightened, only intensifying their effect.

"Sirene." He whispered her name. Their lips were on the same level and drawing closer. "About your boyfriends, the men Darcy writes about. You don't . . . with all of them, with . . . many of them . . . you know—"

"Friday night?"

"That's right. Darcy's just exaggerating. You're not really—"

"Not really what?"

Now the ebbing magenta silk had caught his wandering eyes. Fascinated, he watched while Darcy felt the fabric's slow, inevitable slide halfway down her arm. Steven's forefinger tapped nervously on her bare skin, then found the groove between the bones at the very top of her shoulder, the one his finger fit into as if into a glove. The tap evolved into a rhythmic, unconscious stroking.

"No," he said, his expression as disoriented as his words. "You're not . . . I'm not . . ."

A dull matchlike burn ignited deep in Darcy's body. The furnace of her heart pumped in four-four time, as if in thrall to a rhythm far more demanding than any Danny Dove could cajole from the upright Baldwin. Steven's stroking finger made itself at home in the small subtle notch of her shouldertop. The sensation was exquisite.

They swayed together, lips almost touching. Darcy's face tilted to avoid his glasses. Sirene should have removed them long before this.

"You're sure?" Darcy asked. Not Sirene, but Darcy asked, who wanted to be wanted for being Darcy. "You're sure you don't want to . . . ?"

"No!" He released her so quickly, she nearly fell over.

Steven had already wheeled to face the mantel. His fist, white-knuckled, pounded soft denial on the huge weather-cracked timber. When he opened it, the Crystal Phoenix matchbook lay on his palm.

"I'll start a fire." He bent quickly to the grate, forcing her to step back from the fireplace. "Nights get cold on the desert, even in the fall."

"Yes." Her frozen tone of voice alone ratified his comment.

By the time the Crystal Phoenix's efficient matches had coaxed a fringe of flame around the top log, Darcy's internal fires were firmly banked.

Steven rose and ran a hand through the thick hair at his temple. He glanced very quickly at her dress.

"Do you need a sweater?"

She shook her head. "I'm fine," she said. "Plenty warm. What did you want to tell me, then?"

"Only that—" He cleared his throat as he did when opening a class. "Only that there's a whole world outside the dressing room of a Las Vegas revue. I don't know how you and Darcy can be so different."

"We're sisters, not soul mates," Sirene retorted.

He leaned intently over the sofa back, his strong hands splayed on the now-rumpled blanket. Professor Stevenson Eliot Austen had always been most passionate as a teacher.

"What do you *read*?" he demanded.

Sirene stepped forward uncertainly as the swelling flames heaved toward the chimney behind her, their sudden heat tinging her already rouged cheeks with genuine warmth.

"Darcy's stories," she began, as if hoping for approval.

"Good, good."

"And the Chamber of Commerce *Visitor's Guide to Las Vegas*."

He nodded, not encouraged but urging her on.

Sirene took fire. "The *TV Guide*! And, and sometimes, when she's not looking, Darcy's diary. And the supermarket horoscope book . . . I'm a Gemini."

"Mere visual exercises, not real books, Sirene.

"Do you know how many books there are in this room?" he asked. She shook her head. "Well, I don't either, but it's a lot; and they're on all sorts of subjects—fiction, history, language."

He guided her to a solid wall of books. He pulled out one butter-soft leather-bound volume, its pages edged in gold. His palm repeatedly smoothed the surface in a gesture that made Darcy swallow as he placed the book softly in her hands.

"This one's over a hundred years old. A collection of poems by Shelley, who died at thirty. This book has outlived him by two generations. There are *stories* in all these books, Sirene. Look at them, handle them. Give them a chance."

"You sound like my agent hustling me to producers for a job," Sirene said wryly. But she took the book, flipping the gilt-edged pages until their golden glimmer fanned her face.

"I get enough poe-try from Nostradamus." She handed it back.

"Nostradamus? The famous 16th-century astrologer?" Steven looked hopeful. "Perhaps the humble horoscope is your path to knowledge after all."

"Last I knew," Sirene mused, "Nostradamus was just this flaky bookie on the Strip who talks like something outa Mother Goose."

Sirene whirled gracefully to confront the bookcases, the side slit of her skirt revealing a flash of white thigh. She ran her nails over the book spines, finally pouncing on one title.

"*Lady Chatterly's Lover*. Now that one I've heard

about." The long red-lacquered nails were paging through the unexpurgated edition.

"That's . . . uh, that's literature."

Sirene's dubious eyes darted up from the pages.

"Really. Literature, so help me God," he said.

"Hmmm. This looks like pretty hot literature to me, Professor, all that white flesh and horizontal recreation."

He snatched back the book. "It's literature, I tell you! It may deal with the sensuous side of life, but profoundly. It's nothing like those tawdry books one finds on the supermarket racks."

"Hey." Sirene's hands posed Mae-West-style on her hips, pinching in the loose lines of the silk dress against the streamlined structure beneath.

"I read a few of those. How do you know what's in 'em, Professor? Aren't you judging a book by its cover? How do you know that what they're about isn't a heck of a lot more real to people today than all these old books that've been studied to death by people who don't remember—or maybe never knew—anything about what's what."

"Like . . ."

"Like . . ." Sirene's flirtatious tongue reglossed her already gleaming red lips. "Like sex and love and all that stuff in *Lady Chatterly's Lover*. I may not be a brain, but I know a thing or two about that."

He stared at her as he slipped the Lawrence novel back into its slot between Durrell and W. H. Auden. "I bet you do."

"Now this," Sirene went on boldly, "I bet this is a real good book. Read me something out of it."

He glanced at the title. *Love Lyrics*.

"This is seventeenth-century poetry, Sirene. Cavalier lyrics. I'm not sure—"

"I am." She leaned back against the shelves, her face tilted at the ceiling. "I bet that book's got the right stuff. Read me some, Steven. Convert me," she challenged passionately, with a direct glance he couldn't quite meet.

So he looked down, flipped open a page, and began reading aloud. His voice dropped to the deep, intense range in which he sought to convey the beauty of the written word to his students.

"'When as in silks my Julia goes,'"—he glanced across the shimmering azalea-bright fabric sheathing his listener—

"'Then, then, methinks, how sweetly flows/ That liquifaction of her clothes.'"

Sirene's inch-long lashes snapped open. "What's 'liquifaction'?"

"An archaic word . . . not used anymore. The poet is attempting to convey how the silk moves around his mistress's body, how it ebbs and flows like water. Liquid."

"Say, that Julia chick sounds like she can *move*," Sirene said admiringly, performing an all-too-expert silken shimmy that transfixed, then repelled, Steven's gaze.

"That poem doesn't say much," he said quickly, his voice oddly choked. He clapped the book shut. "No. Sirene—"

"Yes?" Darcy leaned against the books, feeling the leather-bound spirits of Shelley and Byron, of Herbert and Lovelace, of the Brontës and Jane Austen, seeping from their buttressing spines into hers. Her eyes were closed.

"Sirene. I'm trying to be reasonable about this." Steven's voice was torn with tension, a blend of confusion and desire.

She opened her eyes. He had forgotten the books and was reading her now—her face, her body, her thoughts. Lord, she hoped he wasn't reading her thoughts!

"You can't be reasonable about this, Steven. Not even a little bit."

"I don't want to hurt anyone. You. Me. Darcy."

"Darcy's a big girl," she whispered. "She might surprise you."

"Poor little Darcy." He spoke with bitter self-reproach as he turned his face away. "I tell her to stop writing about her sister Sirene, and here I am, aching to make love to her."

"You are? Really?"

His sweeping self-contempt kept him from noticing the naive pleasure of her response. He continued berating himself.

"It's not fair to Darcy, or to you! But there's something about you. It's a purely carnal attraction, I'm afraid. We have nothing in common—nothing!" He paced in front of her like a man leashed by the magnetic pull of her body.

"We have Darcy," she said quietly.

He stopped and stared at her again, as if expecting her to change into a more intellectually palatable form.

"I'm very fond of Darcy," he said in some distress. "I respect her talent, her intelligence. I wouldn't want to do anything to hurt her."

"Why do you think making love to me would hurt Darcy?" Sirene smiled and reached up to pull off his glasses. "You're not reading anymore, sweet. You don't need these. I'm close enough so you can see me perfectly."

His head dropped in defeat. "Heaven help me."

"Heaven helps those who help themselves. I heard that somewhere once," Sirene cooed confidently. She glimmered, sparkled, scintillated directly at him. "So help yourself."

Chapter

Seven

"Good morning."

Steven stood in the bedroom doorway—filled it like a revelation. He was wearing khaki pants and a sweater the color of mist-gray purple heather photographed in soft focus on postcards of Scotland. He also wore a slightly askew smile composed of one part shyness and three parts sex appeal that stripped the awkward morning-after of all its pretensions.

"Some Friday night," Darcy said, rubbing her eyes delicately. "Did I miss anything good?"

His smile grew wicked with memory. "Not too much."

"You, uh, dragged me in here afterwards?"

He nodded.

Darcy whistled softly. "I'm impressed. I'm a big girl. You should see Danny Dove, trying to demonstrate a lift with me. Hernia city."

"You're lighter than you look."

"And you're stronger," she said admiringly.

"Must come from grading papers." His eyes dropped. "I put your, ah, things in the bathroom. I thought you'd want a shower before breakfast."

"Sure thing." She sprang out of bed, expertly flipping the blanket over her shoulder Indian-princess style. "I'm still a little stiff."

They regarded each other, not sure whether to retreat into unspoken embarrassment or advance into shared bawdy reminiscence.

"I won't comment on that," he volunteered. "Come to the kitchen when you're ready."

"Right," Darcy said, grinning insouciantly.

She bounced into the adjacent bathroom as soon as he had left. Her clothes, such as they were, hung from a behind-the-door hook. It was a no-nonsense bathroom, white fixtures all in a row, marine-blue tile, and a split shower curtain with a plentitude of penguins marching across a transparent plastic background.

She sang in the shower, wondering how she would look in designer penguin if Steven happened to peek in. But he didn't, and she was just as glad.

She liked the bathroom; there wasn't anything extraneous in it. Darcy leaned into her image in the chrome-framed medicine-cabinet mirror. She wished she could wash off the old makeup, but didn't dare. It was too soon to strip off her mask. She leaned so close that her lashes almost buffed the mirror.

"Steven," she admitted forthrightly, "I love your house!" She leaned nearer yet, so she could hardly focus on herself. Her voice lowered. "I love *you!*"

Her hands clapped over her mouth. Her eyes widened to Carol Channing dimensions. She was alone with the shower steam and her thoughts.

"I love you," she whispered. She spun in the small room, her bare feet feeling every groove in the tiled floor, and spiraled herself into a roll of penguinized Saranwrap.

"I love you," she whispered, coiled into her own arms and the shower curtain. Unrolling with a dancer's fluid skill, she snatched up a towel and rubbed her cheek on its reassuring terry cloth stubble. "I do. Honest I do."

Back at the mirror Darcy dampened her flying tendrils and pushed them back into the smooth off-the-face order that Sirene favored. Her stomach growled unexpectedly. Good Lord, but she was hungry! She sure hoped Steven could cook too.

The smell of bacon being done to death crushed her optimism. Wrapping a large blue bath towel around her torso, Darcy rummaged in the bedroom bureau until she found some wooly windowpane socks to pull on and hotfooted it for the kitchen.

Steven squinted owlishly at the black iron frypan that smoked on the stove.

Darcy grabbed a hotpad, pinched it over the cast-iron handle, and escorted the frypan hastily to the back stoop.

"It got carried away with itself," he explained behind her. "I thought a hearty breakfast of eggs and bacon after, after..." His thoughts became censorable and died as quick a death as the bacon.

Outside, the desert morning was brewing a sun-steeped rose-gold glow of pungent herbal magic. Far away, the mountains hovered smoky blue on the horizon.

"It's all right, Doc," Darcy said briskly, returning the cooled pan back to the stove. "I'll drain and chop this stuff into an omelet. It'll be just like Bac-Os."

"Oh." Steven seemed glad enough to surrender the breakfast project. What he did not seem ready to abandon was a certain anxiety about her appearance.

"Sirene... are you sure that, um, thing won't... come off?"

"Not if I keep tucking it in tighter, like this," she said blithely, demonstrating with a savage jerk before rewrapping the terry cloth under her arm.

He glanced next to her feet.

"I found them in a drawer of unmatched socks." She wriggled her toes in the oversized stocking feet while draining grease into the kitchen sink. "Do they match?"

He donned his glasses—at hand on the kitchen table—to check it out and came up empty. "I can't tell. I don't suppose it matters, but you do resemble a teenage bag lady right now."

"That's very good. An apt description, Professor. But your floors are cold, and I don't want to totter around on my instep-grinders. Besides"—she sidled against him while returning with eggs from the refrigerator—"I thought we were friends now and didn't have to be so formal."

His warm-palmed hands wrapped her bare upper arms as gingerly as she cradled the uncooked breakfast eggs.

"Of course we're friends," he answered carefully, "but maybe you'd better concentrate on cooking."

One characteristic the elusive Sirene shared with her sister was an ability to function practically. Soon she and Steven were seated at the tiny dinette, their forks dissecting a fluffy omelet laced with peppers, cheese, onions, and bacon bits.

"What d'you usually eat for breakfast?" Darcy asked sunnily, drinking her grapefruit juice.

"Cereal and milk," he answered sheepishly. "It's fast."

"So are you, baby," Sirene interjected with a wink.

"Er, Sirene," he began.

"Yes?" She peered pertly over her steaming cup of black coffee, knowing he wasn't used to staring at bare-shouldered ladies across his tiny breakfast table.

Steven put down his implements and met her gaze.

"We haven't discussed some things. Like whether you're protected—"

"Sure I am," Sirene interjected lightly. "The Crystal Phoenix has a top security force."

"Not *that*," he said sternly. "You know what I mean. Are you protected from—?"

"Heavens, yes, Steven. Don't look so guilty. I know how to take care of myself. I'm on the pill."

"Oh." He looked more disappointed than relieved by her assurance. "I suppose it's, it's the fact that you . . . that you have a somewhat liberated lifestyle."

"No." She put down her fork and met his eyes with her own. "It's the opposite. It's the fact that I'm a dancer. Dancers can't afford physical irregularities in their schedule. Old Man Rhythm doesn't look kindly on natural ups and downs. So, a lot of us take the pill as a matter of routine." She smiled. "But it's nice of you to ask."

"Good God, why shouldn't I ask? I come charging into your life and somehow keep ending up in bed with you. Instead of unraveling Darcy's mind as I meant to do, I keep undressing you, as I certainly never intended—"

"Oh." Sirene pouted thoughtfully as she sipped the hot coffee. "Do you want to dress me this morning?" she inquired throatily. "Would *that* make you feel better, poor man?"

He glowered over his glasses. "Probably, but not in the way I meant. You must start taking these things— your personal liaisons seriously, Sirene."

"Why?"

"Because 'Life is real! Life is earnest!' as Longfellow said. You must live it with discipline and order."

"Longfellow, huh? I'll tell you what," she returned seriously, chewing her toast. "Why don't I go put my clothes on; that ought to help your distraction."

She rose, swept their empty plates to sinkside, and paused in the doorway to the living room.

"You know what I think is bothering you, Doc?" she said over a shoulder that seemed more naked than bare. "Too much 'liquifaction.'" She exited with a sweeping wink of one overstated eyelash.

Steven leaned back in the light kitchen chair and absently reached for his untouched coffee. An automatic mouthful seared his lips and sprayed into his napkin.

Everything around him, he mused glumly at the sink as he bolted a glass of cold water, was becoming, like Sirene, too damn hot to handle.

But she was subdued and decorous when she reappeared, even if her dress still sizzled with late-night sheen and supple motion. He glanced at the delicate high heels.

"My first class isn't until one, so I don't have to get into town right away. If you think your footwear can handle it, there's something—someone—I'd like you to meet out back."

"Sure," Sirene agreed. "I'd love to eyeball any skeletons you keep in your closet, Doc." Her fingernail etched a path down the center of his sweater.

"This is hardly a skeleton," he remarked as he led her to the back of the lot. A profusion of bushes and trees ringed the yard, giving the illusion of domesticated greenery. Beyond this tightknit oasis, the sere desert landscape unrolled, with only the intermittent profile of a tall Joshua-tree yucca offering any shade higher than a creosote or sagebrush bush might accommodate a pocket gopher.

A small shed stood under some trees. They paused at a split-rail fence as Steven put his fingers to his lips and whistled.

Swaying out from the thick shade came the surefooted form of a rangy gray horse.

"Oh, I love him—her—it!" Darcy exclaimed, her voice naked of Sirene's usual *blasé* tones. "A horse! Steven, no wonder you love it here."

"I never said that I did," he said, curious.

"Oh, but you do; you can't hide it. I didn't know you rode. What's his name?"

"He's an Appaloosa stallion. See the white dappling of 'snow' on the hindquarters? I call him Quaker." He studied her interest-shined face. "Maybe you'd like to come out and ride him sometime."

"Oh, yes. Only—"

Steven's eyebrows raised quizzically.

Darcy curled her fingernails tightly into her palm and stroked the horse's velvet-haired pinkish muzzle with her knuckles. Its texture reminded her of intimacies among her own species. She answered Steven's mute question with an embarrassingly girlish rush of words.

"Only... dancing and horseback riding don't mix. You use different muscles. Doing one will ruin the other."

"I see."

Darcy saw too; she could see him withdrawing from her forever behind his elbow patches and his pipes. Steven was hunting for common ground, some mutual interest to explain or excuse their uncommon physical alliance. And Darcy didn't dare extend him the comforting tether of her writing, her ready knowledge of poets. She couldn't even offer him the tiny sop of Sirene's horse craziness because horseback riding was incompatible with her dancing. It occurred to Darcy that a lot of things had always been incompatible with her dancing.

"No, you don't see," she burst out. "I love him! I'd love to visit him here. Maybe a sedate walk around the yard—oh, I don't know. Maybe all that about dancing and riding not mixing are old wives' tales."

"I didn't mean to upset you." Steven smiled and put his arms around her. The sweater's teasing foggy texture felt wonderful against her lightly clad body. Sirene pushed Darcy boldly into his embrace while Quaker nickered dismay at his sudden conversion from centerpiece to equine background fixture.

"You don't fool me, Sirene," Steven went on, his voice strangely tender. "I've seen through your act."

Darcy froze in the dear, warm, fuzzy circle of his arms. "You have?"

"It took me awhile to figure it out," he added with charming sternness. "But it suddenly came up like thunder out of China 'cross the bay! I seemed to sense some fey aspect of Darcy glimmering in you."

Her hands clutched the tenuous carapace of his sweater as her breath caught in her throat.

"At first, I could only glimpse it now and again. And

that's when I realized that all that flash was only an act."

"And you're not angry with me?" she asked cautiously.

He chuckled into her ear. "How could I be angry with you for merely being human? Heaven knows I'm only too human."

His fingers tightened on her ribs. Darcy began calculating shamelessly how late he could be for his first class.

"I know it's been a lonely, hard life you've had, in its way," he was saying.

"No, Steven, I—"

"Now don't interrupt." His fingertips tapped her upturned nose. A meditative light illuminated the satin-gray eyes, as it did in class when he read from his favorite selections. "I can see that, despite the surface glamour of your profession, it calls for tremendous dedication and single-mindedness.

"You are an athlete, an artist," he intoned loftily, embracing his subject as totally as he had her. "You cannot be expected to lead a normal life or to attack life in quite the normal way. I understand," Steven finished, shaking her lightly to reinforce his new insight and conviction.

"Beneath the rhinestones and the feathers lurks a sensitive soul, every bit the match of Darcy's," he insisted. "I was foolish to have worried about her. I see why you fascinate her; you fascinate me. Obviously, I'm very fond of you, Sirene. I expect you to be nothing more than what you are; that's good enough for me."

He sealed his promise by leaning closer and kissing her lips with leisurely surety. "Well?" he demanded, so delighted with his new broad-mindedness that he never noticed her shock.

"I'm, I'm speechless."

"Oh." He seemed momentarily disappointed. "Then perhaps while you're regaining your voice—" He pulled her deeper into his arms for a longer, more consuming kiss.

Sirene responded wholeheartedly, dragging a confused Darcy with her.

It was wonderful, as Darcy had sobbed into the stoic presence of Midnight Louie the week before. She'd never dreamed she'd be wrapped in a lip lock with Professor Stevenson Eliot Austen under a spreading olive tree and the benign liquid-brown gaze of an Appaloosa stud.

Rare desert scents drifted delicately past them on the frayed ends of a soft scarf of wind. Sun dappled through the shade, falling like golden coins.

"You know," Steven said excitedly, "the best way to break it to Darcy might be for the three of us to get together to discuss her stories. That's it! We're all interested in her work, aren't we? Then later, perhaps, we can tell her how, um . . . far our acquaintance has gone. What do you think?"

"It sounds all right," she answered, her mind pedaling madly. He hadn't seen through her at all; he had just decided that Sirene was more complex than she seemed. Damn Sirene—she was simple as two-to-one odds!

"It sounds perfect," Steven happily contradicted her thoughts. "But for now, delicious girl, I'd better get you back to your apartment and me back to campus for my date with thirty-some literal-minded literature students."

The casual weight of his arm across her shoulders as he guided her back to the house was everything Darcy had ever hoped for from Steven, not only ecstasy by night but tender camaraderie by day.

This scenario couldn't have had a happier ending if she had written every word herself, she mused in numb despair. The only problem was, she'd written two heroines into the script, and Steven was a one-woman man.

Steven's hand was patting her arm in an avuncular

fashion that still managed to send her stomach into a nosedive.

"It'll be splendid to have the three of us get together," he crowed, a man basking in the solution to a troubling dilemma. "We can be open about our relationship."

Steven rubbed his hands together in anticipation. "I can hardly wait to see you and Darcy, side by side."

Chapter

Eight

Professor Stevenson Eliot Austen sat on the edge of his desk, his glasses splayed open on some papers beside him, a book propped on his khaki-covered knee, his finger needlessly marking the place while he recited a favorite prose passage from memory.

Spellbound, the class heard him out with unusually respectful attention.

From her customary seat at the very back of the room, Darcy studied him. Steven had favored Sirene with a lingering farewell kiss in the car when they'd parted a few hours before, outside her apartment. Now, his eyes seemed satisfied to overlook Darcy among the student faces so raptly fixed on his.

Of course he would seem more attractive, Darcy thought angrily. He was a man falling in love. For the first time in anyone's memory he'd worn a casual sweater and slacks to class, shedding stiffness from his manner along with his more formal clothes.

Darcy doodled in her journal, oblivious to the resonant voice that had once transfixed only her. Men! They were all alike, she thought self-righteously, hating herself for descending into rank clichés that she would have ruthlessly cut from a page. Show them a makeup-frosted face and a seminude body, and they would all crumble like chocolate-chip cookies. Even Professor Stevenson Eliot Austen. Especially Professor Stevenson Eliot Austen.

When the students finally filed out at the end of

class, she rushed down the aisle stairs behind them, hoping to slip out unnoticed between a couple of classmates.

"Miss McGill."

His call was perfectly timed, his tone impeccably impersonal and not to be ignored.

"Yes?" Darcy risked only the quickest of glances at Steven's face. The glasses shielded his expression again, but he seemed to be in complete control as he spoke.

"Could you walk me to my next class? There are some matters I want to talk to you about."

"No!" Her fingers clenched on her pile of notebooks and texts.

His hand caught her arm bracingly. "Are you feeling all right? I noticed you were very quiet in class. And now you strike me as a little pale."

Maybe you're used to painted faces, she wanted to retort, but bit her lip. "I'm just, just in a hurry."

"This won't take long," he said confidently, using the hand on her arm to guide her out of the building and into the warm October sunshine. Las Vegas temperatures still reached the high seventies at this time of year, but brisk mornings made the balmy afternoons sweeter by comparison.

"I, ah, feel I must apologize," he said when they were safely under the shade of campus trees.

It would have been the epitome of a private academic stroll, except that Darcy's knees were shaking. She felt an imposter; she felt left out of her own love affair. She felt like a liar.

"You apologize?" she heard herself echo at last.

"About—" This wasn't easy for him to say. He shifted the books from under one arm to the other and stared beyond the trees to the doughnut-shaped bulk of the James R. Dickson Library. "About your writing." He stopped to face her. "I didn't understand—about show girls, about how vital the Strip is to the economic lifeblood of Las Vegas, about life, about your sister, Sirene."

"What are you saying?"

"I'm saying that you shouldn't listen to me." A wan smile, small and wee like e.e. cummings's balloon man, softened his serious features. "Which you have not done anyway, thank God. I'm saying that I'm not qualified to judge the subject matter you've chosen to write about. I'm saying that I was narrow-minded, bigoted, an awful prig. You were right and I was wrong. That's all."

Darcy plunked down on a bench with none of her customary élan. "I've never heard of a teacher apologizing to a student before."

"Perhaps I've been instructed by a good teacher," he said rather wryly, settling beside her. His smile broadened into a dazzling one. Darcy fought conflicting urges to pinch his cheeks fondly and to knee him in the stomach.

"Won't you be late for your last class?" she asked instead.

He checked his watch. "They'll wait," he concluded with new serenity, all mellow fellow. "I know you've got obligations, too, but I wanted you to know that I had seen the light, so to speak. Mainly, I've come to realize that I misjudged your sister's world.

"What triggered this sudden conversion?"

"I saw my first hotel revue, for one thing. Quite a show. And some other... things made me think." His hand waved dismissively. "I find it too complicated to explain."

"I bet you do," Darcy muttered.

"What?"

"Nothing. So this means that you—"

"That I was too hasty. I can see that Sirene is the kind of larger-than-life overwhelming personality that might intrigue a writer. I didn't appreciate that at first." A sheepish look accompanied his last words. "In fact, I evolved this theory that you were jealous of Sirene, or trying to live through her."

"You did?" Darcy managed to sound flabbergasted. "Professor, how could you?" she demanded with a touch of impish mirth.

"I know, I know. I was blind, but now I see."

"Amazing," she said.

He glanced sharply at her for signs of sarcasm but saw only a composed, sweetly calm face.

"But you're wrong about Sirene," she added.

"I am? In what way?" A muscle pulsed anxiously in his cheek.

"She's not what you think she is," Darcy murmured demurely.

His laissez-faire posture stiffened. "Not what I think? Of course, I didn't swallow all that fictional embroidery of yours about amorous Arab sheiks and pursuing high rollers—"

"Oh, *that's* perfectly true. They always come around show girls. What's *not* true is that Sirene is as bold and brassy as she appears to be. Actually, she's quite shy."

" 'Shy'?" He choked discreetly, then cleared his throat. "In what way?"

Darcy leveled him with a lengthy hazel stare. "With men."

"With men?"

His voice definitely held a hoarse tone now. Darcy charitably attributed it to too much talking in class.

"Well, think about it," she urged. "All those long hours of practicing ballet when she was growing up, and then the actual growing-up process itself. Imagine being a girl and five-feet-eight at thirteen! Who would ask you to dance at parties—Dr. J?

"And Sirene just kept growing and growing. Oh, it's okay for ballerinas to be a little tall, but nearly six feet? And moving to Las Vegas, where the most widely recognized form of dance means taking off most of your clothes and parading in front of hordes of lascivious men."

"'Lascivious.' Yes, they are that," he interjected guiltily. "You mean that her forward manner—the manner that you portray so masterfully in your stories, that is—is all a front?"

Darcy sighed. "Now that you mention 'front,' you must realize that Sirene was cursed with a good figure, however elongated. Too much 'front' for the ballet stage; she'd fall over. There was only one thing left for a girl who loved to dance and liked to eat—the life of the Las Vegas show girl," Darcy declaimed melodramatically.

"Think how awful it is to have men always ogling your body; I mean, you're finally leading a glamorous life, and all they want is surface, surface, surface. All they want—" Darcy leaned confidently closer and lowered her voice—"is to *sleep* with you."

"Perhaps not *all* men?"

"*All* men." Darcy shook her head sadly. "They're so shallow. They don't care what you think, what your aspirations are. They're all alike." She slipped him a sideways glance as numbing as a mickey. "Of course, I wouldn't be so frank if I didn't know that you're different, Professor, that you would understand, being sensitive to words and people and relationships."

"'Relationships.' Yes, that's a big part of writing, isn't it?" He had gone from mellow to limp. "Sometimes I think I hardly understand anything at all."

His eyes shifted to Darcy's.

"What about you?" he asked. "You were her twin, after all. What was growing up like for you?"

She shrugged. "The same, in some ways, only I spent all my time reading instead of doing *pliés. Pliés*," she explained. "You know, you stand like a pigeon and pump up and down with your knees. It's one the basics of ballet."

"You've lost me." His fingers tapped on the bench's

top rail. "I guess I don't know much about anything, except books."

Darcy noticed with surprise that his arm lay casually on the bench behind her. She felt a vague qualm at having misled him down yet another garden path well planted with half-truths.

"Me too," she agreed bitterly.

"Books are as good a place as any to hide, Darcy," he said softly, his gaze turning suddenly shrewd. "That, I do know a bit about. So when Sirene emerged from her cocoon to spread her terpsichorean wings, you were left in the audience to watch, is that it?"

"In a way. Some of us have to shine, and some of us have to watch."

"Are you shy?" he asked suddenly.

"About some things. Like my writing."

"And I jumped all over it." His fingers lifted from the bench to brush vaguely at her loosened hair. "Poor Darcy—caught between the devil and the deep blue sea."

"Who's the devil?" she asked breathlessly.

"Me, I suppose. And Sirene's the deep blue sea." His voice had softened betrayingly on the last words. Darcy knew a sharp spasm of jealousy. She did envy Sirene! She had manufactured her own rival.

"Darcy." Steven easily read the misery in her eyes. "You're a great survivor, I can tell. You've been such a good sport about my sniping at your stories, about Sirene getting the spotlight. Let's start over, you and I. I'd like to be your friend."

"Sure," Darcy said, standing. "A good sport can always use a friend. Look, I gotta run. Sorry."

And she did. She ran away, leaving Professor Austen late for his class and sitting, surprised, on a campus bench. She ran all the way to the parking lot behind the Humanities Building to her car, then flung her books and papers any which way on the passenger seat.

The Nova burped into gear when she started it and

whipped her through the rush-hour traffic along Tropicana. She got to the Crystal Phoenix just in time to charge through the stage door, wave at Jake, run to the dressing room, pat Louie on his pillow, and crash-land in front of the mirror to paint Sirene back on her face.

"Home before dark," Steven said to the horse he rode. He felt the sunset dwindling to a copper wire of light narrow as a garrote at his back, felt the dangerous desert dark sliding over him like a lizard's inner eyelid.

But Quaker liked a run and knew the way. Familiar silhouettes of Joshua trees flashed by, their cactus arms flexed into right angles as inflexible as any traffic cop's. Steven saw the dark clump that was his acreage swelling ahead and pulled Quaker to a trot.

He walked the animal into the corral and rubbed him down thoroughly in the small shed that served as a stable. Quaker was tough; neither desert sun nor nighttime chill would trouble him. He nickered good-night as Steven walked up to the house. Visions of the raucous, bawdy world Sirene inhabited seared Steven's mind despite the tranquilizer of natural beauty.

Inside, he threw off his windbreaker and left it over a kitchen chairback, a break in an otherwise compulsively neat routine. He cast himself from room to room in the small house, searching for the lost, simply satisfying pursuits that he'd always found to distract him in the evening. He prided himself on being self-sufficient. Now that self seemed fragmented, torn in two, maybe three, directions.

It longed for city lights and wicked ways; it hungered for quiet walks and sensible talks, for a reliable mind and eyes as endlessly soft as dusk when the light goes from hazel to night's brunette beauty.

Brunette Beauty. In his bedroom, Steven studied the cocoa down comforter, undented by any presence since morning. The bedside digital clock told him it was too early to go to sleep, too late to look for a distraction outside the house.

The spare bedroom served as an office. Steven drew the plastic cover off the royal-blue IBM Selectric and ran his fingertips over the keys. When he sat down at it, as he had not done in months, he pulled out a drawer and extracted the entombed corpses of his fiction writing. White and dry they were, these pieces of his past; they rustled like dead leaves, each tucked into its own shroud of clear-plastic folder, each neatly prepared for interment by the local professional typist.

He scanned a few pages and tossed the papers back into the drawer. Literary fiction. Academic exercises, dry as lizard dust. Stories of failed faculty wives and arid intellectual lives. He saw why he had stopped. "Epiphanies" in checkout lines, dissections of infidelity among the chronically unfaithful.

Slowly, his mind churning with mixed images of a peacock-feathered woman and calm, insightful eyes, Steven pulled a fresh white page off his nearby stack of bond. He glanced at the brand on the carton: Neenah Bond. His fingers punched in the byline—Ned Bond.

He sat up straighter and pulled his chair closer to the desk. Light poured its honey down on the platen from the amber-glassed banker's lamp at his right hand. The letters tapped onto the page, bold, extravagant words unrolling with their own impudent purpose and style.

He wrote of the desert and night and Las Vegas, shimmering like a devilish oasis of electricity in the dark. He invented mean streets and meaner men who walked them, trailing danger. He became part Chandler and Lawrence and Cornell Woolrich. Mystery smoked from the barrel of his prose as he pumped word after word onto the pages: death and love and sex and Sirene's earthy "all that stuff" entwined in a murky dance as the silver metal ball spun, stringing letters like black pearls across the white pages.

* * *

Darcy bent over to unbuckle the red-satin T-strap pumps from her red-queen costume.

"I'm beat," Midge said behind her, echoing her thoughts. "You better head straight home and hit the sack," she advised in her dorm-mother voice.

"Sure," Darcy agreed, sitting up with a reddened face. "I haven't got anything on tonight but makeup."

"I was hoping," Trish hinted shamelessly, "that your cute professor might show up again."

"No such luck," Darcy said, standing to jump herself into skintight jeans.

The other women stopped their own re-dressing to watch her with open eyes and minds. Aware of their vigilance, Darcy pulled on a loose sweatshirt over her glitter-dusted Lily of France bra, then grabbed her purse and tote bag from under her chair.

"I've got to run if I'm going to catch up on sleep. Night, all," she threw to them as a parting bone.

She spurted down the corridor, calling out cheery good-nights to everyone she passed. Jake at his desk got a hand wave and a wink as Darcy eeled through the door leading to the casino.

In the desert, Steven stretched and yawned. The movement after immobile hours aroused his senses to ignored cramps and the luxury of returning feeling in his feet and behind. Sirene flashed into his mind; rather, the memory of being with Sirene.

On his piled pages, wish and reality blended. Sirene, for all her integrity and attractions, merged with a woman who could quote Shakespeare. Fantasy reared its lovely, fey, and consoling head—and it wore the eyes of Darcy McGill.

Steven no longer censored his thoughts but embraced his unlikely heroine and swept with her into the gangsters' stretch–Lincoln Continental. The black words stretched limousine-long for line after line, filling page after page until dawn's winged heels rose at his back and kicked their way through his morning windows and into his aching skull like Bruce Lee coming down hard on an errant ninja.

There had been some strange occurrences at the Crystal Phoenix during the night. Van's office had been used by intruders, and Darcy, who stored her books there, had been asked to come back to the hotel to talk about anything she'd seen that might provide a clue. She fretted now on the way home, perhaps because Van had called her at nine that morning when she was used to sleeping until almost noon.

So she was nearly out of her car in the apartment parking lot when she noticed the silver Accord three spaces down. Steven emerged sheepishly.

"How did you—?" she began.

"I found your address in . . . the school records," he said quickly, looking at the asphalt, then checking the length of his nose. It remained perfectly normal, despite his blatant falsehood, although Darcy felt a fleeting urge to tweak it.

"I was going to say," she said, "how did you know when I'd be home?"

"I . . . didn't. I've been waiting."

"All morning?"

"Since nine-thirty."

She checked the neat Seiko on her wrist. "It's lunchtime now, and you were in the hot sun all that time? Better come in."

She observed that he looked more rumpled than his usual charming self as she led him up the exterior staircase to her door. She had noticed the hummock of his jacket slung over the Accord's passenger-seat back. His shirt looked like it had lain wet in a dryer for a week, and his slack tie looked almost as unstrung as his face.

Steven moved into the shade of the air-conditioned apartment with a sigh. He didn't bother to pretend to admire the decor he was supposedly seeing for the first time but headed for the wicker settee and sat.

"Coffee, tea, or milk?" Darcy employed a tone of spritely inquiry.

"Me," he answered absently. "I mean . . . have you any lemonade or club soda or sparkling water?" he continued groggily. When she stared at him, he explained. "I'm afraid I didn't get much sleep last night—not any," he amended.

Her knuckles swung impulsively toward his face, which she now saw bristled with the unfocused look of the unshaven, but his own open hand was already stroking the phenomenon.

"Good Lord, I even forgot to shave. I'm sorry." He looked up, but she had flounced behind the kitchen divider.

"Don't be," her voice urged from beyond the cabinets. Steven saw her dart down the hall and return, then heard the refrigerator door whoosh open and shut. A hopeful look lightened his heavy, sleepless features.

In an instant she had returned to plant a green long-necked bottle of beer on the cocktail table and cast herself down on the—his writerly mind sought the precise description of this small two-seat unit—on the loveseat, Professor Stevenson Eliot Austen duly noted to himself, wincing.

Darcy elevated a small black item. "If you want to shave later—"

He stared, the object coming into focus first, then its meaning. "That's a, a *man's* electric shaver."

Startled, she froze for a moment. Then the flat of her hand lightly admonished his knee.

"Of course it is, silly! They work better. They're designed to get into all those nooks and crannies, like knobby knees. I use it. On my legs." Something occurred to her. "And Sirene's legs have to be baby-smooth for the show."

"Sirene..." he repeated. "One for the money, two for the show, three to get ready, and four to go."

Sirene was a thought that buzzed his brain and then evaporated into the wild blue yonder somewhere over China. Everything seemed seen through a beer bottle, darkly, he thought as he raised the alien libation to his lips. "I seldom drink beer," he commented.

"You need it," Darcy said shrewdly. "Your mind can't get any fuzzier than it is now."

"No," he admitted, slumping back against the plentiful chintz pillows, the beer propped on one slack thigh.

"You look terrible," Darcy said emphatically. "What's wrong?"

Steven ran a hand over his forehead to repel the unruly forelock that had kept tumbling into his eyes on the drive into town. He stared at the beer bottle in his loose grip; it seemed to stare back at him just as glassily.

"I wonder what the university board of regents would think of a professor on their faculty sitting in a student's apartment drinking beer? A female student."

"It's happened before," Darcy snapped. "Steven, what is it? You seem... quite unlike yourself. You seem, well, in an altered state. I know you don't drink much, and I can't imagine you smoking cactus root—"

He was smiling the beatific smile of the self-lost; he didn't even notice that Darcy had called him Steven as naturally as if she'd always done it—or dreamed of doing it—or that she seemed to have a more intimate knowledge of his habits than Darcy McGill should.

"You put it well. A writer born. 'An altered state.' I have been in an altered state. I was writing." His toe nudged the briefcase.

"There it is. It's what I've poured out in the past twelve hours, and it's quite a lot. Funny, I never thought myself garrulous. Anyway, I brought it here because"—he glanced up, the gray eyes murkier than fog—"because I want you to read it, to tell me what you think of it."

Darcy took a deep breath. Steven was watching her carefully now, his focus sharpening with every passing second.

"You're the writing professor," she said carefully.

His eyes stayed relentlessly on her face. "This is not professorial scribbling. It's something quite different. Completely out of character. *You*"—the word had an odd emphasis—"were the only one I could think of to show it to, that I would dare show it to."

"I'm . . . amazed . . . touched," she said, searching for words and finding the precisely right one on the second try. "Steven," she asked softly, "what's happening to you?"

He shook his head ruefully. "I'm afraid I'm having an 'epiphany.'"

"Goodness! Is it fatal?"

He laughed softly. "You know quite well that the word 'epiphany' describes a moment of . . . intense spiritual and emotional enlightenment as depicted in a literary endeavor, in other words, seeing the damn light in black and white!" He leaned forward, instantly energized.

"I've seen it, Darcy! Out on the desert. It knocked me blind. Quaker took me back by himself. I saw that my life, my writing, were just as empty and sterile as all that self-important sand out there. I was drifting, simply drifting, shiftlessly drifting, endlessly rocking."

Darcy caught the beer before it toppled from his hand. Steven's face had fallen sideways onto the sofa pillows, smudges of fatigue mirroring the dark of his lowered eyelashes.

"Why me?" she asked, begged, demanded.

His voice was no more than a drowsy whisper. "I thought that you might understand. *I* don't."

She reached into the briefcase she had seen so often on his desk, under his desk, swinging from his hand as he strode across campus and she had watched from a distance. She had always watched from a distance, Darcy realized; even Sirene was only a mask to keep that distance intact.

She reached into the dark leather depths and pulled out a sheaf of pale papers, feeling like a violator.

"Are you sure you want me to read this? Steven?"

His eyes remained completely closed, but his lips moved. "'Ah, Cynara! Last night betwixt her lips and mine there fell thy shadow... And I was desolate and sick of an old passion...'"

She leaned near to hear it, the brocaded words that made no sense and yet etched ice into her soul.

"'I have been faithful to thee, Cynara! In my fashion.'"

And then he was asleep. Darcy leaned away from him.

The papers trembled slightly in her grasp. Read them? She couldn't. Judge them? Never! What to do? She glanced at his face again. Her hand delicately pushed the thatch of mahogany hair off his smooth forehead. Sleep had melted away the endearing worry lines. Her fingertip skated along the edge of his jaw. She breathed a careful kiss on the skin, baby-smooth enough for the treacherous Sirene, behind his earlobe, then stood and surveyed the situation.

The apartment was cool and dark. He was dead to the world and best left sleeping there. She was due at the Crystal Phoenix around six. She could easily kill the time elsewhere.

Darcy bent to ease his feet up over the wicker armrest and took his shoes off. It wasn't the most comfortable position for sleeping, but she wasn't about to try lugging him to the bed. She wasn't *that* big a girl.

"Now, where did you leave your glasses?" she murmured, looking down fondly at her disheveled charge.

He must have had them for driving—of course! Darcy almost snapped her fingers, then stopped herself. The car. She slipped down to the vehicle, luckily left unlocked,

and searched the dashboard and glove compartment.
Plenty of old parking chits, but no glasses, not even
sunglasses. At last she patted the neatly folded jacket
with absent recognition, and her palm hit pay dirt, a
bulky lump in one pocket. Eureka! What a detective!

Back in her apartment, she left the folded glasses
atop the cocktail table where he'd be sure to see or
stumble over them when he awoke. She whisked the
mostly full beer bottle back to the kitchen, capped it
with aluminum foil, and returned it to the refrigerator.

Her tote bag and purse lay lumpily ready for retrieval
by the door. She paused halfway out into the bright
afternoon sunshine to take one last look at her sleeping
prince. Oh, damn! Her journal and Steven's pages.

She ran back for the sheaf of papers, slapped it atop
her acid-green notebook, and held them like a sloppy
sandwich in indecisive hands. Van's office safe-deposit
box was out of bounds to her now that the hotel
manager's office had been rifled and was kept locked.
She could hide them in her locker, but . . . if anyone saw
Steven's writing when he'd entrusted it to her and even
she didn't want to read it! . . .

She slapped them both into the briefcase, shut it,
and slid it behind the loveseat. They could discuss it
later. She suddenly realized what "later" would be—
when Sirene returned from the last show. Maybe he
would have repented and gone home by then.

Or maybe he'd still be here, waiting with a shaven
face and hungry eyes to take Sirene (the painted hussy!)
into his arms. Darcy's internal early-warning system
shivered in sheer excitement, even though she now
heartily begrudged Sirene her role as sole recipient of
Steven's desire.

Sighing, Darcy slipped out the door again. *Oh, what a
tangled web and all that jazz,* she snarled to herself.
Darcy McGill was dying to have Steven Austen right
where she wanted him—with her and on her and in
her. And Sirene, that seductive figment of her imagina-

tion, her proxy doxy, was as close as Darcy would ever get to attaining that consummation devoutly to be wished.

It was, she concluded, restraining herself from slamming her car door as she left the lot, driven out of her own apartment, a rotten world.

Chapter

Nine

Darcy let her sure feet tap out her haste on the long flight of stairs. She shouldered past canvas-draped costumes on their hallway pegs and shot into the dressing room.

"Golly, Darcy; we were about to call out the Mounties."

"Funny, Jo. I'll make curtain." Darcy slammed herself into her chair and began smearing on pancake. "Oh, Louie . . ." She looked helplessly at the cat ensconced on its cushion. "You're in my way!" She gave the pillow a rough shove into Jo's territory.

"Everything okay?" Midge asked, her eyes reflecting anxiety in her mirror image.

"Frankly. . ." Darcy paused, considering the day's happenings. "No. But I spent the afternoon buying up the West Shopping Mall, so I'm bound to feel better tomorrow."

"Oh, I got the neatest thing there yesterday!" Trish, already painted and dressed, minced over to twist a tube of lipstick open. A violet stick of color exploded from the silver case. "Wild, isn't it?"

"You're not going to wear it on stage?" Darcy demanded, carefully brushing on thick lip color from a small tin. "It'll probably go green under the lights."

"Of course not; it's strictly for daytime—you know, something conservative."

Darcy rolled her eyes and settled down to gluing her false eyelashes into place.

"Better let Darcy play catch-up," Midge advised in a

commanding tone. "We can't afford to be one second off the beat on our entrance, which is—" Her head cocked to a speaker.

"Three minutes, boys and girls," the stage manager announced on cue.

"—too soon," Midge said. "Come on, let's get Darcy's costume into fireman's jump-in order. We can find out why she's late later."

With the concerted aid of her stage sisters, within two minutes a fully made-up and fully semidressed Darcy was charging up the last flight of steps to the backstage area, grading herself for neatness of appearance in the door-mounted mirror and plunging into position with the other show girls in the behind-the-scenes darkness.

In seconds, the orchestra revved up the overture, the curtain parted, and lines of dancers snaked into the blinding brilliance onstage. The show unwound like clockwork.

Back in the dressing room, Darcy pled schoolwork troubles and late assignments and hideous term papers for her dilatory ways. Then it was time to do it all over again. Sometimes being a show girl felt like being a contestant on *Beat the Clock*, and like most TV game-show contestants, show girls often felt they came close to making fools of themselves. But none of the eleventh-second saves or close calls backstage showed.

Darcy shed costume after costume into the cheesecloth safety nets her dresser spread at her feet and donned the next begemmed installment without so much as a hitch of her pantyhose. At times like this, Darcy felt like an overdecorated automaton.

"I'm beat," she admitted in the dressing room after the last show.

While the others tore out of their queen costumes and rammed on street clothes, Darcy dawdled at her mirror.

"I've got to check with Jake for a message anyway,"

she explained, yawning. It had been a long day of unexpected events, from premature rising to tucking in Stevenson Eliot Austen on her wicker loveseat.

Darcy absently pulled Midnight Louie's pillow back into proper position, apologizing for her earlier curtness with a head pat that the cat accepted without expression. "You're getting too fat and lazy to move," she complained fondly.

"Take it easy," advised Midge, the first out the door. Trish and Jo soon followed, leaving Darcy alone amid organized chaos at last.

She studied her mirrored self. Even that looked leaden-faced. A three-sided frame of makeup lights was intended to banish shadows; instead, hollows clung stubbornly to Darcy's features, a look of loss haunting them. Shadows rubbed shoulders in the room reflected behind her, nestled behind hanging costumes and crammed into prop-jammed corners.

She didn't want to go home and couldn't decide if her reluctance was more due to her fear that Steven might still be there or her fear that he might not be there.

"Oh, Louie, could things get any worse?" she asked the dozing cat. He remained mum.

The sharp-edged bar of shadow visible through the crack in the dressing room door widened and then engendered its own shadow. Darcy straightened, watching the door in the mirror.

"Steven?" she whispered, tensing. Of course she should have realized he might have come here. Now there was no choice. Sirene was "on" again, like it or not, and Darcy was consigned to the broom closet of her own overinventive mind.

The shadow spit out its contents, a light-robed man with a swarthy bearded face. Darcy spun to see the stranger. Two others oozed into the room like clotted cream. Her true gentleman caller came last, blinking benignly through his thick-lensed glasses in the harsh lighting.

"You!" Darcy breathed, standing.

Prince Idris-el-Shamsin, first son of the first wife of the Sheik of Shambar, stood in his desert robes, his traditional headdress wound upon his head and circled with jewel-clamped twists of red silk. In a business suit, wearing his glasses, he would have been a nondescript man. Even in the traditional dress he barely resembled the romanticized figure Darcy had etched in her Sirene stories. Yet power perfumed his presence, power taken for granted among rulers of an empty land suddenly oil-rich and populated with an illiterate, nomadic peasantry.

The prince snapped his fingers. A deferential servant advanced with a large shallow case, flourishing it open before Darcy with the air of someone unshielding a blinding uranium glare.

She gasped despite herself. A jeweled gold collar lay arranged on red satin, flanked by long gem-set earrings and underlined by a length of matching bracelet.

The gold alone made a fortune; dimpled with diamonds, sapphires, rubies, and emeralds at every conceivable joint, it totaled a sheik's ransom.

"I can't possibly—"

"You must," the prince said curtly. "It is my bride price for you."

"Bride price? But—"

"You will accompany me to Shambar. I will array you in splendor in my palace, among my wives and other concubines. You will be pleased to serve as my most admired treasure."

"I beg your pardon, Your Highness"—unlike the fictional Sirene, she had never stressed the difference in their height—"but I must decline. It is a most generous offer, and I am—" She glanced to the jewels; for all their worth, they were as overtly gaudy as the gold-foil-backed rhinestones she wore nightly. "I'm overwhelmed, but—"

"It is not an offer," the sheik's son articulated in his

precise British accents. "It is an order. My men will take you quietly to my car and thence to my estate where a private jet awaits to escort us to Shambar. You will like it there—eventually," he promised as an afterthought.

"I'm a United States citizen."

"You are one of my retinue from this moment on. It is better to obey than to pay the price of not obeying." His chillingly matter-of-fact tones threatened only through implication.

Braced against the dressing table, Darcy let her long fingers hunt for a possible weapon. They stumbled over greasy open tins of clown-colored makeup, the long thin form of an eyebrow pencil, and a fat metal tube shaped like an oversized cartridge.

Trish's damned violet lipstick, Darcy realized, carelessly left, as usual, on someone else's table, just as Trish left everyone else's appropriated supplies on hers.

Long fingers expertly worked the top off, the lipstick up. Sideways, Darcy scrawled the shortest, simplest message her mind could manage. She didn't know if she had canceled the painfully drawn letters by writing over them.

But when the prince's men came to escort her out, she managed to roll the lipstick tube silently away in the general direction of Midnight Louie's long concealing fur. She cast the cat a farewell glance, then went to meet them, as meek as a lamb in five-feet-eleven hoofer's clothing, or lack of same, and followed the prince out into the empty hall.

It was two A.M. Night owls would be inside gambling fiercely; the early-to-bed crew had gone long before.

A limousine dark as the night itself purred at the hotel's rear door. The men rushed Darcy into the backseat, sandwiching her between the prince and one guard. Opaque windows emptied the night of even the routine reassurance of parking-lot lights. In utter blackness, the car whisked Darcy away into a bizarre future.

No one noticed. No one cried havoc. No one would know until six o'clock tomorrow night that the Royal Suite Revue was missing one queen of hearts. Her long false fingernails creased her palms. If they had been daggers, she would have used them. They weren't, and she didn't.

Steven lay in darkness, his neck and knees hanging over the edge of what seemed a table. He felt like someone the magician boxes in and saws in half. But he finally sat up and felt the dark until his fingers found a lamp switch.

He blinked in the violent light. When had his living room sprouted chintz-covered furniture? Gradually, the paler blot of a door and a picture window registered on his senses. Darcy's apartment. He checked his luminous watch face. Four-ten. He had slept since coming here at noon, then? His class! He lurched to his feet and blinked at the window again. The curtains were not drawn. The dark outside the glass was night.

Four . . . A.M. Good Lord. His glasses. His disoriented gaze found them folded as neatly as a grasshopper's hind legs on the coffee table.

"That's better," Steven told himself encouragingly. He got up to turn on all the available lights and study the situation.

No one occupied the bedroom he had shared once with Sirene. Perhaps she had gone out with friends after the last show. He backed away from the conflicting memories it contained, part rapture and part denial, and turned to the closed door Sirene had casually indicated was Darcy's room.

He opened the door slowly, then stopped, stunned. A yellow ten-speed bicycle gleamed in the light that leaked from the living room. Shelves held spare blankets and old magazines. It was a storage closet.

"Darcy's room," he told himself, where she supposedly had returned at his request to read his blasted scribblings. A storage closet? Darcy didn't live here? But he had found her here!

Steven shook his head. Sleep had slowed him down, not restored his wits. But he had talked to Darcy—sixteen hours before. He'd given her his manuscript—now, where was that? If he couldn't find that, he'd really think he'd lost his blasted academic mind.

He finally found the briefcase behind the loveseat and, sitting, yanked it open on his knees. Besides the prolific proof of his writing binge, another sheaf of papers came out, bound in Day-Glo green. Its outré color intrigued him enough to flip open the notebook. It split with familiar ease to a particular page.

Steven recognized the handwritten sincerity of a writer's journal. He shut the page quickly, thought, then opened it again. Something was wrong, and if he had to do wrong to find out what, he would. Reading Darcy's journal was a slimy thing to do, but then Sirene had admitted to sneaking a peek, and something might be at stake.

He read the last entries, dated two days before. His eyes enlarged even more behind the magnifying lenses. The words sizzled into the crenellated hide of his brain, not because they sang but because of what they said:

"I don't know what to do to get out of this mess, but one thing's clear: Sirene has got to go. She has become a monster that stands between me and everything I care about—all right, be honest, Pen—between me and Steven. I can't stand the idea of her making love to him anymore, which is pretty weird, but it's how I feel.

"Maybe Sirene could go on a boating jaunt with Prince Idris-el-Shamsin on Echo Bay and drown tragically when a kid on a Jet-Ski rams the boat. Or I could get her out to Hoover Dam and have her fall fatally from a sightseeing parapet.

"I like the Lake Mead idea best; it's deep and quite logical that a body would never be found there. . . ."

There was more, but Steven couldn't read it. His

vision blurred as adrenaline poured into his sleep-numbed fingers, feet, and brain.

"Good God!" He pushed the glasses atop his head and rubbed his eyes. "She's going to kill her sister! Oh, my God!"

He was up, patting for car keys in his pantspockets, leaving all the apartment lights blazing and the door agape behind him as he raced into the car-crowded parking lot, trying to find his own.

Maybe Darcy had decided to eliminate Sirene tonight, Steven worried. Maybe that's why she was gone and Sirene hadn't returned home yet. She mustn't do it! She must be stopped, or it would all mean nothing.

He couldn't think what anything meant, only that he had to save Sirene. The Accord started with a confident grumble. He screeched it out of its slot and guided it into the still-busy early-morning Las Vegas streets with mad, fully conscious recklessness.

Jake was waiting on watch behind his desk like Cerberus at the gates of Hades.

"Oh, it's you, Professor. You're a little late tonight—or early today; you missed her."

"Miss McGill is gone?"

Jake pushed the guard's cap back on his head to polish his spreading bald spot. "Yep. All's clear below. I just checked. Say, have you been on a three-day winning streak, or what?" Jake nodded knowingly at Steven's face.

Steven rubbed anxiety-numbed fingers over what was now a two-day growth of beard, then tore his hand away.

"Do you know of any reason why Miss McGill wouldn't go straight home?"

"I keep track of their comings and goings here, but I'm no after-hours guardian angel. Unless . . . Solitaire Smith in the baccarat room left a note for her. She said she'd see him after the show—"

"The baccarat tables?" Steven demanded. Jake's nod

was enough to propel him through the plain unmarked door that led to the back of the casino.

Even gamblers slacked off in the morning's wee hours. Some twenty-one and craps tables were closed; the baccarat area, announced by gold cursive letters a foot high, looked empty except for idle, black-tied employees.

"One of you gentlemen named Solitaire?" Steven asked as he approached.

They eyed his appearance. Steven glimpsed himself in a gilt-framed mirror. He looked etched in shades of gray, like Ray Milland in *Lost Weekend.*"

"It's important."

"Who's asking?" The man who spoke was the only one attired in a burgundy-velvet evening jacket. Steven turned to him as to a prophet.

"You left a message for Miss McGill tonight. Did you see her after the show?"

The man shook his dark head, offering no more.

Steven's voice lowered. "I'm an instructor of her sister's, at the university English department."

Solitaire looked quizzical. "I didn't know she *had* a sister."

"It doesn't matter! The point is I'm afraid Miss McGill might have . . . Darcy could have—something might have happened to her! What was your message?"

Smith leaned against a fluted white-stone pillar, as unmoved by Steven's desperation as the column itself. But his eyes probed, and finally he answered.

"We had a mob of high rollers at the tables a few hours back. A bevy of Arabs betting heavily. They, uh, they were speaking of a dancer one of them wanted. I thought I heard the name McGill. I speak a smattering of Arabic. That's all. I was going to tip her off."

"Oh, my God!" Steven enunciated clearly for the third time that night. "The son of the sheik."

"You talking about an old film, mate?" Solitaire inquired.

"Yes, an old film," Steven returned. Who would

believe his wild story? No one who hadn't read Darcy's tales of Sirene and the sheik's son, Steven told himself. "I think I'll"—he looked around distractedly—"I think I'll have to find her myself. Thanks."

"No trouble," Solitaire Smith offered. "But if I were you, I'd get some sleep. You look like you've gotten a facial from a kangaroo."

"Sleep, sure. I'll do that." Backing away, Steven caught his balance on the top of a small flight of stairs and retreated under the dubious stares of the baccarat referees.

In moments he was back before Jake.

"I thought I'd . . . check downstairs. Just in case. That all right?"

"Sure, Professor; as long as you don't dress up as the queen of clubs, I don't care what you do down there."

"Right." Steven raced down the stairs the moment he was out of the guard's sight.

Luckily the overhead fluorescents had been left on for the cleaning crew. Steven could hear trash cans banging from the far corners of the understage rat's-maze. He found the dressing room easily.

The room was empty, as Jake had said. Steven stared disconsolately at hanging maribu boas and sagging rhinestone bras. Among the preponderance of rainbow-colored feathers, he finally spotted one object that was not plumed or sequined or rhinestoned.

"If only cats could talk," Steven said, recognizing the big black mascot that had perched in exactly that position during his first encounter with the overwhelming Sirene. "Eh, kitty?"

The animal's self-satisfied face seemed to flinch at this form of address, but Steven was a horse-and-dog man himself and had never had much luck reading feline reactions.

The creature stretched out a languorous paw, then batted at a small gold case, its ears flattened and white whiskers pressed back against its jet-furred muzzle.

"That's a good, playful kitty," Steven told it, sighing as he studied Sirene's abandoned chair and litter-strewn tabletop.

The cat gave the object a sudden savage blow. It rolled toward the table rim, and Steven, being orderly, instinctively stooped to catch it in his palm.

But it stopped before rolling off the edge, and when he picked it up, the shining surface was sticky. Steven looked down to the tabletop. There, scribbled in violet greasepaint, were two cryptic words: "Help, shieks!"

Steven stared. Clearly, Sirene couldn't spell well, but what did sheiks have to do with anything, including her maybe-disappearance?

Shieks . . . The son of the sheik *had returned*! The Idris-el-Chamois from Darcy's journal. Darcy had nothing to do with Sirene's disappearing act yet. It was only, only a wealthy, single-minded, spoiled Arab, son of the sheik of Shambar!

"Oh, my God!" Steven pocketed the lipstick, patted the cat thanks, and darted out the door and up the stairs.

He had to do something, tell someone, go somewhere, but no course rang clear in his mind. Poor Sirene.

Jake was chatting at his desk with a slight, nondescript man. Steven clattered past them, their words catching up to him with dreamlike clarity.

"I'm not placing any bets this week, Nostradamus," Jake was saying firmly. "I'm still flat from last week. Those nags couldn't—"

Jake looked up. A harried Steven had materialized before him again. "I thought you left, Professor."

"Did you say 'Nostradamus'?"

"Sure, but—"

Steven commandeered the little man's arm and dragged him to the door. "Nostradamus, come here; I need you."

"Hey, buddy, watch out for these delicate threads."

Outside the man shook off Steven's grip. "You wouldn't be collaring me for the feds?"

"No, Nostradamus, I'm worried about Miss McGill. My name is Steven Austen; I'm a friend of hers. I just found a message in her dressing room about sheiks. Do you know about the rich son of an Arab sheik, who likes to gamble? Idread-el-Camel or something. I think he may have kidnapped her."

The little man blinked and wiped his forehead with a red bandanna he produced from his pantspocket.

"I know every dude who lays cards down on felt. If he messes with a show girl, it's a rum hand he's dealt."

"Exactly. So who is this guy? And where does he live?"

Nostradamus sank his pointed chin in his palm and ruminated for a moment. Then his glance flashed up bright and on target.

"This dude has a spread where he raises the nags. I know where it is. We'll tail the scalawags!"

"Wonderful!" Steven pounded the bookie on the back, beginning to realize that there was something vaguely familiar in the way the small man phrased his replies.

"How far is it?"

"If you've got handy wheels, we can be there by morning. We'll drop from the dark and grab 'em without warning."

"I'm, ah, delighted that you agree we should handle this ourselves. It really wouldn't do to include the authorities before we had proof. Then you're game to guide me there?"

"With what I know now, you couldn't stop me, mister. Why, I love that little show girl like she was my sister."

"Yes. Er, I'm . . . quite . . . close to her as well. *And* her sister."

"*Sister*, mister?"

Nostradmaus cocked his head, perplexed, but Steven swept him to the Accord.

"Stout fellow," he muttered while starting the engine. "If Custer had had a dozen like you, I'm sure Little Big Horn would have been a different story. Ah"—Steven hesitated before entering the traffic flowing along the Strip—"one thing. Do you think you could knock off the rhyming when you're giving directions? You might lead me astray."

"No way," Nostradamus answered flatly. "José." He smiled.

Nodding numbly, Steven eased the car into the mainstream, then quickly sped onto the highway out of town, north to the empty desert. He was unhappily certain of where Sirene was, he reflected, but what the devil had become of Darcy?

Chapter

Ten

Steven crouched behind a rock-strewn rise, watching the sunrise gradually color the cold gray desert terrain to the shade of a dimpled brown pancake.

Nostradamus hunched beside him.

Ghost-pale gray horses stirred in the grassless, fenced desert turf now that the sun was up, milling expectantly around their troughs. Unless humans kept livestock fed, watered, and shaded, they found the Mojave Desert a stingy mother to all but the few wild and wily mustangs and burros.

"Arabians," Steven muttered again. "Logical. But what's that structure behind the ranch house? It looks like El Rancho Minaret."

Rapidly warming sunlight gilded the edifice's bulb-topped towers and cast strong shadows into its pierced-pattern tiles. It also revealed the building's shape below the architectural decorations—a smooth windowless bunker of pale stucco, ominously featureless except for a wide-timbered door. Before it, two robed men paced back and forth beside a long obsidian-sleek limousine, rifles cradled in their arms and caftans whipping like sailcloth in the morning breeze.

"It's a stronghold," Steven concluded aloud, "that's what it is. And that's *where* she is. I'll go down. You stay here, Nostradamus. If I don't return in a reasonable time, go for help. Take my car."

Nostradamus's mouth opened.

"No reasons, no rhymes," Steven forestalled him.

"We haven't time for it. This is my mess; I'll have to muddle through it. But thanks for showing me the way to—" He glanced again to the bleak bunkerlike structure, "—to Medina on the Mojave."

With a brisk nod and a last push of his glasses to the bridge of his nose, Steven boosted himself over the rise and began the long walk across creosote-bush-dotted desert to the prince's headquarters.

"I'd say that his odds are twenty to one," Nostradamus told the grave, unblinking lizard who had popped its head out of a rocky burrow to soak up some sun. "The university can write off a favorite son."

In the vast panorama beyond the rise, Steven was diminishing into a small moving figure. The horses neighed welcome as he passed their feeding station, lifting twitching noses to display buck teeth. Shortly after, the guards gave a ritual greeting, too, with lifted rifles focused on his breastbone.

Nostradamus waited to see no more. He skittered down the rise, further scuffing the sides of his cream patent-leather wing tips, scrambled into the car, and sent it lurching back along the empty rutted road to town and some kind of help.

Steven, hands raised shoulder-high, approached the guards.

"How do you do? Lovely morning for a walk, isn't it? Ah, kindly tell His Highness that Professor Austen is here to see Miss McGill."

The glowering sun-scorched faces screwed themselves further into brutal disinterest. A rifle barrel rudely prodded Steven in the chest.

"It's impolite to point," he objected mildly. "Please inform your... er, master that I wish to speak with him."

They surveyed his unshaven face, his sand-scoured slacks and rock-scraped palms. Then one shrugged, shouldered his rifle by its leather sling, and vanished behind the wooden door.

Steven smiled winningly at the remaining rifleman and reached into his pocket. The rifle muzzle followed, pressing a perfect circle of threat against his flesh.

"Matches," Steven explained, cautiously pulling out a gold-embossed slick navy matchbook from the Crystal Phoenix. "I forgot they were in this shirtpocket, isn't that odd? Of course, I have no pipe to light—." He looked up as the other Arab returned and gestured him into the shadow of the open door. "Well, hello."

Steven waved the outside guard good-bye while tucking the matches behind his thumb and followed the other man into the welcomely dim interior.

Sand, tracked in on his shoes, grated with his every step on the cool white tiles underfoot. The walls were composed of intricate pattern-pierced blocks that allowed only the most abstract shards of light and sound to penetrate the corridor.

Steven was led through a veiled arch into another circular corridor. He moved about forty feet down the second passage before being ushered through an archway into yet another ring of hallway. This one stretched room-wide and was furnished with Oriental throw rugs, floor-set pillows, and a high-tech array of the latest audio-video equipment.

Onward and inward they went. Steven's methodical mind soon graphed the arrangement of this architectural madness. The place coiled like a maze, a round maze. To get in, one bore left at each archway; to get out, the opposite should work. He cataloged that fact on the assumption that this latterday set of Hansel and Gretel would have to make do without bread crumbs.

Now for the gingerbread house and the oven, he thought wryly, ducking another gauzy hanging and entering the huge circular central chamber he had anticipated.

"Steven!" Sirene's voice wailed in a dirge of startled dread.

She sat on a pillowed high rise across the room,

glittering in her queen-of-hearts ensemble. A brighter, richer gleam shone from the bejeweled gold pieces glinting at her neck and wrist, and dangling from her ears.

Around her, the room unrolled like an Arabian Nights tapestry—richly hung with fabric and color and the winking glint of brass and gemstones. On a dais at the room's far end sat an upholstered baby blue crushed-velvet cocoon—the largest, gaudiest, most self-indulgent king-size waterbed Steven had ever seen.

Its very presence struck horror into his heart.

A short man, bespectacled like himself, held court on an X-chair centered in the space. He immediately noted the direction of Steven's gaze.

"Splendid waterbed, is it not? It has color TV, stereo headboard, VCR, and a telephone, all built in. I ordered it at the Furniture Market in San Francisco, and they customized it especially for me. There is no other like it in the world."

"I'm sure of it," Steven said fervently.

"I collect," the prince further explained, "that which is one of a kind, I think you call it. You Americans are so ingenious with your technology. Everything here is big, bigger, biggest." He glanced at Sirene in her pillowed splendor. "Even your women."

"Yet this one"—Steven let his eyes stray to Sirene—"is a little, er, skinny. I thought the discriminating Arab preferred robust women."

The prince shrugged. "My eye has been educated to Western standards in some things. My Sirene remains a worthy collectible."

"Of course, of course," Steven soothed. "I never meant to question the wisdom of Your Highness's . . . investment."

The prince laughed and leaned forward, his beringed hands spread on his robed knees. "Of course you did, Professor. You came here to bargain her back, did you not?"

"Bargain implies an exchange. I am empty-handed," Steven pointed out, showing his palms. "I came to persuade you to free her."

"Free? She *is* free. I have chosen her. What else would the woman want?"

Steven wet his lips. "That is not our custom—"

"I customize your customs, Professor." The prince's smiling face grew taut. "My father is a collector as well—of American professors, whom he pays handsome sums to teach the royal sons of Shambar. Do not seek to outwit me. I know the turnings of such minds as yours."

"Outwit you? Never! I come only to entreat you, beneficent prince that you are, to return this woman to me."

"Ah." The prince lavished a wasted triumphant glance on his stone-faced retinue. "Now it becomes interesting." His voice snapped out the next words. "She was *your* woman, then?"

Steven glanced at Sirene, already suffering the indignity of captivity and now about to be argued over like a choice piece of sirloin.

"Yes and no," he temporized.

"This is why you Americans lose influence the world over!" the prince raged. "This 'yes and no.' Was she or was she not?"

It occurred to Steven that the prince might mistakenly believe he had acquired a virgin. He swallowed—and committed truth.

"We have been lovers."

The prince roared with laughter. "And you think she would prefer to remain with you, rather than accompany me to my palace in Shambar?"

"Ask her."

Now the prince seemed at a loss. "There are some customs of Shambar it is best not to challenge," he finally said. "A woman's opinion is as a grain of sand—

insignificant and yet likely to be a great irritant in the wrong place."

Sirene stirred indignantly, causing a great clatter of body jewelry. Two guards implanted heavy hands on her restive shoulders.

"Steven, don't reason with this thug; just deck him," she suggested angrily.

Silence ruled the room. Steven sighed, knowing the uselessness of attacking the prince in his den. Prince Idris rubbed his short black beard with a hand on which every finger was knuckled with a ring, even the thumb.

"So. You say she is your woman. Perhaps. I say she is mine. Certainly. Would you fight for your woman, Professor?"

"I suppose so," Steven answered warily.

The prince beamed. "Would you fight . . . Ibrahim?"

The last word was a bellowed summons. From beyond a soft shimmer of translucent curtains came the bare-torsoed bulk of a gigantic man, his muscles hung with excess flesh, his harem trousers lacking only the usual accoutrement of a curve-bladed sword at their sash. Apparently Ibrahim relied on personal force rather than metal weaponry.

"Well?" demanded the prince.

Steven swallowed. He'd never attacked anything more dangerous than a trespassing chuckwalla lizard. Now somehow his manhood was at stake as well as Sirene's future.

He advanced toward the hulking man despite her wailed "Steven, no!" from the sidelines. Then he paused as if to reconsider, turned, and walked back to Idris.

"Would Your Highness hold my glasses?" Steven asked, presenting them with a bow. "I wouldn't want Ibrahim to be accused of the cowardly act of hitting a bespectacled man."

This time the prince's laughter nearly shook the surrounding ring of curtains; the flames in the braziers before them seemed to shrink in the good-humored wind of it.

"I like you, Professor! I like you so much that I will take you, too, back to Shambar. Put on your spectacles and put aside heroics. The royal spawn are forever increasing and presently number four hundred and thirty-eight. My father can always use another American professor. What do you think of that?"

"I think that's better than nothing," Steven reflected quickly, polishing his glasses on his shirttail before redonning them.

Perhaps, in time, he could think of some way to free Sirene. In the meantime, of course, she would be at the beck and call of Idris-el-Chamois, a thought that filled Steven with rage enough to dispense with three Ibrahims.

"And as a boon," the prince was saying, "I will grant you the occasional opportunity to sample the lovely Sirene's delights. Is this not a fair settlement of disputed territory, my friend?"

A sound halfway between a gasp and a sob wrenched the silence. Steven didn't look around to find its source, but his hands tightened into fists.

"No, Your Highness. It is not fair. I would rather face a thousand Ibrahims than violate one woman in my power."

"But she was your lover. Surely, it would be the same."

"Not if she isn't free to refuse—either you, or me."

"What strange customs you have," the prince marveled. "Is the camel who bears me free? The servant who pours my wine? We must all compromise with life."

"Not in this."

Truly puzzled, the prince lowered his voice. "But consider, if she resents her fate, would not the hope of reuniting with a past lover lighten her mind? Although of course I foresee that she will soon come to love my royal self as much as my other concubines."

"Perhaps," Steven conceded. "But it would be a false surcease. I would never be a party to it."

"Hmmmm. Most interesting! We shall have to test that in Shambar."

"It's no use, Steven," Sirene cried from her side of the room. "He's used to absolute power; he can't know or care about Honor."

"Silence!" His face clouded with anger, Idris rose. "I know honor; I merely do not grant your odd notions of it. We will go soon, and I will take only the woman. You incite her to rebellion, Professor, and as such are a dangerous man. Take him out!"

"Wait!" Steven's shout halted the guards. "I'd like to say good-bye to her."

Idris' arms spread wide. "I am a civilized man. Of course. Then you go."

Sirene, subdued, was so white with fatigue that her makeup stood out against her blood-drained skin like an image applied over it.

Steven walked to her quickly. Her eyes followed him, luminous with unshed tears of pure fright. He put his hand to her shoulder—no more than the guards had done.

"Sirene, I—"

"I know you tried. I don't know how you found me, or how you came here. There's so much I have to tell you. Oh, Steven, there's no way out!" Her hands crept up to his.

"Hush. Just listen. Hard. There's a matchbook in my hand. Take it. When they're watching me leave, light the whole book and touch it to the curtains behind you. Then run like hell, and we'll try to get out."

She inhaled quickly, her tight fingers loosening to trace the shape of the matchbook under his hand.

"What did you say?" the prince demanded.

Steven turned, his fingers moving to the heavy necklace's jewel-brailled surface. "Just admiring Sirene's new jewelry."

"My gift," Idris agreed proudly. "Her bride price."

Sirene whimpered her rage and clasped the matchbook in her palms. Her eyes were lucent as they stared up into his, lucent and no longer apparently blue, Steven thought, as if all the color had washed out of her.

Patting her shoulder awkwardly, he stepped away. Immediately two custodial Arabs slipped beside him. Their footsteps echoed on the tiled floor as they brought him before the prince one last time.

"Farewell, Professor," Idris bid with a wave of his gold-knuckled hand. "Do not consider going to the authorities over this. My reach is as long as my memory."

Steven's eyes dropped. He allowed the two men to grasp his arms as they turned him toward the exit. He paused suddenly, twisting his head over his shoulder.

"Your Highness! You said you were a collector of unique things. Did you know she had a sister—a twin sister? She is one of two. Sirene isn't unique."

"Two?" Idris rose, glowering. "None of my agents told me this."

"It's true," Steven said. "I teach her sister at the university. It's how I met Sirene. She's *not* one of a kind."

While Idris frowned indecisively and his retainers looked to him for orders, Steven's guards let their hands drop away. Across the room, a shout drew all eyes that way. A pyramid of flame was climbing the fragile curtains that ringed the chamber. Running from its fiery heart with agile doelike leaps, kicking flaming braziers over as she went, came Sirene.

One guard tried to stand in her way, but a long leg performed the head-high chorus-line kick that ended the second act of the Royal Suite Revue. The guard received a royal knock on the chin that sent his weapon skating far across the slick floor.

Steven snagged Sirene's hand in passing and dashed for the exit archway.

Smoke billowed the curtains behind them, but only sounds pursued them, confused cries and the bellow of an angry prince: "*Not* one of a kind?"

"This way!" Steven yanked Sirene to the right through another arch, running down the passage, then jerking her right again, running and veering right again.

They crashed through the wooden exterior doors, aware of feet drumming the floor behind them. The single exterior guard fell before the violently opened door. Steven, no longer thinking, pulled Sirene after him, heading for an oasis in the desert—the shade and shelter of the few trees grouped together—drawn to the creatures he knew.

The deceptively quiet stable was dim, but the subduded glitter of the tack room beckoned through an open door. Steven dove into the room and whipped a pair of bridles off their hooks. The cries of angry men escalated behind them. He took Sirene's hand again and led her out to the corral. In the shade of a salt cedar, Steven coaxed a startled white mare to statue stillness, then patted the wary muzzle. The bridle slipped on before the mare could lash her dainty head back to evade it.

"Steven, they're coming this way!"

He was up on the mare already, fighting for control as she spun in the rising sandstorm her hooves created. He dropped the second bridle to the sand and thrust one helping hand down to Sirene.

She stared at him, her queen-of-hearts red satin powdered white with dust, the swagging rhinestones winking incongruously.

"You're kidding!"

"Come on!"

"Bareback?"

"Jump up!"

"Who do you think you are, Indiana Jones?"

Dust covered the windows of his glasses, obscuring his eyes. The nervous mare churned the soft turf, showing sickles of eyewhites. Footsteps pounded onto the wooden stable floor behind them.

She took the hand, vaulted into a balletic leap, and found the hard hide of an equine derriere slapping up between her thighs. Steven pulled her forward against his back. He didn't have to tell her to hang on. She wrapped long arms around his midriff, then clasped her own wrists and pressed her face into the darkness above his shoulder blades.

The mare, released from the chaos surrounding her, bounded forward at the urging of his heels. A jolting trot quickly rolled into a canter and then the beast flew over the fence rail as if transformed into Pegasus.

Sand sprayed around them in clouds. Through the mist they saw smoke funneling out of the bunker and agitated men jumping into cars, foremost among them the long black limousine.

"They're crazier than you are," she shouted into Steven's back, but he didn't seem to hear. The great pounding beast under her was stretching its sinuous running muscles; her thighs gripped the uncoiling power as if trying to ride a hurricane. Hooves skimmed the surface of the sand in rhythmic certitude. Lungs bred for endurance heaved mechanically.

At the top of the rise, Steven reined the mare for a moment to look back. Sand-mired jeeps spun in impotent circles. The limo had impaled itself in cactus and creosote bushes to the hubcaps. Men scurried like ants around a collapsing hill, and the vast empty desert extended in all directions to the mountains.

"There's the highway." Steven pointed to a dull gray line bisecting the drab Mojave landscape.

"Well, you've rescued me. What do we do next?"

"Find someone to rescue *us*."

"Dare we rest first?" she asked hopefully.

"In the next dry wash, I think."

His shirt had long since given up its buttons. Her arms hugged bare muscled skin. The sun warmed her back; her forked bare thighs pressed companionably into the clothed backs of his. Her breasts sheltered in the hollows of his shoulder blades.

She sighed and shut her eyes. It seemed over now—the fear, the insanity of her abduction, the wild escape. It seemed over in a very nice way, even if her muscles would rack her for it in the morning. She felt melted in a crucible of love and admiration. She felt like what Prince Idris had wanted Steven to call her—Steven's woman, but by her own free choice. He must love her, she thought, very much.

Sudden stillness interrupted her daydreaming. The living rocking horse beneath her had stopped moving.

"Can you slide off?" Steven was asking solicitously.

"Sure." She tumbled boldly to the ground, then felt her bowed legs wobble. Steven's strong arm was there to balance her; after all, she weighed much less than an Arab mare. She clung, deciding that she could learn to like selective clinging.

He walked the mare into the shade of an overhanging rock and ran a hand along its sweat-darkened side. "Not too bad. I'm sure Nostradamus went for help when he saw the smoke. They'll find us before it's too late for any of us. Watch out for snakes!"

But his sudden warning couldn't keep her from wobbling over on her sadly scuffed dancing shoes, throwing her arms around his neck and pressing her long length against the length of him.

"Steven, you're a hero! I never dreamed that anyone could help me. Steven, I love you!"

She proved it by sinking a rabid kiss into the surprised softness of his mouth. "Oh, Steven, when we get home, I'm going to abduct you into my *boudoir* and hug you and kiss you and call you my very own forever and ever. His Royal Pain didn't know the first thing about collecting uniqueness, compared to me."

His mouth hardened under hers. Hands pried her

arms from around his neck. He pushed her away, breathing harder than the effort required.

"Sirene, I'm . . . I'm sorry. I know you're grateful and a little crazy at the moment, but—"

"'Grateful'! You call this grateful?" She plastered herself to him again, smiling to feel his repelling hands suddenly clasp her arms, to find his mouth succumbing to the grinding hunger of hers.

"Grateful," he said firmly, wrenching his face away. "Sirene, listen. You're a very attractive woman and all—"

"And *all*?"

"But I can't be your lover anymore."

She leaned away, blinking her shock with artificially supplemented lashes. They had clung faithfully through every trial.

"The prince didn't, didn't . . . *do* . . . something?" she asked.

"No!" He looked as shocked as she. "No, not that. You've got to understand, but how can I make you? Sirene"—he took a deeper breath then when he had faced the impending bulk of Ibrahim—"Sirene, I can't love you. I love Darcy."

"Darcy? *Darcy?*"

"Now don't be upset. I know she's your sister; perhaps that just makes it worse. But you see, I loved Darcy all along. I just didn't know it. Otherwise, I'd have never . . . never—"

"Friday night?" she inquired icily despite the sun-heated sand and stone oven in which they stood.

He recognized their euphemism for intimacy, and his face folded like a poker player's last hand.

"I'd never have made love to you if I'd admitted to myself that it was really Darcy I cared for," he tried to explain. "But you were so seductive, and you seemed to delight in pushing me to it. I was weak before, but I won't be weak now. Don't you see? We've both hurt

Darcy very much. I even think she's, she's unhappy enough to contemplate harming you!"

"Darcy?" Sirene sounded even more dumbfounded than before.

Steven winced at the ugly revelations before him.

"I happened to skim some of her journal. She wrote of planning to 'get rid of' you, of a fatal boating accident on Lake Mead. She may need professional help. I'm afraid she's going to need all our love and support."

Sirene pushed off of him, tilting her face accusingly. "You read Darcy's diary?"

"Well, you did too!" he accused back.

"I guess I did." Sirene smiled and moved away, gauging his relief with every step back she took. She thought, visibly, looking from the ground to the sky to the mare. Then she looked at him again, challengingly.

"Steven, if I was such a problem to you and Darcy, why didn't you let Prince Idris's jet whisk me off into the Arabian Nights future he planned? I would have been out of the way forever."

"It . . . never occurred to me. At first, I was afraid Darcy was going to hurt you. When I found that someone else endangered you, I couldn't think of anything but getting you back. You've done nothing but follow your instincts all along. I'm the one that's been untrue to everything I believe in," he added distractedly. "You've a right to hate me, Sirene, and so does Darcy."

"But I don't, Steven," she said soothingly, advancing on him with all her glitter jingling. "I love you."

"You can't," he croaked, trying to claw her arms from around his neck. "It's merely a carnal attraction, a passing whim."

She nibbled lightly at his neck, her fingers walking up his chest, her mobile hips pressing into his.

"Darcy's so ordinary," she pouted. "Darcy's dull, face it, Steven. Too dull for a bold, adventuresome man of the world like yourself. Would Darcy kiss you like this, do *this?* See, you don't need Darcy at all—"

"But I do!" He wrestled free of her. "She's sweet and intelligent. We like the same things—books and writing."

"Have you ever slept with her?"

"Of course not! I've been true to you, so to speak."

"A bird in the hand," Sirene purred, insinuating herself into his arms again, "is worth a question mark in the bush."

"No!" He pushed her off again. "Even if Darcy and I should . . . get together—and it isn't what you and I have had—I'll just have to live with that, Sirene. Sex isn't everything, but love is. You've got to stop this game. That's all it is to you, and I'm easy prey. But I'd never have succumbed to you if I hadn't been yearning for Darcy all along and not daring to admit it—my own student, for heaven's sake!"

"Well, you're in trouble now, buster." Sirene pulled away, it seemed to Steven for good. Her eyes flashed bolts of anger.

"Sirene, you won't tell Darcy about us?"

"I don't have to, Steven." Her head shook with disgust, making the golden earrings chime. "She already knows."

A wicked smile parted her still-glossed lips.

"Steven, my love, my lusty, reluctant lover—" she pinned him against the rock again, her smiling eyes and lips drawing so close, they paralyzed him. "I *am* Darcy!"

"*You're* Darcy?"

She nodded, torn between laughter and tears, and finally, with those last hard-edged words, let Sirene slip away forever. That part of herself seemed to ooze through her fingertips even as Sirene's brazen red fingernails slid slowly down Steven's chest, releasing him.

Darcy felt completely drained. It felt so good to have ended the masquerade. And so awful to think of the confusion Steven must be feeling.

He frowned. "But you're not listed on the revue program as Darcy McGill!"

"It says 'R.C. McGill,' which stands for Ramona

Catherine, just like Sirene said. Darcy's a nickname based on the initials."

"Then . . . then where did the Sirene come from?"

"Sirene was always mythical, Steven," she explained, sighing, "a fiction from the first. But you were so ready to believe in her. . . you seemed to need to. And I had always needed you. So I helped you to believe in what you wanted because I loved you. Can you ever forgive me?"

He looked completely distracted. "Forgive you? My God, if it hadn't have been for this charade, if I hadn't gotten involved with . . . Sirene, you would have been whisked away by that young maniac before anyone had been wiser—"

He stepped back, as if to view her in focus.

"Darcy," he repeated, staring at her adventure-worn stage getups as if it were a space suit and she the alien in it.

"Yes?" Darcy dangled from a hook of suspense even more heart-stopping than being kidnapped.

His expression changed from stupefaction to wonder. Steven grabbed her, his hands tightening on her upper arms.

"Darcy?" he demanded.

"Yes," she admitted.

They stared into each other's eyes.

"Darcy!" This time he said it as if he believe it. "You're Darcy! You've always been Darcy? Even when we—?"

"Yes! Especially when we—"

Steven caught her in an embrace that squeezed her into breathless silence.

"My God," he said, "I'm so glad! I'm so glad you're *both* all right."

Chapter

Eleven

"Drat these eyelashes!" Darcy stripped them roughly from her lids and rolled them on a pencil.

Midge, Jo, and Trish, were nearly ready to depart the dressing room for the night, or morning.

"'Night, Darce," they chanted in turn and slipped out of the dressing room.

Midnight Louie was drowsing on his high-profile pillow.

A moment later, the dressing room door burst open. Steven burst through, bending to kiss the back of Darcy's neck.

"I couldn't wait for you to get home! Look what came today!" He tossed a paperback book with a rather gaudy cover featuring sultry women and granite-faced men toting heavy artillery on the cover.

Darcy regarded this with the amazed pride and joy usually reserved for one's firstborn.

"Oh, Steven, it looks wonderful," she cooed with fond satisfaction. "And they put Ned Bond *above* the title."

"Yes, well, I don't know about the title—"

"What's wrong with *Bullets to Bedsheets*? It's alliterative, catchy—it's got zing. Besides, the publishers must know what they're doing."

"I doubt that," Steven said, "but I'm having a lot of fun with this stuff. It's really awfully liberating to do exactly what everybody told you not to do for years and years. If my university colleagues knew I was the author of *The Nightprowler* series—"

Darcy jabbed one long red false fingernail into the mirror, where it stabbed a taped-up page from a magazine.

"Your academic peers certainly know what *I'm* up to." They spent a moment's silence beaming at the first of Darcy's Sirene stories to see print. The buyer had been a magazine, the price $1,500, and the byline was Darcy McGill Austen. "I just love it that your last name is spelled like Jane Austen's," she said dreamily. "I adore unlikely juxtapositions."

"Speaking of unlikely juxtapositions," Steven said, pulling her up from her chair, "I've got a chilled bottle of champagne in my briefcase outside the door. I suggest I bring it in, lock the door, and we celebrate."

"In here! How imaginative, darling." She wrapped herself around him, arms and legs. "But what about the cat?"

Steven glanced at the massively indifferent Louie. "He'll never tell."

In a minute he had the split of champagne open, Darcy had rinsed out two plastic drinking glasses at the dressing-room sink, and they were toasting their literary successes.

"To Mr. Bond," Darcy invoked throatily.

"To Mrs. Austen."

They giggled together like impish children, then tilted their glasses jointly.

"What would they say at the faculty tea if they knew that the author of *Circle Symbolism in 'Moby Dick'* was really Ned Bond, author of *Bullets to Bedsheets*?" Darcy asked impudently.

Steven set their champagne glasses down and put his hands on Darcy's rhinestoned hips. "What would they say at the faculty tea if they knew that Mrs. Stevenson Austen, short-fiction author and certified show girl, was wearing a rhinestone G-string under her respectable faculty-wife dress?"

Darcy's hips swiveled naughtily under his palms. "They'd probably say that appearances are everything, but I'd answer that it's what's underneath that counts."

"You are as incorrigible as your inestimable sister, the late great Sirene."

"Oh, Professor," she mocked tenderly, coming incorrigibly closer in his arms. "What big . . . words you have."

Midnight Louie Performs an Epilogue

So there I am, trapped. I tell you, in all confidence, that I do not witness so steamy an occasion since I am near the sauna of the Apollo Health Club when Rats McCafferty takes a distinctly unhealthy dose of hot air, thanks to Georgie the Forgery jamming the exit door with a crowbar.

There is no describing what lengths people will go to in front of helpless witnesses from the animal kingdom.

Luckily, I am a dude about town and see more than a few cats on the Strip about their mating rituals, so I am beyond shocking. And I must say that now and again my thoughts roam to certain exploits of a sensual nature in my own past, including one energetic lady of the Siamese persuasion whose come-hither baby blues made me sing the blues in the night until I am dissuaded by some punks brandishing tire irons.

So I cannot blame the professor and his star pupil for carrying on in the dressing room, being it is so late at night that it is early in the morning and being that they are legitimately hitched in holy matrimony.

There is another lady of my acquaintance, Mehitabel by name—it may be you hear of her—who is a great believer in companionate marriage, which is everything but the ceremony. But she is ahead of her time, and I myself think that there is nothing nicer than rings and vows and a little rice underfoot for the right people.

And Professor Steven Austen and the former Miss

Darcy McGill definitely seem like the right people for each other, although I will have to keep an eye on the career of this Ned Bond. It occurs to me that if Mr. Ned Bond becomes as popular a practitioner of the literary art as, say, Mr. Damon Runyon or Mr. Sidney Sheldon, there might be some money to be made doing what comes naturally—that is, keeping my trap shut.

Not that I am thinking of shaking down a friend, but I um no spring kitten now and have to look out for my old age. I cannot sign Medicare checks with these busted paws—I have engaged in a few back-alley pugilistic exercises in my time, purely in the defense of a lady, naturally.

Of course, if the professor is not willing to lay a few mackerels on my plate to keep my mouth shut, I might manage to pick up some sardines from the Evening Snoop, a journal of a national nature that is always on the hunt for a juicy journalistic morsel or two.

It requires acting anonymously, but fame is not my game—I am a retiring fellow and, as always, impeccably discreet.

IF YOU LOVED CRYSTAL DAYS

...the story doesn't end here! Read CRYSTAL NIGHTS for more adventure and romance at the Crystal Phoenix Hotel starring the coolest character in steamy Las Vegas -- Midnight Louie, and

GET A $1.00 REBATE FROM BANTAM BOOKS!

It's easy. Here's all you do:

Buy a copy of CRYSTAL NIGHTS. In the back you'll find the matching **right** half of the tomcat below. Fill out the originals of **both** halves of the coupon (no photocopies or hand drawn facsimiles will be accepted) and mail to: Bantam Books. Dept. SER, 666 Fifth Avenue, New York, NY 10103. We'll mail you a $1.00 check. That's all there is to it!

Offer open only to residents of the United States, Puerto Rico, Canada, and U.S. Military APO's. Refund limited to one per person, family, or household. Void where prohibited, taxed, or restricted. Allow 6 – 8 weeks for mailing of refund. Offer expires September 30, 1990.

Attached are two halves of the tomcat (the left half from CRYSTAL DAYS and the right half from CRYSTAL NIGHTS). Please mail my $1 check to:

NAME: _____

ADDRESS: _____

CITY/STATE: _____ ZIP: _____

NORA ROBERTS

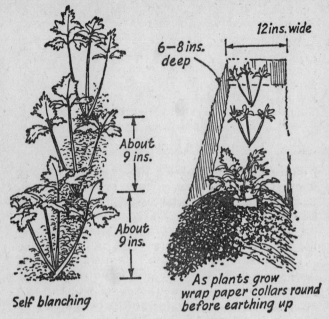

Thoughts about celery

bands, 3 in. wide, round the sticks of celery, to keep them clean.

From June onwards, spray them every three weeks with a combined insecticidal and fungicidal liquid, and it is as well to put slug bait around the plants from July onwards.

SOWING EARLY SEEDS

If you have ordered your seeds, as I always do, in early January, no doubt they have now arrived. I hope you have placed them in an air-tight tin, safe from damp and mice.

There is always the temptation to begin sowing

25

early, but this often results in failures. The only seeds I sow early in the year are those of double-flowering begonias, fibrous-rooted begonias and gloxinias, which are being kept in a warm propagating frame where there is a minimum temperature of 55 deg. F. The next seeds to be sown will be antirrhinum, ageratum and petunia.

Gardeners who have a cool greenhouse, where it is not possible to maintain a minimum temperature of 50 deg. F., will be advised not to sow seeds for a few weeks.

For a seed to germinate and grow successfully it must have moisture, air and reasonably high temperature. Some seeds will, of course, grow at much lower temperatures than others, but most of those we sow indoors or in a greenhouse need temperatures of between 50 and 60 deg. F.

The moisture and air are contained in the soil if we use the correct kind of soil mixture. Ordinary garden soil is not suitable as it will go solid after watering, retain too much moisture and exclude the necessary air. The John Innes seed compost, which I mentioned in my January notes, is ideal.

CHEERING UP THE HOUSE— WINTER COLOUR

February and March are difficult months in which to provide colour for house decoration. Branches of the earliest spring-flowering shrubs, cut and put into water and kept in a warm room for a week or so, will bring a touch of spring to the house.

Twigs of the flowering currant will quickly respond to a little warmth. The sticky buds of the horse chestnut soon begin to unfold and are quite attractive, lasting many weeks in water.

I suggest you plan to grow during the coming spring and summer some everlasting flowers such as helichrysum, acroclinium and statice, so that they can be dried and kept for winter decoration next year.

DIVIDING UP MONTBRETIA AND MICHAELMAS DAISY CLUMPS

I like to lift and divide my Michaelmas daisies every year, and my montbretias every second year. Other herbaceous plants, such as lupins and delphiniums, I transplant, and if necessary divide them at the same time, every third year.

Some people lift and divide hardy border plants in the autumn, but then there is a risk of losing the plants because they will not have sufficient time to get established before winter sets in.

I prefer to lift the clumps and divide them up in February or March, carefully using a garden fork. Use two forks to divide the roots, pushing the forks into the clump with the tines back to back. By pushing the handles together the roots will separate. Divide large clumps into four or six pieces.

Pieces with four or six buds or shoots are large enough to be transplanted, and will provide strong growth with good flowers.

Before transplanting, the soil must be forked over and manure or garden compost mixed into it. Horticultural peat can also be used.

Sprinkle bonemeal over the surface, about a handful per square yard. Firm the soil, by treading it, before planting, and plant each piece firmly. Allow 2 to 3 ft. between plants which grow tall, and 1 to 2 ft. between the shorter ones.

DEALING WITH SLUGS

It is not easy to rid gardens, especially new ones, completely of slugs, but you can reduce their numbers.

Many slugs spend most of their time below soil surface, feeding on roots and underground parts of plants, and therefore are much more difficult to control than those which spend a great deal of their time on the surface.

Slugs move about and feed during damp, mild weather, and then is the best time to put down poison bait.

It is best to put it down in small heaps, and cover them with a piece of slate or tile, to protect the bait from wet weather and prevent it being eaten by birds or domestic animals.

When digging the vegetable garden, flaked naphthalene or other soil fumigant can be mixed

Slug pellets

Dealing with slugs

with the soil. It will not entirely kill the slugs, although it will help to drive them out. To rid the garden of slugs, put down the slug bait at regular intervals of about a week.

MARCH

Planting roses
Pruning a rose bush
Looking after African violets
Pruning shrubs
Growing the best sweet peas
Everlasting flowers
Why not grow your own sweet corn?

PLANTING ROSES

All kinds of roses can be planted between November and early April, whenever the soil is not too wet and sticky. Before planting, firm the soil by treading all over the bed or border, in two different directions, as firm soil is the first step to success. The hole for each rose must be large enough for all the roots to be spread out, so that they are not cramped or turned in towards the stem.

The depth of the hole, of course, depends on the bush itself and the size of the roots. The union between the rose and the briar rootstock should be level with or slightly below ground level when planting is finished. Broken or damaged roots must be cut back, making a clean cut in a slanting direction with a sharp knife or secateurs.

Space the roots out in the hole and work some fine soil between them. Do not put manure or bonemeal in the hole, as they should not come into direct contact with the roots. Half fill the hole with soil, tread it firmly down, then finish filling in the hole, finally making it really firm.

Standard roses need a strong wooden stake to support them, which should be put in before planting. Standard forms of hybrid tea and flori-

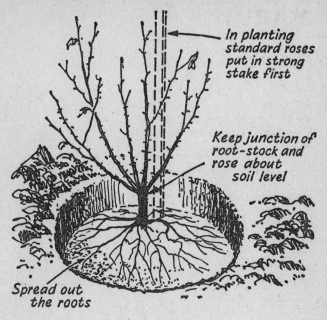

In planting standard roses put in strong stake first

Keep junction of root-stock and rose about soil level

Spread out the roots

Planting roses

bunda roses can be planted between bush roses, and they will add height to the bed or border.

Weeping standards—rambler roses budded on to tall briar stems—are best planted as specimens in the lawn or by the side of a path. Rambler and climbing roses are ideal for training on a house wall, rose arch, individual poles or fences. Many of the well-known hybrid tea roses can be obtained in a climbing form, and perpetual flowering climbing roses give the best value for money.

PRUNING A ROSE BUSH

The success and long life of roses depends almost entirely on pruning. Use a sharp pair of secateurs, because a blunt pair will make a jagged cut and provide entry for disease spores.

Prune hybrid tea and floribunda roses during the latter part of March in the south and midlands, and early April in the northern half of the country.

The pruning of these groups is very similar, the object being to encourage strong young shoots on which flowers will form. All branches of newly-planted hybrid tea roses are cut back to a bud or leaf joint 4 to 10 in. above the soil, and each branch of floribundas to a bud or leaf joint 12 to 15 in. from the ground.

Prune established bushes at the same time. Firstly, cut out to their base all thin, weak shoots. Cut back all branches on hybrid tea bushes which flowered last year to a leaf joint or bud 10 to 12 in. from the older wood, and 12 to 15 in. from the base or older wood on the floribundas.

LOOKING AFTER AFRICAN VIOLETS

If you have an African violet, or, to give it its proper name, saintpaulia, it will need warmth both by day and night, and must be kept in the light, but not direct sunlight.

The best way to keep them is to put a block of wood or some shingle in the bottom of a bowl or container, and pour water in so that the top of the wood or the shingle, when supporting the flower pot, is just above the level of the water. Stand the pot on the wood or shingle, and the plant will benefit from the moisture rising around it.

During the winter, when the plant is making little or no new growth, allow the soil in the pot to get dry, then give it enough lukewarm water to soak the soil right through. Throughout the spring and summer keep the soil just moist.

This plant can be grown from leaves. Break off a fully matured leaf and cut the stem off about an inch below the leaf. Put the stem of the leaf in a mixture of soil, peat and sand in equal parts. Keep the compost moist, and in four to six weeks both roots and new shoots should begin to grow.

PRUNING SHRUBS

Pruning ornamental and flowering shrubs may be regarded as a job for the skilled gardener, but by studying the habits of your shrubs it is a job you can do for yourself.

Many shrubs require little or no pruning, except to keep them tidy. It may prove fatal if you prune the early, purple-flowered daphne, because it does not like being cut.

To prune hydrangeas, except *Hydrangea paniculata*, which is different from the well-known *Hydrangea hortensis*, would mean that you would be cutting away this year's flower buds.

Some other shrubs, if not pruned each year, become straggly and untidy and the flowers are poor.

The general principles are these: shrubs that flower early in the year on the branches produced last year, such as the yellow, winter-flowering *Jasminum nudiflorum*, yellow forsythia and flowering currant, are pruned immediately flowering has finished.

Shrubs that produce their flowers on the current year's growth, such as purple buddleia, hardy fuchsia, blue caryopteris and the creamy *Hydrangea paniculata*, are pruned in late March. All these need drastic pruning, and none more than the buddleia. I cut all its branches back to a bud 12 to 18 in from ground level.

In many parts of the country the branches of hardy fuchsias are killed by frost. I therefore prune them to ground level each spring, and they then flower in profusion from late June onwards.

GROWING THE BEST SWEET PEAS

I gain great satisfaction from growing really good sweet peas which have stems 15 to 18 in. long with four to five blooms on each stem. It is not difficult but does need time and patience, and well-grown sweet peas will flower from June to late August and even into September.

Plants from seed sown outside in late March or early April begin to flower in July. It is possible to buy good sweet pea plants in April or early May from nurserymen and garden stores. Whether you grow your own or buy the plants they will thrive when planted in good, rich soil.

I make a trench which is 18 in deep and wide where I intend to sow or plant them. In the bottom of the trench I put a 3 in. layer of manure, garden compost or peat, to help retain moisture in the soil. Then I add a 6 in. layer of soil, and another layer of manure, peat or compost.

Over this, I sprinkle a large handful of bonemeal for each yard of trench. The trench is then filled in, and some complete organic-based fertilizer sprinkled over the soil, which is then trodden firmly before being sown or planted.

The plants or seed should be spaced 9 in. apart in a double row. Long canes and string will be needed to train each plant up. I grow one single stem from each plant, pinch out the sideshoots from the leaf joints and cut off the tendrils from the ends of the leaves.

The shoots need regular tying with raffia, to the canes or string, or fastening with small rings. The plants like plenty of water in dry weather, and when they begin to flower they need feeding every week with a complete or general organic-based fertilizer.

Colour and varieties are much a matter of personal choice and every year we see new varieties being introduced.

EVERLASTING FLOWERS

From November to April we especially appreciate the value of flowers, when they are scarce and expensive. Like all true gardeners, I dislike the sight of artificial flowers, even in the winter time, and much prefer to have the everlasting ones which we can grow ourselves. The best of all is helichrysum, in which there is a very wide range of colours, such as yellow, purple, rose, peach and red. Acroclinium is also very attractive, with double flowers coloured white, red and pink. Statice can be bought in mixed or separate colours of blue, white, yellow, lavender and pink.

While all three are annuals, and can be sown out of doors in March or April, in all but the coldest districts, I prefer to sow the seed of statice indoors in March and plant the young plants outside at the end of May. They must have a sunny position in good garden soil.

The seeds can be sown in finely raked soil by scattering them very thinly over the surface, and then raking them into the surface soil. The seedlings will have to be thinned to 9 in. apart before they become too crowded.

The secret of having good everlasting flowers is to cut and hang them upside down to dry before the flowers are fully open. I cut helichrysum and acroclinium just as the flower buds are opening, and statice when the colour of the flower is bright.

WHY NOT GROW YOUR OWN SWEET CORN?

Sweet corn has recently become more and more popular, and I can quite understand why. To me it is a real delicacy, a dish I thoroughly enjoy, and so does the whole of my family.

It is not a difficult crop to grow, and during recent years much-improved varieties have been introduced. I grow two sorts, about two dozen plants of each, and they provide more than enough for a family of five.

The varieties are Golden Bantam, which grows 3 to 4 ft. high and produces medium-sized cobs, and Early Golden Market, which grows about 4 ft. high and forms slightly larger cobs. You will find these varieties listed in most seedsmen's catalogues and they are generally available in shops or on the market stalls.

In the midlands and the southern parts of the country the seed can be sown outside in early May. I live in the midlands, in Shrewsbury, and I sow in seed boxes in April and plant out the young plants in late May. To keep a succession over as long a period as possible, I sow the seed outside in early May.

In northern districts it is best to sow the seed in flower pots or boxes in April and keep them in a greenhouse or garden frame until mid-May, when they must be gradually accustomed to outside conditions. Planting outside in these areas may be done in early June.

Sweet corn needs a place where it can get the

full sun. The soil must be dug and some manure, peat or garden compost mixed with it. Before sowing or planting, sprinkle an organic-based fertilizer over the surface of the soil. Allow 2 to 4 oz. per sq. yd. and rake it into the soil surface.

Sow the seed in the place where it is to grow, as it does not transplant well. The plants need to be $1\frac{1}{2}$ ft. apart, with 2 ft. between the rows. The crop should be grown in a block, rather than in single rows, in order to assist pollination.

The first cobs will be ready to gather in early August, and they must be plump and creamy-white when opened. To test their ripeness, press one of the grains with the finger-nail. If the contents spurt out in thick clots, it is ready for gathering.

A final warning word: if you leave the cobs too long before gathering them they may taste mealy.

APRIL

More cut flowers (gladioli and anemone)
April care of the lawn
Sowing time in your vegetable plot (table)
Make room for strawberries
Cyclamen plants last for many years
Replenishing the herb garden
Planting out (salvias, lobelia, geraniums)
Bulbs for a second year

MORE CUT FLOWERS

Every garden should have flowers grown specially
for cutting. One of the best buys is gladioli corms,
and by planting successive batches, some now and
more in a week or two's time, you can have
gladioli for cutting from July to November.

The best varieties for flower decoration are the
primulinus hybrids, miniature and butterfly
gladioli. The spikes of flowers are smaller and
much neater than the large-flowered types. Plant
the corms 6 in apart in rows. I like to make a
trench 4 to 5 in. deep with a spade, and if the soil
is heavy place 1 in of coarse sand along the bottom
of the trench. Then place the gladioli corms on
the sand, 6 in. apart, and rake the soil back over
them.

Anemones are good too, and the dried roots are
plentiful. Plant them in groups between other
plants or in broad rows especially for cutting.
Anemones like a reasonably rich soil and an open
position. Make a trench the width of the spade
and 3 in. deep.

With the soil in the bottom of the trench, mix
some good horticultural peat, composted tree
bark and a light sprinkling of fertilizer. Place

the anemone roots in three rows, one down each side of the trench and one down the centre, allowing 4 to 6 in between the roots in the rows. Cover with 2 in. of soil and put a $\frac{1}{2}$ in. layer of peat and composted tree bark over them. Those planted now should flower from August to October.

APRIL CARE OF THE LAWN

It is several weeks now since the lawn was mown for the first time, and gradually the colour of the grass is improving. From now until the autumn a great deal of grass and plant foods will be taken from the soil through constant mowing. You can only keep a good rich-coloured lawn by feeding and putting back some of the plant foods taken from it.

Choose a showery day and sprinkle a good general or complete fertilizer over the surface of the lawn, allowing a handful for each square yard. Sprinkle it evenly over the grass. Put the fertilizer on the lawn the day after mowing it, otherwise a lot of it may find its way into the grass box of the lawn mower.

The fertilizer will make the grass grow and the weeds as well. Weeds are not a serious problem these days. By using a selective weedkiller they can be destroyed and the grass left unharmed.

To get the best results from selective weedkiller both the grass and weeds must be growing rapidly. Mix the weedkiller with water (according to the maker's instructions) in a watering-can, then spray the lawn with it. Make sure to keep it off those plants growing round the lawn, because it can prove fatal to them.

Almost all weeds will be killed within three

weeks. There are some, however, which are resistant, but it will clear the lawn of daisies, dandelions, plantains and many other troublesome weeds.

One warning about the watering-can into which the weedkiller was placed. It should be thoroughly cleaned out afterwards, as even just the slightest drop will affect the plants.

SOWING TIME IN YOUR VEGETABLE PLOT

April is always a busy month in the vegetable garden. Therefore, I have prepared a chart to guide you with the important business of sowing seed. (See p. 41)

MAKE ROOM FOR STRAWBERRIES

Is it worth while growing strawberries in a small garden? Time and time again I am asked this question, and my answer is always the same, "Yes, if you have the room for about a dozen plants."

First of all, what are the most important requirements for growing good strawberries? A reasonably good soil, an open, sunny position and all the sun they can get. The soil must be dug to the full depth of a spade, and some manure, garden compost or peat should be mixed with it as the digging is done. After digging, bonemeal can be sprinkled over the surface, a large handful for each yard of row will be enough.

The best time to plant is in August or September, when young plants are plentiful, but now is the time to plan where they will be planted. Be sure to buy from a reliable source, and have

VEGETABLES

Seeds to sow	Distance between rows	Distance between plants	Season of use
Peas	3 to 5 ft.	2 to 3 in. in treble rows	June onwards
Beetroot	12 to 15 in.	9 to 12 in.	July onwards
Carrots	12 to 15 in.	9 to 12 in.	,,
Onions	12 to 15 in.	9 to 12 in.	August onwards
Lettuce	12 in.	9 in.	June onwards
Brussels sprouts Cabbage Cauliflower }	12 in. For planting out in May		
Cauliflower (plants)	2 ft.	18 in.	June onwards
Potatoes	2 ft.	18 in.	July onwards
Asparagus	3 ft.	15 in.	Third year after planting
Onions (plants)	15 in.	12 in.	September onwards
Onions (sets)	15 in.	12 in.	,,
Shallots	12 in.	9 in.	August onwards

plants raised from stock which has been certified by the Ministry of Agriculture as being free from virus diseases.

The plants will need spacing out $1\frac{1}{2}$ to 2 ft. apart. Varieties I would recommend are Cambridge Favourite or one of the newer German varieties. When the fruits start to swell, lay clean straw close in under the leaves.

You can also grow strawberries in a barrel in a sunny position. Barrels specially bored with holes for this purpose can be bought. These prepared barrels are $2\frac{1}{2}$ to 3 ft. high, and have 2 in. diameter holes bored round the sides at 9 in. spacings.

The barrel should be filled with good soil, preferably John Innes potting compost. As it is filled, broken bricks should be placed through the centre of the barrel.

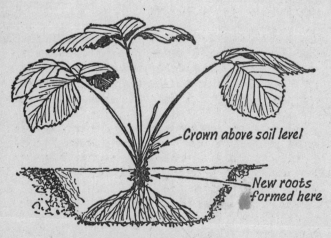

Crown above soil level

New roots formed here

Make room for strawberries

Do not plant strawberry plants so that the crowns are buried; it will cause the plants to rot.

One plant is planted through each hole, and five or six round the top.

A strawberry barrel makes quite an attractive addition to the garden, showing white flowers in May, followed by the bright-red fruits and, later, fine autumn tints of the leaves. The barrel will need lots of water during the spring, summer and autumn.

If you have strawberries in the garden already, now is the time to sprinkle a dessertspoon of a complete organic-based fertilizer on the soil round each plant, and stir it into the surface soil. There are no strawberries, I think, as delicious as those you will gather from your own garden.

CYCLAMEN PLANTS LAST FOR MANY YEARS

It is possible (and I always do) to keep a cyclamen plant for a number of years. When the leaves are turning yellow, and possibly dying off, it need not cause you any concern. It shows that the plant has completed its growth for that season, and is resting.

As the leaves die down, reduce the amount of water until all the leaves have gone, then leave it until the end of June without any water. Keep it on a window-sill until early June, then stand it in the garden, out of the sun.

In early July some of the soil around the corm can be pricked away and replaced with fresh John Innes potting compost No. 1. Give a little water to begin with, and increase it gradually.

From August onwards, add a little fertilizer each week. About the middle of September, replace it on a window-sill, and it should flower from December onwards.

REPLENISHING THE HERB GARDEN

In every garden, whether large of small, there should be a plot set aside for the growing of herbs, preferably near the kitchen door.

Now is the time to replant or replenish the herb garden. Mint is possibly first favourite. After a year or two, however, mint has the tendency to become overcrowded. The old roots can then be replanted at about 9 in. apart. An old, bottomless tin bath, basket or sieve frame sunk into the soil before planting will help to stop the mint roots spreading.

Large clumps of thyme can be lifted and divided up into small portions with roots attached, and these can be planted 12 to 18 in. apart. The bushes of sage tend to get large and untidy too, so pull away young branches with roots on and transplant them to 2 ft. apart.

Chives are useful for flavouring and are very quick to form large clumps. I prefer to lift these and divide them up every spring. The clumps can be separated into pieces with five or six shoots on each and planted 9 in. apart.

Before replanting any of the herbs the soil should be dug, some garden compost or peat mixed in with it and the surface sprinkled with an organic-based fertilizer. It is time now to plant small cloves of garlic and to sow the first parsley. I make a second sowing in late June.

When you harvest the herbs, just before the first flowers on the plant are ready to open,

44

cutting should be done with a sharp knife, preferably on a dry and sunny day and a good length of stalk being taken with them. They should be then tied into bundles and hung up to dry.

PLANTING OUT

Salvias, lobelia and geraniums are half-hardy plants and must be protected until the fear of frost has passed. In the southern half of the country it may be possible to plant outside during the third and fourth week in May, but in the midlands I never consider we are completely safe from frost until the first week in June. In the north it would be very unwise to plant out before early June.

Other plants needing care include French and African marigolds, begonias, fuchsias, nemesia, verbena and ageratum. All these and other plants which have been raised in a greenhouse or somewhere where it is warm must not be planted out straight away, they must be what the gardener calls "gradually hardened off", getting them accustomed to outside conditions.

I transfer them from the greenhouse to the garden frame, giving them a little more ventilation each day until the frame lights are completely left off. It is then a good plan to stand the pots and boxes of plants under a south or west-facing wall, where they will get some protection, for a few days before planting them in the garden.

BULBS FOR A SECOND YEAR

On no account throw away bulbs which have finished flowering, but do not try to grow them in pots or bowls again, because I am afraid you would be very disappointed.

When bulbs are grown in fibre and forced into flower before their normal season it weakens them very considerably, and they need plenty of time to build up again.

The bowls of bulbs which have flowered can be placed outside. Keep them well watered until the leaves turn yellow, and then leave them dry, and the bulbs will then begin their resting period.

When the leaves have completely died the bulbs can be taken from the pots and, if they are dry, be stored away until September when they can be planted out in the garden. You will find that some of them flower the following spring, and nearly all of them the year after. Daffodils and narcissi I find are better for being planted straight out into the garden, leaving them in the clumps with no disturbance to the roots.

My advice is to buy new bulbs each year for pots and bowls, and not run the risk of being disappointed.

MAY

Essential garden tools
Sowing wallflower seed
Sowing for summer—sowing chart for May
Growing flowers in tubs
Planting a hanging basket
Planting time—border bedding plants
The right way to care for cuttings
Window boxes—making and planting
French and runner beans are so easy to grow

ESSENTIAL GARDEN TOOLS

It must be a problem for anyone beginning a
garden to know what tools will be necessary to do
the various gardening jobs. It is, I think, still confusing to those who have been gardening for
some time when they see in shops and catalogues
so many different tools and gadgets.

The most essential tool is a spade, enabling the
soil to be turned over and broken up, and moved
about (should this be necessary), even for mixing
soil, peat and sand for pot plants, and as a means
of edging round beds, borders and the sides of
paths.

A garden fork is next, to fork between plants, dig potatoes, break down large lumps of soil and to move manure or garden compost. From spring onwards a hoe, and I prefer a Dutch hoe, will certainly be needed to keep down weeds and stir the surface soil. A rake is essential when preparing a seed bed, raking up leaves and rubbish and for raking the lawn.

A hedge does, of course, need a pair of shears, and the lawn a mower. Additional items include a trowel and a pair of secateurs. A small sprayer is useful during the spring and summer to keep insect pests and diseases in check.

After using your tools they must be washed clean of any soil, dried, and the metal parts rubbed over with an oily rag to prevent corrosion.

SOWING WALLFLOWER SEED

During May, I often sow the seed of wallflowers. The seed must be sprinkled thinly along shallow drills not more than $\frac{1}{2}$ in. deep. If the soil is dry, water along each row before sowing the seed.

My favourite varieties of wallflowers are Golden Bedder, Orange Bedder and Fire King, because they make dwarf, bushy plants which seem to stand the winter better than the taller ones.

As soon as the seedlings are large enough to be handled, and before they get overcrowded in the rows, they must be planted out separately 9 in. apart so that each one is then able to grow into a sturdy plant before the winter begins.

GARDEN CHART FOR MAY SOWING AND PLANTING		
Flowers to sow	Distance apart	Time of flowering
Sweet Peas for late flowering	6 in. apart in the rows	August onwards
All kinds of hardy annuals and many half-hardy annuals can be sown out of doors this month	Thin seedlings to 9 in. apart	July onwards
Wallflowers	Prick out seedlings 9 in. apart	April to May next year
Sweet Williams	,, ,, ,, ,, ,,	June to July next year
Canterbury Bells	,, ,, ,, ,, ,,	,, ,, ,, ,,
Foxgloves	,, ,, ,, ,, ,,	,, ,, ,, ,,
. . . and to plant		
Chrysanthemums	1½ ft.	August onwards
Sweet Peas	9 in. apart in double rows	July onwards
Gladioli	9 to 12 in. apart, 4 in. deep	,, ,,
Chincherinchees	2 to 4 in. apart in rows 2 to 3 in. deep	September onwards
Geraniums	9 to 12 in. apart	June onwards
Lobelia	6 in. apart	,, ,,
Salvias	12 in. apart	,, ,,
Alyssum	6 in. apart	,, ,,
Dahlias	2 ft. apart	July onwards
All kinds of half-hardy annuals	9 to 12 in. apart	June onwards

Vegetables to sow	Distance apart	Period of use
Peas for succession	3 in. apart in treble rows, 3 ft. between rows	July to September
Runner Beans	9 in. apart in double rows, 4 ft. between the rows	August onwards
French Beans	9 in. apart in double rows, 2 ft. between the rows	,, ,,
Carrots	Thin to 6 in. apart in rows, 12 in. between rows	,, ,,
Beetroot	Thin to 9 in. apart in rows, 12 in. between rows	,, ,,
Lettuce (pinch of seed every fortnight)	Thin to 9 in. apart in rows, 12 in. between rows	June onwards
Endive	Thin to 9 in. apart in rows, 12 in. between rows	September onwards
. . . and to plant		
Marrows (end of month)	3 ft. apart	August to October
Tomatoes (end of month)	1½ ft. apart, 2 ft. between rows	,, ,,
Brussels sprouts	3 ft. apart, 3 ft. between rows	November onwards
Cabbage (Savoy)	2 ft. apart, 2 ft. between rows	,, ,,
Celery	12 in. apart in trench	,, ,,
Onions	9 in. apart, 12 in. between rows	October onwards

GROWING FLOWERS IN TUBS

A bright tub or urn of flowers each side of the front door will add dignity as well as beauty to the house. Both can be bought quite reasonably and can be full of flowers for at least nine months of the year.

The tubs should be at least 18 in. in diameter and 10 to 12 in. deep. Make drainage holes in the bottom of the tub and put in some broken flower pot pieces or pebbles. Use a mixture of soil, peat and sand, to which a fertilizer has been added.

Plant a standard fuchsia in the centre, red or salmon geraniums round the fuchsia, and trailing verbena or lobelia between the geraniums. Other plants to use are salvias, antirrhinums, flowering tobacco plants, marigolds, begonias, pansies and Korean chrysanthemums.

Watering will be necessary every day when the plants are established, and some fertilizer must be added to the water once a week. If you would like a shrub, what could be nicer than a hydrangea, or a camellia with glossy-green leaves and many pink, white or red flowers early in the year?

PLANTING A HANGING BASKET

Plants suitable for a hanging basket, which should be planted in May, are trailing or ivy-leafed geraniums, trailing lobelia, verbena, alyssum, variegated nepeta, petunias and fuchsias.

Choose a basket large enough to hold sufficient soil to grow at least six or eight plants. Line the basket with fresh, green moss to keep in the moisture. Use the John Innes potting compost and press as much as possible into the basket.

Water each plant before putting it in. Some of the trailing plants can be planted through the

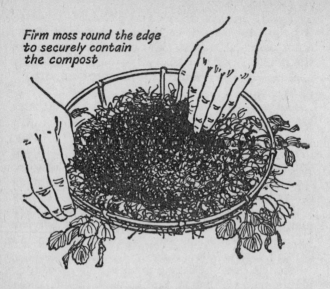

Firm moss round the edge to securely contain the compost

Planting a hanging basket

sides. Do not hang the basket outside until the first week in June, and then choose a sunny position over the front door or in front of the verandah.

Water the basket every day, and about half a gallon of water will not be too much. During the spring and summer add liquid fertilizer, following the maker's instructions, to the water once a week.

PLANTING IN TIME—
BORDER BEDDING PLANTS

During the last weeks of May, most people will have been busy planting out their summer bedding-plants. These will include geraniums, salvias, fuchsias, begonias, asters, antirrhinums, petunias, alyssum and lobelia, which will, if given the proper treatment, flower from late June until September or October.

There is still time to plant them even in June, and this applies in particular to northern districts. Some people make the mistake of planting too early, forgetting that these plants are tender and will not stand up to frost, and we can never say we are safe from frosts until the beginning of June.

The greatest pity of all is perhaps that these plants are being offered for sale from the beginning of April onwards, far too early for planting outside.

There are still plenty of plants available, and if you are buying, choose those with dark green foliage, not necessarily the largest which already have flowers on them.

Fork the soil over in readiness for planting and sprinkle some all-purpose fertilizer over the surface, a handful for each square yard is enough. Next, make the soil firm by treading it all over, and then rake the surface fine and even.

To grow best, each plant must have room in which to grow and develop. Do not waste plants and money by crowding them too close together. Geraniums can be planted 12 to 15 in. apart, salvias and fuchsias 15 to 18 in., petunias, antirrhinums and asters 12 in., and small plants such as alyssum and lobelia 9 to 12 in. apart.

When planting them, be sure to make each hole large enough to hold the plant's roots, and press the soil in really firmly round each one. If the soil is dry, water every plant thoroughly, and then again in two or three days' time.

When they begin to flower, cut off the blooms as they begin to fade. The plants will then give you lasting joy until the frosts begin in the autumn.

THE RIGHT WAY TO
CARE FOR CUTTINGS

I often wonder how many people who take cuttings of their favourite flowering shrubs or plants find that the cuttings die before forming any roots. It is, I am sure, because the plants are not given correct treatment.

If we take a shoot of a plant with leaves on and make it into a cutting we must remember it has no roots with which to take moisture from the soil to replace that which is continually evaporating from the leaves. As the water evaporates from the leaves, the cells of the cutting will become limp, and if this is allowed to continue they will shrivel up completely and die. The first essential is to prevent this loss of moisture. After making the cutting, the stem must be put in a mixture of soil, peat and sand in equal parts, and then moistened.

Cuttings of some plants, i.e. busy lizzie (impatiens), African violet and tradescantia (wandering sailor), will form roots if the stems are kept in water.

Those with their stems in the soil mixture must be kept in a close, humid atmosphere in a propagating frame or polythene bag. The cuttings must have light, but at the same time be shaded from direct sunlight which would increase the evaporation of moisture from the leaves.

A propagating frame need not be an elaborate structure. A box 8 or 9 in. deep is ideal, with an inch of moistened peat on the bottom, and a sheet of glass or polythene over the top to keep the atmosphere inside moist.

If the flower pot or box containing the cuttings is placed in a polythene bag and sealed with a rubber band it will serve the same purpose.

Occasionally, it will be necessary to open the propagating frame for an hour or so to allow some moisture to escape. An excess of moisture could cause a fungus on the stems and leaves of the cuttings which could prove fatal.

Another important point is warmth inside the box or bag to encourage new growth and the formation of the new roots. When the roots have formed, the cuttings must come out into the air and light.

WINDOW BOXES—
MAKING AND PLANTING

Making a window box is not difficult and it need not be expensive. Boards from a large box or crate can be used, or wood can be bought from a timber merchant. These can be screwed or nailed together. It is also possible to buy standard-sized window boxes from garden shops.

The length of the box depends on the width of the window, but it will need to be 9 to 10 in. deep and 8 to 9 in. wide (inside measurements) to hold enough soil to keep the flowers growing.

The box ought to be raised from the window-sill to allow air to circulate underneath. Inside the bottom of the box either leave a space between the boards or drill holes 8 to 9 in. apart to make sure the soil will be well drained. Treat the inside of the box with a wood preservative. Paint the outside of the box in a pastel colour to blend with the flowers and window.

The window box must be firmly fixed to the wall or window frame to make sure it cannot fall or be blown down by strong winds. The box can be fixed with strong screws, and this must be done before it is filled with soil.

Having fixed the box firmly, put a $\frac{1}{2}$ in. layer of broken flower pots, pebbles or cinders in the bottom and cover these with a layer of peat, a $\frac{1}{2}$ in. layer will be enough.

USE THE RIGHT SOIL

Ordinary garden soil is not the best kind to use in a window box, because it will pack together too solidly. The air will be excluded and the soil will get too wet, and then go sour.

It is possible to buy the John Innes potting composts ready mixed, or you can make your own mixture. The formulae for the composts are given in my January notes.

Press the soil firmly in the box, and when completed the top of the soil should be an inch or so below the top of the box to allow room for water.

WHAT TO PLANT

The best of all plants for a sunny window box is the geranium. Or choose the trailing verbena or lobelia, which is ideal for the box front. Petunias are always reliable and the yellow canary creeper is ideal for training up each side of the window.

For a window box not in full sun choose the large, double-flowered tuberous-rooted begonias, the single pink and red fibrous-rooted begonias, petunias and lobelias.

PLANTS FOR WINDOW BOXES

Plant	Flower in	Height in inches	Comments
Geraniums	June to October	18	Appreciate full sun
Geraniums (trailing)	,,	6 to 8	Plant along front of box
Verbena (trailing)	,,	6 to 12	Keep to front of box
Lobelia (trailing)	June to September	4 to 6	Will completely cover the front of the box
Petunias	June to October	6 to 9	Mostly trailing. Most reliable plants
Canary creeper	July to October	36 to 60	Trail round the window
Ageratum	June to September	4 to 6	Dwarf and compact plants
Alyssum	,,	3 to 4	For the front of the box
Salvia	June to October	15 to 18	Form bushy plants
Fuchsias	May to October	6 to 18	Both upright growing and trailing varieties
Begonias	June to October	9 to 15	Prefer a shady window-sill

REGULAR CARE

After planting the flowers, soak the soil in the box thoroughly with water. Give it enough to soak all the soil in the box, and then do not water again until the soil feels dry, and then soak it again.

For the first few waterings you need to have a rose on the spout of the can to prevent the water making holes in the surface of the compost. As soon as the plants begin to grow freely from about mid-June onwards, they will need more water and may have to be watered every day.

From the end of June onwards add some soluble fertilizer to the water. Those plants trained round the window frame will need support. I have made a chart of the many different plants which are excellent for use in window boxes.

FRENCH AND RUNNER BEANS ARE SO EASY TO GROW

French and runner beans are among the easiest vegetables to grow, and few crops will give a better return for the space they occupy. At one time, my wife and I spent hours bottling and preserving both fruit and vegetables each year, but we have now saved ourselves an enormous amount of time by deep freezing, and the most valuable vegetables for the deep freeze are French and runner beans. In any case, they are a favourite of mine.

There are only a few parts of the country where it is safe to sow the seed outside before the middle of May. I usually sow runner beans about the 15th of May. Runner beans are best when given support of some kind which they can twist themselves round and climb. French beans need no support.

Recently, for the runner beans, I tried some large-mesh string netting, and it was most successful. Bean sticks are not easy to obtain in many areas and 8 to 10 ft. long canes are expensive to buy.

Runner beans can be trained up strings supported between two wires, one at ground level and another 8 ft. high. After digging the soil to the depth of a spade and mixing in some manure, compost or peat, I sprinkle over the surface a large handful of a general or complete fertilizer for each yard of the row. I then make a trench the width of the spade and $1\frac{1}{2}$ in deep.

The beans, both of French and runner, are spaced 9 in. apart along each side of the trench, alternating in the rows, and covered over with soil. Apart from putting up the sticks, string or netting, watering in dry weather, and keeping free from weeds, they need no other attention.

I look forward to French beans in July, and even more to runner beans from August until the frosts begin in the autumn.

JUNE

ABOUT TOMATOES

When growing tomatoes, whether outdoor or in the greenhouse, always aim at well-balanced growth.

From time to time stir the soil around the plants to allow air and warmth to penetrate into the soil. Spread some garden compost or horticultural peat on the soil round the plants to prevent moisture evaporating from the soil surface. If the weather is hot and dry, give them a good watering twice a week.

As the sideshoots form in the leaf joints, rub them out while they are small. When the fruits on the first truss are about the size of marbles you can begin to feed the plants with some fertilizer, which should have a high potash content.

The plants can be given this feed once a fortnight to begin with and then once a week as more fruits begin to develop on the second, third and fourth trusses. When you can see the fourth truss of flowers forming on outdoor tomatoes, pinch out the young centre tip of growth.

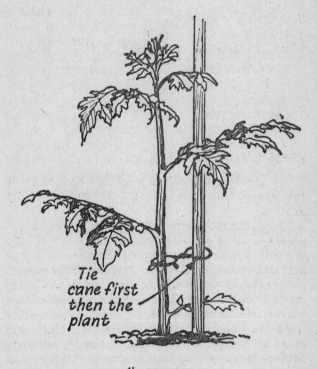

Tie cane first then the plant

About tomatoes

Tomato plants must be securely tied to a stake, to prevent the stem from snapping.

SUMMER CARE OF AZALEAS

Azaleas which were flowered indoors in pots during last winter should be placed outside during the summer. However, do not plant it, but leave it in its pot. Place it where the plant will be in partial shade.

The usual azalea used for winter flowering in pots is *Azalea indica*, which is not hardy to frosts, and must therefore be brought inside again before the frosts during the autumn.

The plant must be watered regularly during the time it is outside as the soil in the pot will dry very quickly in hot weather.

The important point to remember is that azaleas form their buds during the late summer and autumn, and from these buds the flowers during the winter. Whether or not it flowers next winter will depend on the treatment it is given now, during the summer and autumn.

WHEN TO WATER

It is impossible to water everything in the garden thoroughly enough during the summer to be of real value, and it is therefore far better to select plants which will benefit most from being watered. Plants to water are those which were planted during the autumn, winter or early spring, because they will not have the amount of root that the better established plants possess.

If patches of the lawn begin to brown, water with a teaspoon of household detergent dissolved in two gallons of water. Follow with a soaking with clear water.

Dahlias, chrysanthemums, sweet peas, runner beans, celery, outdoor tomatoes and lettuce like plenty of water. The day after watering these plants, stir the soil with a hoe, as this will help to keep the moisture in the soil.

JUNE ROSES

There are a few points to remember if our roses are going to be at their best throughout the summer and well into the autumn.

Firstly, we must be sure to keep the bushes, as well as the standard, climbing and rambler roses, free from pests and diseases. All the roses must be sprayed with an insecticide as well as fungicidal spray. If we use an insecticide containing B.H.C. (benzene hexachloride), derris or pirimiphos-methyl we can add a fungicide to it, to make a combined spray. It is best to spray the rose bushes every two or three weeks for the next month or two.

Even though I sprinkled some all-purpose fertilizer round my roses in March I am now sprinkling a dessertspoonful round each one again to encourage strong and healthy growth. When putting the fertilizer on, make sure that you keep it away from the stems and leaves. When you hoe the soil to control the weeds, the fertilizer will then be stirred into the surface soil.

The standard roses must have a strong support, and the stem must be securely tied to it, or the weight of flowers and leaves may break the main stem, particularly if we get strong winds.

As the new shoots grow from the base of the rambler roses, tie them carefully to the trellis or archway. Far too often, people cut these shoots off, mistaking them for sucker growths. These young shoots will be next year's flowering branches.

The best roses for arches and tall pillars include Parade (pink), Golden Showers, Royal Gold, Casino (yellow), Autumn Sunlight (orange), Danse de Feu (red), Guinée (crimson), Zéphirine Drouhin (pink) and other perpetual flowering varieties.

SOW SPRING SEEDS NOW

During June is is necessary to think about sowing seeds which will flower next year, although with the summer barely started it may seem untimely to think about this job, but unless we do, our gardens will certainly not be as colourful as we would wish them to be. Seeds sown now will produce plants which will be large enough to withstand the winter weather, however severe it may be.

The seeds to sow this month include forget-me-nots, foxgloves, sweet williams, Canterbury bells, daisies and winter-flowering pansies. This may sound a tall order, but a packet of each in mixed colours will provide enough plants for the average garden.

Choose a side border or a piece of land at one end of the vegetable garden and sow the seed in shallow drills 9 in. apart and not more than $\frac{1}{2}$ in. deep. If the soil is very dry, then, as recommended when sowing wallflowers during May, water along the drills before sowing the seed. This will help them to germinate more quickly. Sprinkle the seed very thinly along the drills, put a label at one end of each row and cover the seeds lightly.

To prevent sparrows from disturbing the seed or pecking off the seedlings when they come up, strand some black cotton backwards and forwards over the seed bed. Use pieces of stick to keep the cotton 6 to 8 in. above the soil.

When the seedlings are large enough to be handled they must be transplanted; this is usually towards the end of July. At that time of year there is often a vacant part of the vegetable garden that can be forked over and prepared for these young plants. Plant them 9 in. apart so that each one will have room to develop into a sturdy plant.

STARTING A COMPOST HEAP

From now on in the garden there will be dead flowers and leaves, the remains of crops, lawn mowings, hedge trimmings, etc., all of which are valuable material which on no account must be wasted. They can be made into a compost heap and turned into valuable material to put back into the garden.

A compost heap need not be, in fact it should not be, an untidy rubbish heap which will spoil the appearance of the garden. A properly made compost heap will not be a source of unpleasant odours either.

As the waste material is gathered together, place it in a tidy heap. When it reaches a reasonable size it is time to make a compost heap. The base of the heap should be about 4 ft. long by 3 ft. wide.

Begin by placing a 9 in. deep layer of this waste material on the bottom. Cover this with 1 in. soil, another 9 in. layer of vegetable material, a 1 in. layer of soil, and so on.

After about two months, turn the heap, at the same time mixing all the materials together, and in a further few weeks you will have some valuable compost to put into the soil.

Sulphate of ammonia which is sprinkled over each layer as the heap is made will result in the compost being rich in nitrogen, an essential plant food.

The majority of gardens, and particularly those in the towns, are lacking in humus. Compost is a valuable source of humus, and if peat is used as well the soil will be brought back into a good state of fertility.

When the compost is sufficiently decayed, when it should be the colour of dark earth, it can be dug into the soil.

Compost can be used on top of the soil to form what the experienced gardener calls a mulch. A layer an inch or so deep around shrubs such as rhododendrons and azaleas and between border plants will help to retain moisture in the soil during a dry spell. Roses will also benefit from a layer of compost placed around them.

WHEN YOU GO AWAY ON HOLIDAY

Many people treasure their house plants and window boxes, and are therefore very worried when they go away for a holiday, not knowing how to leave their plants.

One good way is to put a piece of lamp-wick or wool from a jar of water to each plant, pushing the wick or wool into the soil so that the water travels along it from the jar.

Make sure the jar is slightly higher than the plant container. This will ensure the plants will get just enough water to keep them alive if they are placed in a cool, light place; not where the hot sun will shine on them.

I would not recommend standing the pots in a bowl of water, because it will often do more harm than good.

It is now possible to get absorbent sticks to put through the drainage holes in the base of the flower pots and stand them over a reservoir of water.

JULY

MAGNOLIA CUTTINGS

If you have a magnolia in your garden, and its branches droop down to the soil level, it is possible to fasten them down into the soil so that they will form roots, and in time become a new plant. Before fastening down the branch with a wire or wooden peg, cut it halfway through, covering this part with a mixture of soil, peat and sand, and lay a stone over the top.

It should produce roots, and in the autumn of the following year it can be transplanted to another position.

HOW TO APPLY FERTILIZERS

I often think that more money is wasted and more plants are killed every year by the careless use of fertilizers than by any other means.

The golden rule when using fertilizers is little and often. Fertilizers must never come into direct contact with stems or leaves, and they must never be given to a plant, whether in the garden or in a flower pot, when the soil is dry. If it is dry, water the soil thoroughly first. If a powdered fertilizer is used water it into the soil after sprinkling it round the plants.

A plant in a flower pot should never be given fertilizer until the roots can be seen growing through the drainage hole at the bottom, or until you are sure the soil in the pot is well filled with roots. Once a fortnight, as a general rule, is often enough to give fertilizer to plants.

KEEPING YOUR GRASS GREEN

During the hot summer months it is well worth the effort to strive to keep a perfect lawn. A good lawn will not only show the garden off to its best advantage, but the house as well.

From March onwards I mow my lawn every week. In doing so, a great deal of nourishment is taken away from it every week, and the grass cannot be expected to keep on looking healthy through the summer unless something is put back. By this I mean feeding the lawn with a good fertilizer.

In long spells of dry weather, patches of the lawn will turn brown unless watered as well as fed. If the lawn does become very dry it is then very difficult for the water to soak through the surface soil. Therefore, add a little detergent to the water, and lightly water over the lawn first. Follow this by adding more water and it will then soak in without any difficulty.

After watering, sprinkle some good general fertilizer over the surface. Allow a handful for approximately every square yard, and spread it evenly over the surface.

If you choose a showery day there is no necessity to water the fertilizer into the lawn. Should, however, the weather be very dry, water the lawn thoroughly, otherwise the fertilizer may scorch the grass, and this can cause brown patches.

HOW TO GROW THE BEST-EVER MARROWS

Many gardeners pride themselves on growing an extra-large marrow, one which will almost fill their wheelbarrow. It is only the healthy and well-grown plant which will produce such a large marrow, and much depends on the amount of moisture the plant is able to get, together with plant foods.

At one time we used to grow marrows on top of a manure heap, but we are not able to get such large quantities of manure these days.

Put a 2 to 3 in. layer of grass mowings round each marrow plant. Peat may also be used to keep the moisture in the soil. In addition to this, water the plant at least once a week, giving enough water to get right down to the roots.

An hour or so after watering, mix some good general fertilizer with water and give this to each plant. There are both soluble and liquid fertilizers and these must be used according to the maker's instructions. In dry weather spray the leaves over daily with water.

On each plant there will be both male and female flowers. The female flowers are those with the small marrow immediately behind the flower. At midday transfer the pollen from the male flowers, using a camel-hair brush to do the job. Each female flower must be pollinated. As soon as the flowers are pollinated, watering and feeding will help the marrow to develop quickly.

I can remember, when I was at school, growing a very large marrow by feeding it with a sugar solution. A jam-jar of sweetened water was placed near the stem of the marrow and a piece of absorbent wool or thin lamp-wick was threaded through the stem immediately behind the marrow. The other end was placed in the sugar solution so that the water and sugar mixture travelled along the wool or wick and into the marrow stem.

PRUNING RAMBLER ROSES

Rambling roses need to be pruned as soon as flowering is finished. The idea is to encourage as much young growth as possible from the base.

All long branches which have flowered can be cut off a few inches above the ground, and the young, current year's growth trained in on a wall or arch.

SOFT FRUIT FROM THE GARDEN

The season of soft fruit is now, during July, well under way; raspberries are at their best and early black currants are ready for gathering. I have two rows of raspberries, one of the variety Malling Promise, which produces large berries and is early to ripen. The other is Malling Jewel, ripening later and keeping a succession for a few more weeks.

The later fruits of raspberries are often affected with the grub of the raspberry beetle, a small white grub which eats its way into the fruit at a point close to the fruit stalk.

The raspberry beetle lays its eggs in the open flowers. The grubs hatch out and eat their way into the ripening fruits. To prevent this, make one good gathering, picking all the fruit which is changing colour, and spray the canes with an insecticide. Spray the canes in the evening, so as not to cause any harm to bees.

The young canes which will bear next year's growth are growing fast and at this time of the year have a tendency to hide many of the fruits. The canes can be thinned now, leaving the strongest and best.

The canes which are left should be spaced out so that they are 9 to 10 in. apart. All the other canes are cut out to ground level. This will allow the light to penetrate to the fruits, and also ripen off the canes.

Strawberries are now producing runners on which are the young plants. Select the best four to six healthy young plants at the ends of these runners and pin them into the soil, using a piece of wire the shape of a hair-pin.

These little plants will root into the soil, and can be transplanted later on to make a new strawberry plant in August. It is best to plant a few young plants each year. Be sure to use only healthy plants, and they will bear their first fruits the following year.

GROWING CARNATIONS

Border or outdoor flowering carnations need, most of all, a well-drained soil in a nice open position. A heavy clay soil can be improved by mixing with it some mortar rubble and ground limestone.

Manure, garden compost or peat will also help to make any reasonable soil suitable for the plants. A good all-purpose fertilizer containing nitrogen, potash and phosphate will encourage strong and healthy plants.

One of the most serious pests of carnations is aphids, or greenfly as they are also known, which, if not controlled in good time, cripple both the leaves and flower buds. The plants should be sprayed at intervals of three to four weeks with a spray containing either pirimiphos-methyl or B.H.C.

As the flower buds develop there will be not only the one large bud at the tip of each shoot but sideshoots forming round them as well. To grow really fine blooms, these sideshoots must be pinched out when still quite small.

TAKING CUTTINGS

At this time of the year, during July, many of the small alpine and rock plants are easily grown from cuttings. They will form new roots in a matter of a few weeks. Geranium cuttings root very easily, and during the next few weeks we can take cuttings of the flowering ornamental shrubs in the garden. House plants, too, can have cuttings taken from them now.

A box 8 to 9 in. deep can be made into a suitable frame for all the cuttings from outdoor plants. Place the box in a shaded part of the garden and put inside it a 3 in. layer of a mixture of soil, peat and sand in equal parts. Cover the box with a sheet of glass.

To take the cuttings, clean off a few of the bottom leaves, and cut straight through the stem with a sharp knife immediately below a leaf joint. Put the cuttings into the soil, in the box, with half their length of stem below the soil, and press each one in firmly.

AUGUST

Attacking the weeds
Insecticides, fungicides and fertilizers
Maturing tomatoes
Apricot stones
Plant now for the winter
Good climbing plants
Making the most of indoor plants

ATTACKING THE WEEDS

Most gardeners spend at least sixty per cent of their time weeding in one way or another—a job nobody likes.

Recently a chemical called Paraquat has been introduced to the gardening market. This has done much to help agriculture in this country—and, in fact, in all parts of the world. We gardeners can now use this wonder chemical or weedkiller, and I find it reduces the time I have previously spent with a hoe or hand weeding to less than twenty-five per cent of the time normally spent. The chemical, which is in granular form, is mixed with water and sprayed on to the weeds; as soon as it touches the soil it becomes inactive and there is no fear of a build up in the soil. Like all other chemicals this must be used with care and be stored out of the reach of children.

The action of this chemical is to interrupt the normal life processes within the plant; it kills the green leaves and stems in twenty-four to thirty-six hours. It must not, of course, be sprayed on to the green parts of plants or it will kill them too, but it cannot travel through soil so therefore will do no harm to the roots.

There are special sprinkler bars which fix on to the spout of a watering-can for applying the wonder weedkiller and these make its use economical. It can be applied through the rose of a watering-can, but there is more danger of splashing it on to the plants and it is more extravagant. It will do no harm if splashed on to brown stems or mature bark of hedge plants, trees or roses, so can therefore be sprayed right up to the stems of trees and shrubs. It is ideal for paths because if sudden rain should wash it into adjoining beds and borders it will do no harm. The weeds under hedges are easily controlled and, if used with care, so are those round fruit trees and bushes, flowering trees and shrubs, and between other plants.

Perennial weeds with persistent root systems, however, will not be killed with one application. Several sprayings during the course of a season will be necessary. But by constant use such weeds as ground elder, bind weed, couch grass and others will be killed. Planting and seed sowing can be done almost immediately after its use. It has helped me very considerably in my garden and millions of other gardeners will, I am sure, benefit from its use in their gardens.

INSECTICIDES, FUNGICIDES AND FERTILIZERS

To go into a garden shop or store these days and look at the many products on show must, to the average gardener, be most confusing. There are so many different kinds of insecticides, fungicides, fertilizers, and both soluble and liquid plant foods on the market.

I often wonder how many people come out of the shop with the correct product for the particular job they have to do. What the majority of us actually need is an insecticide that will kill most of the insect pests which attack our plants from time to time.

Controlling these pests is an important part of the gardener's task, and I consider one should buy an insecticide which is safe to use and harmless to domestic pets.

An insecticide which contains B.H.C. or pirimiphos-methyl is the best for general purposes, but there are certain plants on which this chemical, like many others, must not be used. Hydrangeas in particular are susceptible to damage from a spray such as this, as are black currants, cucumbers and marrows. For these we must use a derris spray.

If we therefore have these chemicals I have mentioned ready for use when they are needed we should be able to control most pests.

To control mildew on plants and black spot on roses, a fungicide can be bought which can be added to these to make a combined insecticide and fungicidal spray.

With so many fertilizers in the shops, selecting the right one can become confusing, too. There are three essential plant foods, namely nitrogen, potash and phosphate. If we buy a good all-purpose fertilizer, it will contain a fair percentage of these and will do for all plants, fruit, flowers and vegetables, and for the lawn as well.

For pot plants a liquid, or soluble fertilizer which can be added to the water is needed.

MATURING TOMATOES

The outdoor tomato is a plant which is very dependent on our English weather. It is, of course, one which enjoys as much sunshine as it is able to get. There is much we can do to help the crop along and to ensure that it will reach maturity.

By growing the plants in large pots it is possible to move them around to make the most of the sun. As the summer season is so short we cannot expect the plants to carry to maturity more than four trusses (branches of fruit). The tip of each plant must be pinched out at one leaf above where the fourth truss of fruit has formed.

Sideshoots which grow in the leaf joints must be pinched out when they are about an inch or so long. By bending them to one side they will break off easily and not do any damage to the stem.

Watering must be done regularly whenever the soil is dry, giving enough to soak down to the roots. If watering is done irregularly it will result in many of the tomatoes splitting.

Feeding is essential, too, and potash gives the fruits quality as well as hastening their ripening. I find it best to use a soluble fertilizer with a high potash content. Mix this with water and give it to the plants once a week.

Potato blight usually makes its appearance in late June, July and August and the tomato being related to the potato also can be affected by the blight. This will cause brown patches on the fruits, and those affected will not keep when stored.

As a precaution against this disease, I spray my outdoor tomatoes with a colloidal copper fungicide every two weeks from early July.

APRICOT STONES—
PLANT OUT NOW

If you planted apricot stones during the spring they will now, during August, be about 6 in. high, and can be planted out in the garden. Before doing so, however, water the pots thoroughly so that the plants will not wilt.

You can train apricot trees against a wall. If you do, the sideshoots should be pruned this year, and cut back the main shoot by half its length next January.

This will cause many shoots to grow, and you can then select four and train them in a fan shape along the wall. The following year these four shoots should be allowed to produce two shoots each. You will then have an apricot tree with eight main branches within a fairly short space of time.

PLANT NOW FOR
THE WINTER

In the vegetable garden many of the crops we sowed earlier in the year have now reached maturity, and some have already been cleared from the ground. It would be a waste of good ground and valuable plant foods to leave these parts of the garden vacant until next year.

Spring cabbage is one of our most valuable vegetables, coming as it does at a time when many are scarce and expensive. The seeds for spring cabbage can be sown during August. Flowers of Spring and Harbinger are two good varieties.

Sow the seed at one side or end of the garden, so that the young plants can be transplanted to 18 in. apart later next month. Make shallow drills, no more than $\frac{1}{2}$ in. deep, and if the soil is dry, water along the drills before sowing the seed thinly. In about a week the seedlings will be showing above the soil.

From where the early potatoes and early peas have been cleared, sow onions for pulling in the spring. Varieties to sow now include Autumn Queen, Ailsa Craig, Flagon and A.1.

Lettuce, when ready for eating in April and May, is valuable too, and we can also now sow such varieties as Imperial or Arctic. These are quite hardy and will survive the winter in most parts of the country.

It is nice to have flowers for cutting in the spring and early summer, and for this you need to sow the seeds of some hardy annuals now. Among the best for cutting are sweet peas, calendula (pot marigold), cornflowers, larkspur and godetia. Pansies can also be sown. In exposed areas these will be safer if it is possible to protect them with cloches during the severest winter weather.

GOOD CLIMBING PLANTS

From the spring onwards I value the climbing and trailing plants, especially those that flower.

On the wall of my house which faces south I have a glorious deep purple *Clematis jackmanii*. Another lovely clematis is Gipsy Queen, which produces its large, rich blue flowers continuously from May onwards.

I prune all these large-flowered hybrid clematises back to within 3 or 4 ft. of the ground every March, and the new growth is now 15 ft. or more high.

When planting clematis there are one or two important points to bear in mind. Firstly, always buy the plants in flower pots. Plant them any

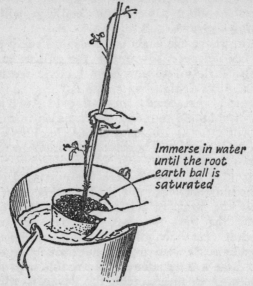

Immerse in water until the root earth ball is saturated

All pot-grown plants benefit by being soaked in water before they are planted.

time between March and September. Mix some ground limestone or old mortar rubble as well as peat with the soil before planting. Clematis love to have their roots under the shade of other shrubs and plants. Should this be impossible, place a large flat stone over the roots.

It is not always necessary to train a clematis up a wall, fence or trellis. It can be planted to train over a terrace wall or a porch. Another good climbing or trailing plant is the beautifully scented honeysuckle. This is a plant which should be purchased in a flower pot too. Virginia creeper is good for covering a large expanse of wall, and the fiery-red leaves look so lovely in the autumn.

Two other good shrubs for a position such as this are the yellow winter-flowering jasminum, and the firethorn (pyracantha) which has white flowers in May and June and bright orange-scarlet berries in autumn and winter.

MAKING THE MOST OF INDOOR PLANTS

The most popular room plants include ivies (green and variegated), tradescantia (wandering sailor), chlorophytum (spider plant), ficus (rubber plant), sansevieria (mother-in-law's tongue), philodendron, rhoicissus (indoor vine) and peperomia. All of them are reasonably easy to grow. There are, however, three good rules when keeping indoor plants.

(1)
Keep all indoor plants in a light position. Variegated plants need more light than those with entirely green foliage. None of them, however, needs direct sunlight.

(2)
Water whenever the soil in the pot is dry, soaking the soil right through. During the spring and summer, add fertilizers to the water once a fortnight.

(3)
Do not leave them near to a window on a cold, frosty night, and at all times keep them out of cold draughts.

Indoor plants need light and careful attention to keep them healthy and attractive. Dust will collect on the leaves and this alone can rob them of a lot of light. Sponge the leaves occasionally with a soft sponge or cloth. A cup of water with the chill taken off and half a teaspoonful of milk added will give the leaves an attractive gloss.

Water the plants whenever the soil is dry,

soaking it right through. Then leave until the soil is dry again. Never allow the pots to stand with their bases in water, and never give the plants fertilizers when the soil in the pot is dry. Water first and then give the fertilizers in solution an hour or so afterwards. Feeding with fertilizers is only necessary during the spring, summer and early autumn.

Many of the indoor plants are readily increased by means of cuttings or offshoots. Young tips of the ivy, philodendron and tradescantia taken off in spring or summer and put into a mixture of soil, peat and sand in equal parts will soon form roots. Tradescantia will root if the cuttings are put into water.

Sansevierias can be increased by dividing the plants in the spring. Chlorophytums will form young plants with roots on the ends of the flower stems. These can be taken off and put into small flower pots.

Try to provide the same conditions for cyclamen as they had when they were in the greenhouse. Place some pebbles in the bottom of an ornamental bowl. Then pour in some water, until it is just below the top of the pebbles.

Stand the cyclamen on the shingle and the moisture rising up round the plant will help to overcome the dry atmosphere of the living-room. Keep it as near to the window as possible, where it can get the direct daylight every day, and keep it in a warm room. See that it is not put in a cold draught.

As the flowers fade, pull them right out from the corm—never cut them off. This also applies to leaves when they begin to turn yellow and die. Whenever the soil in the pot feels dry, give it a good soaking, so that the water soaks right through. Do not give any more water until the soil dries out again.

Water it in the mornings, not in the late evening. When it has finished flowering, usually in February or March, continue giving it the same conditions, and water it regularly until all the leaves begin to die.

From then on, leave the soil completely dry until the end of June or early July, during which time the corm is resting. Begin to water the corm again in early July to start it into growth. So long as the plant has plenty of light, give it water when it needs it, keeping moisture round it the whole time. If it is kept in the warm during the autumn and winter it should flower again from December onwards.

From August to October add a little fertilizer to the water once a fortnight.

SEPTEMBER

HOW TO GROW A PINEAPPLE

Each fresh pineapple we buy has a green top which can be grown into a plant. Cut off the top, leaving a small portion of the top of the fruit attached. Plant it in a flower pot which is about 4 in. in diameter, filled with a mixture of equal parts soil, peat and sand mixed together.

The base of the pineapple top should be about 1 in below the surface of the compost. Give enough water to soak the mixture right through, and keep it in a light window in the warmest room in the house.

Water it again only when the soil in the pot feels really dry. When its roots have filled the pot, transfer it to a larger flower pot. This makes an attractive house plant.

MAKING A NEW LAWN

Round every city and town, and in villages, new houses are springing up. With these houses there are gardens, in which I hope the occupiers will take pride. One of their first considerations will be a lawn, and this is the time of year to make one.

Whether to make the lawn with turves or grass seed is a question continually being asked. The time for laying turf is between November and March. It will cost more than twice as much as compared with making a lawn by sowing seeds. Best-quality turf is very expensive, and with an inferior quality you have to accept weeds, coarse grasses and all that goes with it, and the lawn will never be satisfactory. The preparation for turfing must be the same as for when seed sowing, so why go to all the extra expense? Grass seed can be sown during September and into early October and the lawn will be established before the winter. Another good time for sowing grass seed is from early April to the end of May.

The first important task is to fork out the roots of any perennial weeds. Annual weeds such as chickweed and groundsel will, no doubt, come up with the grass, but these are not serious. When mowing begins they will soon go, or a selective weedkiller can be used to quickly destroy them.

After forking, break the soil down reasonably fine and tread it all over to make it really firm; this will help to break down the lumps of soil, too. Sprinkle over the area of the lawn an organic-based, all-purpose fertilizer, a large handful for each square yard. Next, rake the surface as evenly as possible and it will be ready for sowing.

Buy the best lawn-grass seed, one not containing rye and other coarse grasses, and allow 1 to $1\frac{1}{2}$ oz. per sq. yd. Sprinkle the seed evenly over the surface and lightly rake it in. Nothing more need be done. The birds will take some of the seed but will leave plenty to make a good lawn.

By early next year the lawn will be ready for mowing, and it should be one that will set off not only the garden and flowers but the house as well.

TAKE GERANIUM CUTTINGS NOW

The first severe frost of the autumn will blacken the leaves and stems of geraniums, and those we want to save for next year must be brought inside in good time. The best way is, I consider, to take cuttings now, because rooted cuttings will take up much less room than plants during the winter. There is no need to strip all the shoots off the

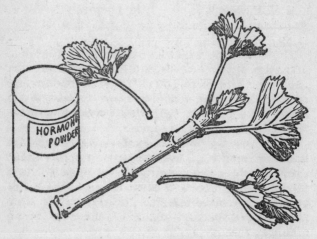

Take geranium cuttings now
Many cuttings will root quickly if their bases are dipped into a hormone rooting powder.

plant, a shoot from here and there will hardly be missed.

Cut the shoots off 6 in. long, and to make the cuttings, cut off the bottom two or three leaves close to the stem and cut off any flower or bud. With a sharp knife, cut straight across just below the bottom leaf joint, and the cuttings are then ready to go into the soil. The best compost for rooting geranium cuttings is a mixture of equal parts soil, peat and coarse sand.

Fill a box 3 to 4 in. deep with the compost, pressing it in moderately firmly. With a pencil, make the holes for the cuttings, 3 in. apart and 2 to 3 in. deep, and put a cutting into each hole. Press the soil round them firmly. Give the box enough water to soak the soil right through, and then stand it under a south- or west-facing wall until early October, then bring it inside.

THE POCKET-HANDKERCHIEF GARDEN

The very small garden is often a problem, because the choice of plants must be limited to make the best use of the space available and yet have the garden colourful and interesting throughout most of the year.

Whatever the size of the garden, it is usually not large enough for the keen gardener who never has enough space for all he would like to grow. First of all, it is important to make full use of any wall or fence for climbing and trailing plants, such as winter-flowering jasmine, climbing roses, clematis or honeysuckle.

Raised beds, made with stones, widen the scope for planting, particularly if places are left between the stones for trailing plants such as aubretia, alpine phlox, rock roses, houseleeks and campanulas.

Only the smallest shrubs must be chosen, and these will give the garden an established appearance. For early spring flowering choose the purple *Daphne mezereum*. *Senecio greyii*, with evergreen, silvery foliage and yellow flowers in the summer, is also very attractive.

Lavender is always welcome and the Munstead variety is dwarf and of a neat habit. *Genista tinctoria plena* has a spreading habit and grows no more than 9 in. high. It is covered in double yellow flowers from June onwards.

Daffodils and narcissi, as well as grape hyacinths and chionodoxas, can be planted between other plants and left in the soil.

Hardy border plants I would choose for a small garden include the daisy-like mauve, pink and blue erigeron, red and pink heuchera, *Sedum spectabile* and dianthus. Small floribunda roses suitable for the very tiny garden are Fashion, Goldilocks, Marlena and Highlight, and, of course, there are the beautiful little miniature roses. A complete small garden can be made with the miniature roses.

A crazy-paving path provides a place for flowering thyme, saxifrage and mossy arenaria between the stones. Tubs and vases widen the scope of a small garden even more. They can be planted with geraniums and lobelia in summer. Hydrangeas and bay trees can also be grown in tubs, as can camellias and rhododendrons.

SAFELY STORED

A good gardener will, during the whole year and especially during the autumn, provide for the winter by storing away those fruits and vegetables which he knows will keep well into the winter, or even until the spring.

Soon now, the first apples and pears will be ready for gathering. Only the perfectly sound fruits must be stored away. Any with blemishes should not be stored. Also, any fruits which are stored before they are properly mature will not have good keeping qualities. They are best left on the tree for a few days longer, rather than gathered a day too soon.

If fruits part readily from the branches, when given a slight upward lift, it can be taken that they are fit for gathering. Be sure to handle each one carefully.

Properly ripened onions will keep in a cool, airy place until the spring. The bulbs must be lifted from the soil and laid out in the sun to complete their ripening.

As the tops of potatoes turn yellow and die the tubers can be lifted, dried and stored in a dark, frostproof place. Before we get too much wet weather, lift the carrots, otherwise the roots may begin to split. Store these in boxes in reasonably dry sand or soil.

Beetroot, like carrots, will, if properly stored, keep through most of the winter. Lift these carefully, twist off the tops so as not to cause the roots to bleed and store them like the carrots.

Before the frosts begin, which may be at the end of this month, the outdoor tomatoes must be gathered and brought inside. Those already changing colour will ripen in a few days, and the green ones can stand in a cool room to ripen a few at a time. With care, you can have tomatoes until well into November.

Parsnips and leeks can be left in the ground, as it is safe to dig them up when you need them.

FLOWERS FOR CHRISTMAS—
FORCING BULBS

Everyone appreciates a pot or bowl of flowering bulbs at Christmas time. It is at least a reminder that spring is not too far away. Flowers are always scarce and expensive at Christmas and both hyacinths and narcissi help with the many decorations which have to be done in the home.

There are many people who will say it is beyond them to get the bulbs in flower in time for Christmas, but this is not so if the right kinds are bought and if they are planted in the bowls early enough.

I shall have mine planted in the bowls before the end of September. They do need time to form their roots, and secondly their leaf and flower growth.

In the bulb catalogues, shops and stores you will see bulbs labelled "specially prepared" or "treated for early forcing". These bulbs will cost a few pence more than the ordinary range of bulbs, and this is not a stunt to sell them at a higher price—it means that they have been harvested and ripened off early, and in some cases pre-cooled to encourage early flowering. Those I find easiest to have in flower for Christmas are the Cornish pre-cooled daffodils.

Whatever we do, a bulb must have a certain resting period. Pre-cooling shortens this resting period, so enabling us to have bulbs in flower for Christmas, several weeks or even months before their normal season. The prepared or pre-cooled bulbs are soon sold out each year, so my advice is to buy now.

I have listed the bulbs I consider best for Christmas flowering, and put them in the order of those easiest to have in flower.

Roman hyacinths (white, blue and pink)

Fairy hyacinth—Blue Pearl
Rosalie hyacinth (deep rose)
Christmas Bells hyacinth (silver-blue)
Narcissus—Paper White Grandiflora
Narcissus—Grand Soleil d'Or (deep yellow and
    orange)
Specially treated hyacinth Bismark (blue)
Jan Bos hyacinth (red)
L'Innocence hyacinth (white)
Daffodil Golden Harvest (Cornish pre-cooled)

These can be followed in the early New Year
with pre-cooled daffodils and tulips in many
different varieties.

It is not wise to plant mixed bowls of bulbs or
even mixed varieties of one kind, because the
time of flowering in most cases is different and
the beauty of the bowl will be spoiled by some
flowers fading while others are only just beginning to come out.

Specially mixed bulb fibre can be bought at
quite reasonable prices. I must say I prefer the
bulb fibre, as it does retain the moisture so much
better. Vermiculite is now being used very considerably for growing bulbs in bowls.

If using the bulb fibre it must be moistened
before putting it into the bowls; place it in a
bucket or household bowl and pour water over it
to moisten it right through. Stir the fibre round
to mix it thoroughly and then test it for moisture
content by squeezing a handful. If it contains
enough moisture, then water will show through
your fingers when it is squeezed, but it must not
contain so much water that it runs over your
fingers.

Press the fibre into the pots or bowls moderately firmly, and when putting in the bulbs they
can be almost touching. The top or nose of each
hyacinth must be left showing above the surface

5 bulbs in a 7 inch bowl

Leave tips just showing after filling bowl with fibre

Flowers for Christmas—forcing bulbs

of the fibre, and large daffodil and narcissi bulbs can have their tops showing too.

No more water should be put on the fibre, after planting the bulbs, until it begins to show signs of drying, and even then only enough to just moisten it. Be careful not to make the fibre in the bowls wet and soggy, or the bulbs may rot.

The care of the bulbs for the first eight to ten weeks is the most important of all, and the success or failure of them will depend on the treatment they are given.

They must first of all be encouraged to form roots into the fibre, and for the first eight weeks they must be kept in a cool, dark position. A cellar is an ideal place, but failing this a dark cupboard under the stairs will be suitable.

Roots will grow first and then the shoots begin to show, and when these are 2 or 3 in. high the bowls must be brought into the light.

To place them straight away into a warm room could result in failure; for a further two to four weeks a light window-sill in a cool room is best. When the flower buds begin to show above the bulbs they can be transferred to a warm room, again placing them on the window-sill.

Growing bulbs must never be kept in the room away from the light because the growth will become thin and drawn, and the flowers may fail to open.

The flowers of the hyacinth will need support, and I find the best way is to use florist's stub wire, 9 to 12 in. long. Push the wire, one for each flower, into the bulbs or fibre. Bend it to form a loop at the top and place the loop round the stem. The wires, if placed on the inside, will be inconspicuous and will not spoil the appearance.

If at fortnightly intervals one or two bowls are brought into the warm you will have a succession of flowering bulbs through the winter.

GROWING BULBS OUT OF DOORS

There is not a more pleasing sight in our gardens than daffodils and narcissi growing and flowering in the grass, under trees and round shrubs. Special mixtures of both daffodils and narcissi can be purchased at quite reasonable prices for naturalizing in the grass. The bulbs should be planted 3 to 4 in. below the turf, and the time for doing this is September and October.

Daffodils and narcissi will grow in almost any kind of soil, and are a joy when planted between other plants such as roses or shrubs. It may be necessary to lift and divide the bulbs, which will increase in number, every five or six years. This should only be done as the leaves are yellowing and dying.

Hyacinths are best planted along the front of beds or borders, or in a flower bed to themselves.

Plant the bulbs 3 in. deep and 6 in. apart in September or October.

Tulips can be planted in groups or between other plants and will add colour and beauty to the garden during April and May. Plant them in November, at 3 to 4 in. deep. Both tulips and hyacinths can be lifted as the leaves begin to die. Dry them and store in a cool, airy place until planting time comes round again.

MAKING A GARDEN POOL

A garden pool, however small, enables us to grow so many beautiful and interesting plants, and there is no reason for the water to become stagnant if you include in the planting oxygenating plants to keep the water sweet and clean. The water should then only need topping up, and not renewing.

The best known of the oxygenating plants is the pond weed, *Elodea crispa*, and another excellent plant is *Vallisneria spiralis*. The vallisneria will have to be planted in soil at the bottom of the pool, but the elodea weed may be fastened to a piece of stone with a rubber band and dropped into the water. The plant will then begin to grow.

A pond need not be deep, 10 to 12 in. in the deepest part and only 4 in. in the shallow part is quite adequate. There are prefabricated pools which can be bought too.

OCTOBER

LOOKING AFTER DAHLIAS

Dahlias can be left in the garden until their tops have been blackened by frost, but if you wish to plant spring-flowering plants they can be lifted about the end of October.

Cut their tops off to about 6 to 9 in. above the ground. Lift each root carefully with the garden fork, and be very careful not to damage the tubers.

Place the roots stem downwards for a week or two in a cool and airy place. This will allow any moisture collecting in the hollow stem to drain away. When they are thoroughly dry the tubers can be placed in boxes with straw or newspaper around them.

They must be kept in a cool but frostproof place, where they can remain until the latter part of April.

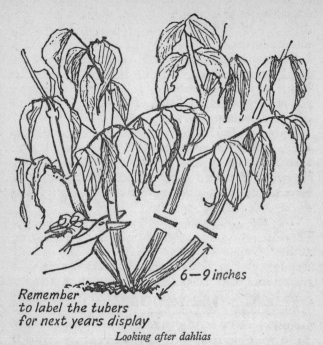

Remember
to label the tubers
for next years display

Looking after dahlias

MINIATURE GARDENS

Most people love tiny things, and miniature gardens especially are a delight. These can be grown successfully indoors and out, and people without gardens will find great pleasure in growing a miniature garden in a large dish.

A miniature garden must have miniature plants and trees, with small pieces of rock and stone, because everything must be in proportion.

Here's how to plant your own tiny garden. The garden can be either a sink or trough garden, or an even smaller one in a dish or pan. From a builder's yard it is possible to buy an old sink quite cheaply and this can be painted over with a mixture of cement and water to make it look rustic.

The main thing to remember in choosing a

container is that plants and small trees, etc., are the point of interest and the container should go almost unnoticed.

Another important point when considering the container is drainage. If you have chosen a sink it will have its own drainage hole, but a dish or pan should be deep enough to take a layer of charcoal under the main soil.

If your container has no other means of drainage, put a layer of charcoal in the bottom, then over that put a thin layer of pebbles. A sink should have a 3 in. layer of pebbles or pieces of broken flower pot over the bottom to ensure that water can drain away easily.

Over this, put a layer of rough peat or leaves. The soil need not be too rich, and the following mixture would be ideal: three parts soil passed through a $\frac{1}{2}$ in. riddle, two parts horticultural granulated peat, two parts coarse sand or grit, all parts by bulk. To this, add a handful of bonemeal to each bucketful, and no other fertilizers are needed.

Fill the container to the top, pressing the soil mixture in firmly. In a sink or trough, make one or two small mounds to form hills and valleys. Place small pieces of natural rock here and there, half the rock at least being buried beneath the soil to give the appearance of a natural rock outcrop.

On a pan or dish, two small pieces of rock should be sufficient. The miniature garden is then ready for planting.

Plant the small trees and shrubs first on the side of a slope or to the back as you would see them growing on a natural hillside. Set cobweb plants between crevices in the rocks and low-growing plants such as thymus in the low spaces between the slopes and rocks.

Plant a saxifraga to one side so that it falls over

PLANTS FOR A MINIATURE GARDEN

Trees and shrubs

Juniperus communis compressa	Spire-like and very slow growing
Juniperus horizontalis	Trailing
Chamaecyparis obtusa nana gracilis	Neat and compact bright green conifers

Plants

Gentiana acaulis	Gentian blue
Saxifraga aizoon rosea	Compact rosettes with clear pink flowers
Saxifraga jenkinsae	Shell pink flowers
Saxifraga naagii	Golden-yellow flowers
Sedum coral carpet	A neat little plant which the name aptly describes
Ramonda pyrenaica	Lavender-blue flowers
Thymus serpyllum	Lilac-pink flowers
Arenaria purpurascens	Lilac flowers
Dianthus alpinus	Deep rose flowers
Fuschia pumila Var. Tom Thumb	Purple and scarlet flowers
Gentiana verna	Brilliant blue

Bulbs and corms

Narcissus bulbocodium	Rich yellow
Narcissus triandrus albus	Creamy-white flowers
Cyclamen neapolitanum	Pink flowers
Iris reticulata	Deep violet
Crocus Var. Cloth of Gold	Deep golden-yellow flowers

the edge. Set bulbs or corms in small groups to grow up through and between the other plants.

The ideal place for the hardy cyclamen is under a miniature tree. Press each plant in firmly and when you have finished give the garden enough water to soak the soil right through.

While it is most important to have good drainage it is also important to water the garden thoroughly and carefully to keep the plants growing and thriving.

During the growing seasons of spring, summer and autumn, the plants and small trees and shrubs will need a plentiful supply of moisture the whole time.

Through the dark days of late autumn and winter they will need much less water and will no doubt get all the moisture they need from rain and snow if they are out of doors. It is at this time that good drainage is so necessary. It is fatal to all but a few plants to stand in water.

Whenever the soil feels dry, and this will be quite frequently if the weather is warm or they stand in a warm room, give them enough water to soak the soil right through, then leave it until it feels dry again.

For the first year, at any rate, the garden will need no fertilizer. During the second and third year only a very diluted fertilizer should be given about twice in the late spring.

PLANTING A CACTI GARDEN

There is a host of cacti and succulents of curious and interesting shapes to choose from when planting a cacti garden. Many of the better ones come from such families as the mammillaria, echinocereus, coryphantha, echinopsis, euphorbia, cereus and notocactus.

They all require good drainage, and an earthenware pan or bowl with holes in the bottom is ideal. Place some broken flower-pot pieces in the bottom of the container.

Use a soil mixture as follows: three parts soil, two parts coarse sand and one part peat. Add to this mixture a tablespoon of bonemeal to about a bowlful of this mixture. Plant the small cacti and succulents 2 or 3 in. apart and press them in. After planting, cover the surface with sand and water well.

During the spring, summer and autumn, water whenever the soil feels dry. Keep the soil dry during the winter.

KEEPING GERANIUMS DURING THE WINTER

It is not easy to keep geraniums from year to year without a heated greenhouse, but with care it can be done. The geranium plants must be lifted from the garden before we get severe frosts.

Pick off any dead leaves, flowers and buds. All large leaves must be broken off close to the main stem. The roots can then be planted in either boxes or pots. Put a 1 in. layer of cinder ashes in the bottom and cover this with 1 in. of soil.

Place in the roots and cover with more soil. Give the box enough water to soak the soil right through. They can then be left until the soil is really dry and then given the same amount of water as before.

For a few weeks they can be kept in the garden or garden shed if there is direct daylight there. Before severe weather begins bring them into the house and find a light place for them. They can be planted out again during the latter part of May.

STORING POTATOES

It is unwise to lift potatoes we wish to keep through the winter if their skins have not yet set. Test by scraping away the soil and rubbing a thumb-nail firmly over the tubers—the skin should remain firm and not scrape off.

If the tops of the potatoes have been affected by the blight fungus, which causes black spots on the leaves and stems, cut them off and burn them before the disease is able to find its way into the soil.

Always use the garden fork to lift potatoes. Push it into the soil well away from the roots so that none of the tubers are pierced. Lift the fork and throw the soil and potatoes forward, and leave them on top of the ground just long enough to dry. If they are left too long they will begin to go green and much of the crop will be spoiled.

Sort out only the good-sized tubers for storing away and put the small and diseased ones into another container for immediate use. As the sound tubers are gathered together rub off as much of the soil as possible and store them away from light or frost. Put them into sacks in the garden shed or cellar, covering the bags with layers of newspaper or straw. If sacks are not available they can be heaped in the shed with layers of newspaper under and over them.

Another way is to make a clamp in the garden. Put the potatoes in a heap on layers of newspapers or about 5 in. of straw and put the same amount of newspaper or straw over the heap. This must be covered with five or six inches of soil.

A HEDGE EVERY TIME

You may find it a problem to decide whether a fence or hedge would make a better boundary for the garden. As a gardener I would say a hedge every time. I know it takes time to grow, but when it is established it is cheaper to maintain than a fence.

An evergreen hedge provides more shelter during the winter than one which sheds its leaves. In most parts of the country privet retains its leaves throughout the winter. However, a privet hedge needs clipping at least three or four times during the summer.

I would never recommend laurel because it does not make a good hedge. A most attractive hedge is that of the cupressus, although it is not quite so quick to form a hedge as privet. But once it has reached the required size it only requires clipping once a year. It is an ideal background for other plants. A similar shrub which needs the same treatment is *Thuya lobbii*.

The small-leaved *Lonicera nitida* is just right for a hedge up to 3 ft in height. Beech, although not evergreen, retains its golden-brown leaves through the winter and this, too, will form a good hedge but is rather slow in growth. It needs clipping once a year.

As a boundary hedge to keep out children and animals there is nothing better than the hawthorn sometimes called quickthorn. This is reasonably fast growing and once it has reached the required height and width, clipping in July or August is enough to keep it neat and tidy.

The time to plant a hedge is from late October to April.

PLANT YOUR FRUIT TREES NOW

When planting fruit trees it is worth while making a hole larger than is actually required, so that the roots can spread out to their full extent. There is no need to dig the hole too deep, however, 9 to 12 in. is enough for most young fruit trees. The soil in the bottom of the hole should be broken up with a fork so that surplus water can drain away. Dig it over to the depth of the fork.

If the soil is light and sandy, mix some manure, compost or peat with the earth in the bottom of the hole. Mix two large handfuls of bonemeal with the soil that is to be returned to cover the roots.

All young trees need a strong stake to support them for the first few years; this should be driven into the bottom of the hole before the tree goes in.

CARING FOR YOUR
CHRYSANTHEMUMS

Chrysanthemums are usually appreciated to the full from November onwards, and more particularly if they are in flower at Christmas time. The ones I grow for Christmas flowering are the Favourite varieties, of which there are eight or more different colours. These have been recently brought into the greenhouse because a few degrees of frost on them would kill the buds.

They need careful watering from now on and once a week I add a little liquid or soluble fertilizer to the water until the colour of the petals can be seen.

Disbudding must still be done, leaving only one bud on each stem unless sprays of flowers are preferred.

Should you not have a greenhouse, then stand each pot on a plate or saucer and keep the plant as near to a window as possible. In the greenhouse the atmosphere must be kept reasonably dry when the flowers begin to open, otherwise damp may badly mark the petals.

On cold, damp nights some heat will be necessary to keep the atmosphere dry, and, of course, the chrysanthemums must be protected from frost.

GROWING TREES AND SHRUBS FROM CUTTINGS

Propagation is, I think, the most interesting part of gardening. Most popular flowering shrubs are quite easily grown from cuttings, but evergreens, and conifers in particular, are not so easy, as they take longer to form their roots.

The privet is possibly the easiest of all and so popular for planting as a hedge. Young branches 9 to 12 in. long, pulled off the privet bushes now and put half their length into the soil, will form roots by the spring, and this applies to laurel too.

There are many fascinating and attractive cupressus and other conifers which can be propagated. I find the most successful way is to put the cuttings into flower pots.

Only very small shoots about 2 to 3 in. long are needed to make the cuttings. Pull these shoots away from the larger branches with a small portion of the older wood or what is called a "heel" attached to the cuttings. Trim off any loose wood and bark and dip the base of each cutting into water and then into a hormone rooting powder.

Half fill a flower pot, 6 in. in diameter, with a mixture of peat, soil and sand in equal parts and press it in firmly. Put the cuttings in with half their length below the soil and soak right through with water.

Put over the top of the pot a piece of glass or a

polythene bag and plunge the pot into the soil in a partially shaded part of the garden. It can remain there all winter but should be watered whenever the soil in the pot gets dry.

Growing trees and shrubs from cuttings

Trim the base of the cutting to just below a leaf joint, remove the lower leaves and dibber it firmly into a pot.

KEEPING THE ROCK GARDEN TIDY

At this season of the year the rock garden looks untidy and dull, and yet tucked away under fallen leaves are some of the most interesting little plants in the garden. But for them to remain covered for too long may prove fatal.

October is the best time to have a general clean-up so that the rock garden looks an interesting feature even during the dark days of late autumn and winter. Clear away all the leaves and put them in one corner for digging into another part of the garden.

Any rampant-growing plants which are smothering the smaller rock plants can be trimmed back. Fork over the soil to freshen it up between the plants and once again the rock garden will look neat and interesting.

There is some planting we can do now to be sure of a bright and early display of colour in the spring. One of the first to come into flower in my rock garden is the *Iris reticulata*. The rich, violet-purple flowers with a golden-yellow blotch on each petal come out in February and early March. Bulbs of these can be planted now.

These are followed by the bright blue chiono-doxa, and soon afterwards by the long yellow trumpet-like flowers of the *Narcissus cyclamineus*, the fascinating flowers of the pale yellow hoop petticoat narcissi, and the creamy-white flowers of *Narcissus triandus albus*. The bulbs of all these are cheap and can be planted now.

NOVEMBER

Growing early rhubarb
Small garden trees
Fruit growing—a long-term policy
Take rose cuttings now
Sow before winter
Making the best use of your winter vegetables
Blackberries and loganberries
Use roses for a background

GROWING EARLY RHUBARB

The earliest, forced rhubarb is usually the most appreciated of all, far more than that which we can pull as we want it later on. The earliest rhubarb must be brought inside to be forced, and after a week or two in a warm greenhouse there are soon sticks large enough for pulling.

The plants to lift for forcing must be strong, well-established roots which have had an opportunity to form large strong buds or crowns. The roots for forcing can be lifted during November and left on the surface for a week or so exposed to the weather; it appears to improve their forcing qualities. Rhubarb forms thick, brown, fleshy roots, so when they are lifted they must be carefully handled and damaged as little as possible.

A dark cellar will make an ideal place for the roots, but it will take longer for the young sticks to grow there than if brought into a warm greenhouse. If you have a greenhouse the roots can be put under the greenhouse staging with some sacking around to exclude the light. The roots must be packed round with either moistened peat or soil, and if they are lightly damped over every day or so that is all they will need.

When pulling is finished I prefer to throw the roots away because forcing does weaken them very considerably. The roots forced or covered last year must not be used for early rhubarb again this year.

If there are not the facilities for bringing rhubarb roots inside they can be left in the ground and covered with an upturned bucket or large box in the New Year. The bucket or box must be covered with a thick covering of straw or leaves to keep out the cold and so that the crowns will be in complete darkness.

SMALL GARDEN TREES

Should trees be planted in a small garden? I would certainly say yes, in all but the smallest gardens. There are many beautiful trees which will not grow too big.

The large double and single-flowering cherries are the first to be considered, and then there are the weeping cherries, which have their branches wreathed in double pink or single white flowers in the spring.

The flowering crabs, too, add colour to the garden in spring with flowers of pink, red and purplish crimson. *Pyrus eleyi* has rich crimson flowers in spring, followed by small deep red apple-like fruits in the later summer.

When planting a tree such as this, a hole must be made large enough for the roots to be spread out without being cramped. The depth of the hole will depend, of course, on the size of the roots. The soil mark on the stem must be just level with the soil surface.

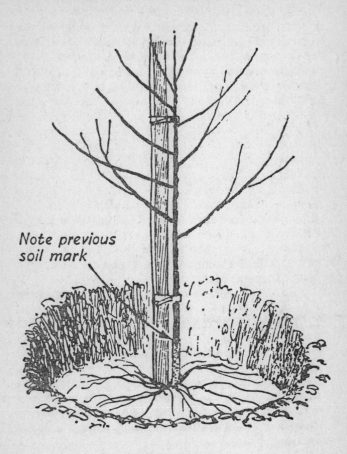

Note previous soil mark

Small garden trees

All trees, when being planted, must have their roots spread out and the soil replaced firmly over them. The soil level on the stem should be at the same level as before.

It will need support the first year or so. A strong stake must be put into the hole before the tree. When planting is finished securely fasten the tree to the stake, and place a piece of rubber tyre or sacking between the stem of the tree and the stake to prevent chafing the bark. The soil round and over the roots must be made really firm by treading.

FRUIT GROWING—
A LONG TERM POLICY

Fruit growing is a long-term policy, and this, I think, has a tendency to deter people from planting fruit trees. The time which elapses between planting, say, apple and pear trees and gathering the first fruits depends to a great extent on the kind of tree chosen.

Apple and pear trees are grown on different types of root-stock which have an influence on the growth of the tree and when it will produce its first fruit.

When buying a fruit tree, do not simply ask for an apple or pear tree, but ask for a Cox's Orange Pippin apple on a type nine, type 106 or type two rootstock, or a Conference pear on a quince A rootstock. These rootstocks, in particular, have a dwarfing effect on the tree and promote early fruiting.

Under normal circumstances it should be possible to gather fruit from trees such as these the second year after planting. It would be unfair to allow the trees to bear fruit the first summer after being planted.

Choice of variety is important, too. A Cox's Orange Pippin apple will not bear fruit unless there is another tree nearby which flowers at the same time, so that the bees and insects can carry the pollen from tree to tree.

If you are planting only one pear tree then plant a Conference pear, it is then not necessary to have another pear tree nearby for pollinating.

TAKE ROSE CUTTINGS NOW

A question that I am often asked is whether roses can be grown from cuttings. The bush roses we buy are grown on a briar rootstock because it is a faster way of producing a good-sized bush, and successful transplanting is easier.

You can, however, grow bush, climbing and rambler roses from cuttings and now is the time to put them in. A greenhouse or frame are unnecessary; they can be put in under the shelter of a wall or hedge. A branch about 12 in. long which has flowered during the summer or autumn makes an ideal cutting. Pull it away from a thicker branch with a portion of the older branch attached. The gardener calls this a "heel".

To prepare the cutting, cut off about 3 or 4 in. of the top of the branch, cutting straight across just above a leaf joint or bud. With a sharp knife cut off any loose bark or pieces of wood from the base and trim over the surface to make it smooth.

To assist the formation of roots on the cutting you can use a hormone rooting powder. Dip the bottom $\frac{1}{2}$ in. of the cutting first into water then into the rooting powder.

To plant them, make a "V" shaped trench 4 or 5 in. deep. Sprinkle some coarse sand along the bottom of the trench and put the cuttings in 3 in. apart, with the base of each one in the sand.

Push back the soil and tread along each side of

the cuttings to make them really firm. Those that form roots will begin to produce shoots and leaves in the spring and can be transplanted the following autumn.

SOW BEFORE WINTER

This is the time of the year when the vegetable garden looks untidy, and in many cases empty; it is an excellent opportunity for a general clean up before the bad weather really begins. The potatoes, carrots, beetroot and onions are now safely stored away and there are large patches of bare earth.

The runner beans must be cleared away and the bean sticks stacked neatly in one corner until next year. Any refuse still remaining must, with the autumn leaves, be put on to the compost heap.

Parsnips and leeks, which will stand up to any amount of frost and snow, will remain in the garden, also celery, Brussels sprouts, cabbage, savoy and both heading and sprouting broccoli, as well as the spring cabbage and autumn-sown onions.

All these are very valuable crops, coming as they do when fresh vegetables are scarce and expensive. Some plants of the hardy winter lettuce can still be planted. There are two varieties which I like, Imperial and Arctic; both are hardy and will produce good-hearting lettuces in April and May.

Sow a couple of rows of broad beans now which will be ready for gathering long before those sown in the spring. Make a trench the width of the spade and $1\frac{1}{2}$ in deep. Space the beans 6 in. apart along each side of the trench and cover them over.

At one end of the row plant several beans to one side. If there are any failures, these can be carefully lifted with the trowel in the spring and planted to fill up the gaps. The variety I would recommend is Aquadulce.

Broad beans should come safely through the worst winter weather without protection.

MAKING THE BEST USE OF YOUR WINTER VEGETABLES

During November, fresh vegetables are often in good supply: there are plenty of Brussels sprouts, savoy cabbage, good-quality winter cauliflower and quite a variety of root vegetables.

Most gardeners and allotment holders have plenty of green vegetables to gather as and when they are wanted, but later on when the winter comes, and particularly around Christmas time, they will not be so plentiful. The prices will gradually begin to rise and the quality will not be so good. Therefore, the vegetables in your own garden should be made to last as long as possible.

Parsnips are best left in the ground to dig as you need them, and they are sweeter after a sharp frost. Leeks, too, can be left in the ground until as late as March of next year.

When you gather the Brussels sprouts take five or six sprouts from each plant at a time, always gathering from the bottom of the stem first. If you take care not to damage the tops and the large leaves, you should have sprouts until well into March.

Once savoy and January King form their solid hearts they will stand for a few weeks, but the savoy cabbage in particular must be used before the hearts begin to split.

The curds of winter cauliflower are forming fast and these are very delicious. Turn the leaves over the curds by breaking the mid-ribs. This will protect them from frost and bad weather, keeping them a creamy-white for several weeks.

BLACKBERRIES AND LOGANBERRIES

In every home fresh fruit is always in great demand and if we can prolong the season of soft fruits, so much the better. With loganberries and the cultivated blackberries the season can be extended well into September.

There are many gardens which are not large enough to grow raspberries and black currants, but some gardens have a wall or fence on which can be trained both loganberries and blackberries.

The loganberries begin to ripen in late July and August when raspberries have mostly finished, and blackberries ripen in August and September.

The cultivated blackberries produce large juicy berries and I consider that they should be much more widely grown than they are at present. The best place for them is on an east or west-facing wall or fence, but they can also sometimes be seen cropping well on a northern aspect.

The time for planting loganberries and blackberries is November or March, but do not expect to be gathering fruit the summer after planting. During this time they will be producing new canes or branches on which they will bear the fruit the following year. Before planting, mix some manure, garden compost or peat, as well as a large handful of bonemeal, with the soil.

Plant as near to the fence or wall as possible. The hole must be large enough and deep enough to spread out all the roots and after putting some fine soil between the roots, fill in with the remaining soil and tread it in really firmly.

The branches on the plant when you buy them must be cut back to approximately half their length. If planting against a wall, fix a wooden trellis or horizontal wires across the wall on which to train the new shoots as they grow; these must be carefully tied to the supports because the fruit will be produced on these the following year.

USE ROSES FOR A BACKGROUND

From now until March is the time to plant roses. So many people think of the hybrid tea and floribunda bush roses and forget the beautiful climbing and rambler roses which can make the garden so much more colourful.

A climbing rose trained up the wall of the house will fill the rooms with a delightful scent. A rose-covered trellis can be used to separate the flower garden from the part where we grow the vegetables and it will form a good background for other roses and flowers.

Flowering pillars can also be formed by training them up 8 to 10 ft. tall poles, and a rose archway looks beautiful too.

Climbing roses require no more treatment than the ordinary bush roses. The soil must be broken up with the spade or fork to a depth of 10 or 12 in., and some manure or good horticultural peat mixed with it, as well as a large handful of bonemeal for each plant.

There is no need to drive nails in all over the wall of the house to train the roses on. Stretch some wires over the wall from vine eyes or pins which can be plugged into the wall.

The roses as they grow can then be tied to the wires. Those on a fence, trellis or rose arch can be tied to the wooden supports.

Rambler roses must be pruned as soon as flowering is finished by cutting out all the long trailing growths which have flowered. The new young branches which will grow from ground level are trained on to take their place. Climbing roses can be pruned in autumn or spring, cutting back the side branches to a bud 1 in. from the main stem.

A climbing rose I like is Zéphirine Drouhin with beautiful sweetly scented flowers which are a deep rose-pink colour.

DECEMBER

CHRISTMAS ROSES ARE EASY TO GROW

The Christmas rose is one of the nicest flowers we have at Christmas time, and it is hardy and easy to grow. Planting time for this plant is between now and next March, and it will then be in flower the following Christmas.

The roots are not expensive and they will grow almost anywhere in the garden. They do not object to partial shade, but the best of all positions is against a wall which faces to the south or west.

Before planting, mix some horticultural peat or garden compost and a large handful of bonemeal thoroughly into the soil. If the soil is a heavy clay, mix mortar rubble or coarse sand into the soil as well.

In early December I place a large sheet of glass supported by bricks over the plants, or a cloche, to keep the flowers clean. This is very important in industrial areas. When gathering Christmas roses, pull the flowers so you get as long a stem as possible.

SAVE YOUR GARDEN WASTE

Whenever I see or smell the smoke of a garden bonfire I wonder how much valuable organic material, which should be put back into the soil, is being wasted.

In the average garden there is very little waste for burning. In the winter time there are the hard woody prunings from the fruit trees, shrubs and other trees in the garden. These, I know, do take a considerable time to decompose so there is an excuse for burning them.

The only other garden waste we can find an excuse for burning, however, is diseased plant material which would, if put back into the soil, infest it with disease. Many gardens and allotments are badly infected with the clubroot fungus of cabbage and other members of that family.

To put these affected plants on the compost heap only results in putting more disease into the soil, and they therefore should be burned.

In every garden there is waste material of all kinds, such as dead and dying flowers, flower stems, grass mowings, leaves from various vegetable crops, as well as leaves from the trees and shrubs. In addition to these there is always a certain amount of vegetable waste from the kitchen. All these can be used to keep the soil in the garden in good heart. This especially applies to a town garden.

To make the compost heap, start by putting a 9 in. layer of the vegetable waste on the ground. Then, a sprinkling of sulphate of ammonia, a 1 in. layer of soil and another 9 in. layer of waste is placed on the original layer. The compost heap is made up of these layers, until all the waste material is used up.

FORCING MINT

After Christmas, and in the New Year, mint and other herbs will be constantly in demand, and whenever possible it is best to be able to gather them from the garden.

Mint can be forced into early growth, and it is possibly the most popular of all the herbs and flavourings. In many gardens there is a bed of mint, and the underground stems and buds on the outside of the bed are usually the strongest, and are therefore the ones to lift for forcing into early growth.

When lifting the roots, select the thickest pieces which have buds or young shoots, and plant in a box. Put a 2 in. layer of soil in the box, which should be approximately 14 in. by 9 or 10 in. wide and 4 to 6 in. deep. Lay the underground stems or roots on the soil, and cover with another 2 in. layer of soil. If the soil is dry give it a thorough watering.

The box can then be placed under the staging in a warm greenhouse, in the garage, or better still in a spare room of the house. If it can be kept where the temperature is 50 to 60 deg. F., the young shoots will soon begin to grow. Whenever the soil looks or feels dry, water it again, and it will not be long before the shoots will be large enough to gather for use.

As the first shoots show above the soil, move the box to a light place, and it should provide enough mint for the average household until that in the garden begins to grow.

CHRISTMAS DECORATIONS FROM THE GARDEN

The few weeks before Christmas are usually a very busy time for us all. There are so many preparations to be made for the Christmas festivities, and the decorations are one of the most important items.

With a little thought and planning there is much that even the smallest garden can provide towards the decorations. The garden may, at this time of the year, look dull and uninteresting, but there are various seed heads left on the hardy border plants which can be used in the decorations.

I make a point of collecting some of the spiky heads of the veronica, some of the brown cones of the taller rudbeckia, the flat heads of the achillea, and the round spiny heads of the echinops. These I cover with either thin flour paste or transparent glue, and while they are still wet, I sprinkle them with some glitter.

Small pieces of ivy growing up the garden wall or up the stems of trees are useful to make small arrangements with the glittered seed heads, berries and evergreens.

Small twigs with large fat buds can be used too, the buds can be painted with silver or gold paint. There is usually no shortage of berries on the holly, and there are often plenty on the firethorn or pyracantha, as well as on the cotoneaster and other berrying shrubs. The hedgerows, too, are bright with the berries of the hawthorn and the hips of the wild roses.

When using these and evergreens, such as holly and ivy, for a small arrangement to place on the mantelshelf where it is warm, put moist earth or sand in the container to keep them fresh as long as possible.

FLOWERS FOR CHRISTMAS

At Christmas time, when flowers are expensive, we look to the garden to see what it will provide. The best known, perhaps, is the yellow winter-flowering jasminum, which grows best against a north-facing wall. To make sure of having twigs of these covered in the bright yellow flowers, I cut pieces a week or ten days before Christmas and put them in water in a moderate to cool room.

Another shrub, which produces clusters of pinkish-white flowers from now onwards, is the *Viburnum fragrans*. Cut twigs a few days before they are needed.

A good flowering tree is the winter-flowering cherry, *Prunus subhirtella autumnalis*. This has double pinkish-white flowers in winter, and twigs with the large buds which when cut and put in water are soon covered with delicate flowers.

The best of all winter-flowering shrubs is possibly the *Mahonia japonica*, the winter-flowering berberis. This has long racemes of lemon-yellow flowers and a scent like lily of the valley. If you have not these shrubs and plants in the garden this year, plant them before March.

A FINAL NOTE FROM PERCY THROWER

The dark days of winter give us an opportunity to look back over the past year, to weigh up our successes and failures in the garden, and to look ahead to the New Year. Whatever his successes may have been, the good gardener will never be satisfied, and should aim at even better things in the coming year.

What should the gardener's New Year resolutions be? Firstly, I would say, to have a garden more beautiful than ever. Secondly, to have better crops of fruit and vegetables, and lastly, to try, and I purposely say try, to keep the garden work up to date. Successful gardening is, I think, not so much having green fingers, but having a love for the plants we grow, and a lot of common sense.

We must do all we can to get the soil in our garden in good condition, and this can only be done by using organic material such as manure, garden compost or peat to keep the soil well supplied with humus. This is one of the basic principles of good gardening, and if we begin in this way, then we can be sure of getting full value for the money we spend on fertilizers.

We must try to do the right things at the right time, seed sowing, planting, thinning, hoeing, and the various other regular jobs which have to be done. We know, for instance, that from spring to autumn the lawn will need mowing almost every week.

Another job we should regularly do is to look over our plants and crops for insect pests such as greenfly and caterpillars, and fungus diseases such as mildew. If necessary, spray before the pests and diseases have a chance to damage the plants. My teaching when I started my gardening career many years ago was, "Prevention is better than cure", and I practise that to this very day.

INDEX